FROM DEEP INSIDE THE JUNGLE, THE TRAP WAS SPRUNG!

Twin fingers of deadly green tracer fire from the hidden Chi-Com 12.7mm machine guns reached up at Warlokk's helicopter. Fire sparked along the middle of the Cobra fuselage as the armor-piercing rounds caught it in mid-dive. Greasy black smoke erupted from the exhaust of the howling turbine.

"Lead!" Warlokk screamed in his throat mike as he battled the controls. "I'm hit!"

The Cobra fell out of the sky in a skidding turn.

High above the battlefield, in his own gunship, Alphabet saw Warlokk's ship go down to the chopper-killing guns. Without thinking, his right hand twisted the throttle to maximum RPMs. He dropped the collective and stomped down on the rudder pedal to kick the tail around.

The North Vietnamese gunners on the fifty-ones aimed at the new target. They had killed one Yankee machine so far. They would get this one, too.

With a stream of Chi-Com bullets arcing toward it, the Cobra dropped to its target like a diving hawk

Other books in the **Chopper 1** series:

CHOPPER 1

#15 WARRIOR SKY

Jack Hawkins

IVY BOOKS • NEW YORK

Special thanks to **Michael W. Kasner**

Ivy Books
Published by Ballantine Books

Produced by Butterfield Press, Inc.
96 Morton Street
New York, New York 10014

Library of Congress Catalog Card Number: 88-91136

ISBN:0-8041-0319-4

Manufactured in the United States of America

First Edition: July 1989

To H.J. and Leone for their unwavering support.
And, as always, to Claudia.

AUTHOR'S NOTE

When the Marines recaptured the city of Hue in February 1968, the Tet offensive was over. All that remained was to relieve the Marine garrison at Khe Sanh, which had been taken under siege a week before Tet exploded in the rest of South Vietnam.

During the first few weeks after the recapture of Hue, the First Air Cav continued Operation Jeb Stuart. New fire-bases were built and the skytroopers fanned out, relentlessly pursuing fragmented NVA forces in their new area of operations. Search and clear, cordon and search, and night hunter-killer operations harassed the enemy and prevented them from reestablishing themselves in the coastal plains. When they were forced to retreat to the mountains, the Air Cav went after them in hot pursuit.

During the forty-two-day period of Jeb Stuart, the Air Cav killed more than 3,200 enemy for a loss of 276 Americans killed and another 1,498 wounded. More serious than the loss of men, however, was the loss of helicopters. Twenty-four had been destroyed and another seventy-six damaged beyond repair during the operation. The availability of air assets dropped to an all-time low for the division.

This became critical when the Air Cav was ordered to prepare for Operation Pegasus, the relief of Khe Sanh.

Thirty days were to pass from the time of that order to the time that the operation could be launched.

While the Air Cav worked to bring themselves back up to strength, six thousand beleaguered Marines at Khe Sanh continued to hold their ground. Outnumbered by at least six to one, hammered by daily artillery and rocket attacks and frequent ground assaults, these men wrote another valiant chapter to the glorious history of their corps.

Everyone from the press to Congress predicted a disaster at Khe Sanh, fearing that the base would fall like the French fortress at Dien Bien Phu in 1954. They did not take into consideration the courage of the American fighting men, who saw to it that history would not be repeated.

One of the primary factors that prevented a disaster at Khe Sanh was the massive amount of air support that was brought to bear on the thirty or forty thousand hard-hat North Vietnamese regulars ringing the base—particularly the Arc Light strikes from the high-flying B-52 Bombers. In 2,548 sorties, the Buffs dropped over 54,000 tons of H.E. on the enemy positions.

Another factor was the dedication of the airmen of the Air Force Airlift Command in Southeast Asia. Their courage and dedication kept the Marines supplied against almost insurmountable odds of bad weather and massive enemy antiaircraft fire. What they accomplished was nothing short of a wartime miracle. When the tales of Khe Sanh are told, these men can never be forgotten.

On April 1, 1968, the sky turned dark with hundreds of choppers as history's largest heliborne operation kicked off. Pegasus was the first time that an entire airmobile division went into action at the same place at the time. The earth shook from the beating of their rotors as they turned toward Khe Sanh. Within a week, the remnants of five NVA divisions fled back to their sanctuaries in Laos. The siege at Khe Sanh was broken.

As always, with the exception of well-known historical figures, all of the characters in this book are fictional and any semblance to persons living or dead is purely unintentional.

The outcome of these battles, however, is not at all fictional. Let it never be forgotten that the American fighting man won his battles in Vietnam, including the seventy-seven-day battle for Khe Sanh.

Jack Hawkins
Portland, Oregon
January 1989

CHAPTER 1

North of Hue, 3 March 1968

The o.d.-painted UH-1D Huey slick skimmed low over the flooded rice paddies of the coastal plains north of Hue. It suddenly banked to the left, giving the door gunner in back a better field of fire. On the ground, two North Vietnamese soldiers frantically tried to flee the certain death that was about to strike them down.

One of the runners stopped and raised his AK in a vain attempt to defend himself, but he was too late. The M-60D doorgun in the rear of the chopper hammered. A solid stream of red 7.62mm tracers lanced down, striking the two men in the rice paddy. Both of them fell flat on their faces in the muddy brown water and quickly sank beneath the surface.

Over the beating of the chopper's rotors, a shout of victory came over the intercom from the man behind the smoking doorgun. Sergeant Treat Brody was finally back where he belonged, behind the doorgun of a chopper chasing dinks across the open ground.

Brody was a trim, sun-bronzed ex-Californian with a wild shock of blond hair and a long, bushy mustache. He looked like he would be more at home catching a wave on a surfboard in California instead of standing in the door gunner's pocket of a Huey slick in the skies over Vietnam. And in fact, before he came to Southeast Asia, he had prowled the beaches of Malibu with his surfboard over his shoulder. That had been almost two years ago. Since then, Brody had found new sport as a door gunner and grunt with the Blues, the Aero Rifle Platoon of Echo Company of the First Battalion of the 7th U.S. Air Cavalry.

On the shoulder of his faded jungle fatigue jacket, he wore the big o.d.-and-black "Horse Blanket" patch of the First Air Cavalry Division, the Pony Soldiers. Above his left breast pocket was sewn the wreathed musket of the CIB, the coveted Combat Infantryman's Badge. The front of the flight helmet he wore was emblazoned with the words Hog Heaven painted in red and yellow.

Brody was proud of his membership in the Hog Heaven fraternity. To join that elite group, a door gunner had to have over a hundred confirmed personal VC kills with his Hog, the M-60 doorgun. He had made his hundred in just a little over six months after arriving in Nam.

In the early battles of the Ia Drang and A Shau valleys, it had been easy to rack up an impressive score. Later, when the VC and NVA had learned that choppers were death in the sky and hid from them, Brody continued to kill, but had long since stopped counting bodies.

All Treat Brody lived for was to fly and fight with the Air Cav. He had become addicted to the adrenaline of combat, and the war had become his entire life. That was why he had reenlisted in the Army for six years and extended his tour in Nam for the third time.

The grunts riding in the open doors of the slick heard Brody's war cry and grinned. Since the end of the Tet offensive and the recapture of Hue, the Blues had been chasing fleeing NVA all over the coastal plains north of Hue. The scattered enemy units were desperately trying to regroup after the massive ass-kicking they had received during Tet. The Air Cav was doing their best to make that as difficult as possible. Every time the NVA tried to dig in, the choppers were right on top of them, blasting them out of their bunkers. The Cav was determined to clear their AO of the enemy.

The chopper came around again and flared out for a landing on the paddy dike. Overhead, two UH-1C Huey Hog gunships flew in an orbit around the slick, ready to blast anything that moved. Three of the grunts quickly unassed the slick to check the two NVA bodies and to collect their weapons.

The first man off the chopper was a dark-skinned, black-haired grunt in a black-and-green striped camouflage uniform, a tiger suit. SP/4 Chance Broken Arrow was a modern-day Comanche warrior from Montana who took great pride in his Plains Indian ancestry. He also took his role in the war very seriously. To him, crawling around out in the jungle was like playing cowboy-and-Indians with real guns. But the way this Indian played it, the North Vietnamese were the Cowboys.

When the grunts were deep in the jungle, Broken Arrow always walked point for his squad. No one made him do it. As far as he was concerned, it was the proper role for a Comanche warrior. Instead of carrying an issue M-16 rifle on that dangerous assignment, he packed a sawed-off Remington twelve-gauge pump riot gun.

He took his work so seriously that he hand-loaded the ammunition for his sawed-off pump gun. The issue ammo was fine for hunting and civilian user back in the world, but they didn't pack half enough punch. Not for hunting gooks in the Nam. Broken Arrow was in the habit of replacing the nine .36-caliber lead balls in the Army-issue shotgun shells with twelve .25-caliber steel ball bearings. He then created his own magnum loads by adding extra gunpowder. Whipping the pump gun's slide back and forth so fast that the shotgun sounded like it was firing on full automatic, the Indian could clear a path in front of him half the size of a football field.

Around the Echo Company Blues, the Indian was known as "Two-Step," a nickname he had earned when he had been bitten by a krait snake. Of the thirty-three species of snakes that were found in Vietnam, thirty-one were poisonous. The most deadly of all was the krait, commonly known as the "Two-Step." Usually, after a man was bitten by the small, light green snake, he only took two more steps before falling over on his face, stone-cold dead.

Somehow, though, Broken Arrow survived the snake's venom. There had been a Dustoff medevac chopper nearby and he had been rushed to the Big Air Cav hospital in An Khe. While he was recuperating, Platoon Sergeant Leo Zack had hung the nickname on him and it had stuck. Now everyone called him Two-Step and, ignorant of the snake-bite incident, most of the troops thought that it was his authentic Indian name.

At the Indian's side was a Chicano packing an M-60 machine gun, SP/4 Juan "Corky" Cordova. He carried the linked ammo belts for his gun wrapped around his chest like a Mexican bandit in a Western movie. A thick, drooping Pancho Villa mustache and blue bandanna tied around his neck added to the bandit look.

Having spent almost two years in the Nam, Corky looked at the world with a seasoned grunt's philosophy. Cordova was a product of the Los Angeles barrios, the son of illegal immigrants, and he had a real chip on his shoulder about that. As far as he was concerned, he was every inch as much of an American as any Anglo he had ever met, and he consistently went out of his way to prove it. Corky had already been an experienced street fighter when he enlisted in the Army. He volunteered for infantry duty in the Nam to further make his point about being a good American.

Now, however, the Chicano machine gunner had finally decided that he was done with it. He had survived almost two years in the Blues humping his pig, as the M-60 machine gun was called. In that time, he had earned the CIB, a couple of Bronze Stars, a Purple Heart, and enough Air Medals from hitting hot LZs to fill a canteen cup. He was just waiting out the last three weeks until his DEROS, his return to the States, While he was waiting, though, he didn't mind killing a few more dinks if the opportunity arose.

The third man in the group was a skinny, freckle-faced, redheaded kid who seemed far too young to be in Vietnam. He looked like he should have been in a Boy Scout troop, not an ass-kicking grunt outfit like the Aero Rifle Platoon of an Air Cav Company.

PFC Ralph Burns went by the nickname Farmer because he came from a potato farm outside Pocatello, Idaho. Growing up in the sticks, Farmer had always had an intense curiosity about the world that extended far beyond his family's plowed fields. Much of his free time had been spent in the city library looking at photographs of exotic foreign lands in *National Geographic* magazines. He longed to visit these faraway places and that longing had driven him to visit the Army recruiter's office in Boise the day after he turned eighteen. He was sick and tired of looking at nothing but potato fields as far as the eye could see.

The way he figured it, there was no sense in him spending the rest of his life looking at pictures in the magazines when he wasn't plowing a field or waiting for potatoes to grow. He could join the Army, see the world, and even get paid for it at the same time. As far as the young farm boy had been concerned, it was a good deal.

At first, except for greatly expanding the young soldier's vocabulary, Farmer's experiences in Vietnam seemed not to have changed him. His insatiable curiosity had remained intact and his capacity for satisfying that curiosity had seemed unlimited. When he found out that Vietnam offered an almost inexhaustible supply of exotic girls for him to sample, he tried to work his way through as many of them as humanly possible.

However, Farmer had changed. The realities of the war had finally broken through his wide-eyed farm-boy mentality when one of the men in the squad, Gardner, had been killed during Tet. Gardner had been the only real friend Farmer had ever had. Farmer was so pissed that he had been locked up in the psycho ward at the hospital for a few days.

5

He had been able to convince the doctors that he was all right, and finally they let him out.

For all his farm boy openness, Farmer was also a very good actor. By no stretch of the imagination should he have been considered sane, not even in Vietnam. He was filled with a burning rage to kill that went far beyond how other grunts felt about the war.

When the chopper touched down, he rushed out in the rice paddy and grabbed one of the fallen NVA by the hair. He jerked the man's head up out of the muddy water.

"Fuck!" he spat, shaking his head in disappointment. "He's dead."

"Of course he's fucking dead," Corky said, looking at him. "What'd you expect? Brody caught him with a full burst."

"Fuck! I wanted to kill him myself."

Farmer dropped the corpse and went to check the other one. He was dead, too. Again Farmer was disappointed. He mucked around in the mud until he found the two AK-47 assault rifles the NVA had been carrying and stepped back onto the rice dike.

"Let's go," Two-Step said, scanning the tree line a hundred meters away. The Indian didn't like being exposed the way they were. If he couldn't be deep in the jungle, where he could hide, he wanted to be back up in the air.

The slick pilot had kept the rotors turning. When the three men returned, the chopper was back up in the sky in seconds to continue searching for the enemy.

High overhead and a few klicks away, First Lieutenant Mike Alexander, the Blues' platoon leader, brought his field glasses back up to his eyes and scanned the wood line beyond the rice fields. Those two NVA Brody had killed had been headed somewhere. If he was lucky, his men might find the enemy unit holed up somewhere close by.

Alexander was a slim, intense young man very much in love with his work. He had spent the first two years of his Army career in Germany with a Mechanized Infantry battalion of the 8th Division, crashing around the frozen woods in his armored personnel carrier. He had loved the "haul ass, bypass, and call for gas" life of mechanized warfare, but as soon as he arrived in Nam and made his first helicopter air assault with the Cav, he found something that he liked even better. Airmobile warfare.

Today, however, Alexander was a bit frustrated. Except for the two stragglers that Brody had cut down, they'd had no joy at all. He was just about to call for the return to Camp Evans when he got a radio call from the chopper carrying Master Sergeant Leo Zack, the Blues' platoon sergeant, and the men of the First Squad.

"Blue Six, Blue Six," Sergeant Zack called. "This is Blue Five. Over."

"Blue Six, go," Alexander answered.

"This is Five, we may have something over here. I've got signs of recent digging at the edge of a wooded area. Over."

"Six, Roger, send the coordinates. Over."

"This is Five, we're at seven three five. Break. Four Si—"

The faint sound of machine-gun fire suddenly broke in over Zack's radio transmission. It was followed by hissing static.

"This is Six," Alexander called. "You were cut off. Say again. Over."

He released the push-to-talk switch on the radio handset. Nothing.

"Blue Five, Blue Five, this is Blue Six. How copy? Over."

The rushing sound of *squelch* echoed in the handset. The radio on the other end was dead.

CHAPTER 2

Camp Evans

Captain Roger "Rat" Gaines pushed the black Stetson hat to the back of his head and looked around the EM club. The usually dimly lit, smoky bar looked strangely different in the harsh light of day. His company first sergeant, "Top" Richardson, was supervising a work detail cleaning the place up and getting it ready for the big company party that night. Rat had stopped in to see how the work was progressing.

Gaines was the company commander of Echo Company, First of the 7th Cavalry, and he loved his job. Echo Company was an Air Cavalry company consisting of the Aero Rifle Platoon, the Blue Team, and Python Flight, the red team that flew a mix of Huey Hogs and Cobra gunships.

Exactly like the horse cavalry troops of the 7th Cavalry back in the days of General Custer, the modern 7th Air Cav Company was a fast-moving, hard-hitting recon and ready reaction force. On just a moment's notice, Gaines could get the grunts of his Blue Team in the air and, supported by his own gunships, get them anywhere they were needed to kick ass and take names.

That kind of shoot-from-the-hip, quick-in-and-quick-out action turned Gaines on. From one day to the next, he rarely had any idea what his company was going to be asked to do next. Whatever mission his people were given, he was confident that they'd be more than able to take care of it.

Today, however, he felt a little at sea. He wasn't facing a battle or a desperate rescue mission, but something far worse—his engagement party.

The smooth-talking Gaines was almost a movie-perfect picture of a carefree bachelor officer. He was a little too short and stocky to be called handsome, but Gaines had a way with women. Born to an old-line Atlanta family, he had all the mannerisms and charm of a classic southern gentleman. His intense green eyes and carefree grin had charmed more than one bird off her limb and into his bed. There were at least two dozen women from Atlanta to Saigon who would have laughed themselves sick if anyone had told them that the infamous Rat Gaines was getting married.

"Impossible!" they would have said in unison. "No fucking way."

That's what Gaines himself had thought until quite recently. He was still somewhat shocked that he had actually asked his beautiful nurse, Lisa Maddox, to marry him, but he had no regrets. Lisa was not only one of the most beautiful women he had ever met, she was also the only woman he had never grown tired of. There was something about the mix of intelligence, toughness, and beauty that totally intrigued him.

He was very much aware that his proposal had been prompted in great part by the fact that Lisa was finally going back to the States. Even if she had not been wounded last month and would be staying on in Nam, he knew that sooner or later he would have wanted to see about making their wartime relationship a more permanent part of his life.

As it was, the shock of her having been wounded during Tet had brought home to him the stark fact that life in a war zone was a very iffy thing. Faced with the thought of that he might have lost her permanently, he had automatically asked her to marry him. The fact that she had said yes had still been a surprise to him. Now he had to go through the social rituals that went hand in hand with getting hitched. The company party that night was one of those rituals.

He would much rather have had a quiet last night alone with Lisa before she returned to the States. She had liked the idea of the party. Since Rat was going to marry her and live with her the rest of his life, the least he could do was to give the men of the battalion a chance to say good-bye to their favorite nurse.

He looked over and saw his first sergeant walking over to him. "Everything's well under control, sir," Top Richardson reported to Gaines. "We'll be ready to go by seventeen hundred."

"Great," Gaines replied. "All I have to do now is get myself ready for this Chinese fire drill."

The first sergeant grinned. He had been married four times, twice to women in the Army. "You'll make it, sir. We all have to do it one time or the other. It's just like getting shot at for the first time."

"That's what I'm afraid of."

Army nurse, First Lieutenant Lisa Maddox, cursed in an earthy, very unladylike manner as she tried to adjust the prosthesis on her right leg. The prosthesis replaced what had been shattered by an NVA .51-caliber machine-gun round a little over a month earlier.

"This fucking peg leg," she muttered to herself. "If they can shoot rockets into space, they ought to be able to design one of these goddamned things so it fits properly."

Lisa was the daughter of a high-ranking general officer who commanded a desk down at MACV headquarters in Saigon. General Maddox had been furious with her when she had volunteered to go to Nam in the first place.

The general had been concerned that she would get hurt, and almost from the first day that she had arrived, he had pressured her to get her to leave the Air Cav and take a transfer down to the 3d Field Hospital, a short distance from his office. He wanted her closer to him, living where she could sleep on clean sheets and not have to face the daily dangers of combat in a forward-area hospital.

Lisa had refused to leave the Air Cav. She considered herself a part of the division. She wanted to stay to help the men that she had grown close to. She had seen it as her duty, and she would not turn away from it.

In return, the men of the Air Cav, particularly the men of the First of the 7th, worshiped the blond nurse. She was a beautiful, green-eyed reminder of the wives and girl friends they had all left behind in the States. For many of them, she was also the angel of mercy who bandaged their wound and helped them be brave when it hurt too much.

She had done the best that she could for the men she served, but the war had finally caught up with her and taken her leg. Lisa had been in Vietnam too long to have any illusions about the realities of the war. She was probably better acquainted with the horrors of the war than many combat infantrymen. Her time in Vietnam had been spent with the unending stream of wounded, blasted bodies of young men who came into her hospital.

Because she spent a great deal of her off-duty time working at several of the Catholic orphanages in the An Khe, Bong Son and Pleiku area, she had seen the effects of the war on the Vietnamese people as well. She had seen the wounded children, hurt both by communist and American fire. She had seen the hollow-eyed victims of communist atrocities as well as American bombing raids that hit the wrong targets. Lisa had seen more of the war than many grunts did, and now the war had brushed a little too close. After all these months, she was finally going to go back to the States.

She had just gotten the prosthesis in place when there was a light knock on the door to her room in the hospital. "Come in."

A gray-haired full bull, Colonel Hardell, the hospital commander, walked in. "The party's on for tonight, isn't it?"

"Yes, sir," Lisa answered brightly. "Seventeen hundred hours in the EM club."

"Is your dad coming down?"

"No." She shook her head. "He's all tied up right now and can't get away."

"Well," Hardell said, smiling. "I'll be there and I can tell him what he missed."

Hardell was an old family friend. He and Lisa's father had been in the academy at the same time and had been stationed together several times over the years. Lisa had grown up calling him Uncle Ernie and he had always treated her like the daughter he never had. He would be more than happy to stand in for General Maddox at the party that night.

Hardell noticed that Lisa was looking better than she had in days. Her long blond hair was combed out and fell down over her shoulders in a perfect counterpoint to her deep green eyes. Most Army nurses kept their hair cut short so it wouldn't interfere with their work, but Lisa had chosen to put up with the hassle of leaving hers long and uncut. The glossy blond mane was her only concession to femininity, and served to remind her that war or not, she was still a woman.

As a man, the colonel heartily approved of Lisa's decision and, like every other man who had ever seen her hair flowing down her back, he was struck by her beauty. He also knew that now, of all times, it was important that she look and feel beautiful. She needed to know that she was still a desirable woman even if she was missing half of her leg. When she had first woken up in the hospital to find that she had been crippled, the thing she had feared most had been that Rat Gaines would no longer love her.

Colonel Hardell had sensed what was troubling her and had helped her work through it. First he had given her a stern lecture. Then he had allowed Gaines to visit her after hours in her room. Obviously, his manipulations had paid off.

"I haven't seen you looking this happy in a long time, Lisa."

12

The nurse laughed. "Aren't all women supposed to be happy when they get married, sir?"

"See," Hardell answered. "I told you that Captain Gaines is an honorable man."

"He was almost too honorable," she laughed. "Him and his southern-gentleman routine. I had to threaten to scream if he didn't get into bed with me. He was afraid that he was going to hurt me."

The colonel laughed, "Well, it worked out just fine, didn't it?"

Lisa grinned.

"When are you going to get married?" he asked.

"Next month, when he takes his R and R in Hawaii. We were going to do it here, but then Dad came up with an assignment for me at the big hospital in the islands, and I have to leave now. I'm going to be in charge of an amputee ward."

"That's great, I hadn't heard about that."

"Dad's still working on the orders, but he says that it's a firm assignment. I'll report there after I take a couple weeks' leave."

"I see that it still helps to have friends in high places."

Lisa grinned. "Doesn't it just?"

"And I understand that you're flying out in the morning?"

"Right. I've got to take the early courier flight to Da Nang so I can get processed and get on a ten o'clock Freedom Bird."

"Are you glad to be going?"

A slight frown crossed Lisa's face. "To be honest with you, sir, I don't really know. I've been here so long that I'm not sure if I remember how to act when there isn't a war going on."

Hardell laughed. "You'll remember soon enough, I promise you. It'll all come back so fast that you won't even know that you were away."

"I sure hope so."

CHAPTER 3

North of Hue, 3 March

The muscular black sergeant hugged the mud on the side of the rice dike. AK fire slamming into the other side kicked dirt into the air. He had lost his helmet in the crash of the chopper, and his shaved head gleamed in the afternoon sun.

To the men of the Blues, Master Sergeant Leo Zack was known as Leo the Lionhearted, but the Vietnamese had named him the Black Buddha because of his shaved head. By either name, however, the veteran of the Korean War as well as two years with the Air Cav in Vietnam, was a real force to be reckoned with around the First of the 7th Cav.

Right now, however, none of that really seemed to matter a hell of a lot. He was pinned down by the dinks who had shot him out of the sky, and there was a real good chance that he was going to get his ass wasted if he wasn't very careful.

The pilot of the slick he had been flying in had gotten careless, doing a low-level recon of the wood line. He had flown in a little too close and it had cost him a burst of RPD machine-gun fire up the ass.

It put the Huey right down on the ground in a crash landing. The pilot was wounded and one of the grunts had a broken arm, but that was about the extent of the casualties. Except, however, for the antenna to the squad's Prick-25 radio. It had been snapped off at the base, and Zack couldn't get through to anyone. He also couldn't get back to the chopper to try to use its radios. The dinks were just waiting for him to try that.

Right now, Zack had seven grunts and three unwounded chopper crewmen trying to hold off an unknown number of NVA in the wood line. If they didn't get help they were going to find themselves in a world of serious trouble.

When Alexander couldn't reestablish radio contact with Zack, he radioed Cliff Gabriel, who was flying Brody's slick.

"I've lost contact with Blue Five. He was sending me coordinates of a possible enemy position when he was cut off. I want you to search the area around seven three five, four six whatever. I didn't get the last number. Over."

"This is Three Five, Roger," Gabe called back. "Be advised that my gunships are bingo fuel and have returned to PK-seventeen to refuel. Over."

Alexander cursed under his breath. That was all he needed, a loss of fire support. "This is Blue Six, Roger copy. Tell 'em to haul ass back here as soon as they're done. Over."

"Three Five, Roger. Out."

Alexander got on the horn to the battalion TOC, tactical operations center, back at Camp Evans to tell them the situation. Meanwhile, Gabe started searching the area of the coordinates Zack had sent in a few minutes earlier. "There they are!" he called back on the intercom.

Brody looked down and saw the slick sitting in a rice paddy only a hundred meters or so from a wood line. It didn't appear to have been hit too badly, but that was hard to tell from the air. He also saw the crew and the grunts huddled behind the rice dike. Green AK tracer fire played over the top of the dike.

"Gabe!" Brody yelled up over the intercom. "Fly past their front and I'll hose 'em down."

The pilot rogered and banked the slick around for a high-speed run. Brody leaned into his M-60 doorgun and sent a stream of red 7.62mm tracers reaching down into the jungle below. An answering burst of green tracer fire came back up at him.

"Machine gun on the left!" he yelled.

"Got it," Gabe snapped back. While the copilot called in their sighting, Gabe racked the slick around sharply to line up for a run at the gun. Brody leaned out into the slipstream straining against his lifeline, and poured fire into the enemy position.

Soon the overused barrel of his doorgun smoked in the cool downblast of the rotors, and the floor of the door gunner's pocket was littered with empty 7.62mm brass and machine-gun belt links. The last of the ammo belt ran through the breech and the gun fell silent. Brody reached down to the rack of ammo cans at his feet and ripped open the lid on another can of 7.62mm linked belts. Flipping up the feed-tray cover on the hot sixty, he laid the ammo belt in place and snapped the cover back down. He reached down to the right side of the gun and hauled back on the charging handle, pulling the bolt to the rear. He was ready to go again.

Gabe completed his low-level turn and banked hard to bring the chopper screaming down again. He had to keep the pressure off the guys behind the dikes until his gunships got there.

The C-and-C ship finally arrived overhead, and Alexander saw Gabe's slick start his second run. He turned to his artillery forward observer, SP/4 Bernie Rabdo, better known as the Bunny Rabbit, who was seated next to him. "Can you get some fire on that? I'll get Gabe out of there and you call it in."

Alexander had just finished warning Gabe to clear out of the area when he saw that Bunny was still frantically searching his map for the coordinates of the downed ship. Bunny

16

was one of the best FOs in the business, but he was not well practiced at directing artillery fire from the air. On the ground he was an ace cannon shooter, but there was something about reading a map from the air that he had not quite gotten the hang of.

Alexander impatiently stabbed his finger down on the map and Bunny nodded. The FO quickly wrote the six-digit coordinates on the combat acetate map cover and keyed the handset to his radio.

"Red Leg Delta, Red Leg Delta," Bunny called urgently. "This is Blue Two Tango, Blue Two Tango. Fire mission. Over."

"Two Tango, this is Delta," came the return call from PK-17, the closest artillery firebase. "I hear you Ham and Limas. Send your traffic. Over."

"This is Two Tango. The target is troops in a wood line at seven three five, four six eight. I need one oh five, H.E., danger close. Pop one and I'll adjust from the air. Over."

"This is Delta, Roger. I copy seven three five, four six eight. One oh five, H.E., danger close. Will adjust. Tango, are you sure about the danger close? Over."

"This is Tango. Roger, good copy. I say again danger close. Get it coming," he shouted. "They're up to their asses in dinks down there. Over."

"This is Delta. Wait one. Out."

It took longer than usual for the 105mm howitzer battery to get into action. Usually, the guns could have the first round on the way in a minute or so. But Bunny was calling for the most dangerous cannon shot of all, the artillery's version of a bayonet charge; something that was done only in extreme circumstances. He was calling for the rounds to come in danger close, less than one hundred meters from the rice dike that the men were hiding behind. The calculations from the fire direction center had to be exactly on target. If someone in the FDC misplaced a decimal point and one of the shells impacted on the dike instead of in the wood line, Zack and his people down there would be dead before they even had time to realize that someone had fucked up.

It seemed like an eternity before the thin voice on the radio said, "Blue Two Tango, this is Red Leg Delta. Shot over."

"This is Tango, shot out." Bunny acknowledged that the first round was on the way. He couldn't hear the rushing sound of the round over the noise of the rotors and had to rely on the FDC telling him that it was due to land. "This is Delta. Splash. Over."

"Roger. Splash. Out"

The burst of the marking round coincided with Delta's warning of splash. It was almost on target, just a little behind and off to the right.

"Delta, this is Two Tango," Bunny radioed the corrections. "From registration, drop one hundred, left one hundred, fire for effect. Over."

"Delta, Roger. Drop one hundred, left one hundred, fire for effect. Out." There was a long pause before Bravo came back on the air.

"Tango, this is Delta. Shot over."

This time, Bunny could hear the rounds come in with the sound of a dozen speeding trains. The forward edge of the tree line blossomed with bursts of dirty black smoke and angry red flames.

"Delta, this is Tango," Bunny radioed over the thundering detonations. "You're right on target. Keep it coming!"

"This is Delta, Roger."

Red-hot shards of shrapnel whizzed through the air, slicing into the jungle. A foot-long, jagged piece of steel slammed into the muddy dike a few inches from Zack's head, sizzling and steaming in the damp earth.

This was a little too close for comfort, but at least it kept the dinks' heads down. All too soon, the artillery fire cut off and the AKs started up again. Over the sound of the AKs, Zack heard approaching rotors. The artillery had cut off to let the gunships come in.

" 'Bout fucking time," Zack growled as he glanced up.

18

A single Cobra was bearing down on the wood line in front of them. It was the most beautiful sight he had ever seen. The rest of the gun team was still half a klick behind him.

The front of the gunship suddenly looked like it had burst into flames. It was the gunner, triggering off everything that he had, all at once. The thumper in the turret spit 40mm grenades, the side-mounted miniguns blazed fire at 4,000 rounds a minute, and he volleyed 2.75-inch H.E. rockets from the pylon-mounted pods, one right after another. The recoil from all the weapons firing at once was almost enough to stop the diving chopper dead in its tracks.

The tree line in front of him exploded. Zack ducked. He couldn't see who was at the controls, but it had to be Lawless Warlokk. No one else was crazy enough to make a banzai firing run like that.

The gunship flashed on past them, chased by green tracer fire from the AKs. The NVA were pissed.

Warlokk pulled the nose of his ship up sharply, banked her over on her side, and savagely kicked the tail around. The heavily laden gunship staggered in the sky, hanging right on the edge of a stall, her rotors unloading and losing lift. Warlokk was far too low and flying much too slowly to try that kind of maneuver, but right at the last moment, he got her back under control. Snapping his ship back upright, he bore back down on the jungle again, his guns blazing.

By this time, the rest of the gunship team had arrived. They paired off to start their runs, coming in from the opposite direction. For a short time, the gunships had it all their own way, whiplashing the hidden enemy from both directions. Then it got serious.

With the gunships doing their best to keep the gooks' heads down, Gabe swooped his Huey down low to the ground and flared out to land on the other side of the downed chopper. As soon as the troop ship was committed and couldn't pull away, a storm of AK fire reached out for it.

Before the skids had even touched the ground, Brody grabbed his M-16 from the rack behind his head and jumped out of the open side door. "Go! Go! Go!" he yelled, waving his men forward.

The grunts followed him, screaming their war cries as they leaped from the slick into a storm of fire.

The weight of the ruck on his back drove Brody to his knees in the paddy. AK tracer rounds flashed over his head. He ducked and rolled out of the line of fire. To his left, Corky was in a gun fighter's crouch, hosing down the wood line with long bursts from his Pig. The barrel of the M-60 was already smoking. Farmer was beside him, adding fire from his rifle to that of the machine gun, while the rest of the squad ran for the cover of the dike in front of them.

Zack looked around the rice paddy. The grunts were stopped cold. Even with the gunships working out, the gooks were still zeroed in on them. In just a few seconds, they were going to start taking casualties. It was time to get the boys off their asses and back onto their feet. If they were going to die in this stinking rice paddy, at least they could die standing up.

He pulled an M-26 hand grenade from his ammo pouch and got to his knees. "Grenades!" he bellowed over the storm of rifle and machine-gun fire, throwing the hand frag as far out in front of him as he could. "Give 'em grenades!"

The M-79 grenadiers came to their senses. From their prone position, they started sending a barrage of the deadly little 40mm grenades toward the tree line. The sharp cracks of their explosions could be heard above the roar of small-arms fire. The AK fire slackened just as one of the gunships flashed overhead again.

Dirty white smoke blew back from the rocketpods and 2.75's lanced out from the side of the ship in pairs. The ripping chainsaw sound of the miniguns firing on the fast rate, four thousand rounds a minute, filled the grunts' ears. A solid stream of fire tore into the tree line. Nothing could live through that, and the gooks were no exception.

"Let's get it!" Zack screamed, jumping to his feet and

triggering off a full magazine. The handful of men stood up with him.

"Come on!" the black NCO swept his arm up over his head in a classic Fort Benning Infantry School "follow me" gesture. It never ceased to amaze him, but that always seemed to work. The day he stood up and no one followed him would be the day that he would die in battle. That was not going to be this day or this firefight.

Yelling like maniacs, the Blues charged the wood line, their weapons blazing.

Farmer ran beside his platoon daddy, emptying one magazine after another into the jungle, reloading as he ran. One of the gunships swept past low over their heads, the downblast of its rotors buffeting his face. Hot, empty cartridge cases from the roaring miniguns rained down on him. Farmer laughed. He threw back his head and screamed, "Eat shit and die, motherfucker!"

The bolt of his M-16 locked back. He was out of ammunition. Farmer dropped the empty magazine out of the bottom of the rifle and jammed a loaded one into pace. He hit the bolt release, chambering a round, and lay down on the trigger again. "Motherfucker!" he screamed.

By this time, Zack's charge had taken the Blues to the edge of the woods. The men plunged into the brush only to find that the gooks had vacated the premises for quieter surroundings.

Zack gave the men a minute to catch their breath. Using Brody's radio, he got on the horn to the lieutenant overhead. Alexander wanted them to search the area before they called it a day. Just because this one bunch of gooks had split, it didn't mean that there might not be a few more who had not gotten the message. With First Squad moving out on point, they started clearing the wood line, looking for signs of the enemy unit.

Overhead, the gunships circled like vultures, ready for a target to appear through the open spaces in the scattered brush. In the C-and-C ship, Alexander waited to vector the choppers in to anything that the grunts ran across. It was a dry run. Whoever had been there was gone now.

"Blue Five," Alexander finally called down to Zack. "This is Blue Six. Over."

"Five, go."

"This is Six. Let's wrap it up down there. We don't want to be late for the party. Over."

"Five, Roger. Out."

CHAPTER 4

Camp Evans, 3 March

By 1700 hours, things were rocking and rolling in the 7th Cav's EM club. The juke box was blaring out Eric Burdon and the Animals, and a couple of drunks were already dancing on the tables. It was a little early for that kind of activity, but nobody minded. They were all too busy celebrating and letting it all hang out. After all, the drinks were on Echo Company tonight.

The word about the party had spread quickly throughout Camp Evans, and the club was jammed with people wanting to congratulate Gaines and the nurse—staff REMF's from the brigade headquarters in pressed fatigues and spit-shined boots, Doughnut Dollies in crisp light blue uniforms, infantry officers, chopper mechanics with black grease under their fingernails, and the grunts of the battalion. It was a typical Air Cav party, and almost everybody would get blasted before the night was over.

It had been quite awhile since there had been a big battalion blowout in the 7th Cav, and this was the best excuse they had had to get drunk in weeks. Not only was it a goodbye party for Lisa, it wasn't everyday that the battalion's leading chopper pilot and favorite nurse decided to tie the knot.

Rat had arrived at the party by himself. Lisa was coming over with the rest of the nurses, and he had told her that he would meet her in the club later. He had showered and changed into a clean flight suit, with the big Python Flight insignia on the front and a full-color Air Cav patch on the shoulder. He was wearing his Cavalry yellow ascot and his one pair of polished jump boots. After all, he wanted to look and smell his very best tonight.

"Hey, Rat!" Walt Greenfield, the aviation maintenance officer from the division G-4, walked up to the pilot. "Does getting married mean that you're going to stop flying like a fucking crazy man and smashing up my choppers all the time?"

Gaines threw his left arm over the maintenance officer's shoulder and put his right hand over his heart. "Walt, my man, on my word as a true son of the South, I promise that I'll continue to do my level best to create my fair share of work for your mechanics."

"Thanks a lot, asshole."

"No problem," Gaines grinned. "I'm always glad to help the G-four."

Gaines glanced around the crowded room and spotted his battalion commander, Lieutenant Colonel Maxwell T. Jordan, standing alone at the bar. He walked up to him with his right hand extended. "I'm glad you could make it tonight, sir," he said with a big smile.

Jordan shook his hand and clapped him on the shoulder. "Wouldn't have missed it for the world, Rat," he grinned. "I'm always glad to see one of my bachelor officers finally join the ranks of the rest of us henpecked old married men."

Gaines laughed. "Well, sir, I guess that it had to happen sooner or later."

"Congratulations, anyway." Jordan smiled. "I came early so I could get something to eat before I have to leave for a briefing at Brigade tonight. Something about a warning order for our next operation."

"Whaddaya you think it is, sir?"

"I really don't have a clue." Jordan frowned slightly. "Everything's real hush-hush right now. All I know is that it's something big."

Despite his tone, Jordan wasn't at all worried. He was confident that his battalion could handle anything that the brigade or the dinks threw at them. They had done a magnificent job during the Tet offensive, and he knew that they would perform just as well on their next operation.

Jordan was one of those men who was born to command men in combat. On his first tour in the Nam, he had been a major advising an ARVN Ranger company down in the Delta. He was proud to say that his Ranger company had been one of the best South Vietnamese units in all of the IV Corps area.

His company had specialized in night patrolling and ambushing, something not every ARVN unit wanted to do. In fact, damned few South Vietnamese troops were any good at all at night. But Jordan had figured that if the VC could work at night, then the ARVNs could do it, too—if they had some decent leadership to show them how it was done. Back then, Jordan had been known as "Mack the Knife" for the Randall fighting knife he always wore, and he had trained his ARVNs in silent knife kills on their night raids.

Those had truly been the good old days. One of the worst things about his promotion to lieutenant colonel was that he didn't get to go out in the woods with his troops anymore. Most of the time, the closest he got to field duty was orbiting overhead in his command-and-control ship, directing his infantry companies when they had a contact going.

Commanding a line battalion was the goal of every Regular Army officer, but he had to admit that most of the time it was a royal pain in the ass, with far more bullshit paper work to do than fighting communists. With the Tet offensive finally over, he was looking forward to tackling the mountain of paper work that had grown while he had been busy.

25

Now it looked like he might be able to put it off for a little longer. Things were going to get interesting again with this new operation, and whatever it was, he was ready for it. He reached into his pocket for his ever-present pack of Marlboros and lit one up.

"Well, sir," Gaines said. "We'd better go out back and see how the steaks are doing."

"Lead on."

The barbecue pits, cut-down fifty-five-gallon oil drums mounted on legs, had been set up behind the club, and the Echo Company mess sergeant was personally supervising the grilling of the steaks over glowing coals. He had scrounged thick, Air Force-issue sirloins for the occasion, and he wasn't about to let the other cooks screw up good meat.

"Good evening, Colonel, Captain Gaines," he said as the two men walked up to the grill. "What's your pleasure?"

Jordan looked over the grill. "It looks good. I'll have one medium rare."

"I'll wait on mine, but I'm expecting one still kicking," Gaines said.

"Coming up, Colonel."

The two officers walked over to a nearby, sandbagged mortar bunker to talk while the colonel ate his steak. "You locked on for that poop-and-snoop in the morning?" Jordan asked.

"No sweat, sir, it's just an escort mission," Gaines replied. The Python Flight gunships were to escort a flight of slicks taking Bravo Company on an early-morning insertion for a search-and-clear operation. "We'll be back in a couple of hours."

"By that time, I should have something for you about our next big job."

"I'm looking forward to it," Gaines grinned. "Things have been rather slow around here."

Top Richardson walked up to the two men. "Captain," he said, "Lieutenant Maddox is looking for you."

26

"Sorry, sir," Gaines said with a stage grimace. "Duty calls, got to run."

Jordan laughed. "See, I warned you. It's started already."

When Gaines entered the club, he didn't have to ask where Lisa was. There was a cluster of men in front of the bar, surrounding Lisa and every other off-duty nurse in camp. Rat shouldered his way through the crowd to reach her side.

"We've got to stop meeting like this," he whispered in her ear. He leaned over and nibbled her neck.

"That's fine with me," she smiled up at him. "Your place or mine?"

"Yours. Mine's a mess as always. And you've got the soft mattress."

Lisa laughed. Even though she was sad to be leaving the Air Cav and Vietnam after all these months, this was one of the happiest moments of her life. She shot a glance at the smiling pilot at her side.

"What you say we blow this joint?" he asked.

"But I'm the guest of honor," she protested.

"Screw 'em," Gaines growled.

"I'd rather screw you."

"You're on."

At the far end of the bar, one of the Python Flight pilots, Warrant Officer Joe Schmuchatelli, sipped at a gin and tonic and puffed on a thin cigar while he watched his company commander and Lisa mingle with the well-wishers in the crowd.

Schmuchatelli, better known around the flight line as Alphabet, was drinking alone. His date for the party, a FNG Red Cross girl he had just met, hadn't shown up. Maybe it was just as well. He wasn't really up to any strenuous activity. He was a little hung over from an all-night poker game the night before and was content just to sit back and watch his boss bask in glory.

Joe Schmuchatelli and his company commander came from totally different backgrounds and had completely different personalities, but the thin warrant officer pilot from New Jersey practically worshiped the stocky, southern captain. The reason was simple. Rat Gaines was the best gunship commander that Schmuchatelli had ever met.

Alphabet had flown with quite a few pilots since he first arrived in Vietnam. Some of them had been good and some had been only so-so. But before meeting Gaines, even the good ones had lacked the one quality that made Gaines stand out—his complete single-mindedness about what he was doing. Gaines lived to fly his gunship and to use it to inflict maximum damage on the enemy, and he allowed nothing to get in the way of that objective.

When Alphabet had first come to Python Flight, he had been Gaines's gunner. Much of Rat's attitude had rubbed off on him, as well as his taste in cigars. Now that he was an aircraft commander himself and flew his own Cobra, he did his best to fly and fight like his commander.

Holding Lisa's hand, Gaines walked up to the center of the bar. "Can I have your attention, please!" he shouted. No one paid him the slightest bit of attention. Most of the partygoers couldn't even hear him over the blare of the music.

Before Gaines could shout again, Alphabet reached around behind the cash register, got the .45-caliber automatic pistol out from under the bar, jacked a round into the chamber, and held it straight up into the air over his head.

"The man said that he wants your fucking attention!" he shouted.

The partygoers saw the pistol and shut up fast. When he first came to the 7th Cav, Gaines had gotten a reputation for blowing big holes in ceiling when people didn't listen to him. It looked like that little habit of his had worn off on Alphabet as well.

When everything calmed down, Alphabet casually put the .45 back under the cash register and took another drag on his cigar.

"As most of you already know, " Gaines said, "the

primary purpose of this party tonight is to say good-bye to Lisa.''

"Good-bye, Lisa," someone yelled out.

"Also, for those of you who don't already know, Lisa and I are going to get married next month, so I guess we're engaged.''

That announcement was greeted with cheers as well as a few boos. Rat wasn't bothered by the boos. "Eat your hearts out," he said, grinning.

"Anyway, whatever the reason for this party, on behalf of Echo Company and Python Flight I hope you all have a real good time tonight.''

Cheers rang out.

He turned to go and stopped suddenly. "Oh, one last thing," he said. "Python Guns, be on the flight line at oh seven hundred tomorrow, ready to go to work.''

Loud groans greeted that announcement. "Get stuffed, Rat!" someone shouted. Gaines continued grinning as he steered Lisa through the crowd on their way to the door.

"Well, I guess that's the last we're going to see of Lisa," Cliff Gabriel said, slurring over the words slightly as he raised his drink. The warrant officer-chopper pilot was well on the way to getting drunk.

His drinking companion, another warrant officer-pilot, Lance "Lawless" Warlokk, watched as Gaines and Lisa walked out. "Well," he slurred, no more sober than Gabe. "If you hadn't been such an asshole before Gaines got here, I might have been able to beat his time with her.''

This was an old argument with the two men. Long before Gaines had arrived, they had frequently battled with each other for the honor of Lisa's attention. The fact that the nurse hadn't paid the slightest bit of it to either one of them had made no difference at all. They both acted like schoolboys every time she was around.

"What the fuck you talking about, Lawless," Gabe shot back. "You're the one who was always getting in *my* road.''

"Fuck you, Gunslinger," Warlokk snorted. "You never

had a chance with her and you know it. I was just about to score big with her when Gaines showed up."

"Your ass, too."

When they got back to Lisa's room in the hospital, Rat closed the door behind him and took a deep breath, savoring the smell. Even over the harsh disinfectant odor of the hospital, the room smelled of her. That was something he was really going to miss until he caught up with her in Hawaii next month. Being with Lisa was the best way he knew to get away from the particularly offensive smell of the war. When he was in Lisa's room, it was easy to forget about everything but her.

"You got everything packed?" he asked.

"Yeah." She sat on the edge of the bed, pulled up her fatigue pants leg and started undoing the straps to her prosthesis. "All I've got to do is get down to the chopper pad in the morning."

Gaines watched her take the artificial leg off and lay it on the chair by her bed. Though he had grown used to seeing it, he still felt a twinge of sympathetic pain every time he watched her take it off.

"The flight leaves at oh six forty-five, right?"

"Right." She unbuttoned her fatigue jacket and freed her breasts from their very unmilitary-looking lace bra. "And the Freedom Bird leaves thirty minutes after I get to Da Nang."

He sat down on the bed beside her. "I'm going to miss you, girl." He reached out and pulled her to him, holding her tightly.

"I'm not gone yet," she said slyly.

Gaines grinned and reached for his boot laces. "No, you're not."

CHAPTER 5

South of Hue

The company of the 12th Cav was ambushed early that morning just as they left their overnight lager position. The NVA had spotted them the night before, but rather than hit them when they were all together in the company NDP, the night defensive position, they waited until morning, when they could catch them strung out in a marching formation.

The NVA commander's strategy was sound, and the American point platoon was quickly cut off from the rest of the company and chopped to pieces in a vicious crossfire. Responding to the panicked cries for help from his lieutenant, the company commander quickly called for artillery fire to aid his stricken platoon.

At the artillery firebase, the battery commander was away from the FDC, the fire direction center, and an FNG artillery lieutenant stepped in to do his first real fire mission. As he worked up the data for the guns, one of the FDC sergeants tried to help. The officer shrugged him off. This was his first real shoot and he was going to do it himself, just like he had been taught back in the artillery school at Fort Sill.

He quickly finished and gave the data to the gun crews.

In seconds, the first rounds were on their way. There was one thing, however, that the lieutenant had forgotten to do, something that he had not been taught at Fort Sill.

Because of the great number of choppers in the skies over Vietnam, an air warning was broadcast on a special frequency whenever the guns were to shoot, so aircraft could stay out of the target area. The lieutenant had been told about this procedure when he reported to the unit, but in his excitement, he forgot. The warning was not sent.

The infantry FO had just received the "shot" message from the FDC when he heard the sound of rotors to his front. He looked up in panic to see a Huey slick pass overhead at about three thousand feet. It entered the target area just as he heard "Splash" over the radio handset.

With a blinding flash, the chopper exploded in midair. A boiling ball of flame erupted as the fuel tanks went off. For an instant, the spinning rotor blades continued on their way although they had been blown off the masthead. Burning fragments of helicopter, crew, and passengers rained down on the lush green jungle. The biggest piece was the turbine, still spinning.

The horrified FO closed his eyes while the stunned grunts around him held their breath as the shower of burning metal hit the ground.

"Oh, sweet Jesus!" one of them prayed.

Colonel Jordan stood behind his desk, staring blankly out the window of his headquarters building at Camp Evans. Of all the things that he had ever had to do in his entire Army career, this was going to be the hardest. He glanced down at his watch for the third time in the last five minutes. Where the hell was Rat Gaines?

Jordan had left word down at Python Operations that he was to be called the instant that Captain Gaines landed. When Rat had come to the phone, Jordan had simply told him to report to his office ASAP. That had been ten minutes ago, and he still wasn't here.

Rank differences aside, Jordan really liked Gaines. Of all of his company commanders, he reminded him the most of himself when he had been a young company commander. Gaines was tough, hard charging, no nonsense, and intelligent. The perfect combination for the job of ramrodding an Air Cav company. Jordan couldn't have asked for a better junior officer to work with.

It had been a pleasure for the colonel to work with a man like Gaines. The battalion commander knew how his captain would react to any circumstance. Jordan didn't know, however, how Rat was going to react to what he had to tell him this morning.

He heard a knock on the door of his office. He straightened his fatigue jacket and stood tall before calling out, "Come in."

Gaines entered the room with his usual jaunty walk. A yellow Cavalry ascot was bunched up in the opening of his half-unzipped flight suit and a thin cigar was clamped in the corner of his mouth. "You wanted to see me, sir?" Gaines said around the cigar.

Jordan paused for a moment. His throat was dry and he swallowed. "Roger . . . ," he began.

A shadow passed over Gaines's face. No one called him by his first name unless it was serious.

". . . the chopper taking Lisa to Da Nang ran into an artillery flight path. It exploded in midair. They were all killed instantly."

For a second, he stood there unmoving. The two words *Lisa* and *chopper* raced through the recesses of his mind. They echoed in his ears. Lisa. Chopper. Lisa. Chopper. Then the last word, *killed,* entered his consciousness.

A whispered prayer passed his lips. "No, God! Please, no!"

Gaines closed his eyes for a moment. Maybe when he opened them, this would not be happening. He had to be dreaming. Just an hour ago he had seen her off at the chopper pad. He had put in the paper work for an R and R in Hawaii next month so they could get married. Maybe if he opened his eyes, Jordan would be biting his ass for something that one of his troops had done. She could not be dead.

Gaines opened his eyes and the stricken look on Jordan's face told him all that he needed to know. He felt his legs start to buckle and locked his knees to keep from falling. The cigar dropped from his hand unnoticed. He tried to breathe, but his lungs did not want to work. He felt a great paralyzing weight constricting his chest, and he fought to suck in air.

"Rat?" Jordan said.

Gaines took a deep breath. "I'm all right, sir."

"The graves registration people are at the crash site taking care of the remains now," Jordan said.

Gaines closed his eyes again and erased that part of his memory. He did not want to remember what the colonel had just said. Lisa could never be remains. Just a little over an hour ago, he had held her and kissed her good-bye at the chopper pad. Chopper. Lisa. Killed.

"The artillery did not send the air warning message before the fire mission." Gaines barely heard the colonel's voice. "The chopper was in the artillery flight path and took a direct hit from a one-oh-five. The GR people said they were all dead before they hit the ground."

Lisa. Chopper. Artillery. The words raced through Gaines's mind. He knew that he had to do something about this error, but it was too much for him to deal with now. He would do it later. I'll talk to her about it first, he thought. She'll know what I should do. Lisa! he cried inside. Lisa!

"You'd better have a seat," Jordan said, coming around the end of his desk. Gaines let himself be led to a chair. The colonel opened the bottom drawer of his desk and came out with a bottle of bourbon and a glass. He filled the glass and handed it to Gaines. Rat looked at the glass unseeingly.

"Go ahead," Jordan urged him.

The pilot took the glass. He had never felt such pain before in his life, but he could not drink. The bourbon would ease the pain and that would not be right. Lisa was dead. He wanted to feel the pain.

Jordan sat down behind the desk and waited, totally helpless to do anything for Gaines. Rat's eyes were mere slits, his pupils constricted as he looked into the barren future of his life. He shivered. How long had he been sitting here? It seemed like hours.

"Rat," the colonel said softly, "if you like, I can get Mike Alexander up here to take you back to your quarters. I also want you to let him look after things for a couple days."

The pilot's eyes snapped back into focus. "No, sir," he said slowly in his native southern accent. "I'm much obliged to you, sir, but I'd better be going on about my business."

He slowly stood up, surprised that his legs would carry his weight. "Thank you for telling me, sir," he said.

He turned and started to go.

"Rat?"

He stopped. "Yes, sir?"

Jordan paused. He didn't know what to say. "Get some rest."

"Yes, sir."

As he walked out of the battalion headquarters building, Gaines was vaguely aware that every eye was on him. He straightened his shoulders and squared his hat on his head. Outside, the bright sunlight hurt his eyes and he felt disoriented. He climbed into his jeep and started the engine. He sat for a moment, not knowing where to go next. He automatically pushed down on the clutch, slammed the gear shift into first gear, and pulled out onto the main road through the camp.

When Gaines focused in on his surroundings again, he found himself down on the flight line wandering around the gunships. That he had automatically driven himself to where the aircraft were was no surprise to him. They were a comfort to him.

35

Gaines was the son of a World War II Air Force bomber pilot from Atlanta, Georgia. Since his earliest boyhood days, he had always dreamed of flying fighters. When he was a boy, he had read every book he could get his hands on about World War II fighter pilots. His room had been full of dozens of models of his favorite fighter planes which he had built.

When he graduated from high school, he signed up for Air Force ROTC in college and started pilot training. Things were going very well for the young Gaines until his sophomore year when, to his complete disbelief, he flunked his P-1 category physical examination. The flight surgeon said that he had a slight heart murmur and had disqualified him from further flight training.

Faced with only being able to hold a non-flying job in the Air Force, Gaines quickly switched over to the Army ROTC infantry program. If he couldn't fly and fight his nation's enemies in the air, at least he could fight them on the ground.

Three years into his Army career as an infantry first lieutenant in Germany, Gaines read an article in the *Army Times* saying that the Army was looking for chopper pilots. The war in Vietnam was eating them up at a rapid rate, and the Army was taking practically anyone who wanted to fly "whop-whops." Gaines applied for flight training, passed the physical, and went to Fort Wolters, Texas to learn how to fly rotary-wing aircraft. Helicopters weren't jet fighters, but at last he was in the air.

He graduated close to the top of his class and requested a gunship assignment in Nam. His request had been granted and he quickly found himself in the First Air Cav commanding Python Flight.

This was what he had always wanted. It was not exactly what he had read about as a young boy—chasing Messerschmitts over Europe or splashing Zeros in the Pacific—but he was flying combat missions in a helicopter gunship, and that was how the war was fought in Vietnam. His obsession for flying had left him with little time to think about much of anything else. That was, of course, before he met Lisa.

Gaines had never met a woman he liked as much as he liked flying, so all of his relationships had been rather short. As soon as the woman he was sleeping with started talking about picking china patterns, Rat swiftly vacated her bed.

In Nam, there was no shortage of women whenever he felt the need to touch something soft and feminine. The locals were mostly beautiful, quite willing, and not too expensive. He had sampled many of them, but only as the need arose. He was not about to get tied down. Until, at least, he met Lisa. She had changed everything.

As much as he loved combat flying, he had been ready to give it up to live a peaceful life in the States with her. But now, all that had vanished in the blinding flash of a stray artillery shell, leaving him with only his Cobra gunship.

He walked slowly around his bird, drinking in every line of the sleek killing machine. The AH-1G Cobra was the world's first dedicated helicopter gunship, and it looked every inch the part. Where the Huey C-model gunships were really nothing more than slicks with guns and rocketpods bolted onto them, the Cobra had been designed from the beginning to be an aerial weapons system. The Cobra used the same turbine and broad-cord rotor blades of the D-model slick, but that was where the resemblance ended.

The Cobra was thin like a shark, only thirty-nine inches wide. She had stub wings on each side to carry her ordnance load. The wings also provided lift and took much of the load off the rotor head, making her far faster and much more maneuverable than the Hueys. She also sported a chin turret capable of holding two automatic thumpers, two miniguns, or one of each weapon. That turret, combined with the various underwing weapons loads she could carry, made the Cobra the deadliest chopper ever flown.

This was not his first Cobra. *Sudden Discomfort* had been shot down during the Tet offensive, and his gunner had died.

This bird was its replacement, and he had named her *Tiger's Revenge* after his dead gunner.

After completing his walk-around, he stopped at the right side of the cockpit canopy and opened it. Reaching inside, he pulled out his flight helmet and put it on before climbing into the cockpit. Locking the canopy down, he quickly tightened the shoulder harness and did a rapid preflight. His hand pulled the starter trigger on the collective, and the big 1,100-horsepower Lycoming T-53-13 burst into life. Over his head, the forty-four-foot rotor blades started spinning.

The screaming whine of the turbine behind his head was a welcome sound, the first welcome thing he had heard since he had left Jordan's office. He eased up on the collective control, and the Cobra came to a hover a few inches off the ground. He pushed in on the right rudder pedal, swinging the tail around and nudging forward on the cyclic. He taxied out onto the PSP runway.

Twisting the throttle full up against its stop, Gaines headed down the runway in a gunship takeoff. The panicked voice of the air-traffic controller in the tower came over his helmet radio, but he didn't bother to answer. He didn't have time for flight clearance and permissions today. He had to get up into the clear blue sky, away from things like artillery shells hitting helicopters and killing nurses.

CHAPTER 6

Camp Evans

Halfway down the flight line, Warrant Officer Lance "Lawless" Warlokk watched his commanding officer climb into his Cobra. He spun around and sprinted for his own gunship. He knew about Lisa's death and had been following Gaines to make sure he didn't do anything stupid. He wanted to offer his condolences, but Warlokk was not the most articulate of men, and he hadn't been able to think of anything to say that didn't sound stupid.

Lawless, as his nickname implied, was a hard-drinking, hard-living warrant officer-chopper pilot of the old school. His scarred face reflected the kind of life he had led, and few of the scars were from chopper crashes. Most of them had come from drunken barroom brawls. His reputation as a badass had been well known, and everyone around the battalion had wisely given him a wide berth. Everyone, that was, until he had run into Captain Rat Gaines. The soft-talking southerner didn't move out of the way for anyone.

Python Flight was one of the best Air Cav units in the entire division, but it hadn't always been that way. The only reason it was so good now was because of its current commander, Rat Gaines. In the months since Gaines had taken command of Echo Company, he had transformed the unit from a bunch of drunken assholes into a crack fighting outfit. In the air and on the ground, Gaines demanded—and received—the very best from all his people.

At the beginning, the tough, scar-faced Warlokk had resented both Gaines and the procedures that he had implemented to improve the unit. Warlokk had gone out of his way to make things difficult for him at every opportunity.

Gaines had not been impressed with Warlokk's attitude. Nor with Warlokk's reputation as a badass. As the saying went, the soft-talking southerner walked through the valley, but he feared no evil because he was the meanest motherfucker in the valley.

The scion of an old-line Georgia family, Gaines was used to having things go his way, and he had grown to expect it. He also knew how to enforce cooperation when someone wouldn't listen to his particular brand of reason.

Back home in Georgia, Rat's uncle had been one of the state's biggest moonshiners. While he was in college, the young Gaines had been his uncle's delivery man. He cut his teeth in barroom brawls, making deliveries to out-of-the-way, backwoods Georgia taverns. The lessons he learned there had been put to good use when he first arrived in An Khe and was assigned to command Python Flight.

When Warlokk finally challenged Gaines one night, Rat had welcomed it as a way to consolidate his command. Out behind the An Khe officers' club, he had proceeded to hammer Warlokk into the ground to show him the error of his ways.

Now Rat Gaines had no stauncher supporter than Lance Lawless Warlokk. There was always one thing about a professional badass. When he discovered that there was some guy who could kick his ass ten times out of ten, he quickly made friends. It was the law of the jungle.

Gaines had become the closest thing to a real friend that Warlokk had ever had. And now, of all times, Warlokk wasn't going to let him down. If Gaines was going to fly,

40

then Warlokk would be flying off his wing where he belonged.

He, too, quick-started his Cobra and taxied out onto the runway. By now the air-traffic controller had gotten his field glasses and could read the tail number of Warlokk's machine. "Cobra Six Niner," he radioed. "You do not have clearance to take off. Over."

The pilot did not answer.

"Six Niner, you are not cleared for takeoff."

"Fuck you," Warlokk finally radioed back.

"Six Niner!" Now the tower operator was really excited. "You're going on report for this. Stop right where you are and taxi back to the pad."

"Fuck you and the horse you rode in on."

"Six Niner," the tower screamed. "What's your name, rank, and unit? Over."

Warlokk grinned as he keyed his throat mike. "Evans Tower, this is CWO-four Lance Warlokk. Whiskey, Alpha, Romeo, Lima, Oscar, Kilo, Kilo. How copy? Over."

"Mr. Warlokk, bring that aircraft back. You are not cleared for takeoff."

By now the Cobra was racing down the runway. "Sonny boy," Warlokk calmly called back. He hauled up on the cyclic, causing the rotor blades to bite deeper into the air. "Didn't anybody ever tell you that Lawless Warlokk flies any fucking time he feels like it? Alpha Mike Foxtrot. Over."

The Cobra leaped into the sky, her rotor blades clawing for altitude.

"Six Niner, I did not read your last transmission. Say again. Over."

Warlokk grinned behind his face shield. "This is Six Niner. Roger, Tower, I say again, Alpha Mike Foxtrot. Adios, motherfucker. Six Niner out."

Warlokk searched the clear blue sky. Now where the hell was Rat Gaines?

He caught a dark speck in the distance at five thousand

feet, headed due west. That had to be him. He turned the wick up and took off after him as fast as he could go.

At five thousand feet over the jungle, Gaines's mind raced as he flew the Cobra on a mental autopilot. Flying a chopper is different from flying anything else in the sky, even the Space Shuttle. God did not intend helicopters to fly. They were inherently aerodynamically unstable, and it required a keen mind and two steady hands on the controls at all times to overcome the law of gravity. A chopper pilot couldn't afford to take one hand away for even a second to scratch his ass or he'd find himself falling out of the sky.

Fortunately for Gaines, almost of their own volition his hands did their own thing, leaving the rest of his mind free to seek peace in the clear, blue skies. Clear, blue skies that were full of things like artillery shells, exploding helicopters, and shattered bodies raining to the ground.

He finally felt the tears start in his eyes. He blinked to clear his vision and swallowed against the tightness in his throat. How could the clear blue skies have taken Lisa away from him? Against that backdrop, he released the scream that had been building inside him.

"Lisa!"

The sound tore from his throat like the cry of a wounded animal.

"Lisa!"

The pain that he had been choking down finally overwhelmed him. It felt like he was going to die and he welcomed the feeling. Maybe an unseen artillery shell would fly out of the clear blue sky and strike him down, too. Then the pain would be gone.

"Rat?"

Gaines's head snapped around. Who in the hell was up here with him?

"Rat, it's Lawless," came the voice in his helmet headphones. "I'm off your portside."

42

Gaines looked over his left shoulder and saw the familiar sight of Warlokk's Cobra. "What the fuck you doing here?"

"Thought you might need some company."

"I don't need a fucking baby-sitter," he snapped back. "Return to base."

"That's a negative, Python Lead." Warlokk suddenly got more formal. He had no intention of going back, but he also had a great deal of respect for Gaines's volatile temper. "Crazy Bull Six told me to keep an eye on you. He doesn't want you flying alone right now. Over."

That was a bald-faced lie, but there was no way that Gaines could know that.

"Lance," Gaines almost shouted into his throat mike. "I swear to Christ that if you don't leave me alone, I'm going to shoot your ass down."

Warlokk took a deep breath. That was no idle threat. Gaines was one of the best chopper pilots in Nam and the only one who had ever actually flown a Cobra in combat with another helicopter. "Sorry, boss," he replied calmly. "No can do."

With a cry of anguish, Gaines kicked down on his right rudder pedal and slammed the collective over to the right. Then Cobra whipped into a hard-banked turn, almost standing on its side.

Warlokk hadn't been caught by surprise, however, and followed Gaines's machine through the violent maneuver. He knew that he had to stay with Rat no matter what. If Gaines got into the clear, he just very well might shoot him down like he had threatened. If he was going to survive this, Warlokk had to keep up with Rat so he couldn't bring his guns to bear on him.

Rat Gaines might have been the best snake driver in the Nam, but Warlokk ran a close second. If Rat wanted to get away, he was going to have to work hard for it. Warlokk wasn't about to just give it to him. And if Gaines crashed while trying, the wreckage of Warlokk's gunship would be lying right beside his.

Gaines dumped the cyclic and the Cobra dropped like a

43

stone. Warlokk nosed his ship over and followed him down into the dive. As the airspeed crept up to the limit, Rat hauled back on the collective and cyclic controls at the same time. The Cobra's nose pulled up sharply as it zoomed into an almost vertical climb.

Hinged rotor helicopters like those in the Huey series were severely limited in their flight envelope. Unlike fixed-wing aircraft, there were many aerial maneuvers that they simply could not do. For instance, they could not fly upside down. They also could not roll too far over onto their sides or pull their noses up too sharply. If they did, the hinged rotors could collapse under the aerodynamic stress.

Not even the best pilot in the world could make a helicopter do something that it was not designed to do, but it looked like Gaines was trying, anyway. He had his machine in an almost vertical climb. He was pushing the outside of the envelope, and it was just about to snap shut around him.

Warlokk knew better, but he was trying his best to stay with his flight leader. It was said that there are old chopper pilots and bold chopper pilots, but that there are no old, bold chopper pilots. Gaines was doing his level best to prove that axiom. He was about to become a bold chopper pilot who would never live long enough to grow old.

Warlokk felt the stick in his hand shake as the rotor head started to unload. Ahead of him, he saw Gaines's bird shudder on the edge of rotor collapse.

"Rat!" Warlokk yelled over the radio. "Put your nose down!"

At the last possible moment, Gaines pushed forward on the cyclic and stomped down the rudder pedal to swing the tail around. Even in his grief, Gaines was too good a pilot to willfully destroy a good flying machine. The Cobra's tail snapped up level with the nose, and she went into a hard-banking turn.

Warlokk followed Gaines through the maneuver, keeping a little behind him and off to his portside.

"Captain," he radioed. "Give it up. You're not going to shake me, I'm going to stay with you no matter what. Why

44

don't you come on back with me? We'll talk about it on the ground.''

Rat continued to fly in a wide, banked circle with Warlokk tucked in right behind him in the six-o'clock position.

"Rat, come on home. It's not going to help if you get your ass killed." Warlokk's voice became harsher. "Captain, you've still got a company to run."

Gaines leveled his gunship out and Warlokk saw him raise one hand in acknowledgment from his cockpit. A second later, he got on the radio. "Lance?"

"Yes."

"I'm okay now." Gaines's voice was weary.

"I'll follow you back, sir."

Rat turned the nose of his ship in the direction of Camp Evans and assumed a normal flight path. "Lance?"

"Yes, sir."

"I still don't believe that she's gone."

Warlokk heard the pain in Gaines's voice. "I know, sir. I don't, either."

"Lance?"

"Yes, sir."

"Thanks."

"No sweat, sir."

Like to dragonflies chasing after one another, the Cobras flew through the clear blue sky back to Camp Evans. Warlokk was right. Lisa was dead, but Rat Gaines still had a company to run and a war to fight. There was a reason for him to continue living for at least a little while longer. Gaines decided to see how he felt at the end of the week and decide then if it was still worth it. If not, he could always join Lisa.

CHAPTER 7

Khe Sanh

David Janson hugged the side of the sandbagged bunker as a barrage of NVA 122mm rocket artillery shells fell on the beleaguered Marine base on top of the hill at Khe Sanh. Each thundering explosion shook the small squad bunker like a cat shaking a rat. Fine red dust puffed out of the sandbags, mixing with the overwhelming stench of too many men living underground for far too long. The dust made the reporter cough, but his nose had long since grown accustomed to the rancid, sickly sweet smell of unwashed armpits, fear, and rotting boot socks.

Janson was in his late thirties, far older than the squad of Marine grunts crowded in the bunker with him, and he was trim as only a man living in the field can be. He wore a sun-faded set of sweat-stained jungle fatigues like the Marines, but instead of an M-16 in his hand, he carried three cameras around his neck. David Janson was a reporter covering the story of the siege of the Marine garrison at Khe Sanh.

A big part of the Khe Sanh story were the hundreds of enemy artillery and rocket shells that rained down on the besieged base every day. Since January 21, when the siege began, the NVA had shelled the Marines with 130mm and 152mm Russian-made long-range guns dug deep into the hills surrounding the base. And when the big guns weren't working, deadly 122mm rockets were.

Every day the Marines huddled in their holes with their steel pots jammed down tight on their heads until the shelling was all over. The last explosions faded away and the men in the bunker relaxed enough to start talking.

"Mr. Janson, just why the fuck are you putting up with this shit, man?" one of the Marines leaned forward to ask him. "You've been here before. I've seen you around. So why'd you come back here for more of this shit? None of them other hotshot, asshole, chickenshit reporters are staying here with us. They just fly in, take a few pictures, and get their sweet, lily-white asses back out as fast as they can. Why the fuck are you doing this to yourself, man?"

The man had asked a serious question and Janson answered it seriously.

"Well, as long as you guys are up here doing your job, I think that somebody ought to be letting the people back home know what you're going through. And that's my job."

"I hope the fuck you're getting combat pay for it," a second Marine laughed.

"Yeah, but why you?" the first man continued. "You look like you're smarter than that."

"Well . . ." Janson slowly grinned as he looked around the crowded bunker. "All I can say is that it seemed to be a good idea at the time."

The Marine slowly shook his head as the other grunts laughed at the age-old joke. "Man, you are one bookoo crazy motherfucker. You know that? They ought to lock you up somewhere for your own good."

"Well, I'll tell you what, then," another grunt spoke up. "When they come to take him away, they can take me right along with him. I'm fucking crazy for ever having joined up with this fucking crotch in the first place."

"Fuck you, man," the guy beside him said. "You love

this shit. Admit it. Just the other day I saw you talking to the re-up man.''

"The fuck I was,'' the Marine shot back. "That must have been some other dumb sonofabitch. I ain't about to be talking to no fucking re-up man. You think I'm fucking crazy?''

"You're a grunt, ain't you?''

Everybody in the bunker, including the reporter, laughed at that one. The all-clear siren sounded, and one of the grunts got to his feet.

"Let's go see what Luke the Gook hit this time. I hope to Christ they didn't hit the crapper, I've got to take a dump.''

Janson followed the men out of the bunker. A smoky pall hung over the camp. Scattered fires were burning and the litter parties were already going from one bunker to the next checking for casualties. Janson walked over to where the medics were digging through the rubble of a small bunker that had taken a direct hit from one of the Chi-Com 122mm rockets.

A tanned hand, dusted with the fine red dirt of Khe Sanh, was sticking out of the rubble. The hand wasn't moving. Janson took a couple of quick shots of the medics and then left them to their work. He had learned long ago that it was not a good idea to photograph the dead in front of their still-living friends.

Back when he had been like all too many of the assholes in the Vietnam press corps, just another posturing, smart-mouth journalist looking for the "big story,'' he had taken sensational photographs of dead GIs. But not anymore. He had learned that they deserved respect.

When Janson had first come to Vietnam, he had initially gone up to the First Air Cavalry AO looking for the "Big Story.'' To most Americans, the Air Cav, with their hundreds of choppers, were seen as the glory outfit in the war. The division staff went out of the way to treat the press well so they would continue to get good publicity.

Instead of finding the glory of airmobile operations or

the "big story" with the Air Cav, Janson had gotten a far more important story about young Americans putting their lives on the line to try to save a small country from falling to the communist invaders from the north.

It had almost cost him his own life to get that story, and later, when he had insisted that his editor print what he had seen, it had cost his job at the news bureau. But he had seen the reality of the Vietnam War and it had changed him.

Janson now worked as a free-lance journalist reporting the war from the grunt's viewpoint. And from what he had been reading in the papers and seeing on television lately, he was one of the very few reporters in country who seemed to care about what was happening to the American fighting man.

Now that the Tet offensive had ended, the press was having a field day doing the "Monday-morning quarterback" number on the military. Everyone was so busy trying to lay blame that they had completely forgotten the people who had turned the North Vietnamese surprise attack into the worst defeat that the dinks had suffered in the entire war. The fact that he was interested in the men who were fighting the war was the sole reason why Janson was with the Marines in Khe Sanh.

Vietnam was a war where nothing seemed to make much sense, but Khe Sanh was a strange battle even for the Nam. The self-proclaimed "experts" in the press and Congress all said it was going to be another Dien Bien Phu, a replay of the dramatic battle that had cost the French their war in Vietnam. To Janson, however, what he had seen so far reminded him more of the battle of Verdun, France in the First World War.

When he had lived in Europe, he had visited the Verdun battlefield several times and had been shocked at the destruction that was still visible even though fifty years had passed. Verdun had been a killing field on a scale never before seen in the history of modern warfare. The German army had created a small salient in their own lines, backed by the world's greatest concentration of artillery, and invited the French to attack. Anybody else would have smelled a rat and backed off. But the French, being French, took the bait.

It was said that three-quarters of a million men had died in that small area in just a little over a year. Most of them died in the never-ending artillery barrages and their bodies were never recovered. So many shells were fired that the ground was still poisoned by the residue of the explosives.

Like Verdun, Khe Sanh had also become a killing ground on a grand scale. An economy-of-force operation, the military strategists liked to call it. After years of frustration trying to chase elusive enemy forces around in the jungle, General Westmoreland had wanted to engage the North Vietnamese Army in a major battle where the superiority of American firepower could be brought to bear to inflict a crushing defeat on them. He had chosen Khe Sanh as the site for that battle.

Khe Sanh was a lonely outpost stuck way out in the middle of the northwesternmost corner of Vietnam, just a few klicks from the Laotian border. It was out of the way, so a big battle there wouldn't involve civilian population centers. Another reason it had been chosen was because it straddled a major NVA supply corridor branching off from the Ho Chi Minh Trail. The NVA had to protect that supply line at all costs.

Once Khe Sanh had been home to a small Special Forces camp keeping watch on NVA and VC infiltration, but the Green Berets had moved their camp down the road to Lang Vei when the first of the Marine garrison arrived in late 1966. By early January 1968, General Westmoreland had ordered the Marine garrison reinforced to the point that the NVA would have to see them as a serious threat to their supply operations in I Corps. The Marines had been dangled out there as bait. Just as the French had taken the bait at Verdun, the North Vietnamese high command decided to meet the challenge.

North Vietnamese General Vo Nguyen Giap, who ran the war for Hanoi, quickly moved four NVA divisions, some forty thousand men, backed up by the largest concentration of artillery yet seen in Vietnam, into the hills surrounding the base. Effectively, this cut the Marines off from the rest of Vietnam.

Giap might have wanted to pull off another Dien Bien Phu at Khe Sanh, but instead he was reliving the Battle of Verdun. This time, though, his forces were playing the part of the French. They were walking into a meat grinder.

What Giap had not taken into consideration was the vast American air fleet. Khe Sanh was cut off on the ground, but it was being supplied and supported by air on a scale that had not been seen before in Vietnam. That air support continually pounded the North Vietnamese troops surrounding the base, just as the NVA pounded the Marines with their artillery.

Though Khe Sanh was turning into a great killing ground for the NVA, the battle was not at all one sided. The Marines were getting the shit kicked out of them on a daily basis.

Janson saw that a fire was still raging in one of the cargoplane wrecks that littered the side of the short PSP runway. The NVA artillery periodically closed the runway to takeoffs and landings, so most of the supplies reaching the Marines had to be air-dropped or choppered in. Janson himself had arrived by helicopter and had been fired at all the way in on his final approach. The chopper had quickly loaded up and flown back out through a barrage of antiaircraft fire, packed with wounded Marines.

On February 23, the base suffered through the worst artillery barrage of the siege. Thousands of rounds fell in just a few hours. Six days later, the NVA launched a massive ground attack that reached to within a few meters of the inner perimeter wire before it was stopped. The Marines were holding on by their fingernails, but they were holding. As Janson had seen in Hue, the Marines were at their best when they had their backs to the wall. It was taking a fearsome toll on them, though, and Janson was beginning to wonder if it was worth it.

Janson was not the only one who was worried about Khe Sanh. Unknown to him, just the day before, an urgent meeting had been held in Da Nang. The decision had been made to send the Air Cav to the Marines' rescue.

Now that the Tet offensive was for all intents and purposes ended, General Westmoreland needed to turn the situation at Khe Sanh around. In the urgency of Tet, the surrounded Marine garrison had been forced to take a back seat to the more pressing problems in the cities, and they had been more or less left on their own. It was high time that those gallant men were relieved, and the sooner the better.

President Johnson had been so concerned about Khe Sanh, he had extracted a promise from General Westmoreland that the base would not fall. Now was the time to make good on that promise.

In the meeting, a plan was hammered out that would result in the Air Cav making the first divisional-level airmobile operation in military history. The entire Air Cavalry division would amass and strike deep into the ring of enemy units strangling Khe Sanh. The operation was code-named Pegasus and D-Day was scheduled to kick off on April 2.

That was almost a full month away, but it would take that much time to gather the men and the material needed—and to build the forward bases required to support the operation. Until the Cav could get everything in place, the Marines just had to keep on holding on. There was no way out.

CHAPTER 8

Khe Sanh

David Janson marveled at the beauty of the sunset over Khe Sanh. Smoke and dust in the air filtered the sun's rays down to a warm golden hue. As he looked out over the perimeter, a pair of Navy A4D Skyhawk jet fighter-bombers dove out of the sun to deliver their ordnance on Hill 881 South, one of the major NVA artillery firebases. The falling napalm canisters glinted silver in the dying sunlight as they tumbled down onto their targets. Angry black-and-red fireballs burst into life just as the sun slipped down below the horizon.

"Jesus," one of the Marines in the trench with him breathed. "That's fucking beautiful!"

Janson knew better than to ask the man if he was referring to the sinking sun or the deadly blossoms of flame from the napalm. He knew what the answer would be.

The Fords, as the Skyhawks were called, completed their runs and banked off to return to Da Nang. Daylight was ending and the air strikes wouldn't start again until morning.

The siege was in its forty-third day and the effect on the defenders was greater than anything Janson had ever seen. He had seen men in tight spots before. Hue had certainly been no picnic. But he had never been with men cut off like these grunts were. This was like something straight out of a castle siege in the Middle Ages, not the fluid warfare of the jungle combat he had grown accustomed to.

Jordan's mind kept drifting back to Verdun. The difference, though, was that, unlike at Verdun, these men were cut off. They had no respite from the daily pounding they were taking, no refuge. They did not even have the mental reassurance of a rear area, a place to go where it was safe. All they could do was to huddle in their bunkers and trenches and take it.

"You going to stay with us again tonight, Mr. Janson?"

The reporter turned to see Wee Willie, one of the Marines from the bunker he had been living in for the last few days. "Sure," he answered. "Why not?"

Williams grinned. "Great. We don't ever get in the shit when you're with us."

Janson laughed. "Well, the dinks know that it doesn't look good if they wax a reporter, so they try not to shoot too many of us."

Just then Sergeant Bernowski, the squad leader, walked by. "Willie, you got the early shift tonight."

"No sweat, Bear."

Beronski fit his nickname. He looked like a bear in human form. The hair on his arms was as thick as the hair on his head and he walked with his broad shoulders slumped forward, making his arms hang like the front legs of a bear walking upright. He carried an M-14 rifle because the smaller M-16 was just too short for him to use. Janson felt comfortable with him around.

"Mr. Janson," Bear said. "One of the pogues over at the battalion TOC said he was looking for you."

"Pogue" was the Marine term for what the Army called an REMF, a rear-echelon motherfucker, a non-combatant, the clerks and jerks of an infantry unit. Considering the circumstances, Janson wondered if anyone at Khe Sanh could be called a non-combatant, including himself.

54

"Thanks," the reporter answered. "I'll go see what he wants."

Darkness was falling fast, so he hurried to the battalion headquarters. On the way over, he saw a work detail filling sandbags to rebuild one of the bunkers. It was a full-time job at Khe Sanh. Considering the pounding they were taking from the enemy artillery, the Marines were not well dug in. Many of their positions did not have overhead cover and even those that did were not reinforced to withstand the shelling. Compared to Army defensive positions he had seen, the Marines were not very good at bunker building.

Janson was no knee-jerk critic of the military, but he was beginning to worry about the situation. The more he saw, the more he was beginning to believe that this operation had not been well thought out. The main problem was the use of the Marines for the mission. As he had seen in Hue, the Marines were good offensive fighters, but they did not have the defensive mentality, nor the engineer backup to properly fortify a place like this. Had the Army been at Khe Sanh, they would have burrowed ten feet underground and had another three feet of overhead cover.

The Khe Sanh operation was killing dinks for the generals as planned, but it was also killing many American Marines.

At the Marine battalion headquarters he located the pogue who was looking for him. The adjutant was holding a package that had come in on one of the resupply choppers. In the package were clippings from a couple of his Khe Sanh stories that had been published and a request from the editor for more of the same. It looked like he was in the right place at the right time, for a change.

"Mr. Janson?"

He turned to the adjutant. "When do you want me to lay on your transportation, sir?"

"Transportation?"

"You'll be leaving us soon, won't you?"

Janson laughed. "No. I'm going to sit this one out with you guys."

The adjutant looked at Janson as if he had two heads. He shrugged his shoulders. "Okay. But whenever you want to leave, I need a day's notice to set it up."

"I'll remember." Janson turned to go.

On his way back to the perimeter, he decided to stop off by the Alamo Hilton, the Seabees' bunker, and talk to them for a while. He had always gotten good stories from the Bees.

When Janson came back from the Seabees' bunker several hours later, he couldn't get to sleep. Usually, like any of the grunts he lived with, he could fall asleep any time he stopped moving long enough. He glanced down at his Army-issue plastic Timex watch. The luminous hands on the dial told him that it was just past eleven o'clock, more properly, 2300 hours.

He stood up. Wrapping the arm poncho liner tightly around him, he went out into the trench outside the bunker. The night air was chilly this high up in the mountains, and he was glad that he had the poncho liner. Of all the things that were in use by the military in Vietnam, the poncho liner and the P-38 C-ration can opener were the only two that you could count on to do the job every time.

Outside the bunker, the velvety black night beyond the wire was intermittently lit by flares. Inside the perimeter, the base was blacked out, the only visible light came from a door left ajar in one of the commo bunkers where someone kept radio watch. He quickly looked away from it so as not to wipe out his night vision, but realized that the flare had already done that for him.

Bear's squad was on guard, and the burly squad leader nodded when he recognized Janson. Willie came up to him and offered the reporter a C-ration cracker with cheese spread on it. Janson took the cracker and munched the stale thing down as a gesture of camaraderie. Willie handed him his canteen without even being asked. Janson drank and handed it back.

"Thanks."

"They're up to something tonight, Mr. Janson," Willie said. "We haven't heard them digging."

Another similarity to the situation at Verdun was the ring of trench lines that the NVA had dug all the way around Khe Sanh. In some places, the trenches had come to within thirty meters of the outer ring of wire and branched out to face the American defenses. It was very much like trench warfare in World War I.

The Marines had learned that when they could hear the enemy sappers digging, they could relax. Nothing was going to happen that night. But when all was silent, they worried about what Charlie was up to.

"They're probably just taking a vacation. Maybe they've gone to Vung Tau for the weekend," Janson quipped. "You know, a little *ba-muoi-ba* and boom-boom."

Someone snorted. "Hey, Mr. Janson. Do you know why you never see a gook smile?"

"No."

" 'Cause they don't have a DEROS."

Janson laughed to be polite, but the joke touched on something that had been very apparent to him for quite some time now. The people who were doing most of the fighting in this war, the American GIs, had no real stake in the outcome of this battle or of any other battle, as far as that went. If they survived their year in hell unhurt, they could go home and that would be the end of it for most of them. Those who had been wounded would have to deal with that, and, of course, the dead were past caring. But most GIs really didn't give a shit what the final outcome was going to be.

The Vietnamese, on the other hand, were going to remain no matter what. Yet they often acted like they really didn't care who won the war, either. In the aftermath of Tet, Janson had seen so much corruption and double dealing on the part of the South Vietnamese government that he was beginning to have a grunt's attitude about them. Fuck 'em all, North or South.

The Marines were killing thousands of the enemy at Khe Sanh, but if hundreds of Americans died doing it, the cost was too high. Janson still believed in trying to save the South from communist domination, but he was also coming to believe that the South Vietnamese were going to have to start carrying more of the load themselves.

The NVA sappers leading the attack moved swiftly through the trench network outside the Marine perimeter. The moon was not up. Dressed in black pajamas and head scarves, they were almost invisible as they crept forward on their bellies toward the outer ring of concertina wire in the sector manned by Janson's Marines.

Each sapper carried a pair of ten-pound satchel charges of plastic explosive. The first charge was to be used to blow gaps in the inner ring of wire so the infantry could charge through. The second one was to be shoved through the front aperture of the machine-gun bunkers along the inner defenses. Their only other weapons were Tokarov pistols, stuck in the waistband of their pants. It would be a miracle if even one of them survived their suicide mission tonight.

Behind the sappers, two full companies of North Vietnamese infantry waited in the forward trenches. They carried bamboo assault ladders with them to throw on top of the outer barbed-wire barrier.

A hundred meters behind them, two more NVA companies with RPG launchers and machine gunners were poised to give supporting fire and to reinforce the assault group if they got hung up. The first satchel-charge explosion would be the signal for the attack.

The North Vietnamese sappers were good. On their way through the outer perimeter wire, they located and deactivated most of the trip flares and claymores that the Marines had placed out in front of them. They had just crawled through the tanglefoot at the inside of the ring of concertina wire when Janson joined the Marines standing guard in the trench.

The leading sapper froze in place when a flare popped overhead, and turned his face away from the light. He heard the reporter and the Marines talking not forty feet in front of him and knew that he had to be very careful. He didn't speak English, but he listened for any change in the tone of their voices that would tell him that he had been spotted.

He was so intent on listening that he let his attention falter. As he slithered forward on his belly, his knee brushed against a thin, dark wire set close to the ground. The wire was affixed to a pull-release trigger for a M-18A-1 claymore antipersonnel mine. It was a light touch, but that was all it took to do the job. The blinding flash of the exploding claymore lit up the perimeter in front of Janson.

The mine had been set to fire at a forty-five-degree angle to the wire and was only a few feet away from the sapper. Most of the nine-hundred steel balls in the mine tore through his body. The blast also detonated the satchel charges he was carrying.

The sapper was dead before he even had a chance to know that something had gone wrong.

"Gooks in the wire!" one of the Marines shouted. Grabbing up claymore clackers with both hands, he slammed down on the firing handles of the detonators once, twice, three times.

Two more claymore blasts swept the deadly little steel balls across the front of the wire. More of the sappers died. The Marine machine gunner at the far end of the trench snuggled the butt stock of his M-40 into his shoulder and laid down on the trigger, rapping out quick, short bursts into the wire.

The entire perimeter came alive. Lines of red tracer fire shot out from the marine positions. NVA signal whistles shrilled from the trenches. The waiting assault platoons leaped to their feet and raced for the wire, firing their AK-47's from the hip!

CHAPTER 9

Khe Sanh, 6 March

Over a hundred hand-picked NVA assault troops charged up the hill for the wire, screaming as they came. More Marines dashed out of their sleeping bunkers to reinforce the perimeter as machine guns opened up all along their sector. Lines of red and green tracer fire crisscrossed the wire.

The first 105mm howitzer illumination rounds burst over the perimeter with a faint pop. The flickering yellow-white flare descended on its parachute and lit up a scene straight out of hell.

Dark figures, their AK-47's blazing green tracers, scrambled over the ladders they had thrown up on top of the rolls of concertina wire on the outer perimeter. Claymores exploded with bright flashes. The dark figures screamed as steel balls ripped through their ranks.

Chi-Com stick grenades arched through the air in return and exploded in front of the Marines' bunkers and trenches with dull red thumps. Steady streams of red M-60 tracer fire blazed from the machine-gun bunkers. The thumper gunners fired their 40mm grenade launchers point-blank into the faces of the charging NVA.

When the first artillery flare flickered out and died, more

popped into life above the camp, and the hellish scene came into view again.

The NVA RPG gunners in the trenches took aim at the machine-gun bunkers and fired their weapons. The rocket-propelled, antitank grenades left their launchers. A few meters out of their muzzles, the secondary propellant charges ignited, speeding the deadly rounds on to their targets. The exploding RPG rounds added to the carnage. One bunker in the third squad sector took a rocket through the aperture and exploded with a bone-shaking crump. The machine gun inside fell silent.

The hollow coughing of the 81mm mortars sounded from the gun pits to the rear of the Marine trenches. The rounds landed in the outer wire, blasting several of the enemy off their feet, but they also opened more holes in the wire. More screaming NVA dashed through the break. The mortar gunners fired as fast as they could drop the shells down the tubes, but the dinks were in too close to the friendly positions for them to do much good.

The 81mm mortar was not a point target weapon that could be accurately aimed. It was an area defense weapon. Fired close to the grunts' bunkers, the rounds would probably fall on top of friendlies instead of on the gooks.

The RPG gunners in the trenches saw the muzzle flashes from the mortar pits and brought their rocket launchers to bear on them. The trenches lit up with the back blast as the RPGs fired. The mortar gunners saw the rockets' flares and ducked for cover behind their sandbagged parapet. As soon as the RPG rounds detonated, the gunners on the 81mm changed their point of aim to the enemy trenches farther down the slope. They couldn't help the grunts, but maybe they could take out the RPG gunners. The mortars coughed again.

The North Vietnamese infantry swarmed through the holes in the inner ring of wire. They fanned out in front of the bunkers, looking for a way into the inner perimeter. Bernowski's squad was crouched behind the sandbag parapet of their trench, their M-16's and machine guns adding to the storm of defensive fire.

"Bear!" one of the men shouted. "Look out!"

On their left flank, screaming, dark-uniformed NVA came out of nowhere. In the flickering light of the artillery illumination and the fires, they looked like creatures out of a nightmare.

Bear brought his M-14 rifle up to his shoulder and started firing quick, well-aimed shots. Each time he pulled the trigger, an NVA went down with a 7.62mm bullet in him. On either side of Bernowski, the other Marines blasted away. There was no shortage of targets.

Janson knelt on the bottom of the trench trying to stay out of the way so the Marines could do their thing. He wanted to get back inside the bunker, but every time he got to his feet, a burst of fire drove him back down to cover again.

Williams was doing what he always did in a firefight—pretending that he was on a firing range. Back when he had first come to the Nam, he had been so scared in his first real firefight that he thought he was going to pass out. But the old gunny had slapped him on the shoulder and told him just to pretend that he was back on the firing range in boot camp.

Since then, he had always followed the gunny's advice, and it worked for him. This time, however, he was on a night range and the targets were harder to spot in the flickering light of the artillery flares and the flashes of the explosions.

A dark figure appeared on the right flank of the trench. The dink was pushing a heavy shape on a pole toward the opening in the squad's bunker. Willie took careful aim and fired a quick burst at him. The shadows in front of the bunker were shattered when the pole charge the NVA was carrying detonated with a blinding flash. The hammering concussion slammed the slightly built Marine back against the sandbags. He slumped down to the bottom of the trench, unconscious.

Bear dropped to his side. "Willie," he yelled above the fire storm, shaking the unconscious man. "Willie!"

The young grunt's head lolled limply on his neck.

"You motherfuckers!" Bear screamed. Slamming a fresh magazine into the well of his empty M-14, he jerked back on the charging handle, flipped the selector switch over to full automatic, and laid down on the trigger.

The line of NVA staggered and stopped. A Marine reared back and threw a grenade into their midst. The explosion scattered them.

"Let's get 'em!" Bear screamed.

Jumping up out of their trench, the Marines charged. Faced with howling crazy men, the NVA turned and tried to run back to the outer perimeter wire. Concentrated fire from the bunkers cut into their backs as they broke and scattered for cover.

Six thousand feet in the air, approaching Khe Sanh, Major Skip Dolan banked his camouflage-painted, twin-engined AC-47 Spooky gunship for the run in over the base. By the number of flares hanging in the air, the 4th Air Commando Squadron pilot knew that the Marines were in deep shit down there again. That was the only reason anyone ever called on Spooky. Someone needed to bring some serious smoke down on the bad guys for them.

The AC-47 Spooky gunship Dolan was flying had been designed to do just that. The *A* in front of the old C-47 transport-plane designation indicated that this was one Gooney Bird that wasn't hauling toilet paper anymore. The C-47 was the military version of the most famous transport plane in aviation history, the Douglas DC-3. First flown in 1935, the Gooneys could still be found all over the world hauling cargo. Over fifty air forces worldwide had used the military transport versions for over thirty years.

In Vietnam, however, a new job had been found for the old aerial workhorse, and that was where they had gained the letter *A* in front of their designations; it stood for *attack.*

It meant that the Gooneys had been equipped with machine guns, and not just any old machine guns. Three General Electric SUU-11A/A 7.62mm electric-powered miniguns mounted in the cargo compartment were aimed out the left-hand side of the aircraft. Capable of firing over six thousand rounds a minute, a minigun was usually hampered by a limited ammunition supply. That was not a problem with Spooky. She carried over twenty-four thousand rounds in her cargo section and had three crewmen back there whose sole task was to feed the ever-hungry guns.

With only one gun firing at a time, Spooky could clear an area the size of a football field in two seconds, putting at least one bullet in every last square foot of it. What her fire could do to troops caught out in the open was not a pretty thing to see, but it was effective. That was what she could do with only one minigun working. Spooky was carrying three. He could fire all three at once. Eighteen thousand rounds a minute.

"Hillsboro Control, this is Spooky One Six. I'm on station and ready to go to work. Where do they want me to shoot this time? Over."

"This is Hillsboro Control," came the voice from the flying Tac Air Control Center orbiting high above the western edge of Vietnam. As part of the Khe Sanh air-support operation Niagara, a converted C-130 Hercules transport plane full of radio gear was on station twenty-four hours a day, monitoring radio traffic from the base and passing on their requests for Tac Air support.

"The problem tonight," Hillsboro said, "is in the southern sector. You are cleared to fire on anything outside the wire. Over."

Skip shook his head as he keyed the mike. Same old shit again. He had shot for the Marines at Khe Sanh at least three times a week for almost a month, It was getting to be a little old.

"Roger, Hillsboro, I'm coming up on 'em now. Moonshine will be dropping flares for me any moment now, and I'll be making my run shortly. Out."

Just then, a bright magnesium flare burst into life above him, flooding Khe Sanh with light. The Spooky pilot could clearly see the problem. The southern slope of the hill leading up to the base was crawling with dark-colored figures carrying AK-47's and RPGs.

He flew past the Marine camp until the beacon in the center just passed under his portside engine cowling. Then he kicked the plane over into a hard left-hand pylon turn and looked to his left side window. Mounted in the middle of the window was a Navy Mark 20, model 4 gunsight salvaged out of an A-1E Super Spad. He tightened his turn until the southern outer-perimeter wire was centered in the cross hairs.

His right thumb pressed a switch on the control wheel, and a deep-throated whining roar sounded from the rear of the plane. Two of the miniguns opened up at the same time. The feared sky dragon was speaking.

To the Marines on the ground, the sound was like heavy canvas being ripped apart. Twin fingers of flame reached down to the ground right outside the wire. One round in every five in the minigun ammo belts was a tracer, but the guns fired so fast that twenty tracers went out of the barrels every second. The result looked like a thick finger of red flame reaching down to the ground.

Where the fingers touched, death followed.

In front of the outer wire, the second wave of the NVA attack was charging the gap blown in the fence when the finger of flame brushed over them. In an instant, what had been over two dozen men became a scattered pile of bleeding, ragged dog meat. Most of the assault unit were killed, torn to shreds in the storm of fire.

The flame winked out, but it appeared again a second later farther down the perimeter. Again the ripping sound filled the air.

The Marines held their fire and watched in total fascination. When Spooky was talking, no man wanted to get in her way. Besides, it was the best show in town.

After the second burst of fire, the NVA broke and tried

to run, but their attempt to escape was in vain. It was several hundred meters back down the hill to the nearest cover. In the brief silences between the minigun bursts, a wailing, moaning sound was heard, the cries of dozens of wounded men all screaming at the same time.

Overhead, Dolan kept the gunship in a tight left-hand bank, orbiting his target area while the accompanying Moonshine flare ship continued to illuminate the hillside. As the NVA ran, he opened his orbit up a little to bring the guns to bear.

From his viewpoint high in the sky, where he didn't have to smell the blood or carry the bodies away, the enemy was just an easy target for his guns. And this was by far the best shooting he had had in a long time. He calmly lined up his sight again and pressed the firing button. Finally, the heavy ripping sound abruptly cut off. The pilot keyed his mike. "Hillsboro, this is Spooky One Six. Over."

"This is Hillsboro. Go."

"This is One Six. I'm bingo ammo and am returning to base. Over."

"This is Hillsboro, Roger. Be advised that we may need you again tonight. Over."

"One Six, Roger copy. Out."

When the ripping sound of the miniguns faded away, a strange silence fell over Khe Sanh. All that could be heard were the screams and moans of the wounded and the dying. Slowly, one by one, the grunts opened up again on the surviving attackers. It was a slaughter.

Slightly wounded NVA, stunned by the sudden storm of fire, were gunned down where they stood. The few NVA still left alive scrambled back through the breaks in the wire, frantically trying to escape. Deadly fire from the bunkers cut into their backs as they tried to run. Many of them stayed where they were, hanging lifelessly on the wire.

Above the sound of firing, the voices of the American wounded cried out for the medics. The enemy were in full retreat, but the victory had not been without a heavy cost.

Now that Spooky was clear, the artillery started up again.

They used one gun to keep the illum coming while the others chased the NVA back down the hill with H.E. With the attack broken, the overworked medics scrambled around inside the base, locating and treating the American casualties while the radio operators in the TOC requested priority dustoff for the most seriously wounded. It was risky to bring the medevac choppers in at night, but many of the WIA wouldn't last until daylight.

In the Marine bunker, Williams sat up. His head was killing him. Bear stood over him, his arms folded across his massive chest.

"Jesus, man. What the fuck happened?" Williams reached around and felt the bump on the back of his head.

"You fired up a sapper and when his satchel charge blew up, it knocked you flat on your ass. I think you hit your head," Bear told him with a grin.

"Jesus," the grunt muttered to himself. "That sorry fucker was trying to kill me."

As the first light of a cold, misty dawn broke over Khe Sanh, bleary-eyed, smoke-stained men stumbled out of their bunkers and looked around at the smoking ruins of the base.

The thick morning mist held the acrid smoke close to the ground. Small fires still flickered in piles of building timbers and ammo crates. North Vietnamese bodies littered the outside of the perimeter, slack limbed and bloody, sprawled in the absurd postures of death.

There were no American dead or wounded still lying in the base. They had all been picked up in the night. The most seriously wounded had been dusted off, and the rest had been taken down to the makeshift hospital over by the airstrip.

While Janson walked around the inside of the perimeter, a small patrol left the base to police up the enemy weapons from the dozens of bodies in the wire. The Marines inside the perimeter kept a close eye on the patrol in case they needed support. They paid little attention to the bodies.

Veterans, they had seen burned, blasted, shattered, and shredded bodies, American and Vietnamese, often enough.

This was not the first glimpse of death for Janson, either, but he had to admit that he continued to be impressed with what modern firepower could do to a human body. A far-better-than-average killing had taken place last night. The enemy had been dealt such a staggering blow that they had not even tried to haul off their own dead and wounded.

The Marine grunts moved among the enemy bodies, stripping them of their weapons and magazine carriers and taking the arms back inside the base. Later the captured arms would be evacuated back to the rear areas so that visiting reporters could be impressed.

While the men policed up the battlefield, Jordan sat down to write his impressions of the battle while they were still fresh in his mind.

CHAPTER 10

Andersen Air Force Base, Guam

While the men at Khe Sanh cleaned up after the attack, the First Air Cavalry Division was busy assembling their troops, stockpiling supplies, and constructing the forward airstrips and firebases to support the upcoming Operation Pegasus. During the lull, the United States Air Force was doing everything in their power to help the situation at Khe Sanh.

From the very beginning, General Westmoreland's plan for the defense of the remote base had included massive air support in what he had named Operation Niagara. Westmoreland had assembled the largest aerial task force that had been seen since the invasion of Normandy in World War II. Army, Navy, Marine and Air Force air assets were all brought together under a single air-control facility to coordinate the attacks. Everybody from the forward air controllers, in their little Cessna O-2 Skymasters, to the swift Navy Phantoms and the huge, high-flying, eight-engined B-52's had a chance to get in on the act. On an average day, as many as 350 Tac Air fighter bombers, sixty B-52's, ten jet recon fighters, and twenty or thirty FACs could be found loitering in the skies over Khe Sanh.

While the Air Cav went ahead full speed with their preparations for the relief operation, the massive air support was stepped up even more. The biggest help that the Air Force could provide was called Arc Light, the code name for the B-52 bomber strikes.

Originally designed as a Strategic Air Command intercontinental nuclear-weapons delivery system, the venerable old Boeing B-52 Stratofortress was commonly known as the Buff—short for "big ugly fat fucker." It had been converted to an "Iron Bomber" for use in Southeast Asia. The CBC, conventional bomb carrier versions of the B-52D with the "big belly" modifications, were capable of carrying 105 seven-hundred-fifty-pound high-explosive bombs, over thirty-nine tons. By comparison, the famous B-17 bomber of World War II had only carried a bomb load of slightly over four tons.

The B-52 was one of the most feared weapons in the entire American arsenal, and the enemy had good reason to fear it. The Buff delivered its bombs with pinpoint accuracy from thirty-five thousand feet in the sky; so high that the bomber could not be seen or heard by the troops on the ground. A North Vietnamese unit would be cooling their heels in the jungle without a care in the world, when suddenly their world would end.

They had no way of knowing that they had been spotted by a recon team or that their movements had been picked up by a seismic device planted along the main branches of the Ho Chi Minh Trail. They would be eating a meal or simply resting when a sudden rain of 750-pound bombs from a plane they could neither hear nor see landed on top of them, wiping them off the face of the earth.

At Khe Sanh, the B-52 raids had been perfected to a science. Guided to their targets by a radar station located within the base, the high-flying B-52's delivered their bomb loads with more than pinpoint accuracy. The attacks were so precise, in fact, that the Buffs had even been given the job of close air support, a first for a heavy jet bomber. After a carefully controlled test, they started dropping their bomb

70

loads five hundred meters in front of the Marine positions, giving close air support from thirty-five thousand feet.

While the Air Cav prepared for Pegasus, the word came down from Saigon for the Buffs to increase the pressure on the NVA besieging the Marines. A campaign of around-the-clock bombing was instituted. Every ninety minutes, a flight of three heavily laden B-52's took off from one of their bases on Guam, Okinawa, or Thailand for the long flight to Khe Sanh. Every hour and a half the high-flying Buffs unloaded their high-explosive cargo on the NVA gun positions and trenches. It was devastating, it was unrelenting, and it killed thousands of the enemy dug into the hills around the base.

As effective as it was, however, it did not stop the deadly artillery attacks. The 130mm long-range Russian guns had been dug into a range of low mountains across the border in Laos. Whenever the NVA received word from their intelligence sources that a B-52 raid was airborne, the guns were hauled back into the caves where not even 750-pound bombs could reach them.

And enemy intelligence sources were good. The Russians had stationed several of their "trawlers" in international waters off Okinawa and Guam to keep an eye on the bombers. Whenever a flight of B-52s took off, a warning was flashed to Hanoi. It was crude, but effective.

The warnings allowed the long-range guns to be taken under safe cover, but it didn't do a thing for the poor bastard NVA in the trenches around Khe Sanh. Those dinks were dead meat.

At Andersen Air Force Base, Guam, three B-52 crews prepared to make the six-thousand-mile, twelve-hour, round-trip flight to Khe Sanh. While the crews received their target briefing in an air-conditioned building, out on the flight line sweating ordnance men fitted the last of the twenty-four Mark 82 five-hundred-pound bombs to the external, underwing racks. An additional eighty-four bombs had already been loaded into the internal bomb bays of the planes. On takeoff, the eight J-57 jet engines would strain to the limits of their power to lift the 220-ton loaded weight of the B-52 off the ground.

After the long mission briefing, the six crew members of *Grin and Bare It* were driven out to where their Buff, a B-52D tail number 687, was sitting on the tarmac.

Parked next to a civilian Boeing 747, a B-52 looked small, but sleek. When seen by itself, however, it looked mean and purposeful. Its landing gear was short and it crouched with its belly low on the runway like a tiger ready to spring. Its high, swept-back tail towered forty feet above the ground. Its fuel-laden wings bent gracefully downward, like a hawk coming in for a landing. In this case, the hawk was green and tan camouflaged, with a flat black belly and olive drab high-explosive eggs tucked under its wings along with four jet engines in twin pods. They almost looked too small to propel the big bomber, but they did—at six hundred miles per hour.

One of the Buffs in the three-plane flight this morning had a huge shark's mouth painted under its nose. *Grin and Bare It,* however, wore a small cartoon mouth drawn up in a smile. The word *Grin* was painted right above the smile. The other half of the plane's nickname, *and Bare It,* was painted back by the tail turret next to a cartoon figure of a man bending over with his pants around his ankles.

The six-man crew climbed aboard their bomber and began going over the lengthy preflight checklist. In the extreme rear of the plane, Sergeant "Wild Bill" Murphy quickly checked over his four .50-caliber machine guns in the tail turret, their ammunition supply and the gun aiming the radar. He then settled back to read his copy of the latest *Playboy.* As soon as they were in the air, he would start his nap. There was very little chance of their encountering North Vietnamese MiG fighters over Khe Sanh, but he was along for the ride on the off chance that the Vietnamese People's Air Force decided to deal themselves into the game.

In the nose of the plane, Captain Pete Woodbridge finished reading off the prestart checklist to his copilot First Lieutenant Bob Andrews.

"Let's get this bitch running," the pilot said as he stowed the checklist back in its pocket.

"You're not grinning, Woody."

"Fuck you."

This was the fifth mission the crew had flown in as many days and they were all bone weary. They were due for a two-day stand-down starting the next day, but first they had to fly for twelve hours. Woody was praying for an engine malfunction, but as he well knew, it was not too likely. He had the best damned crew chief in the entire Buff fleet. If he'd had a marginal engine, Red would have changed it during the night. He sighed. There was no way out of it. They were going to have to fly to Khe Sanh.

"Okay, light 'em."

The copilot hit the starter for the number-four engine. With a whine from the starter motor and a cough of black smoke, it burst into life. When the tachometer showed fifteen percent, the pilot moved its throttle to flight idle. With the number-four generator providing internal power, the other seven engines were quickly started.

After a run-up to forty-five percent RPM, Woody radioed the flight leader that he was ready to taxi. The leader rogered and the pilot switched the steering ratio from takeoff land to taxi. When the call came, Woody came off the brakes, and the huge bomber slowly moved to the end of the runway, where it stopped in takeoff position behind the flight leader.

"Flaps full," Woody called out as he switched the steering ratio back to takeoff.

"Flaps going down," Andrews called back. "Ten percent, thirty percent, fifty percent, flaps full."

Woody advanced his throttles, keeping his eyes on the RPM, fuel-flow, and EGT gauges. The Buff quivered under the strain of holding back under the thrust of the screaming J-57's. Everything was in the green. The flight leader took off ahead of them, the wake of its eight-jet engines rocking *Grin and Bare It*.

"We're go," Woody said. He pushed the throttles into the one-hundred-percent position. The screaming engines howled, black smoke pouring out. A brief glance at the gauges and he came off the foot brakes. The B-52 started forward down the concrete runway, quickly gathering speed. With several hundred meters of runway left, the heavily loaded bomber reached rotation speed and lifted gracefully into the sky.

For the next few minutes, the crew was busy pulling up the gear and flaps and setting the engines for the climb to cruising altitude. The three planes flew in a triangular formation with *Grin and Bare It* off the starboard wing of their flight leader. In the tail turret compartment, Wild Bill settled down for his high-altitude nap. He would wake up for the aerial refueling when they rendezvoused with the KC-135 tankers on the way home. Till then, it was sack time.

The three bombers soon reached their cruising altitude of thirty-five thousand feet and settled in for the first leg of their long flight. Five hours later, the B-52's turned for the run into Khe Sanh. In *Grin and Bare It,* the radar navigator prepared for the bomb run, quickly running through his pre-IP checklist. When the radios were locked on the beacon transmitting from Khe Sanh, he fed the navigational information into the bombing computers and reached for his bomb-run (non-nuclear) checklist.

"IP in ninety seconds," the pilot called back.

"Roger."

The radar navigator flicked the switch on the master bomb control panel to auto. Now the computers had control of the bomb drop. He would center the electronic cross hairs of the radar scope on the target beacon and the computer would take into consideration everything from airspeed, ground speed, altitude, and wind drift, flying the plane directly into position to hit the target. When the ballistics were right, the computer would open the bomb-bay doors, drop the load, and close the doors again.

"IP," the pilot called back.

The radar navigator peered through his radar scope at the blip, his thumb resting on the D-2 bomb-release switch, waiting for the word to drop.

"FCI centered," the pilot called back.

"Roger. Bomb doors coming open. Sixty seconds to drop."

The red light came on and the radar navigator's thumb stabbed down on the D-2 switch. "Bombs away," he called.

One by one, the olive drab 750-pound bombs left the wing racks and bomb bay, headed for the NVA trenches around Khe Sanh. In a few seconds, over twenty tons of high explosive would ruin someone's day.

"Doors closing," the radar navigator called out.

"Roger." Woody took control of his plane again and followed the flight leader into a slow-banking turn that would take them back to Guam. Another mission, another twenty-two tons of H.E. It was a great life.

To Janson and the Marines in the bunker at Khe Sanh, the distant roar of over sixty tons of high explosives detonating hardly caught their notice. Arc Light strikes were such a common occurrence they didn't even look up from their card game. Janson hesitated for a second when he felt the faint echo of the concussion as the earth shook under his feet. "Here it is, boys," he said slapping his cards down. "Read 'em and weep."

"Ah shit!" Wee Willie folded his cards. "That's the fifth time you've done that to me today."

Janson grinned. "See what I learned in journalism school? Now pay up."

Williams handed over the can of C-ration fruit cocktail. "Let's go one more hand, okay? That was my last can of fruit."

"Sure," Janson said. "What do you have to bet?"

"How 'bout a pack of Salems?"

"Make it two."

"You're on."

Janson shuffled the cards and dealt a new hand to the Marines around the makeshift table on someone's foot-locker. He knew that he'd wind up giving all of his winnings back to them, but what else did they have to do until night fell?

"How many you need?" he asked Willie.

The young Marine studied his hand. "Ah shit! Gimme three."

"Here ya go."

"Ah shit!" he cursed, studying his hand again. "I guess I'm wasting all my bad luck on poker and saving the good stuff for out there."

CHAPTER 11

Khe Sanh

From his small underground headquarters bunker hidden in the jungle inside the Laotian border, North Vietnamese Lieutenant Colonel Nguyen Van Tran heard the distant rumbling as his artillery opened fire on the American base again. He looked up from the orders he was writing and rubbed his tired eyes. Now that the ill-fated general offensive had been so crushingly defeated by the Yankees, he was busier than ever trying to salvage something from the mess.

Colonel Tran was the operations officer for the 325C NVA Division, and he had accurately forecast that the general offensive against the cities and the Yankee installations in the south was doomed to fail. The old jungle fighter had known that giving up the guerilla hit-and-run tactics, which had proven so effective against both the French and the Americans, in favor of sending troops into conventional battles would never work, particularly in the southern cities.

Tran had fought most of his life to free his country from foreign domination and he would continue the struggle for as long as it took to achieve the final victory. He was a fighter, but he had feared coming head to head with the vastly superior firepower of the American army. His predictions had been accurate, but he had long ago learned to keep his personal opinions to himself, particularly when they went against the thinking in Hanoi.

Hanoi had naively ordered the Viet Cong in the south to launch a general uprising of the population in conjunction with the NVA attacks. Later, the VC were to have taken over the cities that the army had conquered. But Tran knew the mind of the southerners far better than the high command in Hanoi. Most of the South Vietnamese wanted no part of an austere communist government, especially when they could get rich living off the Americans.

Tran had not gotten over the waste of his seasoned troops in the meat grinder of the Tet battles and the setback that it meant to the struggle. As far as he was concerned, the offensive had been planned primarily to add General Giap's name to the list of history's great generals like Zhukov and Patton. In the eyes of the Western world, Giap's guerilla-war victories weren't considered a mark of military greatness. To be considered great, he had to fight and win a conventional land battle. Unfortunately, Giap's attempt at world fame had been written in the blood of thousands of North Vietnamese infantrymen.

As always, though, Tran had done his best. Now that it was all over, it was his duty to pick up the pieces and carry on. His mission was to keep the Americans and their massive air fleet from relieving the besieged Marines at Khe Sanh, and he was not sure that he could do that. Over the last two years of fighting against the First Air Cavalry Division in Binh Dinh Province, Colonel Tran had learned to fear the swarms of Yankee helicopters with good reason.

It had been different back when the Americans had first come to Vietnam in 1965. As an infantry battalion commander in the NVA, Tran had enjoyed his battles with the Yankees in places like the Ia Drang Valley, teaching them the harsh realities of combat in the jungle, just as the French army had been taught before them.

In the beginning, for all their wealth of arms and equipment, the Americans had been like children. But that had all changed very quickly. Even Tran had to admit that the Yankees were brave and that they learned fast. Too damned fast.

Within months of arriving in Vietnam, the American army had become a first-rate fighting force, supported by a seemingly endless swarm of helicopters. Tran feared helicopters and was more than a little paranoid about them. More times than he liked to recall, he had been forced to break contact and flee deep into the jungle to escape them. Today, just the mere sound of their rotors in the distance was enough to make him break out in a cold sweat.

Now that the battles in the cities were over, Tran knew that he would be facing more helicopters than he had ever seen before. He didn't like his new assignment any more than he had liked the plan for the general offensive, but just as he had done ever since he had joined the people's struggle, he would obey his orders to the best of his ability.

Tran had been born to a small shopkeeper and his wife living in the outskirts of Hanoi in 1923. When his family died of the fever, he had been taken in by a French Catholic orphanage and raised under the stern discipline of the priests. He soon learned to hate the French fathers with a passion, but he had been given a good education in their school. When he graduated, he went to work in the publishing trade in the big city.

When the Imperial Japanese Army swarmed into French Indochina at the start of World War II, the young Tran, then eighteen years old, ran away to the countryside to join one of the Vietnamese resistance movements. He fought well during the war years, and shortly before the end, he happened to hear another resistance fighter, Ho Chi Minh, speak at a political rally. Tran had been entranced with Ho's fiery nationalistic message: Vietnam for the Vietnamese. This policy matched Tran's strong anti-foreign feelings perfectly. Though he had not been politically active before, Tran immediately joined Ho's communist Viet Minh party.

At the end of the war, Tran put down his rifle and went back to his presses, printing revolutionary pamphlets for the party. The Viet Minh, however, decided that they needed his military skills more than they did his printer's ink, and Tran soon found himself back in the expanding Viet Minh guerilla army. This time, however, the enemy was the French, who had returned to Indochina to take control of their former colony.

Toward the end of that long, bitter struggle, Tran had the honor of leading an infantry assault group in the night attack that took the stronghold Beatrice from the French Foreign Legion during the critical battle of Dien Bien Phu. When dawn broke over the smoke-filled valley the next morning, he was one of a mere handful of Viet Minh who had survived the fierce, night-long, hand-to-hand battle with the bearded, foreign savages of the Légion Paras.

When the French garrison finally surrendered at Dien Bien Phu, a victorious General Giap had personally promoted Tran to the rank of sergeant for his bravery during the three-month battle.

When the peace treaty was signed and the French evacuated North Vietnam, Tran was recognized for his devotion to the cause. He was sent to Peking and Moscow for intensive military training. After two years of grueling instruction under Russian and Chinese veterans of both World War II and Korean War combat, he returned to his homeland and was commissioned a lieutenant in the new Vietnamese People's Liberation Army.

In the years that followed, Tran had served as an infantry officer in both staff and command positions. Much of his time was spent in what was now the Republic of South Vietnam, working with Viet Cong units that were fighting the U.S.-supported puppet regime. When the American army finally sent combat units into the south to prevent the collapse of the southern government, Tran was posted back to the North Vietnamese Army, where he commanded an infantry battalion fighting the new enemy of the people, the Yankees.

After almost two years of field duty, suffering through one stunning defeat after another, Tran had lost all interest in commanding combat units. He had secured a staff position at a base camp in Cambodia, far from the fighting. But when the 325 NVA Division needed an operations officer, he had been called back into South Vietnam. His new job had come with a promotion, but Tran felt that it was scant compensation for being back in the middle of the war. Particularly right now.

The Tet offensive had been the worst mistake he had ever seen. The only thing that had come of it had been the death of many of his best troops. This new mission was almost as bad for what was left of his division. They had been so terribly mauled in the city fighting that they should have been taken out of the south and allowed to rest and refit in their Cambodian sanctuary, where the Yankees couldn't get to them. Instead, they had been ordered to Khe Sanh to block positions along Route 9, the road leading down into Quang Tri.

When the Yankees came to relieve Khe Sanh, they would have to come up that road. That, at least, was how the planning experts in the high command felt. Tran knew full well, however, that the Yankees would not simply try to push through along the road, fighting for every inch as the French would have done. They would fly over it and land their troops only where they were needed. That was what he had to prepare for, a massive aerial assault.

Tran's left hand went up to massage the persistent ache in the back of his neck. At times like this, he felt every one of his forty-five years. Maybe it was just the unrelenting pressure of trying to do the impossible that was making him feel old. There was so much to be done, and so very little time to do it. He was sure that the Yankees would be knocking on his door within a week or two, and he had to be ready for them. His main problem was keeping his defensive build-up a secret. Undoubtedly, American recon teams would be sent into his area of operations before the Yankees launched their attack.

Already, Yankee reconnaissance aircraft were keeping a close watch on increased supply traffic and the movement

81

of NVA troop units into the Khe Sanh battle area. Anyone who traveled in the open during the day was bound to attract unwelcome attention. That attention could be anything from the propeller-driven Skyraider fighter-bombers to the high-flying B-52 jet bombers. Tran had never seen so many airplanes in his entire career. It looked as if every plane the Yankees had in Southeast Asia was raining bombs upon the Khe Sanh area. Even the cover of night had been taken away from the North Vietnamese. The Yankees were using more and more planes that could see in the dark. Without the cover of night, his troops faced an even more formidable task.

Every man that Tran could spare right now was busy constructing antiaircraft positions and fortifications covering the approach to Khe Sanh along Route 9. He had few units that he could release to send on patrols in the surrounding jungle to ensure that the Yankee ground-recon teams did not penetrate into their area. The units that he did have earmarked for that mission were some of his most experienced jungle fighters, but they were understrength and the area they had to cover was extensive. He just hoped that they were up to the task.

One thing he could do was saturate the area with booby traps to discourage enemy recon teams. In his experience, the Yankees tended to steer clear of heavily booby-trapped areas. It would increase his defensive coverage without having to put more troops out in the jungle.

He got up and walked over to the big map hanging on the dirt wall of his bunker. His finger traced the possible helicopter landing zones along the course that Route 9 took through the low hills surrounding Khe Sanh. That was what he needed to cover most, the landing zones. When the Americans finally did come, they would fly their recon teams in rather than have them approach on foot.

Tran was still studying the map when his sergeant knocked on the door. "Come in."

"Comrade Colonel?" the sergeant said, snapping to attention. "The company commanders are here for the briefing."

"Send them in."

"Yes, Comrade Colonel."

Tran stood as the five officers filed into the room, his dark eyes sweeping over each one of them as they came to attention in front of him.

"Here is the situation you have to deal with," he said as he walked over to the map. "Our forces have besieged Khe Sanh for over two months now, and if we keep the pressure on, the Yankee Marines will crack. There is only one thing that can stop us from achieving as glorious a victory over them as we did over the French at Dien Bien Phu. And that is if the Yankee Air Cavalry can force Route Nine open and relieve them." His finger traced the route of the highway.

"Our defenses against an aerial assault are almost complete now, but there is always the danger from the Yankee recon teams. And if our defenses are discovered, they will turn the B-52 bombers against us as they have turned them against our brave comrades in the trenches at Khe Sanh. All of our work will have been for nothing."

He turned back to face the five officers. "Your mission is to ensure that the Yankees do not penetrate into our area of operation and spy on our defenses. You must not fail in this task, comrades. We have worked too long and too hard for this moment. The outcome at Khe Sanh and the fate of the people's liberation depends on you and each one of your men."

He looked at the officers standing in front of him. "Are there any questions?"

There never were any questions at Tran's briefings.

The colonel's voice rang out. "You all have your maps and your orders. Go now. Talk to your men. Arouse them to do their duties faithfully."

The five company commanders saluted and left the small room. Tran returned to his desk and sat back down. He still had to talk to the local VC force commander when he showed up later. Then he would have done everything in his power to ensure that they were ready for the Yankees when they came.

And come they would. As surely as winter followed summer, the Air Cav would come to the rescue of the Marines at Khe Sanh. Tran would be ready for them.

CHAPTER 12

Camp Evans

Python Flight's new operations shack and ready room at Camp Evans were a welcome change from the small, run-down hut they had been forced to operate out of back at Chu Lai. It was considerably larger and it was newly built, but it wasn't completely home to them the way their old operations shack back at An Khe had been. The run-down shack at Camp Radcliff had been Python Flight's home for almost two years, and it had acquired a comfortable, lived-in feeling.

The men were doing their best, however, to get comfortable in their new home. They had brought their battered lawn furniture with them and most of their faded *Playboy* pin-ups and VC flags to decorate the walls. The one thing that was missing, however, was their heavy old oak pool table. Forced to leave it behind in An Khe, they were trying to get a CH-47 Chinook mission laid on to retrieve it. The problem was that the shit-hooks were tied up and it was hard to find one heading their way with room for the big pool table inside.

The one thing that hadn't changed about the men of Python Flight, however, was their off-duty behavior. They were still as rowdy and boisterous as ever. The noise level in the ready room was deafening as the men shouted to be heard over the blare of a small Japanese transistor radio tuned into AFVN and turned up full blast.

Dead silence fell over the crowded room when the door opened and Rat Gaines walked in. Someone pulled the plug on the radio.

"Okay, boys, let's listen up here," he said unnecessarily. "We've got several things to talk about here today."

Gaines's voice was low and expressionless, and the pilots listened intently. No one had seen much of Gaines since Lisa had been killed: he had more or less let the unit run itself while he hid out in his office. If something was going down that made him call a meeting, it had to be important.

"First off"—he glanced down at the papers in his hand— "we are going to go into an intensive, week-long maintenance stand-down starting today. The purpose of the exercise is to prepare for a major operation that you will be briefed on later. Secondly, all of the Python UH-1C aircraft are to be turned in and will be replaced with AH-1 Cobras."

The gunship pilots' faces lit up and the room shook with cheers. Any gunship jockey with even half a pair of balls lusted after a chance to fly the new Bell AH-1G Cobra. Unlike the UH-1C Huey Hogs, which were merely slicks with a lot of armament hung all over them, the Cobra had been designed from the beginning to be the ass-kickingest machine ever to swing a rotor blade.

The only problem with the Cobras was that up until now, there had only been a handful of them in all of Vietnam, where they were being tested under combat conditions. At the start of the test program, Warlokk had been one of the first two Air Cav pilots chosen to fly the new gunship. The first week he had it, he had been shot down in it. Even though the machine had been recovered and repaired to flight status, the two Air Cav Cobras had been off limits to all of Python Flight until Gaines had been able to talk the test unit into letting him fly one of them himself.

"A shipload of Cobras has just come in-country," Gaines continued. "We have been chosen to completely re-fit with them. That's the good news. The bad news is that our old Hogs will have to be one hundred percent squared away before we are allowed to turn them in. Every last one of their maintenance deficiencies will have to be worked off."

That announcement got loud groans. There was nothing more frustrating than working on a piece of equipment that was going to be given to someone else.

"I also need four crews to ferry the new birds down from An Khe. Volunteers?"

Almost everyone's hands shot up.

"Gabe, I want you to fly the support and maintenance people to Radcliff and then bring them back when they're done."

The veteran pilot nodded affirmatively.

Gaines turned to Warlokk, who was standing over by the open door. "Lance, I want you and Alphabet to pick the pilots and check them out on your ships. Get back to me as soon as you're ready."

Gaines looked around the room. "Are there any questions?"

There were several, mostly about coordinating the turn-in of the old choppers and the maintenance work they needed.

"Okay," Gaines said when they were done. "Let's get out there and get to work on those machines."

"Lance," Gaines turned to the waiting pilot. "I'd like to talk to you in my office."

"Yes, sir."

A few moments later, Gaines closed the door after them and went over to the map on his wall. "This is just between you and me right now."

"Yes, sir."

"Part of this operation includes sending the Blue Team in to recon this area next week." He ran his finger along Route 9 leading into the Khe Sanh. "We've been asked to help the Headhunters of the Ninth Cav on this particular part of the operation.''

"We're going into Khe Sanh, aren't we?"

Gaines turned to look at him with a serious expression on his face. "You didn't hear that from me and keep it to yourself."

In spite of his commander's solemn face, Warlokk grinned.

"Anyway, because the mission AO is out of the artillery fan, part of the operation includes quick-response air cover. Gunships are to be on station or on ramp alert from forward firebases at all times. We'll be operating in two-man light-fire teams, and I want you to fly with me."

Warlokk's expression indicated that he expected nothing else.

"But," Gaines continued, "until then, so we don't get rusty, you and I are going to be flying a lot of maintenance test flights. Without our gunners."

Now Warlokk was confused. "Why?"

Gaines took a deep breath, the expression on his face intense. "Because even if the Blues aren't in contact, I want to go hunting dinks."

Warlokk paused. He didn't quite know what was going on, but whatever it was, he'd go along with it. "Okay," he shrugged. "We'll go hunting."

"And, Lance, this is also just between you and me."

Warlokk grinned. "Whatever you say, boss. When do we start?"

"Hopefully tomorrow morning."

Later that afternoon, in the Blues' 2 Squad tent, Brody and his people were cleaning their weapons and equipment. Even if they were going into a stand-down, they had to be ready in case something went tits up and they had to suit up on a moment's notice.

Brody, for one, would have rather had a mission than a stand-down. They had been hanging around Camp Evans with their thumbs up their asses for most of the last couple of weeks and it had started getting to him. But since they were on a stand-down, he might as well enjoy it. He knew they'd be back in the woods before too long.

Brody wiped the last of the LSA off his rifle and looked over to where Cordova had his M-60 torn down. He wasn't so sure that Corky was going to be very happy to go out on their next mission.

He, Corky, and Two-Step were the last of the original First of the 7th Aero Rifle Platoon. The rest of the men who had come over with them in 1965 were either dead or in a VA hospital somewhere. It would be a real waste if Corky got killed now that he had finally decided to give it up and go home.

Brody got up and walked over to the Chicano machine gunner's bunk. "When we go out the next time, you can stay back if you like." He watched Corky run a brush down the M-60's bore. "I'll talk to Leo and okay it with him."

"No way, man." Corky shook his head. "If you're going out, I'm going with you."

"But you're short. Give yourself a break. What d'you have? Nineteen days and a wake-up?"

Corky stroked his mustache. "Eighteen, my man. Eighteen days, a nice long wake-up and it's *fini* fucking Nam. Shit, man, I'm so short that I can't even be talking to no fucking lifer like you. I might get into a long conversation and miss my plane."

"Asshole."

"But I think I can spare the time to keep an eye on you guys till then."

"Okay, but I'll make sure that you get back in time to catch the plane," Brody promised. He didn't want anything to keep his old buddy from returning home in one piece, but he was always glad to have him and his fire-breathing pig around when the shit hit the fan.

"As soon as you get that thing cleaned up, let's hit Sin City and grab a couple of brews."

9"Sure," Corky grinned. "I haven't hit my PCOD yet,

so let's check out that new place down at the end of the strip. They've got a new girl there that's completely outta sight.''

A man's PCOD, ''pussy cutoff date,'' was the last possible day that he could take a bar girl into one of the back rooms and still finish his medical treatment if she souvenired him a case of the clap. Some of the men were willing to take a risk and cut their PCOD shorter and shorter, but Corky planned on giving himself a full week.

Brody grinned, too. It had been awhile since he'd had a shot of leg himself. ''Sounds like a plan. Want to see if Farmer wants to go along?''

''Sure, why not? He's a real cock hound.''

''Hey, Farmer!'' Brody called out. ''Want to hit the strip for a little boom-boom later?''

Farmer looked up from the big K-Bar knife he was methodically sharpening and shook his head. ''I've got to finish this, Sarge.'' For the last couple of weeks, he had been wearing the fighting knife on his boot top everywhere he went, and he was always sharpening it.

''You've been working on that thing all day, man.''

Farmer tested the knife's edge against the sparse hair on his arm. The hair came off as clean as if it had been cut by a razor. ''It still needs a little more work.''

Brody shook his head. Farmer was getting a little strange, even for a grunt with the Blues.

''Whatever you say, man.''

Brody walked over to Two-Step's bunk. The Indian was lying back with his eyes closed. He opened one eye when Brody kicked the end of the bunk. ''You about ready for a couple hours of in-country R and R?''

''Sure, let's do it.'' Two-Step sat up and reached for his jungle boots.

At the other end of the tent, the last two men in the squad, artillery FO Bunny Rabdo and one of the newer men, PFC Larry Lindberry, were getting their gear ready as well.

As usual, Bunny was going on and on about how he would run the war if he were General Westmoreland. Lindberry listened with only half an ear as he carefully cleaned his rifle. Bunny was a short, wiry, dark-haired New Yorker of Jewish descent, and he was deeply in love with his own voice. If he wasn't asleep, he was talking. Now that Farmer was keeping more and more to himself, Bunny was on his way to becoming the Blues' champion motor mouth.

Lindberry, on the other hand, was one of those people who never seemed to have a hell of a lot to say about anything. He had kept his mouth shut in basic training, he had kept his mouth shut in Camp Alpha, the in-country replacement center, and he had kept his mouth shut when he first came to the Blues. He hadn't even said anything when Brody had nicknamed him Strawberry. As long as he was in Vietnam, he intended to listen to his sergeants, do what he was told to do, and go home as soon as his 365-day tour of duty was over. He had learned a long time ago that nothing ever came from bitching about things that couldn't be changed.

Lindberry was from Pittsburgh, the son of a steel worker, and he had expected to go to work in the steel mills when the draft board caught up with him after he graduated from high school. He didn't really mind being drafted. His father had served in the Army in World War II and he figured that he owed time in the service to his country. He knew that as soon as he did start working in the mills, he would never have another chance to travel around and see a different part of the world.

Lindberry was content to be where he was, doing whatever it was he was told to do. Even if it was just sitting in a tent, cleaning his M-16 while he listened to Bunny's nonstop bitching.

"Hey, Bunny, Strawberry," Brody asked. "You two want to go downtown with us?"

"No, thanks, I think I'll pass," Bunny said.

"Sure, why not?" Lindberry answered. He sure as hell didn't want to hang around the tent and listen to Bunny jack his jaws endlessly. "Just gimme a second here and I'll be ready."

He snapped the receiver shut on his M-16, pushed the

lock pins back into place, and laid it on top of his foot-locker. "Let's get it."

The four grunts caught a ride in the back of a three-quarter to the main gate of Camp Evans and walked to the start of the strip. Even with the disruption of the Tet offensive, the local Vietnamese businessmen had been quick to build a Sin City outside the Air Cav's new home. In fact, many of the old familiar establishments from the Sin City outside Camp Radcliff at An Khe had simply packed up and moved after their best customers. When you had a good thing going, it didn't make sense not to keep it going.

The brightly lit strip of bars, whorehouses, laundries, jeep-washing emporiums, and souvenir shops outside the gate might have been brand-new, but it smelled exactly like the old Sin City.

Corky took a deep breath and grinned. "You smell that?"

Brody smiled back. "Yeah, pussy."

"What're you two talking about?" Strawberry asked, sniffing the breeze. The hot, humid air smelled of old urine, stale beer, cheap perfume, and a hundred other unidentifiable musky odors.

"It just smells like dinks."

Corky laughed.

Brody threw his arm over the younger man's shoulder. "Strawberry, my man, just wait 'til you've been here a little longer, and you'll learn the difference between the smell of just plain old gooks and gooks who're open for business."

He took another deep breath. "This smells like boom-boom. Just stick with us, buddy, and you'll find out to-night."

Lindberry couldn't help but smile himself. As with everything else he'd come across in Vietnam, he wasn't going to argue with an experienced man like Brody. If Brody said it smelled like getting laid, then he'd just follow along and see for himself.

CHAPTER 13

Camp Evans

That afternoon it had finally dawned on Mike Alexander that history was being made in Vietnam and that he was a part of it. When he first came to the country, it had been hard to see the war as historic. As far as he was concerned, military history had always been the battles of World War II, with names like Normandy, Guadalcanal, and Anzio, not some nameless firefights in a nameless jungle in southeast Asia.

The recent fighting during Tet had given the young officer a very different perspective. He finally realized that someday he would be able to read about what he had done just like his own father read about the fighting he had done in World War II.

He went back to getting his equipment squared away for the stand-down. He had a feeling that their next mission would have to do with the Marines at Khe Sanh. Rumors were already circulating about a relief mission.

That was certainly something that would be in future history books, the relief of Khe Sanh. Those poor bastards had been up there for almost two months, getting shelled on a daily basis. Not for the first time, Alexander was very thankful that he was in the Air Cav, not in the Marines or one of the Army's leg infantry divisions. At least as a cavalryman, he'd never have to go through something like that fucking mess at Khe Sanh.

The routine work on his weapons and equipment brought Alexander's mind back to his immediate concerns. This was a task that the young officer always enjoyed. Some officers had their RTOs keep track of their gear, but Alexander had never done that. No one ever cleaned his weapon or looked after his ruck. He always carefully prepared the tools of his trade himself.

He stuffed the last of his reloaded M-16 magazines into the bandolier and put it on top of the gear in his rucksack. That was the last of it. His rifle and pistol were cleaned, his grenades attached to his ammo pouches and his maps of the AO were in the plastic map case. He had his favorite C-ration meals packed, along with several small rolls of C-ration toilet paper in a plastic bag, and several pairs of extra boot socks. He didn't mind going short on chow in the field, but he hated to run out of ass-wipe and dry socks.

His compass, penlight, grease pencils, C-4 stove, malaria pills, and salt tablets were already packed away, and he would fill both of his two-quart canteens when he went for breakfast in the morning just in case. He was done now, ready to relax and enjoy the stand-down.

Alexander laid his ruck on the footlocker at the end of his bunk and grabbed his hat. He didn't feel like writing letters this evening and decided to go over to the club for an early dinner and a couple of beers. On second thought, maybe he'd borrow the first sergeant's jeep and head out to the strip to have a Vietnamese meal for a change.

The jeep was free and Alexander was soon down among the bars, cathouses, and laundries that had sprung up almost like magic outside the new Air Cav basecamp. It never failed to amaze him how well the Vietnamese did at business. He could never figure out how Ho Chi Minh or anyone else ever hoped to make good little communists out of these people. Maybe the VC could convince the ignorant farmers that capitalism is evil, but they'd never sell that communist garbage to the city Vietnamese. They were too busy getting rich.

He stopped the jeep in front of a restaurant and carefully locked the steering wheel with the chain and padlock before stepping out. As an additional precaution, he paid a street urchin a hundred piasters to watch it for him.

Right next to the restaurant was a bar, the Pink Butterfly. Alexander vaguely remembered the name from the An Khe days. It looked like it had relocated so as not to lose its old customers. A stunningly beautiful Vietnamese girl wearing a skintight, red silk dress lounged against the doorway of the bar. The slits in the sides of her dress showed golden skin all the way to the top of her thigh, skin as smooth and as slick as the silk covering it.

Alexander's eyes automatically followed the sleek, subtle curves of her body from her long, jet black hair to her tiny feet in Western high-heeled shoes. He gulped. She was a knockout. In a land known for its beautiful women, she was a real prize.

The girl noticed Alexander's admiring gaze. It was her business to notice such things. "Hello, *Trung uy*," she said in lilting, musical English. "Would you like to come in for a drink?"

Alexander felt himself blush bright red. "Uh . . . No, thanks," he stammered, silently cursing himself for his clumsiness. "I have to eat dinner."

The girl smiled slowly, sensually. He felt her smile like a blow to the crotch. "Maybe later," she said softly. "Ask for me. My name is May Lin."

Alexander hurried on into the restaurant, the girl's laughter ringing in his ears. The waiter saw him to a table and handed him a menu. He stared at it without really reading the quaintly spelled English renderings of the Vietnamese dishes. He felt his face get red again when he remembered how the girl had looked at him.

In a land where it was easier and cheaper to get laid than it was to get a hot shower, Mike Alexander was still a "straight arrow". He had not yet sampled the local beauties. At first, this had not bothered him, he had been too damned busy with his new command of the Blues to have time to worry about women. Then, when he finally knew what he was doing in the woods and had the time to dally, Tet had hit and he had been frantically busy again.

Though he had been in-country for several months, he still hadn't found out what it was about the Vietnamese girls that seemed to drive most Americans slightly crazy. He was no virgin back in the States, but he was still a cherry boy as far as the locals went. He knew that May Lin had somehow sensed this about him, and that was why she had laughed.

When the waiter came back, Alexander ordered the first thing on the menu, not really caring what it was. When his meal came, Alexander discovered that he had ordered ginger fish, a meal that the locals considered to be an aphrodisiac. The fish was hot but delicious, and he washed it down with couple of *ba-muoi-ba* beers to cool his throat. That was another bad move on his part. *Ba-muoi-ba* was not like real beer. It was preserved with formaldehyde, the same stuff used to embalm corpses. It could also embalm the living and do strange things to a man's brain.

Pleasantly full, Alexander paid his tab and stepped back out onto the street. Night had fallen, but the air was still thick and warm. He could feel the slight breeze against his skin and it brought the exotic smell of Vietnam to his nostrils. He glanced over to the Pink Butterfly Bar. For some reason, it was almost empty. There were very few GIs sitting around the tables. Maybe he would go in for one last drink. It would be two weeks before he had another chance again.

He parted the beaded curtain in the doorway and walked in. Inside, the exotic smell was stronger, almost intoxicating. He breathed deeply. May Lin met him halfway to the bar, smiling like a cat. "You remembered me, *Trung uy,* I am happy."

Alexander grinned like an idiot. "Of course I remembered you."

May Lin led him to a table far from the other customers. "May I get you a drink?" she asked.

"A beer, please."

Alexander watched her walk over to the bar. He had never seen a human body move that gracefully in all of his life. He would have paid good money just to watch her walk back and forth across the room. He would have paid even more to see her naked while she walked. That thought caused a tightening in his pants.

May Lin came back with a cold Budweiser and a small glass filled to the top with a yellowish liquid. She placed them both in front of him. "Won't you have a drink, too?" he asked.

Alexander was a straight arrow, but he knew about the bar-girl system. May Lin was paid a percentage of the drinks he bought for her, usually tea or Coke disguised as something else and outrageously priced. It was a rip-off, and everyone knew it, but that was the system throughout all of Asia. If he wanted the girl's company at his table he had to pay for it.

"No, thank you," she smiled.

Alexander was surprised. From what he had heard, this was a first.

May Lin saw the look on his face. "I own this bar," she explained. "So I can do what I want."

"Where did you learn such good English?" he asked.

"In the university. I studied to be a translator."

The girl moved closer to him and changed the subject. "What is your name, *Trung uy*?"

"Mike Alexander."

"Mike, I like that name. How long have you been in Vietnam?"

"Not too long, a couple of months."

"Are you married?"

Alexander felt the heat of her thigh against his leg. "No."

"Do you have a Vietnamese girl friend?"

Now the heat seemed to creep up to his lower belly. He flushed slightly at his reaction. "No."

"That is sad," she said, her dark eyes sympathetic. "A handsome man like you should have many girl friends."

Alexander was flattered. He had never thought of himself as handsome. Fairly good looking, maybe, handsome, never. "I've been very busy," he said.

May Lin laughed musically. "You work too hard. You should never be too busy for love." Her soft hand slid over the top of his thigh and dropped in between his legs. A shiver ran through him and he reached for his beer.

"Why don't you try this?" she asked, holding out the small glass.

"What is it?"

"Pernod. It is French. You will like it."

Alexander brought the glass up to his nose. It smelled strongly of licorice and herbs. He tasted it, holding the heavy, strong taste in his mouth for a moment. The alcohol numbed his gums at the same time that the scent filled the back of his throat. He swallowed.

"Do you like it?"

He chased the Pernod with a quick shot of beer. "It's good," he said breathlessly.

May Lin laughed. "You will like it even more the next time," she said.

He took another, smaller sip. She was right, it was good. The Pernod sent a fuzzy warmness through his belly. He took another. May Lin watched the young officer with a secret smile on her face. Only an American could be talked into drinking Pernod straight, without mixing water in it. They were so barbarically ignorant of civilized customs. At the same time, with some of them, such as this young *trung uy,* the barbarism came with strength and an innocent, wide-eyed wonder.

May Lin's lovers were all very civilized and very accustomed to the sexual wonders of the Orient. But tonight May Lin did not want to be treated in a civilized fashion. She wanted to be the object of wonder and worship by a strong barbarian, and this young long-nose would do nicely. Her hand slipped up his leg. Yes, he would do very nicely.

Alexander didn't really know what he should do next. The combination of the ginger fish, the Pernod, and May Lin's hand had created a problem for him. As with the spiced meal he had eaten, he did not know that Pernod was also considered an aphrodisiac.

He was just about to ask if he could go somewhere alone with her when Brody and several men from the Blues walked in.

"Hey, Ell tee," Brody called out. "How you doing?"

May Lin felt Alexander diminish under her hand. He straightened up in his chair before answering. "Just fine. How are you men tonight?"

"We're doing great, sir, just great. But not as good as you're doing," Brody laughed.

Alexander felt himself redden. The glow in his stomach vanished. May Lin saw her careful seduction of this good-looking American start to fall apart. If she was going to feel his barbarian strength between her legs tonight, she was going to have to get him out of there fast.

She leaned over and whispered in his ear. "Go outside and wait for me. I will come in just a few minutes. We can go to my house."

He nodded. She got up from the table. As she walked past the bar, she said something to the two other girls sitting there. The girls immediately got up and went over to Brody's table. Alexander got up and headed for the door.

"See you men tomorrow," he said gruffly as he passed Brody's table.

"Good night, Ell tee," they called out a little too loudly.

Back on the street, Alexander's legs felt rubbery, and there was a pleasant buzz in his head. The taste of the Pernod was heavy in his mouth, but strangely he wanted another one. Two Vietnamese girls in crotch-length miniskirts walked by and he eyed them with a newfound awareness. They were both cute, in an Oriental way, but nothing compared to the slender, dark-eyed beauty he had just left in the bar.

"I am ready, Mike," came the lilting voice behind him.

May Lin had quickly changed into an embroidered silk *ao-dai*, the national women's costume of Vietnam. The close-fitting tunic dress worn over the black pants was not as revealing as the Chinese-style red dress had been, but it made her look even more exotic. Alexander quickly led her to the jeep and helped her step in. Running around to the driver's seat, he slid in and started the motor.

"Where to?" he asked as he slammed the gear shift lever into first.

"Down the street."

As he pulled away, Alexander could hear the laughter of the grunts in the bar. By morning, the news of his little dalliance would be all over the battalion. He glanced over at May Lin. Her long black hair was blowing in the wind and her smiling face half-turned to him. She reached over and laid her hand in his lap again

Alexander smiled. No matter what rumors got started, it was going to be worth it.

CHAPTER 14

Camp Evans

Lance Lawless Warlokk had his own distinctive way of dealing with people. He cloaked himself in the aura of his reputation as a world-class badass and used it to get things done his way. More often than not, the reputation alone was more than enough to convince a man to cooperate with him. But the reality of his reputation was always very close to the surface if he needed to employ that instead.

This time he wanted information. He was willing to talk Master Sergeant Vince Genelli out of it, but if that didn't work, he was fully prepared to do whatever he had to do to get what he wanted. As far as he was concerned, the man was totally expendable.

It was after duty hours and Genelli, the brigade personnel NCO, was working late in his office.

"Warlokk," Genelli said, shaking his head. "That's 'friendly fire' information and it's FOUO, for official use only. I can't release it to you or anyone else unless I have clearance from the chief of staff."

Warlokk grinned wolfishly. "You'll release it to *me*, old buddy."

"Don't give me any of the 'old buddy' shit, goddamnit," Genelli snapped. "I just can't do it."

Warlokk stood up and leaned across the desk, his faded blue eyes glittering. "You know, Vince, you and me go back a long, long ways and I've always thought of you as a friend. But we've got us a real problem here this evening. If we're friends and all that shit, then it'll be no problem for you to dig into the filing cabinet behind you and hand me that folder."

He paused for a second. "But if we're not friends," he said coldly, "then I'm going to ship your fucking body home and deal with your replacement."

Sergeant Genelli came straight out of his chair. "Goddamn you, Warlokk, don't try to hard-ass me, you sonofabitch!"

"I'm not trying, Vince, I'm doing it," the pilot said softly, sitting back down in front of the desk. "I don't think you understand what's going on here. This is a family matter. I want that information and I'm going to get it one way or other."

He paused for a moment. "Ambushing your ass in some dark alley down in Sin City and leaving your body for the dogs to eat is no problem, if that's the way you want it."

Genelli backed down quickly. He had learned the hard way that if Warlokk decided that he had to kill him, he would. Friendship didn't count much when the family was concerned.

"Jesus Christ!" he muttered, his hands pleading for understanding. "You should have told me that in the first place. What's so fucking important about this one incident, anyway?"

Warlokk locked eyes with him. "It's a long story. And you don't want to know about it."

Genelli agreed. He pulled out a drawer in the filing cabinet behind him, reached in, and brought out a manila folder stamped FOUO across the front. Without a word, he handed it over to Warlokk.

The pilot quickly read through the file and handed it back. "Thanks."

"I don't know what you're up to, but you'd better leave my fucking name out of it."

Warlokk grinned. "Sure, Vince. No sweat. You just remember that you ain't seen me in weeks."

Sergeant Genelli watched the scar-faced pilot walk out as silently as he had come in. Genelli had no idea why Warlokk had wanted to read the file on that artillery friendly-fire incident, but whatever it was, it couldn't be good. He shivered and went back to his paper work.

Outside brigade headquarters, Warlokk got into his borrowed jeep and started it up. His next stop was back at the Python Operations shack. Gaines had been spending most of his off-duty time there since the accident, and Warlokk wanted to see if he could talk him into going somewhere to get a drink. It wasn't healthy for a man to spend all his time working.

Rat Gaines was out on the berm line at the edge of the airstrip. He leaned back against one of the bunkers, took a deep drag on his cigar, and stared out into the darkness beyond the perimeter lights.

The day had not gone well for him. When he and Warlokk had returned back from their fruitless morning flight he had gotten tied up back at his office with a problem about the equipment turnover, and he had not had a chance to get away again.

He heard the outgoing rounds from the artillery batteries at the other end of the camp as the guns fired their scheduled nightly H-and-I, harassment-and-interdiction, fires. Each time one of the howitzers fired he flinched.

Deep in his mind came the unbidden image of an explosion high in the sky.

It had been almost a week now since Lisa had been killed, and the sharp pain of her death was lessening. In its place, however, a stark, aching sense of emptiness was growing and it threatened to overwhelm him.

He had thrown himself into running Echo Company, even starting to do much of the routine Echo Company paper work just to keep his mind occupied. But it wasn't working. It wasn't enough to keep his mind from flashing back to Lisa and the unseen image of a brilliant flash in the sky where a chopper should have been.

The only thing he knew that would erase that image, even for a couple of hours, was a mission; a dangerous, desperate mission. For the past couple of weeks all Python Flight had had to keep them busy were search-and-clear operations against scattered resistance. Gaines needed a backs-to-the-wall, knock-down, drag-out battle somewhere to help him forget for a little while.

He ground the cigar butt out under his boot and started back across the PSP runway to the Python Operations shack. He had to finish the paper work piled up on his desk so he could get away again in the morning for a couple of hours if the battalion commander didn't want to talk to him about another nickel-and-dime problem.

Gaines had always thought that he had a good working relationship with Colonel Jordan, but now he was beginning to wonder. Lately Jordan had been keeping a real close eye on him. Every time he turned around, the colonel wanted to see him about something that normally he would have trusted Gaines to take care of on his own. It seemed as if the colonel didn't trust him to run the company properly anymore.

When Gaines walked into the pilot ready room, he found Warlokk sitting by himself in a corner reading a *Playboy* magazine. The tall, scar-faced pilot had been his shadow for the last several days. He could hardly take a shit without finding Warlokk standing there ready to hand him the paper. He knew that Lance was just trying to be a friend and he really appreciated it, but it was starting to wear a little thin.

"What you need, Lance?"

"I thought I'd invite you over to the club for a drink."

"No, thanks. I've got to get this fucking maintenance survey finished and run it over to the G-four so we can take off in the morning."

"Screw that, Captain, you need a break. Tell that fuckin' Greenfield that if he wants it that badly, he can do it himself."

Gaines almost grinned as he shook his head. "No, I've got to finish this stuff tonight. Maybe we can do it tomorrow night."

Warlokk tossed the magazine aside. "Is there any of that I can help you with?"

Gaines thought for a moment. "You want to check over the dash-thirteens on the choppers we're turning in tomorrow?"

Warlokk grimaced. "Sure, why not? That's the best way to waste time that I can think of."

Warlokk got up and followed Gaines into his office. He took the thick stack of aircraft maintenance logbooks and dash-thirteen forms from the corner of Rat's desk and sat down.

"You'd think, for Christ's sake," Warlokk said as he started through them, "that all us pilots should have to do is to fly, not fuck around doing this kind of candy-ass bullshit."

"This is the new action Army, Lance. Maintenance management, inspections, rodent control, accident exposure reports. If they took all the assholes who shuffle paper work away from their desks and gave them M-16's, this war'd be over in a month."

"Ain't that the fucking truth."

The two men worked in silence for a few minutes.

"Lance?"

"Yes, sir."

"You don't have to follow me around, you know. I'm not an invalid."

Warlokk put his papers down and leaned back in his chair. "Captain . . ."

"Lance, I know what you're doing. You're trying to be a friend and I appreciate it. But . . ."

"Rat, I don't think you know all of it." Warlokk paused and took a deep breath. Before he could speak, Gaines cut in.

"I know the rest, Lance. I know how you felt about her."

A strange, almost guilty look came over Warlokk's scarred face.

"I also know that when you help me get through this, you're helping yourself at the same time."

"Captain . . ."

"It's okay, Lance," Gaines said softly. "Really, it's okay."

"Captain . . ." The tough, scar-faced warrant officer looked like he was about to cry. "I just remembered that there's something I've got to take care of this evening."

"Okay, Lance, I'll catch you on the flight line in the morning."

"Good night, sir."

Gaines watched Warlokk walk out. For the first time since the day Lisa had died, the tears formed in the corners of his eyes. He tried to hold them back, but something about seeing the naked grief on Lance Lawless Warlokk's face struck deep into him. It made him realize that he wasn't the only one who was feeling the way he was.

He put down the maintenance report and started a letter to Lisa's father. He had delayed writing that painful letter, but now it was time.

Mike Alexander was still a little drunk and totally exhausted when he wheeled his jeep into the company area early that morning and walked into his hooch. He had stayed with May Lin throughout the night and she had not let him sleep more than a few hours. Now he finally knew for himself what it was that made the girls of Vietnam so damned enticing, if not downright addictive.

Alexander had never considered himself to be a ladies' man or a great lover, but he had always felt that he could more than hold up his end of the stick in the mattress-pounding department. Until his memorable experience last night, that was.

May Lin had enthusiastically shown him that what he had learned from Suzie Sweet Shorts back in his college campus days bore about as much resemblance to real sex as a child's finger painting did to the Mona Lisa. May Lin had given him a lesson in an ancient art not well known in the Western world, the art of sensual pleasure for pleasure's sake alone. The sole Western contribution to the Oriental lesson had been more of the French Pernod.

Alexander had known that he was in good shape. One did not last as a grunt in the Nam unless he was. But he had not known how good a condition he was in until she showed him. He shook his head and smiled at the memory of his performance. Six times. He had actually made love to her six times! He had protested when she had wanted to go the fourth time.

"Good God, woman," he had said. "I can't do that again!"

She had reached down and wrapped her soft hand around his limp manhood. "Oh yes, he can," she laughed. "The Pernod will see to that."

She had been right.

He sat down on the edge of his bunk and started unlacing his boots. He could still taste the Pernod in his mouth, mixed with the subtle, musky taste of her body. He made a mental note to get himself a bottle of that and keep it on hand for special occasions. It was amazing what a little of that stuff could do for a guy.

CHAPTER 15

Camp Evans

Rat and Warlokk cleared the berm line of Camp Evans early that morning before the ground fog burned away, and climbed to cruising altitude. At three thousand feet, Gaines turned their Cobras to the west, heading for the mountainous area below Khe Sanh. With all of the activity going on around there, he knew that it would be a good hunting ground.

The two Cobra pilots had logged their machines out for maintenance test flights and no one would miss them for several hours. And on a test flight, no one would question what they were doing flying around fully armed without their gunners in the front cockpits.

As Gaines climbed for altitude over Camp Evans, he felt himself slowly slipping into the peace of mind that flying always brought him, the feeling that God was in his heaven and all was well with the world. Even though he was flying an armed fighting machine, looking for someone to kill, he felt at peace. Being high in the sky, so far above the cares and concerns of the world below, calmed him. He reached forward to flick the weapons switches to armed. It was time to go to work.

Within half an hour, the two Cobras located a likely-looking area and dropped down low to the ground to fly up and down the valleys and ravines. The thickly covered hills and ridgelines effectively muffled the beating sound of their rotors, and as they ducked up over a ridge, Gaines caught an NVA unit loitering around in the open, enjoying a leisurely breakfast.

"Surprise," he growled to himself as he triggered the weapons in his nose turret and volleyed rockets from his stub-wing pods. A shower of 7.62mm rounds, 40mm grenades, and 2.75-inch high-explosive rockets flew in the face of the surprised NVA. He only had a chance for a quick glimpse of his target as he flashed overhead, but he saw that he had gotten good hits.

Warlokk was about five hundred meters behind him and he saw the effects of Gaines's weapons just as he was triggering his own. From where he sat, it looked like they had killed at least two dozen men.

The two gunships didn't return for a second pass, but continued on, looking for another target. The name of the game was surprise! They found two more scattered groups of NVA walking the jungle trails and one bunch of dinks setting up a .51-caliber heavy machine gun on a hilltop. They played the game with them as well. Finally Gaines had to call it off because they were running low on fuel and ammunition.

The two Huey Cobra gunships flew in a tight formation as they came swooping in low over the Camp Evans airstrip. At the last moment, they peeled off and entered the landing pattern. From the smoke stains on their noses and underwing pods, it was obvious to watchers on the ground that they had just returned from a combat mission.

When the two Cobras settled down side by side on the Python alert pad and shut down, Gaines and Warlokk climbed out of the cockpits.

"Lance," Gaines called. He laid his flight helmet back inside the chopper before locking the canopy down. "How about seeing that these birds get rearmed this afternoon?"

"Sure thing, Captain." Warlokk turned to go. "Oh, one more thing, sir."

"Yeah?"

"As soon as I get that taken care of, can I have the rest of the afternoon off? There's a couple of things I need to take care of."

"No sweat."

"Thank you very much, sir."

Gaines frowned. Warlokk wasn't usually so formal around him. In fact, most of the time he bordered on the ragged edge of insubordination.

He shrugged and walked off, immediately forgetting the other pilot. Now that he was back on the ground, Gaines's mind automatically went back into the dark hole that he had been living in when he wasn't in the air.

Artillery Second Lieutenant Dick Jones was sitting on the bunk in his hooch at his battalion's rear area in Camp Evans, putting a little polish on his boots when there was a knock on the door.

He tossed the rag aside. "Come in."

A tall, scar-faced soldier wearing SP/4 badges on the collars of an otherwise anonymous fatigue jacket poked his head in. "Lieutenant Jones, sir?"

"Yes, I'm Jones."

"I'm Specialist Johnson from Brigade, sir. The S-one sent me over here to find you. He needs to talk to you right away."

"About what?" Jones frowned.

The tall SP/4 shrugged his shoulders. "I don't know, sir. Something about your family. He said it was important."

Jones hurriedly buttoned up his fatigue jacket and grabbed his hat. "Let's go."

"I have a jeep standing by outside, sir."

On their way out of the artillery battalion area, the lieutenant turned to the specialist. "Just a minute, driver," he said. "I've got to go back and tell the battery commander where I'm going."

"That's already been taken care of, sir," the tall SP/4 said. "Brigade called and talked to him. I'm supposed to get you over there as fast as I can."

Jones was so worried that he didn't notice that his driver was taking him around the end of the airfield instead of straight across the camp to the brigade headquarters. When the jeep pulled in behind one of the ammo bunkers at the edge of the field, however, he came out of his daze. "What are we doing here?"

Warlokk stopped the jeep abruptly and turned to face the officer. Jones suddenly saw that there was a .45-caliber pistol in his hand.

"Get out!" the pilot ordered.

"Hey! What's going on?"

Warlokk laid the pistol up alongside his head. "Get your ass out of the jeep, mister. Now!"

"I'm not going anywhere!" Jones said.

The hammer of the Colt pistol came back with a well-oiled, metallic click, and Jones did exactly as he had been told.

"I don't know what you think you're doing." His voice quivered as he walked in the direction Warlokk indicated with the muzzle of the gun. "But you're not going to get away with this."

"Up against the bunker."

By now Jones was scared shitless. "Who are you?" he asked, his voice barely a whisper. "Why are you doing this?"

Warlokk didn't answer him. For what seemed to the young officer like minutes, he just stood and stared at him. Suddenly, the pilot's left fist snapped out and caught the lieutenant in the side of the face. Jones's head snapped back.

"Hey!"

Jones raised his hands to defend himself, but the muzzle of the pistol was right in his face again, and he lowered his arms as quickly as he had brought them up.

"Do you remember that fire mission last week?" Warlokk's voice was as hard and cold as the steel pistol.

"What fire mission?"

"The one where you failed to broadcast the air warning message?"

Jones blanched.

"I see that you do remember," Warlokk said softly. "Good, that makes this a lot easier."

"What're you talking about?"

"A couple of friends of mine were on that chopper you shot down."

Jones slumped back against the bunker. It all made sense now and he knew that he was in big trouble.

"But that was an accident," he protested. "A mistake. I was cleared of any wrongdoing in that incident."

"Incident? Wrongdoing?" Warlokk snarled. "What the fuck are you talking about? That wasn't 'wrongdoing,' Lieutenant, and that wasn't no 'incident.' That was a massive fuckup."

"But, God, I didn't mean to hurt anybody!"

"Tell that to my dead friends."

Warlokk hammered the officer in the solar plexus as hard as he could. Jones doubled over, retching and gasping for breath. When he raised his head, Warlokk hit him in the face, slamming his head back against the sandbags. He followed it up with a stunning jab to the lower ribs and felt them give way under his fist. Jones slumped to his knees.

Warlokk grabbed a fistful of his collar. "On your fucking feet, asshole," he snapped, jerking him back upright.

Jones brought his hands up in front of his face to protect himself. "Please," he gasped. "I didn't do anything wrong."

"Nothing wrong!"

Warlokk's fist hammered into Jones's ribs again, and the officer went down on his hands and knees. He tried to scramble away, but Warlokk's boot shot out and caught him in the side. The artillery officer went flat on his face in the dirt.

112

In a way, Warlokk was disappointed with Jones's performance. He had hoped for a little more of a fight. That way he could have cheerfully stomped the lieutenant to death. As it was, there was no challenge. Had he been a charitable man, Warlokk would have almost felt sorry for him. But there was little charity in Lance Warlokk. He kicked Jones in the side one more time and then backed off, leaving the man sobbing and retching in the dirt.

"Just remember this, Lieutenant. If you fuck up back at Fort Sill, it doesn't really matter. But if you fuck up over here, somebody can get killed. And if you ever fuck up again and hurt friends of mine, believe me, I'll come back and kill you."

Warlokk turned and started walking to his jeep. "Oh. One more thing." He stopped and turned back. "Don't bother sending the MPs after me, Lieutenant. I don't exist."

A smiling Warlokk walked into the Python Flight operations shack later that afternoon at about 1730 hours. He was dressed in a clean flight suit and, except for having slightly reddened and bruised knuckles, he looked none the worse for wear after his day's work. He sauntered right into Gaines's office and plopped down in the chair without waiting to be invited.

Gaines looked up from the stack of paper work in front of him. "Just make yourself at home," he growled. He looked like shit and had lost weight.

"Captain," Warlokk leaned forward. "What say you and I go and get ourselves a little something to eat. Maybe go down into the ville for some Vietnamese?"

"No, thanks, Lance. I appreciate the offer, but I've got to finish this up."

"Bullshit, Rat!" Warlokk shot back. "That's what you told me yesterday."

"No, goddamnit!"

Warlokk slowly got up out of his chair. "Gaines, you've

been drag-assing around here long enough. You're going to dinner with me if I have to pick you up and carry you. I've already kicked the shit out of one asshole today, and I'm ready to do it again if I have to.''

Rat flared up, but calmed right down when he saw the grin on Warlokk's face. He didn't know what the hell had gotten into him, but he didn't feel like arguing with him tonight. Gaines put his pencil down and leaned back in his chair.

"Okay, okay. But, let's go over to the brigade club. I want to get a steak.''

"Anything you say, boss.''

By the time they arrived at the club, Gaines discovered that he had quite an appetite, after all. He quickly polished off a medium-rare steak and french fries. He even had seconds on the fries. When they had finished their after-dinner coffee, they retired to the bar for a couple of drinks.

"What'll you have, Rat?'' Warlokk asked. "It's on me.''

"When did you start buying?'' Gaines was surprised. Warlokk was well known for being tight-fisted. "Never mind, I'll have Southern Comfort on the rocks.''

They had just ordered another round when a small group of artillery officers entered and sat down on the other side of Warlokk. Their conversation was about a Second Lieutenant Jones who was in the hospital and what had happened to him that afternoon.

"I heard that he got beat up and robbed down in Sin City,'' one of the officers said.

"That's not what the battery first-shirt told me,'' another one of them offered. "He said that he got mugged in a whorehouse.''

"Well, whatever it was,'' said the third one, "he sure as hell got the living shit kicked out of him. He's got three broken ribs.''

Warlokk had a big grin on his face as he listened to their speculation.

"What're you grinning about?'' Gaines asked.

"Nothing. I just thought of something funny.''

114

"Let me in on the joke."

"It's nothing really." Warlokk suddenly turned serious. "Just something that I remembered from better times."

"Here's to better times." Gaines raised his glass.

"I'll drink to that."

CHAPTER 16

Khe Sanh

The pilot of the Fairchild C-123K Provider slammed all four of his throttles forward against the stops. He needed every last horse that he could coax out of his two aging Pratt and Whitney piston engines and the two little J-85 jets hanging under the wings of his bird.

"Get ready!" he called back to the cargo kickers in the rear of the plane.

The four Air Force cargo men in the rear compartment took their positions and snapped the loose ends of their lifelines into the hooks along the interior walls. When they were securely hooked up, the sergeant flipped the switch to lower the rear ramp. With a whine, the ramp locked down into the open position.

With a lurch, the pilot nosed the plane over and dove for the two-thousand-foot Khe Sanh airstrip below him. In the rear of the plane, the cargo kickers saw the hills surrounding the base blossom with black smoke as the enemy anti-aircraft gunners opened up on them. It was such a common occurrence to be shot at on the way into Khe Sanh that the airlift crews had named the flight path Flak Alley.

"Mother of God," one them prayed loudly against the

roar of the engines as the plane dove for the ground. "If you get me out of this, I swear I'll go to church every Sunday."

The other men stood silently and watched the muzzle flashes below them. They had nothing to do until the Provider made its pass over the runway so they could deploy the parachutes tied to the cargo pallets inside their bird. The weather was good, for a change, and the NVA had a clear shot at them. But there was nothing they could do till then, so there was no sense in pissing and moaning about it. They were committed.

Down on the ground, David Janson heard the antiaircraft guns open up on the cargo plane, and dove for cover in the nearest trench. With the ack-ack guns would soon come the routine mortar barrage, and he didn't want to be caught out in the open again when that happened.

Each time a cargo plane or a chopper flew into the base, the NVA gunners on the hills sent a barrage of mortar and artillery shells raining down on the runway. So far they had destroyed four planes and damaged several others. The enemy anti-craft fire was so accurate that the Air Force had forbidden the big four-engine C-130 Herky Birds from making any more resupply landings. Right now all they could be used for was parachuting supplies into the small drop zone outside the perimeter wire.

Instead, the older, almost obsolete C-123's had been given the dangerous task of landing on the airstrip itself. Nicknamed the Provider, the smaller transport plane was really living up to its name, providing for the needs of the men in Khe Sanh. In fact, the C-123's, C-7 Caribous, and the chopper resupply flights were the only things that kept the besieged base from falling like Dien Bien Phu.

The six thousand men trapped inside the perimeter had to have constant food, medicine, and ammunition if they were to continue fighting. The problem with the siege of Dien Bien Phu had been that the French air force had not been up to the task of the massive aerial resupply that was necessary for such an operation to be successful. If Khe

117

Sanh fell, it wasn't going to be because the Air Force hadn't done their heroic best to keep the garrison properly supplied.

The U.S. Air Force's airlift command was the best equipped and most well experienced aerial supply force in the world, having honed their skills in the Berlin airlift and the Pusan perimeter in Korea. That experience was severely put to the test at Khe Sanh, in the most massive airlift in military history.

As the C-123 swooped down over the end of the runway, the pilot dropped his flaps partway and lowered his landing gear, but he did not throttle his engines back one millimeter for the LAPES supply drop. LAPES was the Air Force acronym for "low-altitude parachute extraction system." It was dangerous, but it was the fastest way known to get the goodies to the people on the ground.

As soon as the plane's wheels touched down on the shell-pocked PSP runway, the cargo kickers deployed small pilot chutes out the open rear ramp door. They snapped open in the slipstream and jerked the larger extraction parachutes out into the air. The plane lurched as the big chutes filled. An instant later, a loaded supply pallet came flying out of the rear of the plane and crashed down onto the runway. More chutes and pallets followed it. Each time a pallet landed on the runway, the speeding plane went faster, relieved of the weight.

The last pallet cleared the ramp just as the Provider reached the end of the runway. Freed of the weight of her cargo, the pilot sucked the control stick back into his belly. Jets screaming and three-bladed props churning the air, the C-123 clawed for altitude.

The pilot's eyes were glued to his instrument panel, watching the altimeter slowly unwind. They wouldn't be safe until they had reached at least five thousand feet or more. Over the howl of the engines, he heard the hollow thud of rounds hitting the rear compartment. At least there was a lot of empty space back there to soak up the hits.

The little Provider continued her climb back into the sky,

and the NVA finally quit shooting. On the ground, David Janson got out of his trench and dusted himself off. For once the NVA hadn't mortared the field during a resupply run. They must be saving their ammunition for something special, and the reporter had a real good idea what it was going to be. He could read a history book as well as the next guy.

Tomorrow was March 13, the anniversary of the attack on Dien Bien Phu. The rumor of a major attack was sweeping through the base, and even General Westmoreland was convinced that the NVA would try something. The network of trenches the enemy had been digging outside the perimeter wire were for the assault, and everyone was on edge.

"Din Pin Poo, what's that?" Wee Willie had asked Janson when he heard the rumor.

"Aw, that's just some place where the French got their dicks knocked stiff," one of the other Marines broke in before the reporter could answer. "And everybody thinks it's going to happen again here."

It was a simplistic answer, but it captured the purest essence of the famous battle. The dramatic loss had cost the French their war with the Vietnamese.

"Actually," he informed Willie. "there is a certain similarity between what happened at Dien Bien Phu and what's going on here, but the situation is really not the same."

"Why not?"

Janson had launched into an explanation of the differences between the battles. Unlike the French, the Marines had the high ground at Khe Sanh instead of being in a valley. He talked about the superiority of American firepower, particularly in the air, and the critical role played by the aerial resupply. The French had tried to resupply from the air, too, but they had not had the machines to do it and had failed miserably. "So," Janson concluded. "The feeling is that it can't happen here."

Willie listened carefully. "Well," he asked, with the precision of a grunt's thinking. "If it's not going to happen here, what's everybody so all fired up about?"

Janson had no answer to that.

119

As the reporter continued on his way, the Air Force cargo handlers swarmed out onto the airstrip and climbed up on the pallets, cutting the parachutes loose for reuse and releasing the supplies so the marines could carry them away.

It was just another routine day at Khe Sanh. The day the routine resupply flights didn't make it would be the day it was all over.

"Muller!" Colonel Jordan called out from his office. "Come in here a moment."

The overeager lieutenant peered around the edge of Jordan's door. "Yes, sir?"

"Come in."

The adjutant sharply marched into the room and executed a snappy salute. "Yes, sir," he bellowed.

Jordan wanted to bury his head in his hands and weep. Dear God, of all the second lieutenants in the entire U.S. Army, why did he have to draw this guy to be his adjutant? He really wished that Lieutenant Muller had not been raised on old movies about the British army. The colonel had been trying unsuccessfully for almost six months to get the lieutenant to relax a little and stop acting like a British regimental sergeant major.

"At ease, Muller," he sighed.

"Yes, sir." Muller snapped into the position of parade rest, his hands clasped stiffly behind his back, his eyes staring at the wall above the colonel's head.

"Will you find Captain Gaines and tell him to report to the S-three? Brigade has a mission for the Blues."

"Yes, sir! Is that all, sir?"

"Yes."

Muller saluted again and, executing a snappy about-face, stiffly marched out of the room.

Jordan was working on his paper work a half an hour later when the Echo Company commander appeared. "You wanted to see me sir?"

120

"I told Muller to have you check in with the three; he's got a mission for you."

"That figures," Gaines said. "He told me to report to you."

Jordan shook his head. "Anyway, Brigade wants to move that recon forward to tomorrow morning. You have any problems with that?"

"No, sir, we'll be ready. I've already got two new light-fire teams of Cobras on line now and I'll have a third in operation tomorrow."

"Good. How's the rest of the equipment turnover going?"

Gaines grimaced. "The usual. More bullshit paper work than I want to deal with, but it should be done by the end of the week."

"Good." The colonel paused. "And, Gaines?"

"Yes, sir?"

"Watch those maintenance flights, will you? You're burning through a lot of ordnance."

Gaines's face was expressionless. "Yes, sir. Is that all?"

"Yes. Good hunting tomorrow."

"Yes, sir."

Jordan watched the pilot walk out of his office. He still looked like shit, but at least he was keeping a tight reign on things. Maybe a little too tight. The colonel knew what Gaines was doing with his early-morning flights, but he didn't have the heart to cut them out completely. Maybe now that the Blues were going back in the field, he would have something else to keep his mind occupied for a while.

Platoon Sergeant Leo Zack stuck his shaved head into the 2nd Squad's tent. "Off your dead ass and on your dying feet," he bellowed. "Mission briefing in fifteen minutes."

"But, Sarge, we're supposed to be on stand-down," Corky said.

"Tough shit."

"Where we going?" Two-Step asked.

"They'll tell you at the briefing." Leo looked around the tent. "Where's Brody?"

"I'll get him," Corky offered.

"Do that."

Farmer came out of his nap when Two-Step kicked the end of his bunk. For the last couple of days the young grunt had been sleeping with his K-Bar fighting knife in his hand, and Two-Step didn't want him to wake up and lash out at him with it.

"What is it?" he mumbled.

"Mission briefing in fifteen minutes."

Farmer sat up and glanced at his watch. "Where we going?" he asked, sliding the K-Bar back into the sheath on his boot top.

"Have to wait and see."

Farmer didn't really care where they were going, just as long as it was somewhere out in the jungle where he could kill dinks. In camp he didn't have anything to do, so he slept, and he was getting tired of sleeping all the time. He wanted to kill somebody.

He yawned, scratched his armpit, and started to reach for his boots before he realized that they were on his feet.

He took his canteen from his footlocker and took a long drink of warm, stale water.

"Why don't you grab a shower when we get back?" Two-Step asked.

Farmer looked up at him as if to ask why. He raised his arm and sniffed. He didn't think he smelled that bad, but he'd do it because the Indian had asked him to. When JJ had died, Two-Step had been the only guy in the squad who had really understood. He had tried to talk to him about it and had welcomed him back when he had been released from the psycho ward. Two-Step was a good man, and Farmer was glad to take a shower for him.

"Sure," he said.

The Indian looked at him for a moment, his dark eyes sympathetic. "See you at the briefing."

"They'll tell you at the briefing a two-footer around the tent. Where from?"

Conqueror was ...

I'll ...

CHAPTER 17

Camp Evans

Early the next morning, the sky was a solid blue and the ground mist had already burned off. It was a fine day for an airmobile operation. Alexander, Zack, and the Blues stood at the edge of the alert pad waiting for the word to board the slicks. A little farther down the flight line, the Aero Rifle Platoon of the 9th Cav, the Headhunters, were also waiting for their lift.

The operations plan called for the two platoons to be inserted at different times and in different places as part of the deception plan for their recon mission. To add to the deception, several dummy insertions would be made. They were to stay out of sight while they did their recon, and that meant keeping the dinks from knowing where they were operating.

When he looked around at his men, Alexander felt good. This was not going to be an easy mission. Two weeks in the brush was a real hump, but this was the kind of thing that his people did best. They were an Air Cav Blue Team. Their primary job was to sneak around in the woods, find out where the dinks were, what they were doing, and then call someone in to kick the shit out of them. He couldn't think of a better bunch of grunts do this kind of work.

Alexander had also been given two snipers from Hotel Company of the Cav's 75th Rangers to augment his platoon with a long-range kill capability. The two Ranger snipers had that cold-eyed, casual look that said they could handle themselves under any circumstances.

As the grunts waited for their lift ships, Alexander checked over each man. The inspection wasn't because he didn't trust them to be ready. They were all veteran boonie rats and knew better than to go into the woods only half-assed prepared. He just wanted something to do to keep his mind off last night while he waited. It would be two weeks before he would have a chance to see May Lin again, and he didn't want to think about her until then.

The men from the Blues, with the exception of Broken Arrow, all wore jungle fatigues with brush hats. Their faces and hands had been camouflaged with green and black grease paint. Two-Step wore his usual tiger suit camies and had a camouflage neck scarf tied around his head. Alexander had long since stopped trying to get the Indian grunt to wear a standard uniform. Or to get a regulation haircut, for that matter.

Everyone's ruck was loaded down with a double basic load of ammunition and grenades as well as extra water and rations. They would be humping almost eighty pounds a man, not counting their individual weapons, but they couldn't go with any less. They were going deep into enemy territory and Alexander did not want to blow the mission by having to call for an aerial resupply. They would probably need every last round of ammunition and ration can they were carrying.

Bunny Rabdo was further burdened down with the platoon CP radio and extra batteries. Alexander had borrowed a Prick-77 instead of the Prick-25's that the squads were carrying, because it had a secure voice capability he could use to report back to the battalion. The enemy often listened in on American radio communications, and on this mission, they could not risk any interception of their transmissions.

Brody's squad was a little shorthanded, but they were armed to the teeth. Cordova had their M-60 machine gun and both Farmer and Two-Step were carrying thumpers, the M-79 grenade launchers. Farmer also packed an M-16 slung over his back, and the Indian had his sawed-off shotgun point-man weapon. Everybody was carrying extra bandoliers of the 40mm grenades for the thumpers as well as extra link belts of M-60 machine-gun ammunition.

The Ranger snipers wore the oak-leaf-pattern camouflage uniform and carried their 7.62mm XM-21 sniper rifles with both day and night scopes strapped onto the sides of their rucks. They also carried Army-issue .45-caliber pistols on their belts and a survival knife strapped upside down on their assault harness.

Down at the other end of the pad, Rat Gaines and Lance Warlokk finished their preflight walk-around of their Cobra gunships and waited for the other pilots to complete theirs. Gaines looked better than he had in quite a while. He was almost smiling.

"Everyone's ready," Warlokk said, reporting the status of the choppers scheduled for the flight.

"Good, let's go." Gaines tightened the fingers of his Nomex gloves and pulled his flight helmet on.

"By the way," he said as he stepped up to climb into the cockpit of his bird. "I heard a story about someone kicking the shit out of an artillery officer. You wouldn't happen to know anything about that, would you?"

Warlokk looked innocent. "No, sir. I never heard of him."

"I didn't think so," Gaines laughed.

The pilot looked down the line of slicks and pumped his arm up and down in the move-out signal. "Let's get this show on the road."

At the front end of the line of slicks, Alexander saw Captain Gaines's signal for them to move out. "Okay, people, let's hit it! Saddle up!'' he shouted, reaching down for his pack.

The grunts got to their feet, shouldered their heavy rucks, and scrambled on board the choppers.

Alexander climbed into the lead slick, Cliff Gabriel's ship, and grabbed up the spare flight helmet from the canvas jump seat. He put it on and quickly plugged into the intercom before he took his place in the open door behind the pilot.

''We're go back here,'' he called up.

''Roger that,'' Gabe called back. ''We're waiting for the word from the captain.''

''Python, Python,'' Gaines's voice sounded in Gabe's helmet earphones. ''This is Lead. Crank 'em.''

The slick pilot hit the radio switch. ''Three Eight, Roger. Cranking now.''

Gabe's hands moved swiftly over the switches and controls of his bird, calling out each item to the copilot as he ran through the startup procedure. ''Battery, on. Inverter switch, off. RPM warning light, on. Fuel, both main and start, on. RPM governor, decrease.'' He looked over his shoulder to both sides of the ship. ''Rotor, clear. Light it!''

Reaching down with his right hand, Gabe twisted the throttle open to flight idle and pulled the starting trigger on the collective. In the rear of the bird, the big Lycoming T-53 turbine burst into life with a screeching whine and a smell of burned kerosene. Over their heads, the forty-eight-foot main rotor slowly began to turn, moving faster and faster.

As the turbine RPMs built and the blades came up to speed, the pilot released the start trigger and held the throttle at flight idle as he checked his instruments. Everything was in the green. He twisted the throttle all the way up against the stop.

The whine built to a bone-shaking scream as the turbine ran up all the way to 6,000 RPM. Everything was still in the green. He flipped the RPM switch to increase. The turbine screamed even higher at 6,700 RPMs. He backed off the throttle, slid the armored side of his seat into the forward position, and latched the door. They were ready to take off. As soon as the other two slicks reported that they were cranked and running, Gabe keyed his throat mike. "Python Lead, this is Three Eight, we're go."

When the gunships had all called in, Gaines radioed the control tower. "Evans Control, this is Python Lead. Request permission to take off. Over."

"Python, this is Evans Control. You are cleared for take-off. Over."

"Python Lead, thank you. Out. Python, Python," Gaines radioed the pilots in his flight. "On my command. Pull pitch now!"

At Gaines's command, Gabe hauled up on the collective and nudged forward on the cyclic control. The rotor blades bit into the air, the tail came up and he headed down the runway. As soon as his airspeed was up, Gabe pulled more pitch to the blades with the collective, and they climbed into the clear blue sky. He looked back over his shoulder and saw the other two slicks keeping in tight formation with him. That was good. Gaines liked his people to look sharp in the air.

As soon as the slick cleared the perimeter of the camp and banked away to the north, Brody set about getting ready for war. Flipping up the latch on the feed-tray cover to the M-60 doorgun, he opened it and laid the linked 7.65mm ammunition belt into place. Then he snapped the cover back down.

The ammo in the linked belts were loaded with a mix of ball and tracer ammunition, one round of tracer for every four rounds of ball. That way, when his sixty was talking, he could see where his fire was going and could bring it accurately onto target.

Reaching down to the right side of the gun's breech, he pulled back on the charging handle to jack a round into the chamber. Sliding the handle forward into the latched position, he flipped the safety on. Now he was ready. His gloved hands were wrapped around the spade grips of the gun and his thumbs rested on the triggers.

Alexander sat in the open door of the chopper with his boots hanging down over the side. As the cool morning air buffeted his face and the sound of the rotor blades rang in his ears, he felt his pulse start pounding faster and faster with the adrenaline that raced through his body. There was a feeling about riding in the open door of a slick, locked and loaded for war, that was beyond description. The young officer couldn't put this heart-pounding, gut-twisting feeling into words, and after all this time, he still didn't know if it excited him more than it scared him.

From the air, the countryside looked peaceful and calm. It always did. But he knew how deceptive that was. Were it as peaceful as it looked, he wouldn't be flying around the sky with a chopper load of men armed to the teeth and looking for someone to kill. Alexander was very conscious of the weight of the loaded ruck on his back and the trigger of his sixteen lying under the first finger of his right hand. It was a powerful feeling.

He looked around at the men sitting in the door beside him and saw that they, too, felt some of the same excitement that he did. He could see it in their eyes, and their faces wore the same tight grin that he knew was on his own face. The smile that hid the hammering of their hearts.

Brody, however, caught his eye and gave him a big smirk. Alexander stifled the urge to shoot him the finger. For the last two days, every time he had seen Brody or any of the other men who had spotted him in the bar with May Lin, they all had big shit-eating grins on their face. That was the only bad thing about officers frequenting the same haunts that the troops did. It was hard to maintain discipline when you were caught with your pants down around your feet.

The flight to the Blues' landing zone took almost an hour. When Gabe and the other two slicks approached the LZ, they pulled into a tight orbit off to one side while Gaines and the gunship escorts charged on ahead and swooped down over the jungle clearing to check it out for them.

"Python Three Eight, this is Lead. The Lima Zulu is green. You are go to execute. Over"

"Lead, this is Three Eight, Roger Green," Gabe answered. "Rolling in now. Break. Python Two, Python Three, this is One, follow me down. Over."

The other two slick pilots rogered as Gabe turned onto a final approach and swooped down onto the small LZ. Overhead, Rat's Cobra did figure-eights, its chin turret sweeping from side to side as the gunner looked for trouble. When Gabe flared his ship out a foot from the ground, Alexander pulled his flight helmet off and jammed his brush hat down over his ears.

"Go! Go! Go!" he shouted as he jumped down.

Brody and the grunts in Gabe's slick unassed the bird in less than ten seconds, running low to clear the rotor blades. The other two slicks flared out behind them, bringing Zack and the other two squads. They went to ground in the tall grass with their weapons trained on the wood line as the other choppers quickly off-loaded. In seconds, all three slick drivers pulled pitch and rose back up into the sky. Alexander saw Gabe raise his hand in salute as he flew off.

Now came the planned deception operation. The slicks would fly to other clearings and make several dummy insertions before they returned to Camp Evans, dropping down and landing for a few seconds and pretending to off-load people. A few miles away, a similar flight of slicks and guns would be inserting the Blue Team from the 9th Cav to work their part of the AO.

The same number of choppers, doing the same thing in different places, would confuse any North Vietnamese patrols who might have seen them flying overhead. The enemy wouldn't know that they were actually two different flights, or where they had dropped the troops, or even if they had landed any grunts at all.

129

As soon as the sound of the rotors faded into the distance, the men got to their feet. Sprinting for the cover of the tree line a hundred meters away, they slipped back into the sheltering darkness.

CHAPTER 18

South of Khe Sanh

Once the Blues were safely under cover in the tree line, Zack quickly put them in a patrol formation with Brody's squad taking the point position. One of the snipers went up front with Two-Step while the other one dropped back to the drag position to keep an eye on their back trail with his sniper scope.

Alexander made no radio calls to inform the battalion that they were on their way. On this mission it was essential that they keep their radio traffic to a bare minimum. Gaines would report their successful insertion when he returned to Camp Evans. With the exception of a nightly commo check, they would maintain complete radio silence until they had something to report or they needed help.

After a final glance at the maps, Alexander ordered them to move out. He wanted to be in the primary recon zone by nightfall.

The first two hours were a routine walk in the woods. Since the men were fresh, Alexander kept up a good pace, covering ground as quickly as they could while still keeping their eyes out for signs of trouble. He called a fifteen-minute break after the two hours. Even though the men were fresh, their rucks were heavy and there was no point in exhausting them. They had thirteen days to go.

At the stop, Sergeant Zack took two of the men and went back to take another look at a major trail they had just crossed, a trail that had shown signs of recent heavy foot traffic. A few minutes later, he came back with an empty tin of canned herring packed in Red China and an empty pack of North Vietnamese cigarettes in his hand. His face was grim when he showed his finds to Alexander. The inside of the can was still wet with fish oil. The ants hadn't even had time to clean it.

"I'd say that we had a sizable troop unit stop for a meal back there sometime in the last couple of hours," the sergeant said.

Alexander turned the can over in his hands. On the bottom the message Packed in the People's Republic of China was written in English. He tossed the can back into the brush.

"Which way were they going?"

"Toward Khe Sanh."

Alexander studied his map for a moment. Since the enemy's tracks ran in the same direction they were supposed to go, they would have to take another route into their patrol area.

"What you think about crossing this next ridge?" He pointed to a position on the map. "And trying to move up through the next little valley?"

Zack glanced at the place under the lieutenant's finger. "Looks okay to me, sir."

"Let's get it then."

"Yes, sir."

Zack got the men moving again, this time deeper into the jungle and away from the trail they had intended to follow. It would take them a little longer to get into their patrol area that way, but the mission of a recon team was to look without being seen, and not to get involved in a firefight.

A couple of hours later, the platoon was strung out in a

line, heading down the side of the ridgeline to the east. The sniper up on point with Two-Step stopped to use the scope on his sniper rifle to check out the valley they were about to enter.

He slowly lowered the rifle. "Oh, shit," he said softly. "We got company."

"Where?" Two-Step dropped down beside him.

"Over there to our right, seven, eight hundred meters," the sniper pointed. "They're moving right across our front, about a dozen of them."

"Okay, I see 'em. Hold it up here while I go back and talk to the ell tee."

"Got it."

Alexander and Zack came up to the point, and the sniper pointed out the NVA to them. The lieutenant studied them for a few moments through his field glasses before pulling out his map.

"Sergeant Zack," he said. "We've got them moving both in front of us and behind us. We've got to haul ass out of here and try to get away from those guys."

His finger tapped the map. "I'm going to wait 'til that bunch down there has moved on. Then we'll swing in behind them and cross over the next ridge into the valley behind it."

"Sounds good to me."

"Okay, shift the third squad up on point and tell Brody to hold the rear here while we go on ahead and check it out."

"Yes, sir."

When Alexander and the other two squads moved out, Brody quickly placed his people into an X-shaped ambush on the top of the ridgeline. With that type of ambush formation, no matter which direction the dinks tried to come at them, they could shoot back.

A tense half hour later, Brody received a radio call. "Two, this is Six. I want you to move on out across the valley now. We're on the next ridgeline and we'll be waiting for you. Over."

"This is Two, wilco. Out."

Brody gave the handset back to Bunny and stood up. "Okay, let's go. Two-Step, you take point, I'll do slack. Corky, you and the shooter take drag."

They had only gone another four or five hundred meters down into the valley when the sniper came running back up to him. "We've got four or five dinks tracking us," he panted.

"Bunny," Brody said. "Hand me the horn. I've got to tell the ell tee that we've got company." Brody keyed the mike. "Blue Six, this is Blue Two. Over."

"This is Six, send it," came the curt reply.

"This is Two, we have a small enemy force tracking us. Over."

"Do you need help? Over."

"Not at this time. Over."

"Keep me informed. Six out."

Alexander halted the main body on the other ridge to wait and see what Brody was up against. He didn't need to have someone dogging their tails while they were on a recon mission. If Brody couldn't resolve this quickly, he'd have to call for an extract.

Brody carefully surveyed their location. The vegetation around them was not thick enough for what he had in mind. "We need a good ambush site real quick," he told Two-Step.

The Indian took off down the side of the hill with the six grunts following close behind. At the bottom of the hill, the jungle was thicker. Two-Step stopped and quickly looked around. "Here," he said.

"Okay, get 'em in place on the right while I rig a claymore."

"Got it."

Brody quickly took a claymore from his ruck and set it up with its back to the trunk of a big tree. Lying down behind the antipersonnel mine, he used the built-in sight to aim it at belt-buckle height. When he hit the clacker, the nine hundred steel balls buried in the claymore would blast a bloody swath fifty meters wide down the trail. If anyone survived that, they'd be taken out with small arms.

After sighting the mine, Brody camouflaged it with brush and hid himself behind the neighboring tree. The rest of the grunts had spread themselves out well back in the brush. When Brody detonated the claymore, they would spring out and rake the killing zone with automatic fire. If everything went as planned, it would be all over in thirty seconds or so.

Brody flicked the selector switch of his sixteen down to rock and roll and took an extra magazine out of his ammo pouch. Holding the rifle in his right hand, he picked up the clacker firing device in his left and settled down to wait. If the sniper was right, it wouldn't be very long.

He was barely back down under cover when the NVA point man slowly walked into view. His dark olive uniform and equipment were brand-new, as was his AK-47 assault rifle. That was good. He looked like a fresh kid, not some seasoned old jungle fighter. That would make this much easier.

The NVA point man walked into the edge of the killing zone and stopped for a moment. Since he could see for quite a distance down the trail that Alexander had taken, and it was clear, he turned around and urgently waved his comrades forward.

Brody grinned. He could tell that this rookie dink didn't like being out on point all by himself. He was as nervous as a cat trying to find a place to shit on a tin roof. His eyes darted around from side to side without really seeing anything at all. This dink was just about to find out that he was right. The point was a dangerous place to be.

The NVA waited until his five buddies were only a couple meters behind him before he moved out again. Brody let him go on past his position. He was after the main body and would police the point man later.

The rest of the NVA patrol were rookies, too. They were all crowded together in a nice little bunch. Brody smiled and waited patiently until they were right in the middle of the killing zone. He slammed down on the handle of the firing device.

The mine detonated with a roar and a blinding flash. Nine hundred .25-caliber steel balls swept the jungle trail at waist height. Three of the five North Vietnamese were blown off their feet.

When Two-Step had dropped back into cover, he had checked the load in his shotgun and loosened a hand frag on his ammo pouch. Before the frag from the claymore had even stopped flying, the Indian stepped out, his deadly pump gun held down at his hip. Working the slide as fast as he could, he emptied the shotgun's magazine into the two dinks who had somehow escaped the claymore's blast. The stainless-steel balls tore into them, blowing them off their feet.

Brody dropped the clacker. Spinning around to the left, he brought his M-16 up. The NVA point man had turned halfway around, a look of terror frozen on his face. Brody didn't give him a chance to recover. He dumped half a magazine of 5.56mm into him.

The dink pitched forward onto his face.

Spinning the other way, Brody unloaded the remaining rounds in the magazine into the tangled pile of bodies on the trail. The sixteen's bolt locked back on an empty magazine.

When Farmer heard the roar of Two-Step's shotgun, he dashed out into the open, his sixteen on rock and roll. He sprayed fire into his side of the trail. He emptied the magazine into the unmoving bodies, slammed a fresh one into position, and fired again.

"Cease fire" Brody yelled. "Cease fire."

Silence filled the jungle. Nothing moved for a few moments. Brody dropped the empty magazine from his rifle and slapped a new one into place. He pulled back on the charging handle to chamber a new round, and slowly moved out into the open. The Indian stepped out of the brush beside him, and they quickly checked the six bodies lying in the trail.

"You see a radio?" Brody asked.

"Nope."

Brody turned and saw Farmer bent down over one of the dead NVA, his K-Bar knife in his hand.

"Farmer, knock that shit off."

Farmer straightened up, the knife bloody in his hands and a big grin on his face. "Hey, Sarge! Look what I got."

Brody turned away. He didn't want to have to deal with that. Taking ears was one thing, but Farmer looked like he enjoyed it. He'd have to have a long talk with that young troop when they got back to Camp Evans.

"Bunny," he called out to his RTO. "Call the ell tee. Tell him that we got 'em all and that they didn't have a radio with 'em."

While Bunny passed the message on to Alexander, the grunts quickly checked the bodies for documents.

"Farmer, Strawberry," Brody said. "Get these bodies off the trail fast."

Taking the corpses by the arms and legs, the two men dragged them well back into the thick brush and dumped them out of sight. Their weapons followed. Brody tried to scuff dirt over the wet bloodstains on the trail, but there were just too many of them. Anyone passing by that way would know in an instant that there had been a firefight. Unfortunately, there would be no rain to wash out the telltale signs of blood and the blast mark of the claymore.

"Okay," Brody said, looking back down the trail. "That's it, guys, let's get the fuck outta here before any more of these bastards show up."

By the time Brody and his men rejoined Alexander and the main party, the platoon leader saw that it was getting dark. They were going to have to stop for the night. He was a little concerned because they hadn't covered as much ground on their first day as he would have liked.

He wasn't about to try to move the platoon through the jungle at night. For one thing, it was noisy. Far more important, there was too great a chance of stumbling into someone in the dark. They needed to find some place high enough where they could stay out of the way and watch all approaches.

At first light, they could move out again, but right now, all they could do was find a place to hide. He dropped back to where Zack was walking alongside the radio man.

"I think we should stop," he told the veteran sergeant. "With all the NVA crawling around in this area, there's just too great a chance of us running into them in the dark. We'd better hole up and just wait it out. We'll have our asses in a real crack if we get into a firefight tonight."

Zack looked around at the darkening shadows. "You're right, sir. With three understrength squads, we can't afford to get into a full-scale pissing contest with a passing NVA unit."

"Okay, Sergeant," Alexander said. "As soon as we can find a good spot, we'll overnight and move out again in the morning."

"Yes, sir."

As night fell over the jungle, the Blues reached the top of a small, sparsely covered ridge. "What do you think?" Alexander quietly asked Zack.

The platoon sergeant looked around, down into the already pitch black jungle. "It'll do, sir. We've got good cover and can keep an eye on the approaches."

"Get 'em settled down while we can still see what we're doing."

CHAPTER 19

South of Khe Sanh, 13 March

As each of the Blues reached the top of the small hill, Sergeant Zack had them pull into a tight defensive perimeter. Instead of digging in, as they usually did when they stopped at night, Zack positioned them in a large-patrol star formation.

Digging fighting positions would be very little help if they were hit during the night. It would also be a dead giveaway that they had been there. Without artillery support, there were too few of them to fight it out, so they would have to try to run for it, anyway.

Their best chance of survival was simply to lie low, be long gone from that place in the morning, and not leave a trail.

After dropping their rucks, the men got out their poncho liners and lay down on their bellies in a big circle, facing out with their feet toward the center. They would lie that way all night, awake or asleep. If one of them had to urinate, he would just roll over onto his side, piss, and lie back down. Other than that, no one would move until morning.

During the night, if anyone heard anything or thought

139

that he saw movement, he would tap the boot of the man next to him and point it out to him with hand signals. The man would pass it on down the line to the next man in the circle. No one would say a word until first light. Their weapons were ready in their hands and they had their extra magazines and hand grenades within easy reach. But their survival depended on not being discovered.

In the center of the formation, Alexander lay wide awake, thinking over the events of the day. It had been a real bad beginning to a recon operation, but it wasn't because he had done anything wrong. Since the dinks didn't have a radio, maybe he and his men had gotten away clean and weren't being tracked. He was beginning to think that running a recon in this area with the entire platoon wasn't a real good idea.

The strategy was to move the Blues into an area, break down into smaller teams during the day, but join up at night for mutual defense. It had worked well before, but this time it didn't seem to. There were just too many dinks operating in the area, and moving the platoon in a single body left too much of a trail for the enemy to follow. Alexander wondered if he should split them up in the morning. They might attract less attention that way.

The platoon leader took a deep drink of water from his canteen and tried to get comfortable. It was going to be a long night.

Out in the circle, Farmer smiled and reached into the side pocket of his fatigue pants to make sure that he hadn't lost his souvenirs. If he was lucky, he could get enough ears to make a necklace before this patrol was finished. He had seen one of the men in a LRRP unit wearing a string of sun-dried human ears around his neck when he had first come in-country. Back then he hadn't understood why the man would want to have something like that. Now he did.

If he took the ears, it was easier to keep track of how many dinks he killed.

Farmer started having trouble remembering what had happened when he came off a mission. Lately, all of the firefights seemed to have blended into one big battle. He lost track of how many NVA he killed and he desperately needed to know. He wanted to fully avenge Gardner's death. He didn't know how many Vietnamese he would have to kill before his old buddy could rest in peace, but the number would come to him someday. Until then, he had to keep track of the dead.

He rubbed the grisly souvenirs and smiled again. Maybe he'd even get a chance to take more ears tonight. He tightened his finger around the trigger of his M-16 and stared out into the darkness. It was at times like this that he could remember Gardner best. In the daylight, all he could remember was seeing his friend running across the rice paddy with the wounded nurse in his arms while the deadly 12.7 hammered at him, kicking up big clots of red mud around his feet.

Thinking of the nurse reminded Farmer that she was dead, too, and that he had to collect some ears for her. Most of the time he didn't think of Lisa unless his mind flashed back to that day at Thon La Chu. He saw her in JJ's arms, her face contorted with pain, her blond hair matted with mud, and the bright red blood pulsing from the mangled mess of her leg.

The dinks had hurt her, too. JJ had died saving her. Again Farmer saw in his mind the heavy 12.7 rounds tearing into JJ's back as he handed the wounded nurse to the medic in the waiting Dustoff chopper. As if in slow motion, he saw them explode through Gardner's heaving chest. He saw the stark white of his ribs against the shocking pink of his lungs and the bright, bright red blood.

JJ's blood had splattered all over Farmer when he hauled the limp body of his friend into the Dustoff. The smell had clung to him even after he had showered and changed his uniform. Even tonight, he could smell the hot, sharp smell of fresh blood and Gardner's death.

He reached into his pants pocket again and cupped the severed ears in his pocket. Somehow dink blood didn't smell the same.

In the underground headquarters of the 325C NVA Division, Lieutenant Colonel Tran glared at the five officers standing at attention in front of him. The harsh yellow light of the hissing kerosene lamp made him look even more ferocious.

"Your only reason for living right now," he snarled, "is to keep the Yankee recon teams from learning of the defenses we are constructing." He shook a fistful of papers at them. "You have more than enough men for the task. Yet it appears that an American recon team was not only able to penetrate your security, but that even after they were spotted, they killed the tracking team and escaped."

He rocked back on his heels and glared at the company commanders. "Well? Can any of you tell me how this happened?"

"Comrade Colonel . . ." An older man stepped forward. Captain Xuan was a veteran jungle fighter and a man well known for his bravery against his nation's enemies. "That happened in my sector, and I think those Yankees were Green Berets," he offered as an explanation.

"But you found no bodies," Tran replied. "How do you know that they were the Green Devils?"

"They move through the jungle leaving almost no traces," he explained. "And the ambush of the tracking team was very well done." He paused for a moment. "Also, two of the bodies were missing an ear."

Tran thought for a second. Taking kill trophies was a trademark of the Han mercenaries who worked for the Special Forces, but other Yankees followed the barbaric practice of mutilating the dead, as well.

"That may be true, Xuan," the colonel continued. "But even so, your men should be capable of overcoming a small American recon team, even if they are Green Berets. It is imperative that your men find and neutralize this team before they stumble into the supply depot in your area. It is absolutely vital that it not be found. Do you understand that?"

"Yes, Comrade Colonel."

Tran turned his gaze on the other commanders. "The rest of you take heed as well, I do not want to have this conversation again." He stepped back. "You are dismissed. Return to your duties."

The company commanders saluted and quickly exited the small room. Tran went over to his map again and found the site where the tracking team had been wiped out. Maybe the Yankees had been hit hard enough that they would pull back out and go somewhere else. If they did, no one would learn of the giant supply dump in the jungle.

But Tran had been a professional soldier far too long. He had to be prepared for the worst possible case—that the recon team was hiding in the heart of his most sensitive area. He decided to bring another infantry company in to provide even more security for that particular sector.

He hated to take men away from the work of preparing the defenses along Route 9, but it was necessary. This was certainly not going to be the last Yankee recon team that was going to come snooping around. The next time they showed up, he had to stop them cold. None could be allowed to escape.

If his company commanders did not get this situation under control instantly, he was going to have to take command of the field operations personally. There was too much at stake to trust even a capable man like Xuan. If the Yankees penetrated his security, plans for the battle for Khe Sanh would suffer a serious setback. And if that happened, he would suffer a setback as well. Hanoi would not reward the officer responsible for such a disaster.

The reward Tran was looking for was a transfer out of South Vietnam to a position back in one of the Cambodian sanctuaries. As far as he was concerned, he had seen more than his fair share of fighting for the people's struggle. He felt that he deserved to be safe, where he could pass his

143

experience on to younger men rather than risking his life in a combat unit.

He had been in Cambodia once before, but he had been called back into the combat zone when the 201st Division needed an operations officer. From there, he had been transferred to his present position with the 325C for the Tet offensive.

The attack on Khe Sanh was not progressing as well as the high command would have liked. The big attack that had been planned that day to commemorate glorious victory over the French imperialists and the dreaded Foreign Legion at Dien Bien Phu had to be postponed. The increased B-52 attacks of the last two weeks had decimated the units that had been moved into position for the assault.

Tran shook his head in frustration. He had been at Dien Bien Phu and had seen the proud French forced to bow their heads under the yoke of the People's Army. He feared that he was not going to see the same thing happen at Khe Sanh.

To all the world, it seemed that history was repeating itself, that the proud American Marines would soon fall to the irrepressible power of the People's Army. But Tran really didn't think so.

The Yankee air power alone was enough to make the difference. The French air force had consisted of old World War II transport planes, most of them either captured from the Germans or American rejects. And they did not have the high-flying jet bombers or the vast helicopter fleet. There was still a faint chance that the Khe Sanh garrison would surrender. But if they did, it would be because the American leaders lost their nerve, not because the Marines had been beaten.

No matter, though. Tran had his mission, to deny the use of Route 9 to the Yankees. And if his part of the battle plan was successful, he would still be in a good position to have his request for transfer approved.

* * *

That evening at Camp Evans, Rat Gaines was out on the berm line at the edge of the airstrip, staring out into the darkness beyond the perimeter lights. The soft, orange-red glow of the cigar clamped between his teeth shone against his motionless face.

The day had not gone well for him. When he came back from escorting the Blues to their LZ, he had been tied up again with bullshit paper work, had not had a chance to go flying. He flicked the cigar butt out beyond the wire, watching the sparks flare brightly before dying. Lisa had flared out and died, too.

The pilot turned around and started walking across the PSP runway to the Python Operations shack. There were still a few things that he could get out of the way so he would be free in the morning, in case something came up with the Blues.

When Gaines walked into the pilot ready room, he found, for a change, that Lance Warlokk wasn't lurking around anywhere. The only other person in the building was the night radio operator.

"Anything for me? Gaines asked, sticking his head around the corner of the radio room.

"No, sir," the SP/4 answered.

"I'll be in my office if anyone needs me."

"Yes, sir."

Gaines sat down behind his desk and looked at the overflowing in-boxes. He started reading the first piece of paper, but before he was even halfway through it, he threw it back down. He stared out the window at the darkened airstrip for a long moment. Then he reached into his desk drawer for a couple of sheets of typing paper.

He picked up the typewriter from the table behind his desk and headed for the radio room.

"Can you type?" he asked the RTO.

"Yes, sir, some."

"Good." Gaines handed him the typewriter and the paper. "I need you to do something for me."

CHAPTER 20

West of Khe Sanh

At first light, Zack called the stand-to before Alexander was up. Once he had awakened the men, he went to the lieutenant, who lay curled up under his poncho liner. "Lieutenant," Zack called out softly. "Stand to, sir."

Alexander came instantly awake. "Right, Sarge." Wrapping the poncho liner tightly around him to ward off the morning chill, Alexander sat up and looked around their small hilltop lager site. The sun hadn't risen above the horizon yet. The thick morning mist clung tightly to the ground, giving a mystical, eerie quality to the jungle, muting the brilliant daytime colors to shades of greenish gray.

Most of the men were sitting where they had slept, with their camouflage poncho liners wrapped tightly around them as they tried to eat. They were hungry, but it was a cold breakfast they were having that morning. They could not afford to light even a small C-4 fire to heat coffee. The warm smell of coffee or heated rations would carry through the chill air for a mile or so.

Most of the grunts opened a C-ration can of fruit or a B-2 unit and washed it down with water. Some of them, however, had managed to score some of the prized Lurp rations and were at least having a warm breakfast. Lurps were freeze-dried rations in plastic bags that were designed to be carried by long-range recon units. To rehydrate a Lurp, you tore open a corner of the bag, poured in a little water, re-sealed the bag, and put it under your shirt. A man's body heat would soften the food and bring it up to body temperature, ready to eat in just fifteen minutes or so.

Alexander was never very hungry in the morning, so he made a breakfast of a can of pound cake and a Lurp nut bar before making a canteen cup of cold coffee. He had to have his morning coffee to get his brain started. He would have killed for a cup of hot coffee, but cold coffee would do if that was all he had. Taking the cup with him, he went looking for Sergeant Zack to talk about what they were going to do that day.

The black sergeant was halfway down the side of the hill, taking a look at the trail they had followed last night. Alexander knelt down beside him and pulled his map out of his side pants pocket.

"We're only about six klicks away from our recon area," the lieutenant said. "Maybe two hours in this stuff. What do you think about splitting up into two groups and going in on different axes? That way we can cover more ground and there's less chance of our being spotted."

Zack traced a route on the map. "That sounds good to me, sir. Why don't you take one of the squads and move up through here, while I take the others and do a sweep to the north of you. We can plan on meeting up here." His finger stabbed the map. "Right about dusk."

"That sounds like a plan," Alexander agreed. "I'll take Brody's people and one of the snipers. One thing, though. . . . If we keep running into the same guys that we did yesterday, we may have to get our asses out of here. So keep your eyes out for good PZs just in case."

Zack glanced down at the fog-shrouded jungle around them. "I really don't think that we're going to last two weeks in here, sir."

"Neither do I, Sarge. Neither do I."

Alexander got to his feet and folded the map. "I'll go get Brody's people moving. I want to get going as soon as this ground fog clears up."

An hour later, Alexander, Brody, and the six grunts slipped down the hillside and disappeared into the jungle below. Zack and the remaining fifteen men stayed where they were, covered their rear for half an hour and then headed down.

NVA Captain Xuan stood on the top of the small hill and looked into the jungle below him. The sun was climbing high in the sky, and Xuan mopped the sweat from his forehead. He had been pushing his men hard all morning, trying to pick up the Americans' trail again. Today, though, he had enough radios to properly equip all of his search teams, so when the Yankees were spotted this time, they would not get away.

And spot them they would. Colonel Tran had made it abundantly clear that if they did not, Xuan's head, as well as his job, was in jeopardy. Xuan had known Tran for a long time and he had great respect for the colonel's ability to make good on his threats.

One of Xuan's best scouts, a grizzled old veteran jungle fighter, came up to him. "Comrade Captain," the tracker said. "The Yankees were here last night. Maybe twenty of them."

"Which way did they go?"

"East, Comrade Captain, toward Khe Sanh."

Xuan pulled his map out and checked the location of Colonel Tran's supply depot. As he had feared, it was also to the east of their present location, directly along the route that the Yankees had taken.

That was not good. He knew that he had better relay this information back to Tran right away. Maybe one of the other units was closer to the Americans' route of march and could be maneuvered into position to block them.

As Xuan had expected, Tran ordered him to immediately

148

pursue the Yankees as fast as he could. Blowing on his whistle, Xuan sent his best tracking team double-timing down the jungle trail to the east, while he radioed his other platoons and vectored them into the area where he thought the Americans were headed. He had them now, he thought with a smile. This time they could not possibly escape.

The North Vietnamese tracking team was good, and the trail left by Zack's men was plainly visible, so they moved fast. They had been on the go for several hours nonstop and could sense that they were closing in for the kill. That sense of anticipation, however, made them a little less alert than they should have been. Because the trail was covered with boot prints made by Zack's men, they missed seeing the place where Alexander and Brody's squad had split off on their own.

"Jesus Christ!" Alexander whispered to himself as he peered through his binoculars. "We hit the jackpot!"

The lieutenant, Brody and his squad were halfway up the side of a small hill overlooking a narrow valley below. Hidden back inside the trees on the hillside across the valley was the biggest enemy supply dump that Alexander had ever seen. It had been so carefully camouflaged that it would never be spotted by a plane flying directly overhead.

The NVA had cut down the underbrush under the closely packed trees and had even selectively cut some of the trees themselves to open up the ground underneath. But enough of the trees had been left standing so that their branches effectively formed a solid canopy overhead.

It was only at certain angles that you could spot beyond the screen of brush left along the wood line and see what was under the trees—an angle like the one Alexander had now from their position halfway up the opposite hill. From where he was, he could see dozens of North Vietnamese troops going about their business. It looked like they were issuing the supplies scattered around on the ground rather than stockpiling them for future use.

As he watched, men took long crates from a pile and headed back deeper under the trees with them. Something was going on. Troops were being outfitted for something big. He put the field glasses down and charted the location of the dump on his map.

"Ell tee!" Brody hissed softly, pointing over to the far left. "Look!"

Moving into the wood line at the far end of the valley was a long line of NVA infantry in dark olive green uniforms. Alexander snapped his field glasses up to his eyes. The dinks were all wearing full packs and combat equipment with the distinctive NVA pith helmets. These looked like hard-core NVA Regulars, fresh troops just down from the north. They were probably picking up their ammunition supplies before heading into the trenches around Khe Sanh.

As Alexander watched, at least two companies of troops moved into the supply area. The NVA supply people quickly issued them ammunition and other supplies. In half an hour, they were on the move again, heading west for Khe Sanh.

Alexander motioned Bunny over to his side and took the handset to the radio. "Switch to secure," he whispered.

Bunny set the radio frequency and nodded.

Alexander keyed the mike. "Crazy Bull, Crazy Bull," he spoke softly. "This is Blue Six, Blue Six. Over."

He waited, listening to the hiss of the carrier wave coming in over the handset. He had been afraid of that. They were too far away from Camp Evans to get through. However, he had the frequency for Hillsboro Control, the Air Force flying Tac Air Control Center on station over Khe Sanh.

He pulled out his SOI, found the frequency and call sign for the air controllers, and dialed it into the Prick-77 radio. "Hillsboro Control, Hillsboro Control, this is Blue Six, Blue Six. Over."

"Blue Six, this is Hillsboro control," answered the radio operator in the C-130 flying Tactical Air Control Center orbiting high in the sky to the east. "Send your traffic. Over."

"This is Blue Six. We have located a large basecamp in the hills southwest of Khe Sanh at zero three five, two eight four. It's a big resupply depot, and I've seen two companies of November Victor Alpha moving through it on their way to your location. What's the chance of your getting an air strike down on these guys today? Over."

"This is Hillsboro, I copy supply depot at zero three five, two eight four and troops on the move. It's too short of a notice to get an Arc Light, but I'll see what other assets I have on hand, and I'll get back to you. Over."

"This is Blue Six. Roger, copy. We'll be waiting. Out." Alexander had a big grin on his face when he handed the radio handset back to Bunny. Now they would see some action.

It took a little time to put the air strike together, but the results were well worth it. A little over an hour later, a familiar voice came in over the radio. "Blue Six, Blue Six, this is Mac the Fac, the Bluebird of Happiness, on your push. Over."

Alexander looked up into the sky, but he could not see the small gray Cessna 0-2 Push-Pull spotter plane of the Air Force forward air controller. He must have been keeping station well out of sight so as not to give the NVA any warning of what was coming their way.

"Mac, this is Blue Six," Alexander radioed back. "I hear you loud and clear. How me? Over."

"This is Mac, I've got you five by five. Look, I've got a bunch of thirsty birds just loitering around up here in the sky burning gas. How 'bout giving us something to do? Over."

"This is Six, Roger, glad to have you aboard, Mac. Your target today is a supply depot hidden under camouflage nets and trees on a hillside. The center mass is at zero three five, two eight four. The target runs east and west and is halfway up the side of a hill. Make your runs along that axis and you can't miss 'em. We've seen the usual small-caliber antiaircraft stuff, but nothing major. Over."

"This is Mac, Roger, we'll be on the lookout for it. Like

151

the man in the song says, '. . . get ready, baby, 'cause here it comes.' I've got the whole nine yards today, seven fifties, nape, rockets, and twenty-mike-mikes, so keep your heads down. Over.''

''Roger, we're well clear of the target area, but we have it under observation and can direct the strike. Get it going. Over.''

''This is Bluebird FAC, Roger. Out.''

Alexander had a big grin on his face as he released the push-to-talk switch on the radio microphone and gave it back to Bunny. From where they were hiding, they were going to have a ringside seat for the greatest free show in all of Southeast Asia—an Air Force tactical air strike.

CHAPTER 21

South of Khe Sanh

Master Sergeant Leo Zack was starting to get more than a little concerned. This was the third time this morning that his drag man had reported seeing NVA on their trail. The first time they had been spotted, he just picked up the pace, hoping to lose them in the jungle. The second spotting, however, meant it wasn't working. They were sticking to their trail like stink on shit.

His men double-timed down the faint jungle trail, but they couldn't keep up that pace forever. As he ran, Zack whipped out his map. Two klicks ahead, there was a clearing on a small rise. It looked like a good place to hole up and try to contact the ell tee. All he had to do was get there without the NVA tracking team catching up to them.

Zack decided to try one last time to break away from the dinks. He halted the patrol for a short rest break. As the men fought to catch their breath, he went forward to talk to the sniper. "I want to give you two security men and use you for a stay-behind ambush," he told the Ranger shooter.

"Where's the marry-up point?" the veteran sniper asked, pulling his map out of his pocket.

153

Zack pointed it out on the map and the sniper marked the location. "Who you giving me?"

"Williams and Lopez. They're both real good."

"They'd better fucking be good."

"They are, believe me."

Zack pressed on with the rest of his men and soon left the sniper and his two security men far behind. His plan, if it could be called a plan, wasn't much, but it was the best he could do until he could link up with Alexander and his people. Then, maybe they could get some air support, maybe even an extraction. Either way, though, it wasn't going to be easy.

The stay-behind, the sniper, Williams and Lopez, found a good ambush site on a little rise on the ground overlooking the main trail. With Lopez out on the flanks, Williams was spotting targets for the sniper.

"Left front, two hundred meters," Williams whispered in the sniper's ear.

"Got him." The sniper slowly focused the day scope on his XM-21 rifle, ranging in on Captain Xuan's point man. The sight reticle on the day scope had two stadia marks on the vertical cross hair. When the top mark was lined up with the top of a man's head and the bottom mark with his feet, the target was dead meat.

He took a deep breath, held it, and slowly squeezed the trigger. The silenced rifle spat.

With a strangled cry, the NVA went down on his knees and pitched over onto his face.

"Fuck!" The sniper had missed his aim point and hit the dink in the upper chest. He was still dead, but he had cried out. AKs opened up in the jungle in front of them, firing blind.

The sniper ducked down under cover and waited for the spotter to find another target for him. So far, the gooks didn't know where they were. Not only did the silencer quiet the heavy 7.62mm sniper rifle, it also made it very difficult to spot the muzzle flash.

"Ten o'clock, got two of 'em down low at the base of a tree. Hundred and fifty meters."

"Got it."

The sniper fired at the man on the left, quickly shifted his aim, and fired again. The second man screamed in pain. He had only been wounded. He rolled back behind the tree and started shouting in Vietnamese.

"We'd better haul ass outta here," Williams said. "He's probably telling the others where we are."

"Yeah, let's *di-di-mau*."

The three men crawled backward as fast as they could until they were clear and faded into the brush. Running down the trail, they looked ahead for another good ambush point.

Alexander caught the faint whine of screaming jet engines and glanced up. Two black, batlike shapes flashed overhead, aimed straight for the enemy camp. The rotary bomb bays of the B-57 Night Intruder Canberras rolled open. Fat, o.d.-painted, 750-pound iron bombs fell away.

It sounded like the end of the world had finally come when the bombs crashed down in the middle of the NVA supply depot. The thundering blasts of high explosive ripped the jungle to splinters, dug deep, smoking craters in the ground, and flung men into the air like broken, bleeding dolls.

Pulling out of their steep dives, the two jet attack bombers from the famed Doom Pussy Squadron, the 8th Bombing Squadron stationed in Da Nang, made a graceful banking turn high in the sky at the end of the valley and bore back down on their target.

Normally the twin-jet B-57 Canberra bombers stalked the night skies over North Vietnam and the border regions, interdicting the supply traffic moving along the Ho Chi Minh Trail. Today Mac the Fac had been able to get the four of them to come down south and play in the hills around Khe Sanh. The pilots were glad for a little change of scenery.

155

The North Vietnamese reacted quickly to the sudden attack and ran for the antiaircraft-gun emplacements dug in around the supply dump. Whipping the camouflage nets away from the guns, they frantically tried to train their weapons on the diving jets.

A couple of the guns, the deadly twin-mount 37mm automatic cannon, got off a few hurriedly aimed shots. But the glowing orange tracers of the shells sped harmlessly past the diving Canberras. Most of the gun crews only reached their guns in time to receive the full force of the second attack.

Each Camberra carried four 20mm cannons mounted in the wings, and the hard points on their outer wings had been loaded down with the five-inch high-velocity rockets. The cannon barrels belched flame and the rockets ignited with puffs of dirty white smoke, lancing down from under the bomber's broad wings.

The twenty-mike-mike H.E. cannon shells and the heavy rockets slammed into the gun emplacements, throwing shredded bodies and pieces of blasted anitiaircraft guns high into the air.

The few enemy gunners who survived that onslaught were burned to cinders when the second wave of the attack, another pair of Iron Cranberries playing follow-the-leader, delivered their 500-pound napalm canisters on top of the antiaircraft-gun emplacements. The stench of napalm and burned bodies mingled with the sharp, metallic smell of the explosives.

With the enemy antiaircraft threat blown to smoking rubble, the B-57's were free to continue runs at their leisure. The first flight of two jets made several more low bomb runs, dropping a pair of 750-pounders on each run. The other two jets circled the camp and attacked targets of opportunity—anything that moved. It was a massacre.

From their hiding place on the opposite ridgeline, Alexander and his team watched the B-57's turn the jungle hiding the enemy supply point into a smoking, tangled rubble. It looked to them like the attack was right on target, but it was difficult to see much because of the thick clouds of smoke and dust thrown up by the bomb and rocket explosions.

"Blue Six, this is Mac," came the voice on Bunny's radio. "How're we doing down there? Over."

Alexander took the handset from the FO. "This is Blue Six," he answered. "So far, so good, but the smoke is obscuring the target and it's still a little hard to see much. Over."

Their jet engines screaming, the Canberras swept down low over the jungle again, the 20mm cannons in their wings blazing flame. They dumped the last of their remaining ordnance and rose into the sky, heading east to Da Nang. Their job was over and cold beer was waiting for them at the bar of the Doom Pussy Club. A man could work up a real thirst bombing the shit out of a bunch of gooks.

"Bluebird, this is Six," Alexander called the FAC as he watched the B-57's climb back up into the clear blue sky. "We're not going to be able to do a BDA for you today. There's just too many dinks still running around in the woods. Over."

"This is Mac. No sweat on the BDA, GI. We've got the Cranberry's camera film of the strike and I'll make a pass myself on my way out to have a quick look-see. Thanks for the business. This is Mac the Fac, the Bluebird of Happiness, leaving your area to go help some other defender of freedom."

High in the sky, the small gray 0-2 Cessna Skymaster FAC plane waggled its wings as it went into a dive. The surviving NVA heard the sound of its props as it came screaming down. They started firing everything they had into the air in MAC's path. The pilot dropped down to almost treetop level as he made his run over the smoking ruins of the depot. Chased by glowing green tracer fire, the small plane disappeared behind the hill, seemingly untouched.

Alexander slowly shook his head in amazement. Mac the Fac was more than a little *dinky dau,* but he couldn't help

157

but admire the man. It took a lot of balls to fly over anti-aircraft guns at treetop level in an unarmed plane. Mac either had the biggest balls in-country or he had left his brains in a martini glass at the Nha Trang officer's club. Either way, he put on one of the best shows in-country.

"Okay, Sarge," Alexander said, turning to Brody. "We'd better grab our hats and haul ass outta here. Those guys are really gonna be pissed."

Brody grinned. "Let's do it, ell tee."

The three men quickly faded into the jungle to rejoin Zack and the rest of the platoon.

Rat Gaines and Lance Warlokk were at three thousand feet in their Cobras, heading east for the mountainous area below Khe Sanh again. The hunting had been so good there before that Rat had decided to try it again.

As Gaines climbed for altitude over Camp Evans, he felt himself break out into a smile and slowly slipped into the peace of mind that flying always brought him. This was where he belonged, high in the sky flying his chopper, not doing paper work and busting his ass trying to run Echo Company.

He almost laughed aloud when he thought of the look that Jordan was going to have on his face when he read the request that he be immediately relieved of his command and transferred to a non-command flying assignment.

When he reached forward to flick the weapons switches to the armed position, Gaines had a big shit-eating grin on his face. He glanced over at Warlokk, flying in tight formation off his portside. He squeezed the trigger for the UHF chopper-to-chopper radio transmitter.

"Lawless?"

Warlokk looked over at him. "Yeah."

"Let's take a heading of two eighty and check out those hills to the west of Khe Sanh."

"Roger."

The two Cobras turned as one and dropped down a few

hundred feet. When they reached the hills, they would go into a hunter-killer team mode of operation. One of the gunships would fly flat-out as close to the ground as it could, trolling for fire, while the other one stayed high and spotted. If someone made the mistake of shooting at the low ship, the high ship would drop down and kick the living shit out of them.

It was a simple enough tactic, but it was effective. The dinks never seemed to learn that it was unhealthy to shoot at helicopters.

When the two gunships reached the target area, Gaines tightened the fingers of his Nomex gloves and clicked on his radio. "Lawless, I'm rolling in now."

"Roger," came the terse reply.

Gaines twisted the throttle up against the stop and pushed forward on the cyclic. The Cobra's nose dropped as she headed for the ground, her turbine screaming. Gaines's pulse rate sped up to match his rate of descent as the tangled jungle raced up to meet him. At the last possible moment, he hauled back on the cyclic control and brought his gunship out of the dive just a few meters off the tangled treetops.

Kicking down on the rudder pedals, he snaked his Cobra from side to side and flew flat-out, down a narrow valley between two ridgelines at almost a hundred and fifty knots. Though he was flying so low that he could have been hit by a child throwing a rock, he had far more to fear from running into a tall tree than he did from the dinks. At the speed he was going, he was flying so fast that he would be completely past someone before they had time to react. At the most, all they could do would be to fire a couple of shots after him. That, of course, was precisely what he wanted.

It took a great deal of concentration to fly that fast and that low, and Gaines felt the thin rivulets of sweat break out under his flight helmet. He swept out the end of the valley and zoomed over the ridge into the next ravine. So far, all he had seen was jungle.

The tree cover over the ravine was spotty and he caught

a glimpse of a trail. Kicking down on the rudder pedals to swing the tail of his bird around, he followed it south. The ravine flattened out into a large clearing between two hills. The trail disappeared into the tall elephant grass, but he could see that someone had been using it. The grass was beaten down in a clearly defined path leading into the far tree line.

His gloved fingers tightened on the turret weapon's firing controls, and he dropped down even lower to the ground.

"Lance," he radioed. "Party time!"

The tree line erupted with fire, bright green AK and RPD tracer fire mixed with the glowing orange balls of 12.7mm heavy-machine-gun tracer.

Rat opened up with a return barrage from the turret minigun and thumper. He kicked down on the rudder pedal to throw the Cobra into a skidding turn. Hauling up on the collective, he banked away from the tree line.

This was when he would have liked to have had Alphabet working the weapons for him from the front seat. Flying alone as he was, he could not swing the turret to the side to cover him as he made his turn.

He heard the dull thuds of heavy-caliber rounds hitting the airframe behind him. His eyes swept the instruments and then the sky around him.

Where the hell was Warlokk?

CHAPTER 22

South of Khe Sanh

Lance Warlokk watched with horror as the NVA twelve-point-seven zeroed in on Gaines's gunship. He saw the sparks when the rounds impacted against the armor-plated engine compartment and then walked down the side of the Cobra. He was still too far out for accurate shooting, but he triggered off a pair of 2.5-inch H.E. rockets from each of his side pods.

The rockets ignited and leaped from the pods, trailing dirty white smoke as they bore in on the target. The NVA gunners switched their fire from Rat's fleeing Cobra to face this new threat diving down upon them.

Warlokk peered through his gunsight, his fingers tightening on the firing controls. He flew through a hail of glowing tracer fire, waiting until he was even closer to his target. By now, Gaines should have been able to get away, but Warlokk was too busy to look. If he didn't take out this gun, it was going to get both of them.

The nose of Warlokk's bird disappeared in a burst of flame and white smoke as he triggered everything he had all at once. Rockets volleyed from the side pods, the turret-mounted thumper coughed again and again, and the 7.62mm minigun sounded like a berserk chainsaw.

A hard rain of steel and explosives fell on the heavy-machine-gun position. In an instant, it was enveloped in multiple explosions and billowing flame. Unidentifiable chunks flew up though the black smoke. Lance kicked down the rudder pedals and swept the minigun fire to both sides of the smoking hole in the jungle. When he flew over the smoke, no one shot at him.

As Warlokk climbed out at the end of his run, Gaines swooped down again from his left side and hosed down the tree line just for good measure. The two Cobras then climbed back up into the sky and orbited high above the gun site.

"Captain," Warlokk called over. "You okay?"

"I think so," Gaines called back. "Everything's in the green as far as I can tell, but you'd better take a look at my tail boom."

"Roger."

Warlokk carefully maneuvered in right behind Gaines and flew as close to him as he could in the turbulence of his rotor wake. "You've picked up a couple holes in your elevator, but it doesn't look serious."

Gaines cautiously tried his flight controls. Everything felt fine. "I'm still go," he called back.

"Roger," Warlokk laughed. "What'd you want to do for an encore?"

Gaines grinned to himself. "How about a little more of the same?"

At the first distant sound of firing, Lieutenant Alexander came racing down the trail to the drag position. Zack was in contact.

"Sergeant Brody," he called out.

"I hear it, Ell tee," Brody panted. They had been double-timing through the brush ever since they had gotten

162

Zack's call fifteen minutes ago. "It sounds like they're a little more than a klick ahead us."

Alexander stopped just long enough to let the RTO catch up with him again. With the heavy Prick-77 radio on his back, Bunny was having a hard time keeping up with his lieutenant. The platoon leader snatched the handset from him. "Blue Five, this is Six. Over."

"Five, go." Alexander could plainly hear the sounds of heavy gunfire over the radio. It sounded like everything had gone tits up.

"This is Six, we are less than a klick from you, approaching from due east. Be on the lookout for us. Over."

"Five, Roger. Be advised that the bad guys are between us, so be careful. Over."

"This is Six, Roger copy, we're coming as fast as we can. Out." He tossed the handset back to Bunny and took off running again.

Alexander put on a burst of speed and ran past Brody up to the point, where Two-Step was leading the pack. "Zack says that there's gooks between us," he panted, beginning to get winded himself. He hated to admit it, but it looked like at twenty-six, he was getting a little too old to be running around in the jungle trying to keep up with a bunch of teenage grunts.

"Yes, sir," the running Indian heaved. The pace was starting to wear him out, too.

A burst of AK fire sent both of them sprawling flat on their faces, scrambling for cover.

In his prone position, Alexander ripped off a burst from his sixteen. Behind him he heard Brody yelling at the men, getting them out on the flanks. Another burst of AK fire hit right in front of his head and he started crawling backward. Two-Step had found good cover behind a tree and was returning fire with roaring blasts from his sawed-off shotgun.

Alexander rolled to his left behind a thick clump of bushes. Bullets kicked up dirt where he had been lying. He couldn't see where the dinks were hiding, but so far, all he had heard were the AKs, no machine guns. They might be able to get out of this.

He heard the characteristic thump of an M-79 grenade launcher behind him as Farmer opened up. The deadly 40mm grenade exploded in the trees in front of him, but it didn't make the enemy slack off at all. If anything, the firing intensified.

With a smooth, practiced motion, Farmer jammed another one of the stubby little grenades into the opened breech of the launcher, snapped it shut with a flick of his wrist, and fired again. The grenade sailed away and exploded on the ground, throwing up a puff of dust and black smoke. A sharp scream sounded and Farmer grinned. That was better. He snapped open the breech of the seventy-nine to reload.

Alexander heard muffled shouts in front of him and knew that the dinks were bringing up more people. If they didn't get this situation under control pretty fast, they'd be pinned down.

He pulled an M-26 hand grenade from the ammo pouch on his pistol belt. Holding the spoon down firmly in his left hand, he pulled the pin. Getting to his knees, he ripped off a full magazine of 5.56mm from his M-16, spraying the bullets from side to side. When the rifle's bolt locked to the rear on an empty magazine, he lobbed the frag grenade with his left hand.

The grenade had the desired effect. He heard a scream, and the enemy fire slackened for a moment.

The platoon leader dropped the empty magazine out of the bottom of his sixteen and slapped a new one into place. Pulling back on the charging handle, he peered through the bushes. Spotting a muzzle flash, he opened up on it, burning through half a magazine. No more AK fire came from that position. It looked like they were getting it under control, after all.

He was taking another frag from his ammo pouch when he heard shouts and the heavy hammering of Corky's M-60 on his right front. Brody had gotten the rest of the people around and was hitting them on the flank. He got to his knees and lobbed the grenade to keep the dinks occupied from his side, too. This time, the explosion seemed to have no effect. Time to charge.

Alexander yelled over at Two-Step. The grunt turned his head.

"Let's take 'em!"

The Indian nodded and gathered his feet under him. Alexander slapped a fresh magazine into his weapon and laid down a base fire. Two-Step jumped up. Running in a crouch, he dashed up to the next available cover, pumping the rounds out as he ran.

No shots were fired back at him.

Racking a round into the chamber of his pump gun, he ducked his head around the tree, ready to fire. There was no one there.

"Cease fire!" Brody shouted from the flank. "Cease fire!"

Alexander slowly got to his feet as Brody stepped into the open. "I think we got 'em all, sir," he said. "There were only four of 'em."

"You're shitting me! Only four?" Alexander was surprised. He was sure that they had been facing a least a full squad.

"Okay, Sergeant," he said as the other men stepped onto the trail. "Let's get 'em moving. Zack's waiting for us."

"Blue Five, this is Raven. Over." It was the sniper calling.

Zack took the radio handset from his RTO. "Five, go ahead."

"This is Raven. We're blown and we're coming in. Over."

"This is Five, Roger. Keep coming down the trail till you hit a small clearing. We'll be off to your left front with the clearing at our backs. I think we can hold them here. Over."

"Raven, Roger copy."

The three men ran harder, keeping an eye over their

165

shoulders. The sniper dropped back. "Keep going," he shouted to the security men. "I'll cover you."

The Ranger slipped back into the brush along the side of the trail. The green, tan and brown colors of his camouflage uniform blended in perfectly with the vegetation. He readied a grenade and checked the magazine in his sniper rifle.

Two NVA came pounding down the trail, but he waited until they were right on top of him before triggering off four quick shots. Both of the dinks went down. He waited a second and threw the grenade as hard as he could farther back down the trail.

The explosion was followed by cries of pain. Time to *di-di*!

The sniper got to his feet and dashed up the trail after the others, changing the magazine in his rifle as he ran. He rounded a shallow bend in the trail and saw Zack's position a hundred meters ahead. The two security men had already reached cover when he heard a long burst of AK fire behind him.

Zack's people saw the sniper coming in and cut loose with everything they had to cover him. He was only twenty feet from safety when a round took his leg out from under him. He fell hard, automatically rolling over into a firing position.

He glanced down and saw the round, oozing hole in his pants leg. One of the grunts jumped up from behind a log and dashed out to help the wounded sniper to his feet. The two men raced the last few steps back to cover behind the fallen log.

"You okay?" the grunt panted.

"Fucking dinks!" the sniper spat, reaching for his field dressing.

Taking the K-Bar knife from his assault harness, he ripped the camouflage pant leg open. The round had made a neat circular hole through the muscle on the outside of his right thigh. It was clean, and not bleeding badly. He put the dressing over it, tied the strings around the torn pant leg, and rolled over into a firing position. He'd been hit far worse than that before.

The pursuing NVA had spotted Zack's position and spread out in an assault line in front of it. The grunts could hear the NVA sergeants shouting at their men. The AK fire was heavy, but the Americans were not firing back unless they had a good target. There was no point in wasting ammunition. Even the two machine gunners were being very careful with their sixties, snapping out short bursts instead of firing suppressive fire.

The only man not being careful with his ammunition was the sniper, and he was burning it up at a rapid rate. The only drawback to using the silencer on the XM-21 sniper rifle was that it did not hold up well. When the rifle was fired too quickly, gas pressure built up inside the silencer until it blew the end plate off.

When he felt the silencer give way and his next shot sounded clearly, the sniper reached up to the right side of the rifle's breech and switched the selector over to fully automatic. Now he had a scoped, 7.62mm automatic rifle.

He started snapping out three-round bursts, but it wasn't helping much. The enemy fire wasn't slacking off one bit. There were just too goddamned many dinks out there, and too damned few of them.

"Blue Five, this is Six. Over," Alexander's voice came over the radio.

"Five," Zack shouted above the roar of small-arms fire. "Send it."

"This is Six, I am only a hundred meters behind you. Watch for us, we're coming in!"

"In the rear!" Zack shouted to alert everyone. "Blues coming in!"

Alexander and Brody were the first of the squad to break into the perimeter. The lieutenant made a quick appraisal of the situation, dropped for cover, and yelled for Bunny. The FO scrambled over to him and passed him the radio handset. It was obvious that they needed help. Fast.

Alexander paused for a moment, frantically trying to

think of who in the hell he should call first. Captain Gaines had said that he'd have a gunship team standing by, maybe he should try them first.

"Python, Python," he shouted into the handset, "this is Blue Six, Blue Six. Over."

He released the push-to-talk switch and waited. Nothing. "Python, Python, this is Blue Six. Come in, please."

"Blue Six, Blue Six," came a faint voice over the handset. "This is Python Lead. I hear you weak, but steady. Send it. Over."

"This is Blue Six, we are in contact at zero six three, four zero two, and need air support ASAP. Can you help us out? Over."

There was a brief pause as Gaines plotted Alexander's location. "This is Lead, Roger copy. I'm about fifteen minutes out from your location. Can you hold out that long? Over."

"This is Blue Six, we can hold, but get here as fast as you can, please. We've got our asses in a real crack. Over."

"This is Lead, Roger copy. Do you require extraction at this time? Over."

"This is Six, that's most affirm, Lead. This place is crawling with dinks and they've been tracking us all day. Even if we could get out of this contact, our mission's blown. Over."

"This is Lead, Roger. I'll get the slicks in the air ASAP. Out."

CHAPTER 23

South of Khe Sanh

While Alexander was on the horn, Brody's men spread out on either side of Zack's small group, took cover, and got to work. Brody found a good position behind a log next to Zack.

" 'Bout fucking time you people got back here," the NCO growled.

"Fuck you, Leo," Brody snapped back, bringing his sixteen up to firing position. "We've been a little busy ourselves, man."

Zack had more important things to worry about at the moment than Brody's smart mouth, but he would take it up with him later. Right now, if they didn't gain fire superiority, they were going to get their asses overrun.

"Get those thumpers going!" the platoon sergeant shouted.

Farmer and Lindberry teamed up again. Each time Farmer rose to fire a grenade, Strawberry would calmly lay down a base of fire for him. Lindberry was surprised at how calm he felt under fire this time. Before, he had always been scared that he was going to do something wrong.

This time, he clearly saw his targets, carefully brought

169

fire on them, and watched them go down. It was as if he were moving in slow motion. Strawberry didn't realize it, but he was shot through with the adrenaline of combat, and it had taken complete control of his reflexes. He had turned into a fighting machine, a real grunt.

Out on the left flank, Corky caught movement in front of him and snapped out a quick burst with his sixty. The smoking machine gun clicked silent after only a few rounds.

"Ammo!" he yelled out. "Need some ammo!"

The gunner from the first squad rolled up a two-hundred-round belt and threw it over to him.

"Thanks, *amigo*."

Corky flipped up the feed tray and laid the linked belt in place. Snapping the cover back down, he hauled back on the charging handle and got back to work. His first burst took out his earlier target.

With more guns on line now, the grunts started getting serious. Brody's two thumpers made quite a bit of difference. The deadly little grenades dropped down on top of the hidden NVA as fast as Farmer and Two-Step could pump them out.

"Keep firing!" Zack yelled, raising his head to see how they were doing. A long string of green tracer fire almost took it off. The gooks had finally gotten a machine gun into action, an RPD.

The Russian RPD machine gun fired a lighter cartridge than the American M-60. In the jungle, the shorter range didn't matter. And the RPD fired two hundred rounds a minute faster! It was nothing to mess around with.

It opened up in full song. The bullets chewed into the Americans' position, sending all of them ducking under cover. One grunt in the 3rd Squad took a hit. The Blues' three M-60 gunners tried to take the deadly Russian gun out, but the NVA gunner had them zeroed in. Every time one of the gunners stuck his head up to take a shot at it, the RPD fire sent him back down again.

Zack listened to the characteristic rattle of the RPD. They

had to do something about that motherfucker fast! ''Get that gun!'' he shouted.

The sniper edged the barrel of his rifle around the side of a tree and focused in on the NVA machine-gun nest. They had built a hasty bunker of fallen logs, and it was going to be a difficult shot. Before he could fire, a burst of fire into the side of his tree made him duck back down. That dink gunner was damned good. The sniper shifted his position and tried again.

This time he got a shot at what he thought was the machine gun's spotter, a man crouching beside the gun. It was a snap shot and he missed. The enemy fire was too intense for him to take the time to aim and squeeze the trigger properly.

Under the covering fire of their RPD machine gun, the NVA infantry started creeping closer to the Americans. Two-Step laid his thumper down and checked the load in his pump gun. They were almost close enough for him to use the short-range weapon. But when they got that close, it would all be over.

''Blue Six, Blue Six, this is Python Lead.'' Rat Gaines's voice was loud over Bunny's radio. ''I am inbound to your location. Echo Tango Alpha two Mikes. Pop smoke. Over.''

Alexander snatched up the handset. ''This is Six,'' he shouted back. ''Roger. We're under heavy fire from a machine-gun bunker. We're at the edge of a small clearing, and the target is due west of us. I'm popping smoke now. Over.''

''Somebody throw a smoke!'' he yelled.

One of the grunts quickly ripped a smoke grenade off his assault harness, pulled the pin, and lobbed it out in front of them. Bright green smoke billowed up into the air.

''This is Python, I have lime. Over.''

''This is Six, Roger green. A hundred meters west of that. Over!''

''Roger. Rolling in now.''

Rat brought his gunship around in a hard bank over the small clearing. Since he was flying without a gunner, he had his turret thumper and minigun locked in the straight-ahead position, forcing him to aim the nose of his ship at the target to bring the weapons to bear. Peering through the gunsight at the jungle beyond the column of green smoke, he cut loose with everything that he had left.

The Cobra swept down low over the grunts. The red-and-white-painted shark's mouth on her nose blossomed flame, and the air was filled with the sound of ripping canvas. The mini spat out 7.62mm rounds at the rate of 4,000 rounds a minute. Hot shell cases rained down on the grunts, but they didn't mind.

As Gaines swept in closer, the dinks fired everything they had at the diving gunship. The jungle twinkled with the muzzle flashes of AKs sending a steady stream of fire into the Cobra's flight path.

The pilot hunkered down lower in his armored seat and kicked down on his rudder pedals, snapping the ships' tail from side to side to spread his fire over a wider area. A barrage of 2.75-inch H.E. rockets lanced out from the Cobra's stub-wing pods, trailing dirty white smoke. They slammed into the enemy positions. The jungle erupted with bright red-and-black bursts as the warheads exploded. Smaller puffs of black smoke appeared in between the bigger rocket bursts when the 40mm thumper grenades went off.

It was a seemingly impenetrable wall of fire, but it didn't make the dinks slack off any. Lines of green tracer fire still clawed up at his gunship. Gaines felt the ship take several hits.

Suddenly, he was past the edge of the target area and in the clear. He stomped down on the right rudder pedal and slammed the cyclic over to the side to bring his chopper around as fast as he could. The low-flying Cobra shuddered in the air as it skidded into the hard turn. He knew better than to try that so low to the ground, but he had no choice. He had to get back in position to cover Warlokk when he made his run.

As Gaines hauled *Tiger's Revenge* around to make another pass, Warlokk brought his gunship parallel to Alexander's front in a crazy banzai firing run. The diving Cobra looked like it had burst into flame, but it was just Warlokk triggering off everything that he had all at once.

The thumper in the nose turret spit 40mm grenades, the side-mounted miniguns blazed fire at 4,000 rounds a minute, and he volleyed 2.75-inch H.E. rockets from the pylon-mounted pods one right after another. The recoil was almost enough to stop the diving chopper dead in its tracks.

The jungle in front of Alexander's men exploded in a mass of flame, and the lieutenant involuntarily ducked his head. He couldn't see who was flying that bird, but it had to be Lance Warlokk. No one else was crazy enough to make a firing run like that. The gunship flashed past them, chased by green tracer fire from the AKs. The NVA were pissed.

Warlokk pulled the nose of his ship up sharply, banked her over on her side, and savagely kicked the tail around. The heavily laden gunship staggered in the sky, hanging right on the edge of a stall, her rotors unloading and losing lift. Like his flight leader, he was far too low and flying much too slowly to try that kind of maneuver. At the last moment, Warlokk got her back under control. Snapping his ship back upright, he bore back down on the jungle again.

At the same time, Gaines began his second run with his stub-wing-mounted minigun pods blazing fire. Even with the burst limiters holding down the amount of ammunition going through the six-barreled weapons, the rain of fire they put out was impressive. The combined impact of so many bullets at once shredded the jungle. Anything smaller than a tree was instantly pulped. This included the dinks. For the first time since the firefight had started, the enemy fire slackened a little.

By this time, Warlokk was rolling in on his second run. He bore into the target, flying even lower over the trees this time. The explosions from his rockets threw dirt and debris up into his line of sight. He was two hundred meters out when the surviving dinks picked themselves up from the jungle floor and ran for their lives. They had enjoyed just about all they could stand. It was *di-di* time for Charlie.

Alexander's men cheered and sent volleys of fire into the backs of the fleeing enemy. Gaines and Warlokk let the NVA run away unmolested. They were almost out of ammunition and wanted to keep what little they had left in case someone came back for more.

"Blue Six," Gaines radioed down to Alexander. "This is Lead. Your lift is inbound with a light-fire team to take over for us. Their Echo Tango Alpha is fifteen Mikes. What's your situation down there? Over."

"Six, Roger copy. I've got three walking wounded, all routine. Be advised that this is not a good PZ. I recommend that the slicks stay on station until I can find a better place for a pickup. Over."

"This is Lead, Roger. I can keep 'em around for nearly an hour. Recommend that you try your Sierra Echo, there's a ridgeline a little over a klick away that looks suitable. Over."

"This is Six, Roger, wait one."

Alexander hurriedly checked his map. The ridge to the southeast was shown and it didn't look like too bad of a hump for the wounded. "Python Lead, this is Blue Six. Roger, I've got it spotted and we'll be moving out in zero two. Over."

"This is Lead, Roger. We'll hang around here in case you have any more problems before that other gun team shows up. Over."

"Six, Roger. Thank you, Python. Out."

"Sergeant Zack," Alexander called out. "Let's get 'em moving. The birds are waiting."

It took only twenty-five minutes to reach the ridgeline. As Gaines had said, it was bare enough on top for a single-ship pickup zone. Under the protective cover of the orbiting gunship escort, Brody's people watched their back trail. The first slick touched down and loaded on the wounded and most of 3rd Squad. The second slick took on

Zack and everybody else except Brody's squad and the ell tee.

As soon as the second ship lifted off again, Gabe flew down and flared out for a landing. "Let's go," Alexander shouted as soon as he touched down.

The grunts ran for the slick and clambered inside, quickly followed by their lieutenant. Alexander reached over and tapped the pilot on the shoulder. "We're go," he shouted over the noise of the rotors.

Gabe nodded and pulled pitch to the blades. In seconds, they were airborne and headed south.

Alexander found a place in the open door of the chopper and sat down. He was exhausted and glad to be out of the jungle, but he was also royally pissed. He didn't like being chased out before the mission was over.

Another man who didn't like leaving the jungle behind was Farmer. He, too, felt that he had failed, but his failure was of a different kind. He had failed to collect the ears from his latest kills back in the clearing. He went through the firefight again in his mind step by step to see if he could remember how many dinks he had snuffed this time. Four or five? As he struggled to remember, tears formed in the corners of his eyes and ran unnoticed down his cheeks, streaking the red jungle mud and camouflage paint.

JJ! he cried inside, how many did I get for you?

CHAPTER 24

Camp Evans, 14 March

As the flight of choppers neared Camp Evans, the slick carrying the three wounded men split off from the formation and headed for the Dustoff pad behind the field hospital. The other two choppers and the gunship escort entered the flight path for a normal landing on the runway.

Gabe flared out and greased his slick down to a landing. Hovering, he taxied over to the Python pad and shut down. As the rotor slowly came to a stop, the weary grunts stepped down onto the PSP runway. Though they were glad to be back in camp, there was a sense that they had been beaten, that the NVA had forced them to turn and run. The grunts did not like the feeling.

Mike Alexander took it as a personal affront to his military manhood. Slinging his ruck over his shoulder by one strap, he headed over to the operations shack to talk to Rat Gaines about a plan he had worked up on the flight back. He found the pilot still in his flight suit, dumping the contents of his wall locker into a big cardboard box.

"Come on in, Mike," Gaines said when he saw him approaching. "What's up?"

"I'm pissed, sir," Alexander spat.

Gaines studied his Aero Rifle Platoon leader. Alexander was sweat-stained and filthy. His hands and face were scratched from crashing through the jungle trying to get to the pickup zone. He looked bone-weary and ready to drop, but he also looked mad.

"I want to take another team back in there, sir. I know we were right on top of them, but it's hard to sneak around in the fucking brush when you've got the whole platoon with you. I should have gone in there Special Forces style, with only five people, six at the most."

"You might be right about that," Gaines replied. "You sure as hell stirred up a hornets' nest, so you must have been getting close to something they didn't want you to see."

"That's what I think, and I want to go back in there and find out what it was."

Gaines thought for a moment. "I'll tell you what. Why don't you go talk to the Old Man about your idea. See if you can sell him on it."

"Aren't you going to come with me, sir?" Alexander was puzzled.

Gaines shut the door of his locker and slipped the latch. "I'm not your company commander anymore," he said. "I've asked to be relieved."

Alexander's jaw fell open. "I hope you're shitting me, sir."

Gaines grinned. "Nope. I've enjoyed just about all of this that I can stand. I'm going to find me a job where all I have to do is fly a chopper and not have to worry about anything other than keeping the fucking rotors from falling off."

Alexander didn't know what to say. Like all the rest of the men in the battalion, he had been stunned when Lisa died, and his heart had gone out to Rat Gaines. But this? Rat quitting? He just didn't know what to make of it. "I'll go see him, sir."

"Good luck, Mike."

"You, too, sir."

* * *

"Goddamnit, Muller!" Colonel Jordan bellowed. "Where in the hell is that regulation?"

Jordan could hear Muller's chair slide back as he jumped to the position of attention. "I can't find it, sir."

"You better shag your ass over to Brigade and get a copy of it before I send your young ass down to a line platoon."

"Yes, sir!"

Jordan heard Muller race down the hall as fast as he could run, but he was not amused. He had just been handed a bomb and it was about to blow up in his face.

Gaines's letter requesting that he immediately be relieved of his command due to mental instability was sitting on his desk. By the regulations he had to honor Rat's request. Any time a pilot felt that he had stepped over the line and wasn't safe in the air anymore, he had to be medically examined before he could fly again. Even if the doctors said that Gaines could fly, it would take time and he would have to be replaced down in Python Flight for now.

Jordan had his ass caught between a rock and a fucking hard place, and he was feeling the pinch. He knew that Gaines was just as sane as anyone else who was fighting this crazy war. Sure, he was grieving over Lisa, but the man was sane.

The problem was that if Jordan didn't take action on Rat's request and relieve him, he would be putting his own career on the line. Gaines could always go over his head. And Jordan had to forward the request, anyway, even if he didn't approve it. And if he made Gaines stay in command of the unit, and something did go wrong, it would be Jordan who would have his ass on the line, not Gaines.

"Sir?" the personnel NCO stuck his head around the door. "Lieutenant Alexander's here to see you, sir."

"Send him in."

Colonel Jordan was surprised to see the lieutenant alone. Usually when he came in, he was tagging along behind

Gaines. Alexander stopped the regulation three paces in front of his desk and saluted.

"What brings you here?" Jordan asked, returning the salute.

"Captain Gaines told me that I should talk to you about a plan I have, sir."

"Have a seat," Jordan said. "And tell me all about it."

"Well, sir," the lieutenant began, "I've been thinking about what went wrong on our mission."

When Alexander had finished, Jordan got up and walked over to his map. The plan was sound and he shouldn't have any problem selling it to the Brigade 3. He turned back to Alexander. "Okay, how soon can you get your people ready to go back?"

"I'd like to give them a day or two to rest up first," the platoon leader answered. "But I think we can be back in there by the day after tomorrow."

Jordan thought for a moment. "You get your people squared away and I'll clear this with Brigade."

Alexander smiled grimly. "We'll be waiting, sir."

"By the way," Jordan asked, trying to sound casual. "Did you happen to see Captain Gaines when you were on your way over here?"

Alexander got a very strange look on his face. "Yes, sir, I did," he answered carefully. "He was cleaning out his wall locker in the operations shack."

"I see."

"Will that be all, sir?" Alexander was anxious to leave now.

"Yes, I'll talk to you tomorrow."

As Jordan watched the lieutenant walk out, his mind snapped back to his current problem. What in the hell was he going to do about Rat Gaines?

"Muller!" he bellowed at the top of voice. "Where is that regulation?"

"Coming, sir."

* * *

Outside Jordan's headquarters building, Alexander headed over to the company area. He wanted to give the guys as much warning as he could.

"Ten-hut!" Brody called out when he saw his platoon leader walk up to the squad's GP small tent.

"At ease, men," Alexander said, looking around to see if everyone was there. Only the FO, Bunny, was gone. He hadn't planned on taking him, anyway.

"I'm looking for volunteers," he said with a grin.

Everyone in the tent looked for the fastest way out of the tent. No one with even half a brain volunteered for anything in the Nam.

"What've you got in mind, Ell tee?" Brody asked.

Alexander took a seat on someone's footlocker and took out a smoke. "I don't know about you guys," he said, lighting up. "But I didn't like getting my ass run out of the woods today."

"Me, either," someone growled.

"So how'd you guys like to go back into the woods?" he asked.

"All right!" Corky said.

"What's the plan, sir?"

"The Colonel's trying to get Brigade to okay a real recon this time. Just me and you guys, traveling light and moving fast."

"They should have done that in the first fucking place," Brody said. "These platoon clusterfucks never work out the way they're planned."

"I'll remember that when I'm the battalion commander," Alexander grinned. "No clusterfucks."

"When do we go?"

"Day after tomorrow be too soon?"

"No, sir, we'll be ready."

Alexander stood up. "Great, we'll fun through it all tomorrow afternoon, so you guys don't get too drunk down in Sin City tonight."

"Right, sir, we'll all be in bed by eight."

Alexander laughed. "Clowns."

180

The lieutenant found Zack in the hooch he shared with Top Richardson. "Sarge, can I talk to you for a moment?"

"Certainly, sir. Come on in. Have a seat."

Alexander sat down in the lawn chair.

"What's up, sir?"

The platoon leader looked at the muscular black sergeant for a moment. "I've got another little operation in the works. I'm going back into that area we were in and find out what was so important that they had to run our asses out of there."

Zack was silent for a short moment. "Count me in," he said.

"You don't have to go out on this if you don't want to, Sarge," Alexander said.

Zack grinned. "Well, Lieutenant, it's like this. I don't like being run out of a place any more than you do. They're hiding something in there, and I think that we can find out what it is if we play it real cool."

"Leo the Lionhearted."

Zack laughed. "That's what they call me."

"Anyway, Brody's people volunteered to keep me company, so with you and me, that'll make seven of us."

Zack did a quick count in his head. "Who you leaving back?"

"Bunny. I figured that we'd take turns carrying the radio so we can keep on the move."

"Sounds good to me, sir. When do we go?"

"Day after tomorrow. The colonel's got to clear it with Brigade, and I want to do a mission briefing tomorrow afternoon."

"I'll get the first sergeant to give you the orderly room for the briefing, sir."

Alexander got to his feet. "Good. I'll see you in the morning."

"Right, sir."

Out on the company street, Alexander headed to his own hooch. He would have liked to have gone down to Sin City to see if May Lin was at the bar, but he needed his sleep even more.

Rat Gaines walked into the officers' club and sauntered up to the bar. Every eye in the place was on him. Not only was this the first time that he had been in the club since Lisa had been killed, the word about his resignation had swept through the battalion.

"Bartender," he called out, ignoring the others. "Southern Comfort on the rocks."

"Yes, sir."

When the bartender brought his drink, Gaines looked disdainfully at the four-ounce cocktail glass. "That's the biggest glass you've got?"

"No, sir."

"Then, how about getting me a real drink, for Christ's sake?"

"Yes, sir."

Gaines was very much aware that everyone was looking at him, but he really didn't give a shit. As far as he was concerned, he didn't owe anyone in the world a thing, and that included explanations. He was well into his second drink when he sensed someone behind him.

"Rat?"

He turned to see Lance Warlokk standing there with a very worried expression on his face.

He took a long sip of the whiskey. "Yes?"

"What's this I hear?"

"I give up. What do you hear?"

"Goddammit, Rat." Warlokk was having trouble keeping his cool. "Don't give me that shit. Everyone knows that you've asked to be relieved."

"So?"

" 'So'!" Warlokk exploded. "Is that all you've got to say about it? So'!"

Lance Warlokk was never a patient, subtle man. If Rat Gaines left Python Flight, the unit would fall apart. The

182

only thing that made them so good was the personality and leadership of their commander.

"What the fuck's wrong with you, Rat?"

"That's *Captain* Rat to you," Gaines reminded him.

Warlokk almost choked. "Goddammit, Rat, you can't do that!"

Gaines put his drink down on the bar. "Mister"—his voice was cold, "I can do anything I fucking want, and that includes tearing you a new asshole."

Warlokk looked at him for a long moment, hurt and confusion plain on his face. "Okay, Captain, if that's the way you want it."

He spun around and walked out of the club.

Gaines watched him go. He was sorry Warlokk felt that way, but regardless of what he or anyone else thought, Rat knew that he had made the right decision. Even on the good days when everything was working well, the command of Echo Company had been like a weight around his neck. When she had been alive, even Lisa had complained that he put so much into the company, he didn't have anything left over to give her.

That was why she had gone down to Nha Trang and had her little fling with that Kasnowski guy. Maybe if he hadn't been commanding the fucking company he could have spent more time with her and made her happier. Maybe he could even have gotten the time off to fly her down to Da Nang himself.

Fuck it, he thought, slamming his glass down on the bar. It's fucking over.

CHAPTER 25

Camp Evans

Brody smiled and watched the lieutenant walk away from the tent. Alexander had had a good idea, for a change. Why not go down to Sin City and get totally fucked up? Since everyone had the next day off, they could sleep it off in the morning.

He looked around the tent. "Okay," he announced. "Here's the plan. We get cleaned up and make a run on the strip. Celebrate the fact that our favorite 'bean bandit' is short."

"Short! Fourteen days and a wake-up," Corky called out.

Farmer looked up from sharpening his knife. He had a strange smile on his face. "Yeah," he said. "Let's go down to the ville."

Two-Step was surprised that Farmer wanted to go with them, but he was glad to see this change in his behavior. Maybe the young grunt was finally starting to come out of the funk he'd been in ever since JJ's death. He had actually smiled when he said that he wanted to go.

An hour later, the men had changed into clean uniforms

and were walking down the strip. "Where we gonna go?" Corky asked.

Brody looked around at the shabby, brightly lit buildings with the miniskirted girls standing out in front to entice them. "How about the Black Cat for a change?"

"Sounds fine by me. Let's do it."

The Black Cat was down toward the end of the strip, and it looked no different than the dozen or so bars they had passed on their way to it. The girls were no prettier, and the tables no cleaner than any other place on the strip. The only remarkable thing about it was a larger-than-life painting above the bar of a lewdly posed, naked woman with the head and tail of a black panther superimposed on her body. Brody liked the painting.

The grunts took a table against the back wall and ordered American beer. They fully intended to get fucked up, but they didn't want to have to deal with the *ba-muoi-ba* hangover they would get if they drank the local brew. Having a bad head in the morning was one thing. Having a *ba-muoi-ba* hangover was something else entirely.

The girls at the bar knew Brody and his men and didn't bother going over to them. There'd be no Saigon Tea coming out of these guys. Maybe one or two of them would pay for a trip to the back rooms, but that was all. Treat Brody was known far and wide as a number-one Cheap Charlie.

"Where'd Farmer go?" Two-Step asked as he finished his third beer.

Brody looked around the crowded bar. "Beats the fuck outta me," he shrugged. "It ain't my day to watch him. Who's buying the next round?"

Everybody looked over at Bunny.

"Hey, guys," he protested. "Gimme a break! I bought the last one."

They all turned to look at Lindberry. "Okay, okay," he said, pushing his chair back from the table. "Miller's or Bud, right?"

Out in the back alley behind the Black Cat, Farmer kept to the shadows the same way he did when he was out in the brush. Even though he was less than a quarter of a mile away from the main gate of Camp Evans, as far as he was concerned, he was deep in enemy territory.

He stopped. Crouching down against the back wall of the bar, he reached down to his right boot and loosened the K-bar knife in its sheath. He had a plan for the night. Since he hadn't been able to take the ears from the NVA he had killed that day, maybe he could get some VC ears in Sin City that night.

There were lots of VC in Sin City, but they were harder to find in the strip than they were in the woods. Most of the Vietnamese in Sin City had smiles on their faces and wore civilian clothes. But Farmer knew that they were really VC. He could always tell a VC when he saw one. They had dark eyes and black hair. They were sneaky little bastards who killed people, people like his friend JJ.

He edged around the side of the building and went down the alley. There had to be some VC around there someplace, doing VC things. All Farmer had to do was to find them.

The two Vietnamese "cowboys" crouched behind a low fence at the end of the alley, waiting for a GI to come out of a nearby house. They knew that he was going to appear soon, because the whore inside had started singing a Vietnamese folk song. That was the signal for them to get ready.

The American would be falling-down drunk. The girl would make sure of that.

Vinh, the first "cowboy"—the Vietnamese slang term for a petty gangster—tightened his grip on a length of iron pipe in his hand. This business arrangement with his sister was working out very well so far. In just a little over a week, they had made almost three hundred dollars by robbing her customers.

Usually, the GIs were so drunk that a light tap on the back of the head was all it took to knock them out. After cleaning their pockets, Vinh and Duc, his partner in crime, would drag their victims out into the next alley and leave them for the Yankee MPs to find. So far, none of them had given them any trouble. Vinh laughed. So much for the big, smelly Americans who thought they were so strong and brave.

He had been incensed when he returned from Saigon and learned that his younger sister had been prostituting herself to the long-noses. At first, he wanted to kill her. But when he saw all of the things that she had bought with her money, he relented and had only beaten her. Then he told her that she was going to have to share her ill-gotten wealth, and devised this plan. So far, it had worked very well.

He let her keep half of the money she made from sleeping with the Yankees and warned her not to try to keep any of it from him. His share of her earnings, combined with what he got from her customers, was more money than he made selling dope in the streets of Saigon. It was almost enough to wipe out the shame of what she was doing. He still beat her up, though, whenever he thought of her spreading her legs for them.

A crack of light showed at the door of his sister's house and Vinh got ready. A tall GI emerged, turned back, said something to her, and then staggered out into the dimly lit alley. He looked around as if trying to get his bearings, and staggered down the street.

Vinh and Duc silently got to their feet and followed. They let the Yankee get several meters way from the house. Vinh wore black market American tennis shoes. The rubber soles made no sound. He closed in behind the man and smashed the iron pipe against the side of his neck.

This GI was drunk, but he wasn't quite drunk enough. When Vinh hit him, he let out a bellow of pain and spun around. Duc slashed at him with the big fish knife in his hand, drawing blood from his upper arm. The GI staggered back and Vinh slammed the pipe against his head. The man went down.

Farmer heard the GI yell. Keeping to the shadows, he broke into a run. He dashed around the corner and saw the two Vietnamese bent over the prone body of a GI. One of them was beating him with what looked like a stick.

Farmer's right hand flashed to his boot top and came up with the K-Bar. He was right. There were VC right in Sin City.

Farmer was grinning in the darkness when he came up behind Duc. Light glinted from the knife in the Vietnamese's hand. Farmer stepped closer and stabbed the big blade of the K-Bar deep into the man's lower back. The man screamed shrilly. Farmer twisted the knife as he ripped it back out.

Vinh spun around to see a small figure standing behind Duc. In the dim light, he thought that it was another cowboy horning in on his operation.

"Du ma!" he yelled, raising his pipe.

Farmer grinned even wider. He let the body of the first Vietnamese fall to the ground and crouched down in a knife fighter's stance.

"Come and get it, motherfucker."

Vinh hesitated when he heard the shadowy figure speak English. It didn't matter, though. He'd pick his body clean, too.

The pipe whooshed through the air. Farmer sidestepped out of the way and the pipe clanged against the pavement.

The grunt backed up. The pipe gave his opponent a far greater reach than Farmer had with the eight-inch blade of his knife. Vinh smiled when he saw the American back away. He advanced against the crouching American.

Farmer held the K-Bar knife at his side, point down with the edge turned out, his left arm out in front of him to block, just as he had been taught back in basic training. The VC would have to raise his arm in order to swing the pipe and that would be his opening. All Farmer had to do was block the blow when he stepped in to deliver his strike.

Vinh lashed out. Caught off guard by the speed of the attack, Farmer took the blow against his left shoulder and staggered back a step.

Vinh raised his pipe again. "American dog," he spat. "I kill you."

When the pipe came up again, Farmer lunged, his left arm raised to cover his head. The big knife flashed up, stabbing deep into the Vietnamese's lower belly.

Vinh gasped and tried to strike, but Farmer's arm blocked the blow. The grunt's knife hand jerked upward, ripping the blade through Vinh's intestines and stomach, all the way to his breastbone.

Vinh felt his belly turn to wet fire. The pipe fell from his hands. He staggered back, trying to keep the steaming wet mass of his guts from falling out of the terrible rent in his belly. He screamed only once before the razor-sharp blade of the K-Bar slashed across his throat. Sinking to his knees, he fell onto his face, gurgled once, and died.

Farmer winced as he crouched down to collect the right ear from this dead VC. Pain shot up his left arm, but he still had full movement and he didn't think anything was broken. He backtracked and got the ear from his first kill.

When he was done, he went over to the GI and felt for his pulse. He was still alive. Grabbing him by the arms, he started dragging him out to the main street. He decided to leave him there for the Dustoff to pick up. Farmer wanted to continue his one-man patrol. There had to be more VC than these two punks in Sin City.

Back in the bar, Brody, Corky, and Two-Step were reminiscing about the good old days. Bunny was fascinated by their conversation, but Lindberry had gotten tired of hearing the legendary exploits of men he had never known. He looked around the room. One girl sitting by herself at the bar caught his eye and winked. He blushed and turned away, but quickly looked back.

This time the girl raised the hem of her crotch-length miniskirt, flashing her plump inner thighs and nicely filled-out bikini panties. Lindberry felt himself get red again, but this time he did not turn away.

189

Lindberry was still a cherry boy, a virgin to the sexual pleasures of the Orient, but he was not ignorant of the system. As always, he kept his mouth shut and his ears open when the other men told their cathouse stories. He knew, at least in theory, what he could expect to happen next, and he knew what it was going to cost him.

He quickly checked his wallet to make sure that he had a condom tucked away inside. He did. And he had the five hundred Vietnamese piasters that she was going to charge. Now all he had to do was to get out of his chair and go over to her. That was the hardest part of this operation.

"Hello, GI," the girl said when he walked up. "My name Suzie. What your name?"

"Larry."

The girl's eyes ran up and down his body. "Oh, that a nice name," she said as she spread her legs a little wider. "You like me?"

As the curfew hour approached, Brody looked around the bar. Farmer wasn't back yet. "Where is that little bastard?" he growled.

"He hasn't come back yet," Lindberry said.

Brody sighed. "We'd better try to find him. I don't want the MPs grabbing him."

"Better check the back rooms first," Corky laughed. "That little fucker's probably shacked up again."

"I didn't see him when I was back there," Lindberry said innocently.

Brody's head turned. "Strawberry! My man! You finally lose your cherry?"

Lindberry blushed and everyone laughed.

"Who'd you get?" Corky asked.

"Suzie."

"Good stuff!"

Brody pushed his chair back and stood up. "Enough of this grab-ass, people. We've got to find Farmer and get his young ass back to camp."

CHAPTER 26

Sin City

The five men swept past the hanging beads that separated the back rooms from the bar itself and entered the long, dimly lit hallway flanked with small cubicles on both sides. It was a busy night. The doors to all of the rooms were closed.

"You take that side," Brody told Two-Step. "And I'll check this one."

Brody knocked on the first door.

"What the fuck you want!" someone called out. It was not Farmer.

"Sorry, buddy. Wrong room."

"Fuck you."

He knocked on the next door. No one answered. Opening it, he peered through the crack. All he could see was a Vietnamese girl with her legs spread wide, and a GI's head in between them. "Don't you know that that'll rot your teeth?" Brody chuckled.

"Hey! What the fuck you doing, man?" The GI raised his head.

Brody laughed and shut the door.

The rest of the rooms were the same: GIs busily spending their hard-earned money, and girls waiting for them to hurry up and get finished.

"Shit!" Brody said.

"Let's check out back," Two-Step said. He opened the door leading out to the alley. In the dim light of a naked light bulb, there was nothing to see. The alley was empty.

"Farmer!" Brody called out.

When there was no answer, he turned to the Indian. "Now what?"

Two-Step looked up and down the alley. "He went this way," he said, stepping out to the left.

Brody had learned a long time ago not to question Two-Step when he was tracking someone. In the jungles or the back alleys, the Indian point man operated on hunch and instinct as much as he did on logical reasoning. The strange thing was that he was usually right, even when logic said otherwise. It was Two-Step who found the unconscious American propped up against the side of a small shop. "Treat! Over here!"

He dropped down to check the man's pulse. It was light and fluttering. "This guy's hurt bad. We gotta get him outta here fast."

"Shit!" Brody muttered. "We get the MPs in on this and we'll never be able to find Farmer."

"Bunny and I can get him some help," Lindberry offered. "You keep looking for Farmer."

"Good idea. But remember, you two found this guy when you came down this alley by mistake."

"You got it."

Lindberry and Bunny got on each side of the wounded man and helped him up to his feet. Slinging his arms over their shoulders, they walked him to the main street, looking for a patrol jeep.

As soon as they were gone, Brody, Corky, and Two-Step faded back down the dimly lit alley. None of them were armed. Corky stopped and climbed up the side of a small building to rip down a short piece of two-by-four that was holding up the electrical lines.

"Careful," Two-Step cautioned.

"I got it."

With the comforting weight of the two-by-four at hand, the three men continued down the alley.

Jordan leaned back in his chair and stared at the wall. According to the regulations he had been going through for the last couple of hours, as soon as he received that letter from Gaines, he had to relieve him until the pilot could undergo a medical evaluation. That's what the regs said, and that's what he had to do.

Jordan ran that last thought through his mind again. "As soon as he *received* the letter," he had read. But what if he had not? Jordan smiled. It was the oldest trick in the Army. Letter? What letter? He couldn't very well act on something that he hadn't received.

He thought back. Did anyone know that he had the letter? The duty messenger had handed him a shotgun envelope and he had opened it in his office. Fortunately, Muller was such a klutz that he had not discussed the matter with him when he had asked for the regulations. In fact, he had not discussed it with anyone. Not even Gaines knew that he had actually received it. Gaines and the guy in Echo Company who had typed it up were the only two other people in the battalion who actually knew that the letter even existed. Rumors were flying around like AK fire. The typist had obviously blabbed. But no one really knew anything for certain.

Jordan smiled and folded the letter, stuffed it in his breast pocket, and buttoned the flap down over it. Check and mate. Now it was up to Gaines to make the next move. Sometimes doing nothing was the best tactic of all. Let the other guy make his move first. Hopefully he'll screw up, and when he does, you pin his ears back.

Jordan knew that all he was doing was buying a little time and maybe not even that much. Gaines would be waiting for the orders relieving him of his command, and when they weren't issued, he'd be pounding on Jordan's door, wanting to know where they were.

But that might take a day or two, and it would give Jordan a little while longer to try and find out what in the hell was going on with Rat Gaines. Of all the officers in the battalion, Gaines was the last one that he had ever thought would pull something as stupid as this.

The colonel reached for his hat as he headed out the door. He had been so wrapped up in this thing that he had completely missed dinner. Suddenly he was ravenously hungry. He decided to stop off at the club and see if he could get a cold-cut sandwich or something. His stomach rebelled at the thought of cold pony peter and rat cheese, but he had to eat something.

Farmer's arm was stiffening up in the cold now that he had stopped moving. He was crouched uncomfortably in the dark, keeping an eye on a house where several Vietnamese were playing cards inside.

This was his last chance to find more VC tonight and he was waiting for them to reveal their true identities before he took action. Farmer wasn't at all fooled by the fact that the card players looked like civilians. He was wise to all the clever disguises that old Victor Charlie used.

Everyone he had seen tonight looked like a civilian, even those two VC who had been beating that GI. Well, they hadn't fooled him and he had taken their ears. Now, when the people in the small house made their move to do VC things, he'd be ready for them.

Brody, Corky, and Two-Step had reached the end of the alley. Out of habit, Two-Step pulled back into the shadows as he surveyed the open land and scattered houses at the edge of the built-up area in front of him. The moon was just coming up, casting a silvery glow over the landscape.

"He's out there," Two-Step said quietly. "I know he's out there."

"What's he doing?"

194

The Indian shook his head. "I don't know, but he's there."

"Farmer!" Brody bellowed.

Farmer heard the shout and spun around. It sounded like Brody, but he knew that the night often played tricks on a man's hearing. He turned back to watch the house.

"Farmer!"

Just then, an old woman in the house got up to go to the door. She had heard the shouts and wanted to see what was going on. Farmer saw the door open and tensed himself to spring.

Two-Step saw the shaft of light when the door opened, illuminating a figure crouching against the wall. "That's him!" he shouted. He jumped up and took off, running as fast as he could.

"Hey! Wait up," Brody called out, starting after him.

Two-Step dashed across a hundred meters of open ground and leaped for Farmer just as the grunt reached for the old woman. He caught Farmer's knife hand as the blade flashed down for her neck.

"Farmer!"

The old woman broke away and started babbling in high-pitched Vietnamese. Farmer looked surprised. "What are you doing here?" he asked.

Corky ran up to the woman and tried to get her calmed down while Brody went over where Two-Step was quietly taking to Farmer. Brody grabbed the young grunt by the shoulder and spun him around.

"Jesus, man!" he spat. "What in the fuck do you think you're doing?"

"Killing VC." Farmer calmly reached into his pocket and pulled out the two fresh ears.

"Where'd you get those?"

"From the two VC who beat up a GI. They were going to kill him, so I killed them and took their ears."

Farmer looked over at the old mama-san, whom Corky was trying to calm down. "I wasn't going to kill her," he

195

said. "I was just going to bring her in for questioning. I don't kill female VC unless they're armed."

"Treat," Two-Step broke in. "We'd better *di-di* outta here. The MPs patrol this area out here."

"Corky," Brody called out. "Pay off that old bitch and let's boogie."

Corky put a couple hundred P notes in the old woman's hand and steered her toward her door. She was still bitching a mile a minute as the door swung shut behind her.

The four men ran back to the alley and disappeared in the shadows again. Corky stayed with Farmer while Brody and Two-Step ducked around the corner of the building to clear the way. The squad leader glanced down at the luminous hands of his issue Timex. "Fuck! It's past curfew."

Two-Step automatically checked up and down the alley. "We gotta get him outta here."

"We gotta get *us* outta here, too. I don't want to have to take a ration of shit from some dumb fucking MP about being out after hours."

"Who's got berm guard tonight?"

"Shit, man, I don't know. I haven't been watching the bulletin board lately."

"You want to try it?"

"We get caught doing that and we're really going to be in the shit."

"Farmer's the one who's going to be in the shit if the MPs find two dinks missing their fucking ears. We're going to be right in it with him."

Brody shook his head. "Man, what's wrong with that guy?"

"Let's worry about that later, okay?" Two-Step said. "Right now, let's just get the fuck outta here."

"Okay, take the point."

It was far easier to get back over the wire than any of them had even hoped for. One of Corky's Chicano buddies in Alpha Company was on guard at the rear gate to the camp. He opened it right up for them.

196

"Thanks, Chico," Corky said once they were safely inside.

"De nada."

Once inside the camp, Farmer seemed to come out of he daze he had been in. "I'm really sorry about this, Brody," he said sincerely. "I didn't mean for you to go to all this trouble."

Brody studied him carefully. "Farmer, I swear to God hat the next time you fuck up, I'm going to let the MPs save your ass."

"I'm okay now," Farmer said, his hand clenched around he two ears in his pocket.

"You'd better be."

When Colonel Jordan walked into the noisy, smoke-filled club, a hush fell over the room. No one greeted him or called out for him to come and have a drink with hem. Jesus, he thought, I guess I need to change my deodorant.

"Can I help you, sir?" the bartender greeted him.

"Yeah, what do you have for a sandwich?"

"Bologna and cheddar cheese."

Jordan groaned inside. Pony peter and rat cheese. "Okay, I guess it'll have to do. Gimme one, heavy on the mustard, please. And a beer."

The bartender got the colonel his beer before he went for the sandwich. Jordan took a deep drink and looked around the room. It was still strangely quiet for the club hat he knew. Something was not right.

The bartender returned with the sandwich, a few smashed fragments of potato chips, and a limp dill pickle slice on a ness-hall plate.

"Thanks," Jordan said, lifting the pickle to his mouth. "By the way," he asked on a hunch. "Has Captain Gaines been here tonight?"

"Yes, sir, he left about half an hour ago."

"Thanks." Jordan nodded and returned to his sandwic[h]
Not only was Gaines waiting for the next move, the who[le]
damned battalion was holding its breath.

Jordan smiled and bit into the sandwich.

CHAPTER 27

Khe Sanh

David Janson took a long, deep breath. He couldn't smell himself, but after over two weeks without a shower, he didn't have to know that he was rank. His nose had shut down a long time ago. Living in close proximity in a bunker with men who had been without showers far longer than he had killed his sense of smell real quick.

Water was so strictly rationed in Khe Sanh that all he had been able to do was to run a wet washcloth under his arms and in between his legs every other day or so. He would have killed somebody for a chance to spend even fifteen minutes under a steaming hot shower. At least he had been able to brush his teeth, though. He hated the scummy feeling of dirty teeth.

"Mr. Janson?"

The reporter turned and saw Wee Willie coming his way. "Yeah."

"The Bear sent me to find you. They want you over at the TOC."

"Thanks, Willie. I'll go see what they want."

The reporter stubbed his cigarette butt out on the sandbag and headed over to the Marine battalion command post bunker. It was probably nothing more than another note from his editor requesting more news from the beleaguered base. Even though the siege was well into its second month, the image of the Marines reliving the days of the French at Dien Bien Phu had captured the attention of the American public. The stateside papers wanted more.

The rumored Dien Bien Phu anniversary assault had not materialized on the thirteenth. The entire Marine garrison had stood to in their bunkers all night, waiting, and the artillery batteries had been loaded and trained on their targets. Nothing had happened. Not even the usual harassment shelling. The entire thing had been a complete non-event.

Janson wasn't sorry that the attack had not happened, but his editors back in the States were. It would have been great press. Now, however, they were off chasing the new rumor about the relief effort, and they wanted daily updates on the situation. He could have written that UFOs were reportedly coming to their rescue and it would have been printed in every paper in the country. The "anything for a headline" attitude of the American press never ceased to amaze him.

The Marines in Khe Sanh had even heard the stories of the relief mission. They kept asking him if he knew anything about when they were going to get some help. When he pointed out that since he was living in the same bunkers that they were, he didn't know any more about it than they did, they had been sadly disappointed. In their eyes, as a reporter, he was supposed to know, even if he had to get his information out of thin air.

While he knew nothing concrete, it was obvious that General Westmoreland was going to make an effort to relieve the base. The only questions were when it would take place and who would get the honor of doing it. As to when, Janson knew full well that it took many days for a large force to prepare for that kind of an operation. But it had been well over two weeks now since the Tet offensive had been declared at an end, and he felt certain that their turn would be coming before too much longer. It had to be. The Marines had withstood more than was necessary.

As far as who would get to do the job, he was betting that the relief mission would be given to the Air Cav. That was the only thing he could think of that made much sense. The Marines in I Corps couldn't be pulled down to do it. Their combat strength was tied up along the DMZ.

Even if they were free, they didn't have the aerial assets needed to do the job. Marine units would have to fight their way up the hills of Route 9 on foot, one hill at a time. That could take weeks or even months, depending how much of a fight the NVA wanted to give them. The Air Cav, on the other hand, could fly their grunts in behind enemy fortifications and air-lift the required artillery to fire-support missions for the fast-moving infantry. If anyone was going to turn the situation around at Khe Sanh, it was going to have to be the Air Cav.

The more Janson thought about the relief rumor, the more he was beginning to think that he might be in the wrong place. His editors were screaming for stories from Khe Sanh, but they were rehashing old news.

Maybe he should start trying to get out of Khe Sanh and hook back up with the Air cav. Mack Jordan would probably let him bunk up with the First of the 7th, as he had done during Tet. It would be good to see Jordan and see how his assorted collection of madmen and crazies had been doing lately. People like Rat Gaines and that mob down in Rat's Blue Team always made good copy.

As he started over to the Marine CP, Janson concentrated on the logistics of getting back to the press camp in Nha Trang long enough to get reoutfitted before joining up with the Cav. He was so deep in thought that he didn't hear the whistle of the incoming 122mm rockets until the first one impacted barely twenty meters in front of him.

The crushing hammer blow of the rocket's detonation sent Janson crashing into the sandbags. A sharp burning pain bit deeply into his side as he fell to his knees.

"Oh, fuck," he muttered, a puzzled expression on h[is] face. "I'm hit."

"Mr. Janson!" Willie yelled from the trench. "Mr. Ja[n]son."

The reporter tried to get to his feet, but suddenly he ha[d] no strength. He toppled to the ground. The last thing [he] remembered was Willie crawling through the smoke towa[rd] him.

When Janson awoke, it was late afternoon. He looke[d] around and saw that he was in the makeshift emergenc[y] surgical suite at the aid station by the airstrip. Medical pe[r]sonnel in blood-spattered surgical greens were moving fro[m] patient to patient, checking IV drips and taking pulses. [He] was vaguely aware of a burning sensation in his lower bell[y.]

When a Marine corpsman saw that he was awake, [he] came right over. "You're okay now, sir," he said, trying [to] reassure him.

Janson knew that he was okay or he wouldn't have woke[n] up, at least not in Khe Sanh. Unless, of course, Khe San[h] was hell.

"How bad is it?" he asked.

The medic looked at the casualty tag tied around h[is] neck. "Not that bad. Just a little frag in the lower inte[s]tine."

Janson grimaced. A belly wound. That was never goo[d,] particularly in the Nam.

"We'll have you outta here on the next Dustoff and you'[ll] be in a field hospital full of pretty nurses before you kno[w] it."

"Hey, Mr. Janson," a familiar voice called out from th[e] bed next to his.

He turned his head and saw Wee Willie sitting up wit[h] a big grin on his face. "What are you doing here?"

"I'm going on the Dustoff with you," he said proudl[y.] He held up a leg and displayed a bloody bandage tied aroun[d] the knee.

"What happened?"

Willie looked away. "I got hit by one of those rockets, too."

"He got hit when he crawled out to drag you back under cover," Bernowski said, walking up to the foot of Janson's cot.

"Ah, Bear," Willie protested. "You weren't supposed to tell him that."

"Actually," Bear continued, "he crawled over to you and shielded you with his body when another one-twenty-two landed close by."

Janson looked over at the wounded young Marine. Willie looked acutely embarrassed. "Thanks."

"No sweat, Mr. Janson, It wasn't nothin'. Really, it wasn't."

Janson looked up at Willie's hulking squad leader. "Bear, how do I go about getting Willie written up for having saved my life?"

"I can take care of that for you, sir,"

"Will you please? I'll forward my own recommendation as soon as I get back to my typewriter."

"That'll help, particularly since I'm going to write him up for an Article Fifteen for willingfully damaging government property. If he hadn't ran out there to get you, he wouldn't have been hit, and the Corps would still have another PFC grunt out on the line."

"Hey, Bear! You can't do that to me!" Willie protested.

"I told you to keep your head down, dammit. Now I'm another man short."

"But think of it this way, Bernowski," Janson said. "Now I can write more press releases, and you know the Corps likes the publicity."

Bear grinned. "You have a point there."

Just then, one of the medics came in with the word that the medevac flight was on its way in. Janson, Willie, and the other casualties were all strapped down to their litters.

"Mr. Janson," Bear said. "You let us know what happens to you."

"I will. You keep your head down, now."

203

"You got that shit right."

"See you later, Willie."

"Right, Bear."

The medics carried Janson's litter out to a gathering point on the edge of the runway. The pilots didn't like to stay on the ground any longer than was absolutely necessary while the patients were being loaded. The average time to take on a medevac load was running just under four minutes from touchdown to takeoff.

While they waited, Willie kept up a steady chatter about how safe it was to fly in and out of Khe Sanh. He kept saying over and over that none of the medevac planes had been shot down. Yet. The young grunt was desperately trying to reassure himself. Janson couldn't find it in his heart to remind the grunt that there was always a first time for everything.

A distant black speck in the sky grew closer and closer until Janson recognized one of the old, faithful, twin-engined C-123 Providers. When the plane came in range, the NVA ack-ack guns on the hills opened up. The plane ducked down through the barrage of flak and lined up on the end of the runway, her rear ramp, landing gear, and flaps down.

At the other end of the base, the Marine artillery started firing counter-battery fire against the antiaircraft guns to cover the plane as it landed. With a squeal of brakes, the Provider touched down on the pockmarked PSP runway. In seconds, it had slowed and taxied over to where the medevac patients waited behind the sandbagged blast walls.

"Go! Go! Go!" the Air Force men yelled from the open ramp of the plane.

The Marine corpsmen grabbed the handles of their litters and ran for the ramp. The litters were handed up to the blue-suiters who rushed them inside the plane and quickly strapped them down. As soon as all was secure, the pilot threw his throttles all the way forward and stood on the brakes.

The old rattletrap Provider shuddered and shook as the

two big props clawed the air and the two little J-85 jet engines screamed. When the pilot came off the brakes, the C-123 leaped forward as if it had been shot from a gun. The plane had been on the ground only a little over three minutes when it rotated and pointed its nose into the sky.

Behind the plane, the Marine artillery batteries doubled the intensity of their counter-battery fire to keep the enemy gunners' heads down. From where he lay in the darkened belly of the plane, Janson could see out the closing ramp as Khe Sanh was quickly left behind. For once, he was not sorry to be leaving a story.

"See, Mr. Janson," Willie yelled over the roar of the engines. "I told you we'd get out of here okay."

Janson just smiled.

Colonel Nguyen Van Tran read over the radio message from Captain Xuan for the third time. He was disappointed that the Yankee recon unit had not been annihilated, but at least they were gone. Now, as soon as he tracked down the other team that had been reported working in the southwest hills around Route 9, the Khe Sanh operation would be secure again. At least for a while. The Yankees would be back, however, probably within only a few days.

He rubbed the ache in his neck. As hard as he had tried to isolate the Khe Sanh sector, he had a nasty feeling that it wasn't working. He knew that the Yankees were getting in, anyway, and scouting out his defenses. This was always the problem when you were engaged in a static defense operation like this. No matter how good your security, it was always vulnerable to small teams sneaking around in the jungle. Hopefully the extensive booby-trapping program he had ordered would make things even more difficult for the bastards.

He was beginning to become more than a little concerned by the reports that had started coming in to his division command post, reports that said the Yankee Air

Cavalry was opening several firebases to the east of Khe Sanh.

The one that particularly worried him was being built in the valley along Route 9, just to the north of Ca Lu. The intelligence reports claimed that the Yankees had built a five-hundred-meter paved runway as well as fuel- and ammunition-storage facilities in only eleven days.

That report was nonsense, of course. But even an idiot could see that the Americans were preparing to attack the People's Arm units ringing Khe Sanh, and this made his problem even more immediate. He had urgently requested that the new base be attacked immediately, but so far no action had been taken. The division commander was very reluctant to move troops from his defensive positions.

Tran was expecting to be attacked any day but he had to keep the Yankees at bay until the Marine garrison at Khe Sanh fell. And it would fall. Even the American newspapers were calling the operation a complete disaster. All the People's Army had to do was keep the pressure on, and the Yankees would collapse.

CHAPTER 28

Camp Evans

Rat Gaines slept in late the next morning. When he finally got up he took a leisurely shower before changing into a clean set of pressed jungle fatigues and his best pair of Cocran jump boots. He packed his belongings into a duffel bag and set it by the door. The minute he got the official word, he was out of there.

When everything was ready, he grabbed his hat, walked out to his jeep, and slid in behind the wheel. The sun was shining. It was a nice day for a ride in the country. He decided to stop off in the ville and have a little Vietnamese food for lunch.

It would take the colonel a little while to get all of the paper work ready, but by the time he got back, his orders would have been cut. He could wrap this thing up and be gone in a flash, leaving it all behind like he had never even been there.

He didn't really have the foggiest notion of where the hell he'd be going next, but he knew that it would be someplace where he didn't have to look at people and things that reminded him of Lisa all the time. Maybe he could get a job flying for one of those VIP transport units down at Tan

Son Nhut or Nha Trang. He laughed out loud when he thought of flying a bunch of lard-assed colonels and generals around all day.

What a life that would be; nine to five, good food, hot showers and never having to put up with the hassles and bullshit paperwork required to keep a combat unit up and running.

Thinking about Python Flight made him look down toward the flight line. He could see the mechanics swarming over the choppers. Without even thinking, he pulled off the road to watch for a moment. He started to wonder how the guys were doing this morning with the scheduled turnover of the old machines, but he ruthlessly squelched that thought.

"It's not my fucking problem," he growled. "Not anymore."

He slammed the gearshift into first and drove off, headed for the main gate. His lunch was waiting for him and he didn't want to be late.

Down on the flight line, Lance Warlokk had seen the jeep stop for a while before driving off again. Even though it had been too far away for him to see who was behind the wheel, he knew that it was Rat Gaines.

Warlokk had reported for work that morning as if nothing were wrong. When he looked around Python Operations, Gaines had been nowhere in sight. The pilots and crew, however, had all been standing around in the ready room waiting for something to happen.

"Why the fuck aren't you people out there working on those birds?" Warlokk had asked.

"Hey, Lawless!" someone called out. "What's the word? Did Rat quit on us or not?"

Warlokk bristled. It was one thing when he got on Rat's case, but these assholes weren't going to do it. At least not when he was around. "You'd better watch your mouth, boy."

"Well, did he?"

Warlokk didn't bother to answer the man. "You people'd

better get your asses out on that fucking flight line now!" he bellowed. "We've got a lot of work to do today."

The men filed out to go about their tasks. They knew better than to cross Lawless Warlokk. Warlokk stayed down on the fight line and made sure that they did their work, too. He didn't know what Gaines was up to, but he wasn't going to let Python Flight go to hell in his absence.

In the Echo Company area that afternoon, Brody and his people left Lieutenant Alexander's briefing and went back to their tent to get their gear together. They were moving out the next morning.

"What do you think about this mission, Treat?" Corky asked.

Brody looked up from cleaning the broken-down M-16 rifle in front of him and shrugged. "It makes more sense than the first go-around. I never did like those platoon-sized clusterfucks, anyway. If we're going to to do a recon, we don't need to have a bunch of assholes stumbling around in the woods with us." He shook his head. "Shit, man, that was almost as bad as being in a line company."

Corky laughed. "I thought you said that there was nothing as bad as being in a line company."

"You got that shit right, but this last little trip damn near changed my mind."

All of the men in the Blues considered themselves an elite unit compared to the other infantry platoons in the battalion. And Brody's people considered themselves to be the elite squad of the Blues. As such, they liked to work by themselves.

"You want out of this?" Brody asked. "Just say the word, man."

"No, like I said before, I'll hang in there with the rest of you guys till this shit's over."

"How much longer you got now?"

Corky glanced down at his watch. "Fourteen days, sixteen hours, and four minutes till the big, shiny Freedom Bird takes my young ass outta here.''

Brody shook his head and laughed. ''You don't count the seconds?''

''Only pussies count the seconds.'' Corky grinned. ''Real men don't sweat the small stuff.''

''Right.''

When Corky got up and walked off, Brody went back to cleaning his rifle. The Colt M-16 was a good weapon. When it was fired on full automatic, its small-caliber, high-velocity rounds could cut a man in half. But the M-16 had not been designed for use in the Nam. It didn't like dirt and mud at all. The smallest speck of dirt, sand, or hard carbon in the wrong place could leave a soldier with an inert chunk of metal and plastic in his hands when he least expected it.

It could get a man killed fast, so Brody went to great lengths to clean his piece thoroughly. When the cleaning ritual was done and every last part of the weapon was sparkling, he reassembled it and sprayed a short burst of WD-40 on the bolt.

Then he turned to reloading his sixteen magazines from the open can of 5.56mm ammunition at his feet. When he had loaded up enough to fill five bandoliers, he took out the magazine he had specially made for himself, a modified Russian AK-47 assault rifle magazine.

The AK mag had been extensively reworked so that it would fit into the magazine well of an American M-16. Its throat had been ground down so that it would fit into the narrower magazine well of the sixteen. Then the original AK magazine catch had been ground off and a square hole cut into the sight side so it would clip into the magazine catch of the American rifle.

The modification worked because the 7.62mm AK-47 and the 5.56mm M-16 cartridges were almost the same length, the AK round being just a little longer and much fatter. When it was filled with AK ammunition, the Russian magazine held thirty rounds, but Brody was able to load thirty-eight of the skinnier M-16 rounds into it. That was over twice the capacity of the issue magazines.

The Army was aware that the twenty-round M-16 magazine was inadequate, and a new thirty-round replacement magazine was supposedly being field-tested with elite units. But that didn't do Brody any good. He wanted to have extra firepower when he stepped off the chopper now, not when the Army got around to deciding to issue the new mags.

They had stirred up a hornet's nest out in the jungle, and they were going right back into it. The veteran grunt had a definite feeling that they had actually gotten off light the last time around. The dinks were going to be waiting for them as soon as they poked their noses back in there.

Over in the corner by the door, Two-Step was putting together a new batch of tailor-made ammunition for his Remington pump gun. He had burned through a lot of rounds on the last outing, and he needed to build up his supply again. Usually, he only made up a hundred rounds at a time, but this time he wanted to have at least two hundred when he went out again.

Working a dozen at a time, the Indian opened the issue shotgun shells and took out the lead balls and the gunpowder. First he measured out a new powder load ten percent greater than the standard and poured it back into the empty hulls to make his own Magnum loads. Then he counted out twelve .25-caliber stainless-steel ball bearings for each shell. Since the ball bearings were lighter than the lead balls they replaced, they traveled farther and hit harder. Also, unlike lead balls, which deformed when they hit something, the steel balls kept their shape. The plowed right on through and kept going. Once, Two-Step had killed two NVA with a single blast of the pump gun. The steel balls had torn all the way through the first man's chest and gone on to kill the man standing behind him.

While Two-Step's hands automatically performed the familiar tasks, his mind wandered off in another direction. For the first time in months, he thought about his grandfather, the man who had taught him to walk proudly on the path of the warrior. He wondered what his grandfather would have said about Farmer. He knew the old man would not have approved.

The taking of trophies from honorable kills was an old Indian custom. Usually, though, the traditional trophies had been weapons or items of clothing. Unknown to most people, the practice of taking scalps was something that the Indians had learned from the white man. The French had introduced them to it during the French and Indian Wars of the 1700s.

Two-Step had no moral problem with the practice of taking VC ears, and he knew that it was often done, particularly by men in the sniper and LRRP units. But he didn't like Farmer's obsession with it. Not only was the practice unsanitary, it was completely against Army regulations. Farmer risked a court martial if he got caught at it.

He was particularly concerned by Farmer's little raid in Sin City last night. He really didn't mind that two petty Vietnamese gangsters had been killed, not in the least. As far as he was concerned, if they were all killed, the country would be better off. It was *why* they had been killed. Farmer had gone out specifically to make a trophy kill. That was not the act of a warrior. It was the act of a psychopath.

Two-Step shook his head. The young grunt had come a long way in the short time since he had joined up with the Blues. The innocent, smiling kid from the farm had turned into a real head case. If Farmer wasn't real careful, he'd be going home in a straitjacket— if he didn't get himself killed doing something crazy first.

That was the real problem with Farmer's current mental condition. In a combat situation, anytime that a man became obsessed with something, he lost his edge. Surviving on a battlefield, particularly one as chancy as the jungles of Southeast Asia, required that a man be mentally and physically alert at all times. Any obsession, even one for staying alive, dulled the senses. When a man was as obsessed as Farmer was, he was a walking dead man.

Two-Step wasn't quite sure what he should do about the

young grunt, or if there was even anything to be done. He talked to Brody about him after they had gotten back into the camp last night, but Treat had only wanted to keep a closer eye on him. Brody felt sure that the kid would snap out of it once they got back in the field.

Two-Step wasn't too sure about that, but Brody was the squad leader, so he'd go along with his decision for now.

The object of Two-Step's concern was sacked out again. When Brody and the others had gotten him back into the camp last night, Farmer had just crawled into his bunk and gone straight to sleep. He hadn't even taken his boots off. He had gotten up for the ell tee's mission briefing, but that was all. As soon as the briefing was over, he had crawled into his sack and gone back to sleep again.

On the next bunk, Lindberry covertly glanced over at Farmer as he got his gear ready. He had thought about waking him up to see if he was okay, but he hesitated. Brody and the other veterans in the squad were keeping an eye on Farmer, so Lindberry let it go. If they weren't worried, then he wouldn't, either.

He wasn't really sure how he felt about Farmer's trophies, however. He had seen enough combat by now that he had gotten over his initial FNG squeamishness about the dead, particularly the NVA dead. But he had been shocked when Farmer took the dried ears out to show him. It was just a little more than he had been prepared to deal with.

He didn't really know what to say and he didn't want to touch them when Farmer handed them to him. Lindberry liked Farmer, but he was beginning to wonder if he shouldn't be taken out of the field. Maybe he needed to be sent to the rear, someplace where he could relax.

CHAPTER 29

Camp Evans

The sun was setting when Rat Gaines finally returned to Camp Evans. He had enjoyed a leisurely lunch down in the village and then taken a long ride into the countryside. It had been fun, running around without a care in the world. It had also been fun running around without a weapon. Gaines knew that he should have at least carried a pistol with him, but the way he had been feeling, if he had gotten wasted, it would have ended this whole fucking mess.

Now that he was back, his brief vacation was over, he had some business to take care of. He stopped off at his old orderly room and stuck his head around the side of the door. "Top?" he said.

First Sergeant Richardson looked up from his paper work. "Captain Gaines, everyone's been looking for you all day, sir."

Gaines ignored his remark. "Did I get anything from battalion today?"

Richardson rummaged around in his overflowing in-box. "No, sir."

"Did the Old Man call for me?"

Top shook his head. "No, sir."

"Shit!"

"Uh, sir?"

"Yes."

"I've been hearing things, sir, and I just kinda wondered . . ."

"They're true, Top," Gaines grinned. "Every fucking last one of them."

"Then, sir, what—"

"Sorry, Top," Gaines cut him off in midsentence. "Gotta run."

Richardson shook his head as he watched his CO walk out. Gaines had proven himself to be one hell of a fine officer and a good company commander, but he had obviously gone completely off the deep end. It was a real crying shame that his fiancée had been killed, but that was war. Gaines needed to pull himself together and get back to the matter at hand, running Echo Company.

Gaines climbed back in behind the wheel of his jeep and drove over to the battalion headquarters. When he walked into the outer office, Gaines noticed that Lieutenant Muller was a little slow jumping to his feet when he walked in the room. Usually the adjutant was out of his chair and standing at attention as though he were rocket propelled. Some of the officers had even given him a new nickname—Spring Butt.

"The colonel in?" Gaines asked.

Muller swallowed before he answered. "He told me to tell you that he's at Brigade, sir!"

Muller's eyes were locked in the straight-ahead position, and he said his piece as if it were memorized. Gaines knew he was lying.

"You cut any orders on me today?"

Muller blinked. "No, sir."

Gaines smiled. Now he knew the game. Jordan was trying to sandbag him. He could live with that. Jordan needed to have someone running Echo Company, and Mike Alexander couldn't step in to do it, since he was already tied up with the Blues. If Rat just stayed out of the company orderly room and the Python Operations shack, Jordan would have to cut the orders to get a replacement in to do the work.

"At ease, Lieutenant," Gaines said as he turned to leave.

"Captain Gaines, sir?"

Gaines stopped and turned back. "Yes?"

Muller hesitated. "Uh . . . nothing, sir."

"I didn't think so."

Back out in the parking lot, Gaines got in his jeep and fired it up. Putting it in reverse, he backed out of the parking lot. He automatically started for the officers' club, but hesitated. If he went in there, he'd probably run into Warlokk, and he didn't want to go through it with him again. He spun the wheel and headed in the opposite direction, down to the flight line. He'd go walking around the choppers and remember what it was like to fly without a care in the world.

The flight line was dimly lit by the lights from the maintenance hangers where the mechanics were putting the finishing touches on their long day's work. The last two weeks had been an exhausting grind for the division's grease monkeys and supply people, and the end was not yet in sight.

Wear and tear as well as increased combat damage suffered during the Tet offensive had crippled the division's chopper fleet. They were at the lowest level of combat-ready machines that they had been in since they had first come in-country. New helicopters were flying in every day to replace combat-damaged and just plain worn-out equipment, but there was still a lot of work to be done, even on brand-new machines.

By now everyone had heard about the new operation to relieve the garrison at Khe Sanh. With all the construction going on and the massive movements of men and material, it was hard to keep it a secret. Particularly the construction at LZ Stud, the new division forward CP.

The Cav was going to war again, and that meant that the people who kept the division flying were busting their butts working late.

Gaines was drawn toward the big maintenance hangars,

where several new Cobras were parked right inside the circle of lights. These machines were shiny bright, their rotor blades unscarred, their dull skins unspotted with bullet-hole patches. There were no oil leaks underneath them, and the plexiglass canopies were clear and unblemished. They were beautiful.

Gaines was running his hand over the sleek flank of one of the new Cobras when he heard someone walk up behind him. "I thought that was you," he heard Walt Greenfield say.

The maintenance officer looked exhausted. His fatigues were dirty and stained, his eyes were red, and he badly needed a shave.

"Walt, my man." Gaines greeted him with a laugh. "You look like two pounds of shit in a one-pound bag."

Walt didn't blink an eye. He was used to taking friendly abuse from Rat Gaines. But he had something else on his mind this evening.

"I've been hearing some real strange things about you," he said. "Rumor has it that you're hanging up your guns for good."

Gaines's face tightened. "Walt," he said. "It's a long story."

Greenfield flung his arms out to encompass the crowded hangar. "Well, since I've got nothing else to do tonight, why don't you come in, have a drink, and tell Uncle Walt all about it. I've even got a bottle of Wild Turkey in the office."

"I don't want to keep you from your work." Gaines protested.

"Fuck it, it'll be here tomorrow. I want to find out what the fuck's wrong with you."

Walt told his NCO that he didn't want to be disturbed and closed the door to his office. "You want that Turkey with or without?"

"Straight."

Greenfield poured a brown plastic mess hall coffee cup

full and handed it to Gaines. He poured himself half a cup and topped it off with coffee.

"That's a real waste of good whiskey," Gaines commented dryly.

Walt took a sip and made a face. "Actually, if the coffee wasn't so fucking bad around here, I wouldn't have to put this shit in it at all."

The two men drank in silence for a moment. Greenfield was the first to break the silence. "How long has it been?" he asked.

Gaines knew without asking what he was talking about. "A little over two weeks," he replied.

"It's a real bitch, man."

Gaines didn't answer. No reply was necessary.

Walt leaned forward in his chair. "Rat," he said, "I like you, so I'm going to tell you something. You're fucking up by the numbers, boy."

Gaines looked up at the maintenance officer. Of all the men he knew, Walt could get away with telling him that. "How's that?"

"You can't run away from it."

Walt took another drink and refilled his cup with straight booze. "Believe me, I know."

"Why do you say that?"

"I don't usually advertise this," Walt said softly. "But I was married once. Back in the days when I was a young butter-bar."

"I didn't know that."

Walt locked eyes with the pilot. "I was stationed in Germany and she was killed in a car crash on the Death Strip. One of those massive pileups in the fog on the Autobahn right outside of Frankfurt. She was trapped in the wreckage of her car and burned to death before they could put the fire out."

"Jesus, Walt, I'm sorry."

Greenfield raised his hands. "It's okay, it's been years now. And you know, weeks go by here without my even thinking of her."

218

Gaines was silent.

"I guess that the point I'm trying to make is that I tried to run away from it, too. I hated everything German for years and I almost resigned from the Army. You see, I was pulling battalion duty officer the night she was killed. If I'd been home, I would have been driving her where she was going and I might have been able to avoid the accident." He paused. "Or at least I would have been killed right along with her."

Greenfield took a long drink. "Either way, I wouldn't have lost her."

"Walt, I didn't know. I'm really sorry."

"Let me finish."

Gaines sat back.

Greenfield took a long drink from his cup. "Anyway, I couldn't take it anymore. I got myself transferred to the States and took the first slot I could get over here. I ran, but it didn't help."

Gaines was silent for a moment. When he spoke, his voice was strained. "Walt, I've got to get outta here. Everywhere I turn, I see her, everyplace I go reminds me of her." He took a long drink. "And every time I see a fucking cannon cocker, I want to kill the sonofabitch."

Walt pushed the bottle across the desk top toward him. Gaines refilled his cup.

"I know the feeling, but it's part of the process. You have to get past it."

"What process?"

"Saying good-bye."

Gaines felt his eyes water up. "Goddammit! I don't want to say good-bye!"

"I know, but you have to."

Gaines slammed his hand down on the desk top. "Fuck that. I don't want to forget."

"I didn't say anything about forgetting," Walt snapped. "You aren't ever going to forget. But if you're worth a shit to yourself or anyone else, you'll say good-bye and get on with the rest of your life."

"But that's the thing. I really don't want to do that."

"I know you don't, or you wouldn't be doing what you're doing."

"What do you mean?"

"How many times have you gotten drunk since she was killed?"

"I haven't."

"I didn't think so."

"What're you talking about?"

"If you get drunk it'll go away for a while, and you don't want it to do that."

"What are you, Greenfield, some kinda fucking shrink?"

Walt grinned. "No. I'm just some poor bastard who already went through what you're going through now. I've been there and I did just exactly what you're doing. I inflicted as much pain on myself as I possibly could, but it didn't work. In the end, I was still alive."

"Damn you, Walt Greenfield."

The maintenance officer grinned. "Rat, if you weren't such a lovable asshole, I wouldn't even be wasting my time with you."

"So what's next, Doctor?"

"Well, I was kinda thinking that maybe you and I oughta get all sorts of fucked up tonight. You know, puking, falling down, crawling in the gutter, blind, fucking drunk."

Rat took another drink. "It's not a bad idea, but it's not going to change my mind. I'm still outta here the minute Jordan cuts my orders."

Walt waved the bottle in the air. "Who said anything about changing your mind? You're a big boy now. You can do anything you want. We're just going to have a drink to celebrate the fact that you won't be fucking up any more of my choppers."

"I'll drink to that."

Walt upended the bottle into his cup. "Oops, that one's dead, better switch to the good stuff." He reached into his desk drawer, pulled out a bottle of cheap brandy, and handed it over.

Gaines glanced at the label and slowly shook his head. "Now I know why you can't ever get one of my choppers fixed right the first time. Anybody who'd drink this stuff would eat shit, chase rabbits, and bark at the moon."

"It goes real good with the coffee they make around here."

"I'll bet it does."

CHAPTER 30

Camp Evans

It was a far different-looking bunch of grunts down on the alert pad the next morning than the ones who had flown out only three days ago. For one thing, instead of the whole Aero Rifle Platoon being suited up and ready to go, there were only eight men: Alexander, Zack, Brody, Two-Step, Corky, Bunny, Farmer, and Lindberry. When Bunny had heard that he was being left behind, he had pitched such a fit that Alexander had added him to the mission.

Also, they were traveling much lighter than before. Their rucks held only their ammunition and a five-day supply of freeze-dried Lurp rations. This time they were going to move fast and keep on the move. At the end of the five days, if they still needed to continue their recon, they would take a fly past an aerial resupply drop and keep on going.

For another thing, they looked like a real LRRP team this time, instead of Air Cav grunts. All of the men wore camouflage greasepaint on their faces and hands, and Brody had scrounged a set of oak-leaf-pattern camouflage fatigues from one of his Ranger sniper buddies. Two-Step, of course, was in his customary tiger stripe camies.

Only Alexander was wearing his usual brush hat. The

rest of the men wore olive drab headcloths fashioned out of arm slings issued by the medics. The headcloths wouldn't keep the sun out of their eyes, but they blended into the jungle foliage better and acted as a sweatband at the same time.

They were also armed to the teeth. Everyone except Bunny and Zack were carrying some kind of secondary weapon. Corky had his .45 pistol backup. Farmer, Two-Step, and Lindberry all packed thumpers along with their usual pieces. Alexander had managed to procure a CAR-15 submachine gun for short-range work and had his M-16 slung over his back. Brody had his M-16 with the big magazine, and a Browning 9mm pistol.

Since there were so few of them, they would make the insertion in one slick, with only Warlokk's Cobra for escort. It was a good plan, but it had a catch. They would attract far less attention with just the two choppers, but if their planned insertion turned out to be a hot LZ, they would find themselves in an instant world of shit. If anything went wrong, it would take too long to get help.

As Warlokk preflighted his gunship, he kept glancing at his watch and looking up and down the flight line. For some reason, he had half expected that Gaines would show up for the mission, if nothing else, just to see his men off. He was still hoping that Rat's strange behavior was something that he would have gotten out of his system by now. When it was time to go, there was still no Rat Gaines anywhere to be seen.

"Hey, Gabe!" Warlokk called out. "Let's do it."

The slick pilot nodded and climbed up into his bird. "Show time, Ell tee," he shouted over the electric whine of his starter motor as he pulled the start trigger on the collective.

Alexander gave him a thumbs-up, and the men clambered up into the back of the slick. Gabe was carrying two other men on the doorguns, so Brody found a seat in the troop compartment instead of going back into the gunner's pocket. On the way to the LZ, the men would sit inside the

223

machine instead of in the open doors, with their feet hanging out. That way, if anyone saw them fly by, it wouldn't be as noticeable that the slick was carrying troops inside.

Gabe pulled up on the collective and taxied out to the runway. When Warlokk called, he brought the tail up and nudged forward on the cyclic. The Blues were going to war again.

Severely hungover, Rat Gaines woke abruptly when the two choppers passed low over his hooch, their rotor blast shaking the roof. His head felt like someone had used it for a punching bag, his eyes ached, and his mouth tasted like Attila the Hun had camped in it overnight. He sat up and painfully swung his legs over the edge of his bunk.

When the bottle of cheap brandy had been emptied last night, Walt had brought out the coup de grace for the evening, a bottle of Everclear, a commercially produced white lightning.

Gaines had been a little reluctant to continue on that stuff. Having worked for his moonshining uncle, he knew better. But Walt had tauntingly challenged his southern honor, and he had taken the bait. Now that he thought of it, Greenfield had drunk very little of the stuff himself. Smart man. He ran his tongue around the inside of his mouth and gagged.

He reached down for his canteen and then remembered that he had already packed it away in his duffel bag. With a groan, he got to his feet and slowly staggered out to the Lister bag that hung right outside the orderly room. He poured water into his cupped hands and drank deeply. The instant the water hit his stomach, he wished that he hadn't.

He finished rinsing his mouth and spit the water out. His stomach churned. He ran back to his hooch and lay back down.

As soon as his stomach settled down, he slipped into his shower sandals, grabbed his towel, and headed out. The sun hadn't been up long enough to warm the water in the discarded aircraft drop tank that served as the shower water supply. Gaines suffered stoically through the cold water. It was a fitting punishment for what he had done to himself.

Back in his hooch, he dressed quickly and went outside to find his jeep. He had no idea where he might have left it, but it was parked in his usual spot in front of the orderly room. It was even locked up properly. He patted his pocket and discovered that he did not have his keys.

Top Richardson looked up when Gaines walked into the orderly room. "Captain, I've got your jeep keys. A driver from Division Maintenance delivered the vehicle this morning."

Another mystery solved.

"Thanks, Top. Anything from battalion for me?"

"Not yet, sir," the first sergeant answered. "If you tell me what you're expecting, sir, I can give them a call about it."

"That's all right, Top," Gaines said. He poured himself a cup of coffee from the ever-brewing pot on top of the filing cabinet. "I'll take care of it."

Gaines shuddered as he took a sip. Top Richardson was famous for his coffee. When the mechanics ran out of degreaser, they came to him for a refill. Gaines took his coffee into his office and sat down. He looked at his desk with a puzzled expression on his face. The top of it was clean, for a change.

"Top," he called out. "Can you come in here for a minute?"

"Yes, sir."

"Close the door behind you," Gaines said when the first sergeant entered the room. "And have a seat." He waited until Richardson had sat. "Top, who's been taking care of my paper work?" Gaines's voice was cold.

"Well, sir, me and the clerks have been trying to see that things get out in time."

"Who's been signing my name?"

"Bunting has, sir." Top locked eyes with Gaines. "On my okay."

Gaines took another drink of the rancid coffee and shuddered. "Top, you and I have gotten along pretty well, I think."

"Yes, sir, I think we have."

"Then why are you doing this to me?"

"Doing what, sir?"

"Dammit, you know that I'm trying to get the fuck out of this place."

"Yes, sir, I've heard that." The disapproval was thick in the old NCO's voice.

Gaines sighed and leaned back in his chair. "Okay, Top, tell me about it."

The first sergeant looked down at his spit-shined boots for a moment. This was hard for him to do, but he felt that it had to be said.

"Well, Captain," he began. "As you know, I've been in this man's army for twenty-five years now. I've seen a lot of young officers come and go in my time. Most of them have been good men, but even good men sometimes have their difficulties. In your case, sir, my job is to see that your work gets done and sent out on time."

Gaines sat silently for a long moment. "Top, I appreciate that, I really do. But I don't think that you understand."

The first sergeant broke in. "I think I understand perfectly, sir. You lost your lady and you don't know how to deal with it."

Gaines bit off an angry retort. Jesus Christ, he thought, am I that transparent to everyone in the battalion?

"That's part of it," he admitted. "But I'm also very tired, Top. I need a break from this shit for a while."

"But what about the men in the company, Captain?" Richardson said evenly, his eyes locked on Gaines. "Who's going to give them a break?"

"Goddammit, Top, don't do that to me. I don't need that shit right now."

"I think you do, sir."

Gaines didn't know how to answer that. It was the inevitable issue of command responsibility. The troops always come first. This was the thing that made the American army different from any other army that had ever existed. In the American army, the troops were supposed to come first. It didn't always work that way in practice, but it was supposed to.

"Top . . ."

Richardson got to this feet. "If you'll excuse me, sir, I've got to get back to work."

Gaines watched his First Sergeant walk out. That's the best ass-chewing I've ever gotten, he thought. Now what am I going to do?

Warlokk's Cobra gunship and Gabe's slick flew along the normal flight path that was used for the daily resupply flights to Khe Sanh. Anyone seeing them fly over would think that they were just two more of the dozens of choppers that went in and out each day.

As soon as they had crossed into the area of the Blues' aborted recon mission, Warlokk made a sudden dive for the ground. Gabe nosed his slick over and followed him down. The gunship made a fast pass over a small opening in the jungle, and Warlokk racked his Cobra into a hard-banked orbit right above it. Gabe slid in under him for a hot landing.

"LZ coming up!" he called to the grunts.

Before Gabe had even flared out, Alexander and the rest of the men had shouldered their rucksacks, flicked their weapon's safeties off, and were standing out on the skids. The pilot touched down and they leaped off, running bent over to clear the rotor blades.

With a quick glance over his shoulder to make sure that everyone had unassed the bird, Gabe pulled pitch and the slick rose back up into the air. They had been on the ground for such a short time that no one could have known that he had dropped the men off unless they had been watching from the edge of the small clearing.

As soon as his skids had cleared the treetops, Gabe

swung the slick around and followed Warlokk's Cobra as it climbed back up into the sky. In seconds the two choppers were back at cruising altitude, heading for Khe Sanh again, just one more resupply flight out of dozens that went in and out every day.

Alexander slowly stood up and looked around the small clearing. It looked clear. Now they were really on their own. The platoon leader caught Two-Step's eyes and nodded his head. Without a word, the Indian grunt took up the point position and moved into the nearby tree line. Alexander and the other men followed.

From a hilltop two klicks away, NVA Captain Xuan watched the slick rise back up into the air and rejoin the Cobra gunship. The troop ship had only been on the ground for sixty seconds, but even a minute was more than enough time for it to have off-loaded another recon team. He had lost sight of the helicopter when it had landed in the small clearing, but in his gut, he knew.

He quickly checked his map before calling for his radio operator and vectoring his tracking teams into the landing zone. This time he had them.

CHAPTER 31

West of Khe Sanh

Alexander wanted to move fast for the first day, so he and Two-Step swapped off walking the point position every hour or so. Alexander was taking his turn leading the patrol again when he reached a broad stream. After carefully checking out both sides, he pulled back into the brush along the near bank. Two-Step, who had been walking in the slack position right behind the point, dropped down beside him.

"What is it?" he asked quietly.

Alexander studied the stream for a moment before turning to the Indian. "It may sound crazy, but I've got a nasty feeling that we're being tracked."

Two-Step didn't think it sounded crazy, not in the least. For one thing it made perfectly good sense. And secondly, he took hunches seriously, both his own or anyone else's.

"What do you want to do?" he asked.

"I want to try to lose them by going down the stream," Alexander smiled broadly. "Get the rest of the guys up here quick."

When the men had assembled, Alexander quickly told them his plan. Everyone had big grins on their faces as they put the Lieutenant's little plan into operation.

"Comrade Captain," the North Vietnamese scout said fearfully. "The Yankees have vanished."

"What do you mean 'vanished'?" Xuan snapped. "Men don't just vanish, you fool. Find out where they have gone!"

"But, Comrade, the tracks on the trail disappear one by one, until they are all gone and the trail is bare again."

"Show me."

The scout was right. The muddy banks of the slow-moving stream clearly showed where six or seven men had crossed over and climbed out on the opposite side. But as their boot prints led deeper into the jungle on the other side, they became fewer and fewer until they had completely disappeared.

Xuan frowned. He did not believe in demons. This had to be some kind of Yankee imperialist trick. "Fan out," he shouted. "Look for more signs."

The men frantically searched the jungle on both sides of the stream for a hundred meters from the crossing point, but they could not find a thing. Angry, Xuan sent them ever farther afield. The Yankees had to be found.

While Captain Xuan waited impatiently for his men to discover a new trail, he bent down over the muddy boot prints and carefully examined them. One of the prints showed a double image, as if the boot had stepped down twice in the same place. At first he thought that one man had merely stepped into the tracks of another man, but then he noticed that the boot that had made this print had a notch cut into the heel. The same notch showed in both impressions.

Puzzled, the NVA officer examined another one of the prints. It, too, showed a faint double impression. Suddenly it struck him. The Yankees had crossed the stream, walked into the jungle, and backed out, carefully stepping in their own boot prints. They hadn't disappeared, they had simply moved back into the stream to break their trail.

Xuan admired the clever ploy, but it had cost him valuable time. He called for his men to reassemble. If the Americans knew they were tracking them, and it certainly looked like they did, his men were going to have to be more cautious. But he could not let caution keep him from pursuing the Yankees as quickly as he could. Colonel Tran would not view caution as a good excuse if the enemy got away.

Alexander remained up on point as they cautiously moved down the stream. In most places the muddy water was no more than waist-deep, but there were hidden sinkholes on the bottom that threatened to drown a man if he wasn't careful.

Bunny was in a state of absolute terror. He couldn't swim and hated water. Anything more than a bathtub full sent him into a blind panic. He watched the brown water curling against his thighs, almost holding his breath and waiting to step into a hole. He fought down the urge to run for the bank. His foot slipped on an unseen rock. Off-balanced by the weight of the heavy radio on his back, he started to fall. A strong hand grabbed his radio harness and jerked him back onto his feet.

He looked back to see a grinning Sergeant Zack holding a finger to his lips in a "be quiet" signal. Bunny shivered and continued on his way, being very careful where he placed his feet.

About half a klick farther downstream, the banks rose until they were well above the heads of the men. Alexander halted the patrol and checked out the jungle along both sides. This was going to be real tricky. With the level of the ground up over their heads blocking their line of sight, they could not keep an eye on the jungle as they advanced. If there were dinks lying in ambush for them, they would be trapped, with no place to run.

Signaling Two-Step to stay well back, Alexander started out, moving slowly down through the cut banks. Holding his M-16 at the port-arms position, he scanned the high jungle on each side with every step, being careful to move slowly so as not to make splashing sounds.

Two-Step let the lieutenant get fifty feet ahead before he started after him. Following the stream was one hell of a good idea, but if it backfired on them, they would all die in the water. It would be like shooting ducks in a pond.

The water level was higher in the cut, and Bunny fought back a rising tide of fear as it rose well past his waist, almost to his chest. If he stumbled, he'd drown for sure. Zack reached forward and laid his hand on the grunt's shoulder. Bunny felt his panic subside. If he went down, the Black Buddha would save him.

When Alexander saw the banks slope down to the surface of the stream, he breathed easier. Suddenly a crash in the tree above his head froze his blood. Fired by adrenaline, his heart racing, Alexander spun around, frantically trying to bring his rifle up in time. His feet slipped in the mud and he went down to his knees at the same time that the butt of the M-16 came to his shoulder. His finger tightened around the trigger when he saw the face of an inquisitive monkey poke through the foliage. Another monkey dropped down through the tree limbs, curious as to what these humans were doing walking though the water like a bunch of idiots.

Right behind Alexander, Two-step choked off a laugh. The soaked lieutenant got back up to his feet. This was good training. At least the ell tee had quick reflexes.

After traveling a little over two klicks farther down the stream, Alexander came upon a rocky outcropping. This was exactly what he had been looking for.

"Here!" he hissed, motioning for the men to climb out over the rocks. As soon as the sun dried the wet boot prints on the outcropping, there would be no sign at all of having passed that way. Once more, to all appearances, they would have vanished.

Before they moved out, however, the men quickly checked each other over for leeches. Even though the bottoms of their jungle fatigue pants were tied tightly around their ankles, several of the bloodsuckers had managed to get past one way or the other.

"Get that thing off me!" Bunny said in disgust, looking at the thumb-think, blood-gorged leech fastened on his thigh.

"Just be glad it isn't on your balls," Brody laughed. He squirted a small spray of Army-issue insect repellent on the animal. "That really smarts."

The bug juice caused the leech to release its grip and drop off his leg. Bunny started to grind it into the rock under his boot.

"No," Brody kicked his foot away. "The dinks might find it."

The RTO kicked the slimy thing back into the water instead. Then he shuddered.

When the leech check was finished, they faded into the jungle, with Two-Step back up on point. They moved to the west as fast as they could. The terrain was starting to get more difficult as they approached the ring of hills around Khe Sanh—the hills that were hiding five well-dug-in NVA divisions.

The men pressed on until midday, when they reached the top of a ridge a little over three klicks from Route 9. They had been humping the brush without a break for almost four hours. Alexander called an hour's halt to eat and rest up. He wanted his people rested when they moved out again. As close as they were to the heavily defended area around the highway, he wanted everyone on their toes. This was no place for people who were half-dead on their feet.

At the halt, Zack wearily shrugged his ruck off and sat down with his back to a tree trunk. Taking the sweat rag from around his neck, he mopped his face and shaven head. Damn! he thought. I'm getting too old for this shit. Trying to keep up with these fucking kids is breaking my old RA ass.

"Hi, Sarge," Farmer said as he plopped down beside him.

This was a good example of what Zack had been thinking about; a nineteen-year-old kid in perfect physical condition. He was hardly even sweating.

"You think we're going to get in contact today?" Farmer asked.

Zack uncapped his canteen and took a long drink. "Jesus, I sure as hell hope not."

Farmer looked real disappointed. So far the day had been a complete bust as far as he was concerned. "But we're going to be right into the middle of them, aren't we?" he asked hopefully.

Zack gave him a long look. "We're on a recon. We can't afford to get in no pissing contest. There just ain't enough of us for shit like that."

Farmer smiled, but his eyes held a strange look. "We'll do okay if we run into any dinks, Sarge. We always do."

Zack made a note to himself to talk to Brody about this troop when they got back to the camp. He had been acting just a little too gung ho lately. Enthusiasm was a good trait, particularly for a grunt in the Blues, but it looked like Farmer was taking his work a little too seriously.

"We're here to look, goddammit, not fight. Remember that."

Farmer smiled that strange smile again. "I will, Sarge, I will."

NVA Captain Xuan was almost beside himself with rage. Even though his men had searched both sides of the stream bank for almost two kilometers downstream, they had not been able to find a new set of tracks for the Yankee recon team.

After threatening his sergeant with a distinctly unpleasant death if he didn't find them, Xuan calmed down a little bit. He realized that he was up against a well-trained team, probably Green Berets again, and that he was going to have to outsmart them.

He took out his map and traced the route that the Americans had taken before they had "disappeared" in the

234

stream. If they continued traveling in the same general direction, they had to be headed for the fortified positions along Route 9. The route they were taking, however, took them up and down a series of small hills and ridgelines. The long way to their objective.

Referring to his map again, he checked his current location and saw that if he swung out to the north, there was a long valley he could take that terminated right next to the NVA defensive ring. If they hurried, they should be able to arrive there before the Yankees did. Then he could move his men into blocking positions in front of the enemy.

He smiled to himself. That made much more sense than stumbling around out in the jungle looking for vanishing boot prints.

"Van!" he yelled for his senior sergeant. "Get the men. We move out now!"

Alexander and Zack lay in a clump of brush fifty feet down from the crest of a ridge overlooking Route 9. The narrow mountain road snaked through a pass between their ridge and a big hill on the other side. This was what they had come for. The hill opposite them was crawling with North Vietnamese troops.

As he watched through the field glasses, Alexander saw antiaircraft guns being dug in and camouflaged. He saw other troops digging trenches and firing pits for heavy mortars. From just the troops that he could see on this one side of the hilltop, it looked to him that at least a battalion was ringing it.

What amazed him the most was that they were working out in the open in heavily overcast daylight. This high in the mountains, thick clouds were building effectively, preventing aerial surveillance by high-flying aircraft. The antiaircraft guns could more than deal with any low-flying choppers that blundered into the area.

Alexander lowered the glasses and made a few notations

on the acetate covering of his map. "It looks like we hit the jackpot, Sergeant."

Zack shook his head in disbelief. "You know, sir, in the two years I've been here, I've never seen anything like that. This is a once-in-a-lifetime shot to take out an entire battalion."

"If I can get an Arc Light strike out of the blue-suiters," Alexander said. "That's the key to this thing; seven-fifties, and lots of 'em."

He quickly folded the map and stuffed it back in his pocket. "Let's get back to the radio and call this in."

The two men carefully crawled back down to the hidden position where Alexander had left the rest of the team. Two-Step picked them up coming through the brush and waved them in.

"What'd you find?" he asked when he saw the grin on Alexander's face.

The lieutenant reached for the handset. "Just an entire battalion clusterfucked right out in the open."

CHAPTER 32

West of Khe Sanh

Alexander finished his call to Hillsboro Control, the flying Tac Air controller high in the sky over Khe Sanh, and handed the microphone back to Bunny.

"Okay, guys," he said. "Listen up, here's the plan. The Air Force just happens to have a flight of B-52's that they can divert to our target."

Brody whistled softly. "That's going to bring some serious smoke down on their asses."

Alexander grinned broadly. "You got that shit right, Brody. Anyway, we're going to hang around 'til they get here."

"How long is that going to be?" Zack asked with a frown.

"Three hours."

"That's a long time to stay in one place." The veteran NCO looked worried. "This fucking place is crawling with dinks."

"I know, Sarge, but this is too good a target and they have to do a fix on our radio transmission for their bombing computers."

"Okay, I'll get the men into position."

The long wait got on everyone's nerves, but they knew that it was worthwhile. Finally, after what seemed like days, a thin voice came in over the radio speaker.

"Blue Six, this is Big Thunder Two Niner on your frequency. How do you hear me? Over."

Alexander snatched the microphone out of Bunny's hand. "Big Thunder, this is Blue Six. I read you five by five. How me? Over."

"This is Thunder Two Niner. I've got you weak but steady. Can you give me a long count? Over."

"This is Six, Roger. Long count follows. One, two, three, four, five . . ." Alexander slowly counted to ten, then back down to one. "Long count finished. How copy? Over."

"This is Thunder Two Niner. I have a good fix on your location. Give me an azimuth to your target. Over."

"This is Six, azimuth is three three niner degrees. Over."

"This is Thunder, Roger three three niner. Our Echo Tango Alpha is two eight minutes. First bomb on target will be three one. How copy? Over."

"This is Blue Six, we'll be here. Anything further? Over."

"This is Big Thunder Two Niner, negative. Just keep your heads down. Out."

The men knew that the bombs were coming, but it was still a shock when the first blossom of dark gray smoke, shot through with angry red flames, burst into life on the hilltop. It took a couple of seconds for the sound of the explosion to reach them. Before it did, another bomb had hit, and then another.

The air was rent with a long, loud rumble as explosion followed explosion, and the ground shook with the concussion. It was like being in the middle of an earthquake.

"Sweet suffering Jesus," Lindberry said in awe. He had never seen anything like it.

Farmer's face wore the intense, twisted smile that he always had when he thought of killing dinks.

238

Unlike a single bomb blast that fades quickly, the ground continued to shake as bomb after bomb hit directly on the target. Within seconds, the hilltop was obscured in smoke, but the explosions continued. Two-Step and Alexander held their hands over their ears to block the sound of the blasts, but they felt the shock through their bodies. When the roar finally ended, a thick pall of smoke and dust hung over the hilltop, hiding the damage caused by the Arc Light strike.

"Jesus," Lindberry said. "I'm sure glad the dinks don't have B-52's."

"You got that shit right," Corky said, shaking his head. "Man, can you imagine all that shit coming down on you?"

"Okay, boys and girls," Zack growled. "The show's over. We got to get our asses outta here ASAP. Charlie has to know that somebody called that in on him, and he's going to be pissed."

Brody laughed. "Better them than me."

"Fuck 'em," Farmer spat.

Captain Xuan cursed the night. His scouts had lost the trail of the Yankee recon team again in the dark. Whoever they were, they were good at covering their trail. He had no choice now but to stop and make camp until first light. At dawn, they would move out again and try once more to pick up the trail.

As Xuan gave orders for his exhausted troops to halt for the night, he was confident that he would catch up with the Yankees in the morning. The only thing that bothered him was that they seemed to moving directly for the defenses the division was preparing along Route 9, south of Khe Sanh.

Several North Vietnamese battalions were moving into that area to take up the positions that had been prepared. If the Yankees caught them on the move and reported their locations, they could call the dreaded B-52's down on them. Xuan had to catch up with the Yankees in the morning and eliminate them once and for all. If he didn't, Tran would have his head on a pole in front of the division headquarters.

The North Vietnamese officer called for his radio operator. As much as he hated to do it, he had to report to Tran that they were halted until morning.

Lieutenant Colonel Nguyen Van Tran cursed when he read the transcription of the radio message from Captain Xuan. Xuan was a good man, but he and his men were badly overextended.

The recon team he had been tracking had to be the one that called the air strike down on the hilltop position of his 26th Regiment. That air strike had cost them dearly. Over half of the regiment had been either killed or wounded. And their carefully dug positions had been smashed to smoking rubble.

Tran took the B-52 air strike as a personal affront. He had personally ordered the regiment to work out in the open, counting on the overcast skies to hide them from the high-flying Yankee spy planes. It had been a risk, but he never thought that they would be spotted by a ground recon team. Till then, he'd had no reports of any Yankees operating in that area.

Now Tran was angry. He wanted those men tracked down and killed. But, as with all too many things lately, the NVA officer knew that if he wanted this operation done properly, he was going to have to take personal charge of it. He called for his orderly.

"Yes, Comrade Colonel?"

"Get my field equipment and three days' rations ready immediately. I will be joining Captain Xuan's company tonight."

"At once, Comrade Colonel."

"Also, get me a radio operator and tell the duty courier to be ready to lead me to Xuan's camp."

"Yes, sir."

Tran grabbed a copy of the map that recorded the areas

where he had ordered the booby traps emplaced, folded it tightly, and put it in his pocket. Maybe he and Xuan could maneuver the Yankees into the booby traps. Then they would be taken care of.

Tran smiled a thin, tight smile. Well-positioned booby traps could be worth an entire company of infantry to him if he could steer the Yankees that way.

Alexander called a halt for the night before it was too dark to move under good cover. After leaving the site of the Arc Light strike, they had taken to the jungle to put as many klicks between them and that hill as they could.

The men were exhausted as they made themselves comfortable for the night. Zack was too tired to even pour water into a Lurp ration for dinner. He was going to have to think seriously about getting a job doing something other than running around in the woods. This was strictly a kid's game and he finally admitted that he was getting too old for it anymore. Maybe he could get a job in the S-3 shop as an operations NCO. He hated paper work, but this was breaking his ass.

Farmer, though young, was also tired, but that did not put a damper on his appetite. In fact, he had the best appetite he had had in days. There was something about seeing all those dinks getting blown to smithereens that made him very hungry.

He ripped the tops off two Lurp ration bags and poured water into them. Before they had even had a chance to rehydrate, he was digging into them, stuffing the food in his mouth.

Lance Warlokk was furious. The last batch of choppers that were to have been turned over had not passed the maintenance inspection.

"Goddamnit, sir," he said to Walt Greenfield. "We've been busting our butts working off the deficiencies on those fucking things."

"I know your men have been working hard, Mr. Warlokk," Greenfield said patiently. "But the fact remains that the dash-thirteens are not up to date, and I cannot take them until they are."

Warlokk was short-tempered, but he was also smart enough to know that if he pissed the maintenance officer off any more, they would probably never get those goddamned helicopters though the inspection.

"Okay, sir," he said wearily. "We'll get back on them in the morning."

"And, Warlokk?"

"Sir?"

"Make sure that your people log the maintenance in properly."

"Yes, sir," Warlokk sighed. Those fucking logbooks were going to be the death of him yet.

Lance got back into his jeep and started off across the tarmac to Python Operations. He could tell that it was going to be another long night. He cursed Rat Gaines. He was the officer responsible for the turnover, and he wasn't doing anything.

Warlokk had finally lost all sympathy for his commander. He had tried his best to help him through Lisa's death, but it had not helped that he could see. The next time he saw Gaines he decided he was going to punch him right in the fucking mouth. Maybe that would help instead.

He pulled the jeep into the parking space in front of Python Operations and reached down to shut it off. Cursing violently under his breath, he changed his mind. He hammered the gearshift into reverse and slammed down on the gas pedal. That fucking paper work would still be there when he went to work tomorrow morning. He needed a drink tonight.

There were a few people in the battalion club when he walked in. He got a bourbon and branch water and took it over to a table in the far corner of the room. Some young WO-1 pilot walked over to the juke box and started to drop in a dime. Warlokk got up and, reaching past him, jerked the plug out of the wall.

"The fucking thing's busted," he growled.

The younger man took one look at Warlokk's scarred

face and walked away without saying a word. He thought of himself as a hot-rock pilot, but he didn't feel like tangling with someone who was obviously seriously pissed off. There were easier ways to get his head busted.

Warlokk was well into his second drink when Walt Greenfield came up and sat down at his table. "Let me buy you a drink," Walt said.

"Sure." Warlokk looked up. "Bourbon and branch water."

Warlokk liked Walt and didn't hold it against him that the paper work was overwhelming him. Walt hadn't invented the damned system. He was as much a victim of it as anyone else.

Walt returned with two glasses in his hands. "When do you think that your glorious leader is going to get his head out of his ass and come back to work?"

Warlokk shook his head. "Fucked if I know. Jesus, I don't know how he has put up with this level of shit for so long. If I was him, I would have bugged out a long time before this."

Walt laughed. "That's why they pay us commissioned officers more than they do you warrants. It's supposed to make up for the pain and suffering of command."

Warlokk snorted. "Man, you couldn't pay me to put up with that shit. I'm supposed to be a fucking airplane driver, not a goddamned paper pusher."

"That's all that Rat wants to be," Walt said. "Just an airplane driver."

"Smart man."

"By the way," Walt said. "The Cobras for your heavy-gun team have been diverted. That's the bad news. The good news is that you can hold off on working off all the deficiencies on the Hogs for a while."

"Thank God," Warlokk suddenly crowed, raising his glass. "This calls for another drink."

CHAPTER 33

West of Khe Sanh

Sergeant Zack woke the men for the stand-to-arms before the sun had even risen over the hills. They quickly gulped down a cold breakfast while Alexander did a map reconnaissance of the area he wanted to cover, another hilltop overlooking Route 9.

The B-52 strike yesterday had been such a success that he wanted to find another target for the high-flying bombers today. If they moved in closer toward Khe Sanh, they would undoubtedly run across more troop concentrations.

"What do you think, Sarge?" he asked Zack.

The black NCO quickly looked over the map. "Sounds good to me, sir," he said. "The only thing, though, is there a PZ in that area?"

Alexander checked his notes from the mission briefing. "It looks like we could make it to Papa Zulu Two Niner, if the shit hits the fan."

Zack checked Pickup Zone 29. It was halfway between where they were and the hill that the Alexander wanted to take a look at. "It looks good to me."

"Okay, Sarge, let's get them moving."

* * *

NVA Lieutenant Colonel Tran drank hot tea from an enameled tin cup while he took radio reports from his tracking teams. He now had three companies in the field looking for the Americans. He had moved them into position last night. At first light, they had started searching the area he had chosen. He was taking a gamble by concentrating all of his efforts in this one area, but something told him that this was where the Yankees were operating.

After that successful air attack yesterday, Tran felt that they would have pressed on to get even closer to Khe Sanh, scouting out more of the NVA defenses to attack them as well. That was where he was counting on them to be, between the area of the air strike and the inner ring of positions overlooking Route 9. If his hunch was right, he had them.

He finished his tea and checked his map one last time before calling for his sergeant. It was time to close the noose around the Yankees. If any of them could be captured, he would put nooses around their necks and slowly strangle them.

By the time the sergeant got his men assembled, Tran had received a report from one of the tracking teams. They had found signs of a small group of men moving directly toward their present positions. Tran quickly vectored his units. His hunch had paid off.

"Quickly," he shouted to the sergeant. "We move out now!"

Two-Step crouched down low in the clump of bushes and watched a platoon-size North Vietnamese patrol heading straight for them. The black and green stripes of his tiger suit and the green and tan splotches of his face paint made him almost invisible against the leaves. He was well hidden, but it wasn't going to help much this time. He had fucked up.

245

Because of the tangled thickness of the jungle they were traveling through, he hadn't spotted the NVA patrol moving their way until it was far too late to evade them. Now all they could do was fight their way out. There was just too great a chance that the dinks would hear or see them if they attempted to cut and run for it.

The enemy was so close that they had not even had a chance to put out any of their claymore mines to even up the odds a little. They would have to fight this battle with their small arms and grenades.

The other men were spread out behind him in a classic L-shaped ambush, their fingers poised on their triggers and their grenades close at hand. They were outnumbered by at least two to one, and the only way they were going to get out of this in one piece was to achieve complete surprise.

At the Indian's side, Brody focused the sights of his M-16 on the last man in line. Since he was the best shot in the squad, he would try to take out the men farther back in the rear of the formation, while the others took care of the point element. His first shot would be the signal for the rest of the men to open up on them.

He set his sights high on the man's chest and then waited until the point man was well within the killing zone. He took a deep breath and tightened his finger around the trigger.

The rifle spat.

At the rear of the enemy patrol, the North Vietnamese soldier went over his back. Brody shifted his point of aim and fired again.

The jungle erupted with gunfire as everyone opened up at almost the same time. Three of the enemy went down in the first burst, but the other dinks dove for cover and immediately returned a heavy volume of fire.

Two-Step's sawed-off shotgun roared again and again as he whipped the slide back and forth until the weapon was empty. The stainless-steel balls shredded the foliage and tore into the men hiding behind the underbrush.

He dropped down under cover and frantically stuffed

shotgun shells into the tubular magazine under the barrel. AK fire tore into the tree, shredding the bark and sending splinters flying. Racking the slide back to chamber a round, the Indian popped back up and emptied the gun into them again.

From the short end of the L, Farmer fired his grenade launcher almost point blank into the brush in front of him, hoping that the rounds would travel far enough to arm themselves. With the forest's canopy hanging over them, he could not arch his deadly little 40 mike-mike grenades up into the air as he usually did. They would hit the tree branches and explode.

The first round exploded, but the second one didn't. He didn't even try it a third time. Dropping the seventy-nine, he reached around behind his back and swung his sixteen around.

He triggered off a quick burst as a gook stuck his head up to throw a Chi-Com stick grenade. The 5.56 rounds caught the Vietnamese in the chest as the grenade left his hand.

"Grenade!" Farmer yelled, throwing himself to the ground.

Under the adrenaline rush, Farmer's personal time went into slow motion. It seemed to take forever for the Chinese grenade to land. He could see it tumbling over and over in the air, looking like a soup can stuck on the end of a short piece of broomstick. He knew that the black powder fuse train was sputtering, he could almost see the faint trail of smoke it left in the air. He threw his arms up over his head.

With a dull crump, the Chi-Com stick bomb exploded. A heavy piece of frag slammed into his back, momentarily stunning him. He rolled off to the side and came up firing, his sixteen blazing in his hands.

In the middle of the long arm of the L, Zack took his time and placed well-aimed shots into anything that he saw moving. Arms, heads, legs; it didn't matter. If it moved, he put a bullet in it.

After two well-aimed single shots, Brody switched over

to rock and roll. He emptied his modified AK magazine in a long burst of automatic fire and ducked back down to reload. He dropped the empty magazine out of the bottom of his rifle, slapped a loaded seventeen-round magazine in its place, and pulled back on the charging handle to chamber a round.

An AK bullet slapped into the tree by his head, throwing wood splinters into his face. He snatched a grenade from his ammo pouch, pulled the pin, and tossed the hand frag out in front of him.

The instant that it exploded, he jumped out and sprayed a full magazine load of 5.56mm into the killing zone. When the bolt locked to the rear on an empty magazine, he dropped back down again. More AK fire followed him. He rolled to the right just as a round tore into the ground where he had been lying. It was beginning to look like they just might have bitten off a little more than they could chew this time around.

The hollow crump of a Chi-Com grenade and the shower of dirt and debris from the explosion spurred Brody into new action. He snatched another hand grenade from his pouch, pulled the pin, and, holding it in his left hand, stuck the muzzle of his rifle around the edge of the tree. He triggered off half of the magazine in one long burst, tossed the grenade as far as he could, and ripped off the rest of the magazine. The explosion was followed by a high-pitched scream.

He dropped the empty magazine and reloaded before he crawled off to the side to take up a new position behind a fallen log. He peered around the end of it and saw a man's leg through a break in the dense foliage. A leg wearing an olive NVA uniform.

He thumped the selector switch on his rifle back down to the semi-auto position and, taking careful aim, put a bullet in the leg.

The dink screamed when the 5.56mm round went through his thigh. He rolled over, twisting around to duck back under cover.

248

Brody flicked the switch back down to rock and roll and sent a short three-round burst after him, but he had disappeared.

The firing was still intense. Over the chatter of Corky's smoking M-60 machine gun, Brody heard the coughing roar of Two-Step's sawed-off shotgun going off again and again. It sounded like he might have a little more business than he could handle by himself.

Keeping low, Brody dodged through the brush toward the sound of the Indian's gun. He parted the leaves in front of him and almost ran into an NVA trying to make his way around on Two-Step's flank. Brody's boot stepped on a fallen tree branch and it broke with a snap. The dink spun around at the noise and saw him at the same time. It was a race to see who could get down on the trigger first.

Brody won.

His long burst tore into the middle of the NVA. Some of the rounds hit the AK, knocking it out of his hands. The man gave a short grunt and went down to his knees, his belly shot open. Brody put another quick burst into his head and moved on.

By the time he reached Two-Step's side, the Indian was standing alone. Four NVA bodies lay sprawled in front of him, victims of his deadly shotgun.

Two-Step reloaded and the two grunts moved back to rejoin the others at the ambush site. They had just crawled up into position on each side of Corky, when the Chicano's smoking pig fell silent.

Suddenly the jungle was quiet.

After a few seconds, Alexander cautiously stepped out from his position, his weapon at the ready and his finger on the trigger. He looked both up and down the trail, but there was no movement anywhere in the killing zone. Their ambush had been totally successful.

The lieutenant silently waved the men forward to check the kill zone. The grunts went from one dead North Vietnamese soldier to the next, making sure that they were dead and then searching the bodies for documents.

249

Alexander found the enemy radio man and was pleased that his radio had been destroyed. He vaguely remembered seeing the man go down in the initial burst of fire. The bad news was that the RTO had the radio handset in his hands, as if he had been transmitting when he had been killed. If he had been making a call to their headquarters, the dinks on the other end of the call would have been able to hear the gunfire. There was nothing to be done for it now, except to get the hell out of the area as fast as they could.

"Brody," Farmer called out softly, kneeling on the ground beside a tree, his rifle aimed at one of the NVA. "This motherfucker's still alive."

Brody walked over and saw an older North Vietnamese soldier lying on his back with a bullet wound in one of his legs. His hair was cut short, he looked well fed, and, like the rest of them, his uniform was fairly new. He was an NVA regular, not Viet Cong. There was fear in the man's dark eyes, and he held his hands clasped in front of him in a plea for mercy.

"Kill 'im." Brody said, drawing a finger across his throat. There was no way that they were going to take prisoners on this mission. They sure as hell couldn't call for a Dustoff to evacuate him. That would bring every dink in the area right down on top of them.

Farmer smiled as he pulled his K-Bar knife from the sheath tied to his boot top. The wounded man saw the knife and struggled to sit up.

"Wait," he said in fairly good English. "I am an officer. I have information."

From across the trail, Zack looked up and saw what was happening. "Farmer!" he shouted as the grunt reached for the NVA. "Wait!"

Reluctantly, Farmer lowered the knife, his disappointment evident. Zack walked up to the prisoner with a big smile on his face.

"Well, well," the black sergeant said. "If it isn't my old friend Major Tran. How the hell are you, you slope-headed sonofabitch?"

CHAPTER 34

West of Khe Sanh

Tran's eyes widened with shock when he saw Zack's shaved head. He recoiled, trying to push himself backward.

"Do you know this man, Sergeant Zack?" Alexander asked.

"Yes, sir," Zack said grimly. "I sure as hell do. A little less than a year ago, this slope-headed motherfucker kept me in a cage for a week and tried to beat me to death."

"Who is he?"

"I am the operations officer for the Three Hundred Twenty-fifth Division of the glorious People's Liberation Army," Tran answered.

The North Vietnamese officer knew that his only chance to stay alive was to impress this young Yankee officer with his importance. He also knew that the black sergeant wanted nothing more in the world than to slaughter him right where he lay.

Alexander studied the prisoner for a moment. "Bandage his leg," he ordered.

"Yes, sir," Zack answered reluctantly. "Strawberry, patch him up."

Lindberry knelt beside the NVA officer and took the field

251

dressing from the pouch on his field belt. This was the first time that he had seen one of the enemy alive and up close. And he was not impressed. To him, Colonel Tran looked no different than any of the other Vietnamese papa-sans who burned shit in the American basecamps or hauled the garbage away. He looked a little better fed and wore an NVA olive uniform, but that was about it.

Using a little more force than was really necessary, he tore open Tran's pant leg, exposing the wound. The round had gone clear through, tearing the muscle, but missing the bone. He hurriedly tied the dressing over the wound and backed away from him.

Even though the prisoner didn't look impressive, Lindberry didn't like the feel of Tran's eyes in him. There was something about the cold, hard look in them that raised the hair on the back of his neck. He shivered, but continued his work.

While Lindberry bandaged their prisoner, Alexander got on the horn back to the battalion. Since they were so far from Camp Evans, he had to retransmit through a communications relay that had been specially set up for the recon teams working in the Khe Sanh sector. After the usual delay while the call was retransmitted, he got through to Crazy Bull Three, the battalion operations officer.

"Blue Six, this is Crazy Bull Three," came the voice over the handset. "Do you have traffic for this station? Over."

"This is Blue Six, Roger," Alexander answered. "I am at zero seven three, two six one. I have a November Victor Alpha in custody who claims to be an Oscar Five. Over."

"This is Bull Six, say again rank, over."

"This is Six," Alexander replied, smiling at the astonishment in Three's voice. "Oscar Five as in Light Bird. Over."

"This is Three, good work. Get him to Papa Zulu Two Niner ASAP. I'll get the extract going. Over."

"This is Blue Six, wilco," Alexander said. "Anything further? Over."

"This is Bull Three, negative. Out."

While Alexander was getting his instructions, Farmer went back to searching the corpses, particularly the ones that he had personally killed. He knelt by the first one and, with a deft swipe of his razor-sharp knife, cut off the right ear and stuffed it in his pants pocket. He had made a good killing today. He was smiling broadly when he went over to the next body.

Two-Step had taken up the drag position at their rear, scanning the area behind them with the lieutenant's field glasses. With as much noise as they had made, if anyone had been within hearing range of the fierce firefight, they would be hotfooting it in their direction. Also, he had a nagging feeling that he had caught a glimpse of someone crawling away at the start of the ambush. He had been too busy killing people at the time to check it out, but if he was right, they had to be extra careful.

He checked out the sides of the ambush site and then turned to look back along their trail again. He caught a glimpse of movement and froze. It was just a flash of something lighter than the surrounding foliage, but that was enough.

"Ell tee!" he hissed, waving the grunts to take cover. "We got company."

The grunts instantly hit the dirt and fanned out to meet the new threat. Alexander slid in beside the Indian and took the field glasses from him. "Where?"

Two-Step pointed off to their left. "Coming down the side of the ridge."

Alexander focused the glasses. "Shit! Someone must have gotten away. We'd better get our asses outta here ASAP."

"What about him, sir?" Zack asked, jerking his thumb back to point at Tran.

"He's coming with us," Alexander said without hesitation. "The Three says he wants us to get him to the pickup zone ASAP so he can be interrogated. He's sending the slicks in to get us."

"You sure about taking him along, sir?"

"Sarge," Alexander admonished him. "You know bette[r] than that. That guy's a big shot in the NVA. He's got t[o] have one hell of a lot of information that we can sure use."

"Yes, sir." Zack's eyes blazed as he looked at his pla[toon] toon leader. "But if he causes me any trouble, I'm going t[o] waste his sorry ass."

"Only if he compromises the mission, Sergeant," Al[ex]exander said sternly.

Zack looked away. "Yes, sir."

The seven-man patrol started moving out as fast as the[y] could go. They did not have time to hide the bodies. The[y] could only move and move fast, hoping to outrun the sec[ond]ond enemy unit that was coming in behind them.

Back at Camp Evans, Python Operations exploded into ac[tion] tion when the call came from the S-3. Warlokk came storm[ing]ing out of the radio room at a dead run, yelling at the top[] of his lungs for the gunship pilots to follow him. He foun[d] Gabe already out on the flight line and told him to cran[k] up, too.

In seconds, the air was thick with the smell of burning[] JP-4 as the three Cobras of Warlokk's light gun team, the[] five Huey Hogs of the heavy team, and Gabe's slick fire[d] up their turbines. As soon as every rotor was turning, War[] lokk gave the word to taxi out onto the runway for takeoff.

As usual, the control tower people were more worrie[d] about procedure than they were about Alexander being ou[t] in the jungle with a bunch of dinks hot on his ass. Also[,] they did not know that Lance Warlokk was leading Pytho[n] Flight.

"Evans Control, this is Python Lead," he radioed. "Re[quest]quest permission to take off."

"Python, this is Control. The runway is closed at thi[s] time, we have traffic inbound. Over."

"Tower, this is Python Lead." Warlokk scanned the sk[y]

as he radioed back. "I have troops in contact. Request priority over other traffic. Over."

"This is Evans Control, that's a negative, Python. Inbound is Saber Six, do you roger? Over."

Without even bothering to waste his breath on an answer, Warlokk switched the radio over to talk to the other machines in his flight.

"Python, Python," he called to them. "This is Lead, pull pitch now."

As if they were being flown by one mind, the nine choppers of Python Flight raised their tails and started down the runway. The guy in the control tower went completely bug shit.

"Python, this is the tower," he screamed. "Abort! Abort!"

Warlokk wasn't even listening to him when he hauled up on the collective and lifted off the PSP.

"Damnit, Python, you have to do what I say! I'm the control tower."

Warlokk gave the tower a raspberry and banked away to the east and Khe Sanh.

Colonel Tran, his hands tied tightly behind him with someone's neck scarf, was directly in the middle of Alexander's group as they ran down the trail headed for the PZ. Zack was running right along beside him, hoping that Tran would make a run for it. He wanted an excuse to blow his sorry ass away. He was afraid, though, that the North Vietnamese colonel was much too smart to try anything as stupid as that.

Zack was pissed to the max. He knew for a fact that as soon as Tran went through interrogation by the military intelligence people of the Cav, he'd be turned over to the South Vietnamese authorities. That was like putting a fox in the henhouse. As soon as VC agents in the South Vietnamese army learned who he was, they'd spirit him out of whatever prisoner-of-war camp he was being held in. The bastard would be back on the job within two months at the very most.

Zack spat. It was going to happen that way just as sure as shit stank. It took everything that he had not to just waste the slope-headed sonofabitch right here.

Panting for breath, Tran smiled to himself as he ran. The Yankees were taking him straight into the area where Xuan was operating with his three platoons. All he had to do was to keep his wits about him and stay on the lookout for his troops.

As he ran, he twisted his hands, testing the strength of his bonds. The thin cloth tore at the skin of his wrists, but he didn't even notice it. The cloth gave way a little bit with each twist. He ignored the pain in his wrists and continued trying to free himself.

The Yankees edged out around a small clearing, and Tran saw the almost imperceptible NVA marking signs along the trail. They were deep inside Xuan's territory now and he had to be at maximum alert. He had to spot the ambush before the Yankees did.

Just a second later, Tran saw a flash of movement at the edge of the clearing. It was Xuan's men! He shoved Zack aside and dove for cover just as the ambush was sprung. In their haste, or because they had seen that Tran was with the Americans, the NVA had opened fire a little too soon. Had they waited another minute or two, they could have taken all the Yankees out in the first burst. As it was, Tran's bid for freedom startled the Americans, and they were halfway to the ground when the first shots rang out.

AK fire exploded overhead as Tran rolled to get as far away from Zack as he could. Frantically, he twisted his wrists against the cloth binding. Fear gave him strength. The sweat-rotted cloth ripped apart.

"Comrades!" he shouted as his hands tore free of his bonds. "It's me, Colonel Tran! I'm over here! Don't shoot me!"

The NVA officer leaped to his feet and ran crouched

over, zigzagging across the short distance to the edge of the jungle and safety.

"Tran! You motherfucker!"

Zack snapped his sixteen up and zeroed in on Tran's fleeing figure. A sudden burst of AK fire passed his head and he flinched as his finger closed on the trigger. The shots went wide.

Startled by the burst of fire, Tran dodged to the other side of the trail. In his headlong flight into the brush, his boot brushed against a trip wire set low to the ground.

Suddenly the foliage in front of him parted. Propelled by the tension of a thick green bamboo pole bent back to almost the breaking point, a two-foot square platform, studded with dozens of sharpened bamboo spikes, slashed forward at waist height. Tran's eyes barely had time to register the movement before the malay whip caught him in mid-stride.

This was one of the most deadly weapons in the NVA arsenal of jungle-warfare booby traps. Since it was made of bamboo, it was very difficult to detect against a backdrop of tangled jungle foliage. And the bamboo-pole spring might as well have been made of steel. It could snap the trap shut in less than a tenth of a second, faster than the eye could see.

The heavy-spiked head of the malay whip swept Tran off his feet and slammed him into the tree trunk that served as a back stop for the deadly booby trap. When the tree stopped him, the bamboo stakes on the head of the booby trap kept going. They tore through him, pinning him to the tree.

By the odd chance of fate, the fire-sharpened stakes missed the major blood vessels and arteries that would have ended Tran's life instantly. They also missed severing his spine, which would have also brought him instant oblivion. They tore through the muscles, guts, and minor nerves of his lower body, bringing him a pain like none he had ever known. Tran's high-pitched screams echoed over the roar of the weapons. They were the screams of a man's worst nightmare come true.

He tried to push himself away from the embrace of the booby trap, but that only brought even more pain. His screams turned to a high-pitched wail. Over the storm of small-arms fire, Tran's pain rang out true and clear. Zack shuddered at the sound and raised his sixteen.

Even a bastard like Tran deserved a cleaner death than that. Zack took careful aim and slowly squeezed the trigger.

Tran's scream broke off in mid-breath as the 5.56mm bullet smashed into his head, exploding the brain in his skull. He was dead before he even stopped screaming.

CHAPTER 35

West of Khe Sanh

Captain Xuan heard his colonel's screams cut off abruptly. The feared Tran was finally dead, but Xuan would see that his death was avenged. He had hated and feared the colonel, but Tran was one of these who had been the backbone of the glorious People's Revolution and he deserved to be avenged. The air was rent with three shrill blasts from an NVA whistle, the signal for the assault.

"Attack!" Xuan shouted. "Attack! Let none of them escape!"

Alexander and the men of Brody's squad readied their weapons as they braced themselves for the assault. They knew as well as the dinks what that whistle signal meant. Men were going to die there real soon, and it was probably going to be them.

Warlokk and Alphabet's Cobras had gotten well out ahead of the pack by the time they reached the area of Pickup Zone Two Niner. Warlokk banked sharply to the left to fly the last few klicks up the valley. He got on the horn to Alexander.

"Blue Six, Blue Six, this is Python Lead. Over."

"This is Six Tango, go," Bunny answered for Lieutenant Alexander.

"This is Lead. I am about five minutes away from your location, ready to roll in with two gun teams. What's your situation down there? Over."

"This is Six Tango," Bunny answered calmly. Just because he would be dead by the time the choppers got there was no reason to lose his cool. "Be advised that we are facing at least a full company of November Victor Alpha. They have us pinned down and we are in the process of being overrun right at this moment. Other than that, we're doing just fine and are running low on ammo. Over."

Warlokk chuckled. At last someone had a sense of humor. He hoped that whoever it was made it through this. "Roger copy, Six Tango. You just hang on down there. We're coming as fast as we can. Out."

Warlokk keyed his throat mike and called back to the slower heavy gun team. "Python Hogs, this is Lead. You'd better turn the wick up, boys, they're really hurting down there."

A few seconds later, Warlokk spotted the faint traces of gun smoke coming from the clearing in the distance.

"Six Tango," Warlokk called. "This is Lead, I think I have you spotted. Pop smoke. Over."

A few seconds later, a thick column of bright green smoke rose from the clearing.

"Tango, Lead. I have lime. Over."

"This is Six Tango. Roger green. Hurry up, please. Out."

With Warlokk leading the pack, the two Cobras dropped out of the sky like diving hawks.

"Three Seven," Warlokk called back to Alphabet, as the nose of his Cobra came around and lined up on the far edge of the clearing. "This is Lead. I'm rolling in now. Cover my ass."

"Roger."

"Okay, gunner, hose 'em down."

In the front cockpit of Warlokk's Cobra, the gunner's gloved fingers tightened on the triggers to his nose turret. Swinging it from side to side, he sprayed short bursts of 7.62mm minigun interspaced with a few thumper rounds. If anyone was hiding in there, they'd run for their lives or shoot back. Either way was okay with him.

This time, however, the dinks didn't feel like running. Fingers of glowing green AK-47 tracer fire reached up from the jungle, followed by the dirty black smoke trail of an RPG round.

"Break! Break!" Warlokk screamed into his throat mike as he threw the Cobra out of the line of fire. Those bastards were serious!

He kicked down on the right rudder pedal and slammed the cyclic over into the upper right-hand corner. The Cobra banked up onto her right side as the tail came around in a sharp turn.

Alexander saw the green AK and RPD tracer fire reach up for the lead Cobra as the pilot threw his machine to the side to get out of the way of the storm of fire. As he watched, the second Cobra sped up and bore in, her rocketpods and guns blazing.

A section of the tree line at least a hundred meters long suddenly erupted in smoke and flame. Rockets and 40mm shells tore into the trees. The explosions sent shredded limbs and pieces of tree trunks flying into the air.

In the front cockpit of Alphabet's ship, the gunner played his firing controls like a master. The turret swung from side to side, spraying 7.62mm rounds and 40-mike-mike grenades like a garden hose spraying water.

H.E. rockets shot out of the stub-wing pods in pairs as Alphabet brought his gunship in on a gentle curve over the edge of the trees. When he pulled out of his firing run, Warlokk was tucked in right behind him, ready to start his second run. Somebody had to keep these people busy until the Hogs could get there.

As Warlokk dropped down, he jinked his ship violently from side to side, frantically trying to find a clear path between the lines of fire. Somehow he emerged at the end of his run seemingly unscathed. Now it was Alphabet's turn again.

"Lead, this is the Hog Driver," came the call on Warlokk's chopper-to-chopper radio frequency. "We're on station now. Over."

"Roger, Hogs." Warlokk looked over his shoulder and saw the five-ship Huey Hog heavy fire team. They had finally caught up with the faster Cobras. "Go to work in the wood line to the east. Over."

"Hogs, Roger. Out."

While the Cobras pulled up and banked out of the way, the Hogs dropped down over the clearing. Flying parallel to the tree line, they started hammering on the rest of Xuan's company.

One of the Hog drivers saw the muzzle flash of an RPG rocket launcher and lined it up in his gunsight. Triggering his 2.75-inch rocketpods, he sent half a dozen H.E. rockets racing straight down for it. One of them detonated in the rocket ammunition stockpile, and it exploded with a blinding flash.

The concussion of the exploding RPG rounds rocked the Huey in the air as it flew over the launcher site.

Another Hog spotted Xuan's command group under the trees and opened up on them with everything he had. The rockets, 40mm grenades, and minigun rounds turned that little part of the jungle into a killing ground. When he flew past it, nothing was left but a smoking hole in the ground.

Xuan, however, was not killed. He had left his radio operator to take personal command of one of the machine guns.

When the Hogs had cleared the area, Warlokk brought his Cobra around in a hard bank over the small clearing. He was flat down on the deck doing well over a hundred miles an hour, spitting death into the tangled jungle below. His rockets slammed into the NVA positions. The explosions threw bloody body parts into the trees. A thick cloud

262

of smoke rose up into the sky. He pulled up and hauled his Cobra around to make another pass.

In one of the NVA machine-gun positions, a red-hot, jagged shard of steel sliced into the NVA machine gunner at Captain Xuan's side. Blood and tissue spattered him as the man died. They had almost had the Yankees, but there was no way that Xuan's men could stand up against the gunships.

Xuan was determined not to let the Yankees get away with this. They had killed Tran and had to be punished. He pulled the RPD machine gun out from under the gunner's body and checked to see that the magazine drum was full. He raced out into the open, carrying the gun. Propping the barrel up on a low-hanging limb, he waited until Alphabet swept down closer. He centered the diving Cobra in his sights, remembering to give the speeding machine plenty of lead as he squeezed the trigger.

"Yankee, you die!" he screamed as the RPD started its deadly chatter.

The stream of bright green 7.62mm tracer flashed past Alphabet's canopy.

"What the fuck!" Alphabet shouted as he stomped down on the rudder pedal, wrenching his ship out of the line of fire. He felt the Cobra take hits on the armor plating around the cockpit. The overworked turbine screamed as he frantically pulled maximum pitch and overrevved. He had to get out of there.

More tracer rounds flashed past. The Cobra shuddered and took more hits. Alphabet felt a vibration in the cyclic. The rotors were damaged.

He was frantically jinking the ship from side to side when, out of the corner of his eye, he saw another Cobra dive past him, her rotors a blur. Rockets lanced from the pods under her stub wings and the thumper in her nose turret belched flame into the jungle.

It was Warlokk!

In the front seat of Warlokk's gunship, the gunner played

his firing controls like a master, saturating the area that the tracers were coming from so that Alphabet could get away.

Xuan shifted the fire of his RPD to meet this new threat. Warlokk saw him lean out from behind his tree with the machine gun. Reflexively, he hit the commander's override and triggered off a salvo of 2.75's. One of the speeding rockets caught the North Vietnamese officer dead center in the chest.

When the flash of the explosion settled, there was no more Captain Xuan with an RPD machine gun, and there was no more tree, either.

With their commander dead, the surviving NVA didn't feel like dying anymore. Now that the gunships were on station and doing what they did best, turning dinks into carrion, the NVA infantry faltered under the intense, unrelenting fire. By ones and twos they started breaking away, fading back into the dense jungle as fast as they could run.

The grunts in the clearing didn't let up on the dinks, either. Rising up to their knees, they sent a barrage of fire into their backs. Everywhere the NVA turned, they were being slaughtered.

With a final pass, Warlokk climbed back up into a low orbit over the clearing while Alphabet took up his station beside him.

"How do I look, Lead?" Alphabet radioed over to Warlokk.

Lance checked the other chopper for damage. "Not too bad, but keep an eye on things 'til we get home, over." Warlokk searched the sky until he found Gabe's slick orbiting high over the battle site. "Three Eight, this is Lead, I think they're ready for a pickup. Over."

"Three Eight, Roger. Break. Blue Six, this is the old Gunslinger. Pop a smoke for me and I'll get you out of there. Over."

Bunny quickly rogered and tossed a smoke out into the clearing in front of them.

"This is Three Eight," came Gabe's return call. "I have banana. Over."

"This is Six Tango, Roger yellow. Out."

The grunts slowly got to their feet and waited for their ride home.

Leo Zack slumped back against the doorframe of the Huey. Once more he had been chased out of the woods, but this time he had a smile on his face. He really didn't mind leaving at all. It had been a worthwhile trip for him. He'd suffered from recurring nightmares after being imprisoned in Tran's cage. He would wake up, his heart pounding and covered with sweat. Tran's death had settled a very old score for him, and he was satisfied.

Corky was also happy to be on the slick headed home. He had only two weeks to go and with a little luck, the Blues would spend most of that time around Camp Evans waiting for something to happen.

One of the grunts on the slick was not pleased to be out of the woods. Farmer had only taken eight ears this trip, and he hadn't been able to harvest any from the last battle.

Alexander was pissed that Tran had died and now he would not be able to bring him back as his prisoner. It would have been a real coup to walk into headquarters with an NVA light colonel in tow. Nonetheless, he wasn't completely unhappy with the mission. They had walked in the valley of the shadow one more time and they had kicked ass.

He stuck his head out of the door as far as he could and let the rotor blast dry the sweat from his face. There was always the next time. And from what he had heard before they had left, the next one was going to be a real thrill. Khe Sanh.

It was too bad that once again the mission had been cut short, but at least this way, the men would get a chance to rest up for the big one. Also, it occurred to him that he could go into Sin City for dinner again and see if May Lin was around.

CHAPTER 36

Camp Evans

David Janson stepped off the chopper at the Python flight pad carrying his bulging duffel bag with him. He winced when he threw the heavy load up over his shoulder. The wound in his side was still not completely healed. The doctors in Da Nang had wanted him to stay in bed a few more days, but he had checked himself out of the Navy hospital. There was a big story coming up and he didn't want to miss out on it.

He walked into the Python operations shack and set the duffel bag on the floor by the doorway before continuing on into Gaines's office. He was surprised to find Lance Warlokk sitting behind Rat's desk, glumly facing a stack of paper work.

"Where's Rat?" the reported asked.

Warlokk looked up with a disgusted scowl on his face. "Fucked if I know," he snapped. "He's decided to quit on me."

Rat Gaines quit? Janson couldn't quite believe what he was hearing. That didn't sound anything like the Gaines he knew. He took a seat in the folding chair by the desk.

He had a puzzled expression on his face as he looked at

the pile of papers on the desk. "What the hell's been going on around here, anyway?"

Warlokk tossed his ball-point down and leaned back in his chair.

"Well, for one thing, Lisa Maddox got killed."

"Oh, Jesus, what happened?"

In terse sentences, Warlokk told the reporter about the artillery accident.

"Oh, my God," Janson said softly, shaking his head. "How's Gaines taking it?"

"I told you, the asshole quit on me."

Janson slowly coaxed the rest of the story out of the warrant officer-pilot.

"You don't have any idea where I might find him, do you?"

"Try the club. He's been hanging around there a lot the last couple of days."

"Thanks." Jordan stood to go.

"If you find him," Warlokk said, returning to his paper work, "tell him that things are going to hell in a handbag around here. And if he doesn't get his ass back here pretty soon, there's not going to be anything left for him to come back to."

"I'll tell him," Janson promised. "By the way, is there any way that I can get a ride over to battalion with my bags? I picked up a little frag last week."

Warlokk tossed him a key. "Take my jeep, Echo Three. I'm going to be here all fucking day."

"I'll get it right back to you."

"Do that."

Janson carried his bag out to the jeep and threw it in the passenger's seat. Starting the engine, he backed out of the parking lot and turned toward the club. As he drove, his mind weighed the pros and cons of writing a story about Lisa's death.

It was a good human-interest story with a tragic ending. The editors would love it. But the problem was that any editor who got the copy would twist the story around and make an antiwar piece out of it. So on second thought, he decided not to write it. He knew that Lisa wouldn't want her death made into something that could be used to blame the Army for negligence. And Rat wouldn't like to see his name in print that way.

The club was almost empty, for a change, and he spotted Gaines sitting alone. "Mind if I join you?" he asked as he walked up.

Gaines looked up. "Well, if it isn't the press! Have a seat."

Janson had never seen Gaines like this. The pilot looked like he had aged several years. His uniform was dirty and he was badly in need of a shave. There was little left of the famous Rat Gaines "go get 'em" attitude that he had grown to really admire. Janson was looking at a crushed man.

"I heard about Lisa," Janson started cautiously. "I don't know what to say."

Gaines took a deep drink. "There's not much to say. She's gone and I'm going."

"When are you leaving?"

"Fucked if I know," Gaines answered bitterly. "Jordan doesn't want to let me go. He's playing stupid games with me."

"Can you blame him? He doesn't want to lose you down in Python Flight."

"Shit! Anyone can do what I'm doing. I'm not the only O-Three pilot in the goddamned Army. Let him get someone else in to run that fuckin' mob, and let me get the hell out of here."

"What do you want to do?"

"I don't know," Gaines said quietly. "All I want is to find someplace where I can fly a chopper and not have to screw around with all the bullshit."

He paused. "Someplace where I don't see Lisa every time I turn around."

There was nothing Janson could say. "Is there anything I can do?"

268

Gaines tossed off the last of his drink. "No, thanks, I can't think of a thing."

Janson stood up. "I guess I'd better motor on back. I got a big day ahead of me tomorrow. Take care, Rat."

"You, too."

Later that night, Rat Gaines slept fitfully, tossing and turning on the narrow bunk in his hooch. As he slept, his mind worked overtime, carrying him from one dream scene to the next.

His dreams took him to an officers' club. All the men in the club were dressed in jungle fatigues or flight suits, but it was not any club he had ever seen in Vietnam. It looked more like the Stag Bar at Fort Benning or the clubhouse at the Benning swimming pool. The room was full of beautiful women in evening gowns and party dresses, their hair done up in elaborate hairdos.

Gaines was one of those rare people who had the ability to censor his dreams, to stand outside what he was seeing in his mind and to analyze and question it. As he moved through the crowded room, he wondered what he was doing back at Benning. But it didn't bother him. He was aware that he was only dreaming, and it was pleasant enough.

As always in a dream, though, something was wrong. In this case, he couldn't find the bar. He walked around the room, watching the crowd, when he spotted a girl in jungle fatigues and long blond hair. His heart raced.

Lisa!

It couldn't be, she was dead!

He fought his way through the crowd, elbowing and shoving people out of the way, but he couldn't get any closer to her.

"Lisa!" he called out.

The girl turned and smiled at him. It was her! She raised a hand and waved.

Suddenly he was at her side. She looked strikingly beautiful. Her eyes were calm and her long blond mane flowed down her back.

His throat was suddenly dry. "Lisa! My God! What are you doing here?'

She smiled and took a drink from the glass in her hand. "I just stopped by to see you."

"But how did you know that I'd be here?"

She smiled secretly. "I just knew."

Rat was stunned. She was dead. He knew she was dead. How could she be standing here?

"Where have you been?" he asked, his voice sounding strange to his ears.

She smiled that same smile again. "Oh . . . I've been on a trip."

Even in his dream, Gaines knew better than to ask where. And he also knew better than to ask how she had been able to come to this party. There were some things better not known, even in the safety of a dream. He didn't care, just as long as she was there.

"Oh, love," he said, longing to hold her, but afraid to reach out. "I've missed you so much."

She reached up and touched his face, wetting her fingers with his tears. "I've missed you, too, Roger. How have you been?"

Now his tears came full force. He swept her into his arms and held her to him, savoring the feeling of her body pressed tightly against him. Suddenly he realized that her prosthesis was gone. It was her own leg again that he felt against his. He almost pulled back from her. Now he was certain. She was dead and she shouldn't be here. Everyone else in the room was alive.

"It's okay." She smiled again as if she had sensed his sudden understanding. "I'm really here and I can stay with you for a while."

Suddenly Gaines was in the big Air Cav club back at Camp Radcliff, where he had first met Lisa. They were sitting at their favorite table as they had done so many times. Gaines was wearing a flight suit and had a drink in his hand,

270

as well. Lisa was smiling as he reached over and took her hand.

For what seemed like hours, he didn't say a word, he just held her hand and drank in her presence. The smell of her perfume washed over him, a warm scent that he had sorely missed.

"Lisa," he finally said, "it's been so lonely here without you."

"I know." She squeezed his hand. "It's been lonely for me, too. Look," she said suddenly, her green eyes gazing over his shoulder. "It's Tiger."

Gaines turned and saw Tiger O'Leary standing at the bar. His face wore its usual confident smile. He looked real good for a man who had taken a .51-caliber round through the back. Tiger raised his glass to Gaines in a salute.

Rat was stunned. O'Leary had been killed during Tet. Gaines looked more closely at the other men in the club. At a table in the far corner, Snakeman Fletcher sat talking with JJ Gardner and another man whose name he couldn't remember. Was everyone in this club dead?

Gaines was consumed with horror. What was he doing in a house of the dead? His mind started to panic, but Lisa held tightly to his hand.

"It's all right, Roger," she said. "You're safe with me."

Then they were transported outside the club and were watching the sun set over Camp Radcliff. On the Golf Course, dozens of choppers were lifting off, flying in the direction of the dying sun.

"It's beautiful here." he said.

"It's always beautiful here."

Gaines couldn't think of anything to say. He was content for the first time in weeks. It was more than enough for him to just stand there, hold Lisa, and watch the sun go down. He wanted to stay there for the rest of eternity.

Suddenly Lisa pulled away from him. She glanced down at her watch. "I'm sorry, but I have to go now."

"Oh no! Please!"

She smiled and touched his face gently. "No, Roger. I

have to go back now. I'm sorry, but there's still a lot of work for me to do. Remember how it was in An Khe? Both of us had important things to do that kept us apart so much of the time.''

"I'm sorry," he said. "I wanted to spend the time with you, I really did."

"I know you did. But that's okay. You had a very important job to do and so did I. It's the same now. I have my work and you have yours, but I'll come back to see you whenever I can."

"But you're here now! Why can't you stay with me?"

"We'll be together later," she said softly. "I promise you, we'll be together. Good-bye, Rat."

Suddenly she vanished.

"Lisa!" he screamed.

"Lisa!"

Gaines woke and sat up. Tears ran unnoticed down his face and his pillow was soaked. Swinging his legs over the side of his bunk, he fumbled in the pocket of his fatigue jacket and found a cigar. His hands shook as he unwrapped it and thumbed his Zippo to life. Holding the flame to the end of the cigar, he sucked deeply, dragging the smoke into his lungs.

As the tears ran down his face, he smelled her perfume again. Rat Gaines was a very rational man, but there were things in the world that defy all rationality and logic. For the first time since he had become an adult, Rat Gaines truly believed that there was a life after death. And he believed Lisa's promise. He would see her again. Someday, somewhere, somehow, he would be with her again.

He ground the cigar out on the concrete floor and lay back down. In seconds he was sleeping soundly again. The tears had dried and he had a smile on his face.

CHAPTER 37

Camp Evans

Early the next morning, Rat Gaines walked into the battalion headquarters, swept past a startled Lieutenant Muller, and knocked on the door to Colonel Jordan's office. He was clean-shaven and wearing a flight suit with the colorful Python Flight patch above the right breast pocket.

"Come in."

Rat stood in the open door. "Do you have a minute, Colonel?"

Jordan looked up. "Sure, Gaines, come on in and have a seat."

Gaines walked into the office and sat down on the edge of the chair like he was afraid that it was going to bite him.

"What can I do for you today?" the colonel asked, his voice unfriendly.

"Ah . . . sir," Rat began nervously. "Well . . . first I'd like to apologize for my behavior over the last couple of days."

Jordon didn't respond. He wasn't going to make this easy.

"I don't know what to say except that I'm sorry I've been such a pain in the ass and I'd like to withdraw my letter of resignation, if I still can, sir."

Jordan finally grinned. He just couldn't help it. "Letter? What letter, Rat?"

Gaines looked blank. Where in hell did Jordan think he had been for the last week or so, on R and R? Then he saw the smile on the battalion commander's face.

"Is the company commander's job down at Echo Company still open, sir?"

"It was never closed, as far as I was concerned, Rat." Jordan stood, his right hand extended. "You're still the CO down there."

Gaines stood to shake his hand. "Thank you, sir. I really appreciate that."

"Okay," Jordan said gruffly. "Now that the pleasantries are over, how about getting your ass down there and getting that mob squared away. We've got a major operation going on in a week and I don't think your people are ready for it."

"Yes, sir." Gaines turned to go.

"Rat."

"Sir?"

"You may want this." Jordan held out the resignation letter.

"No, thanks, sir," he shook his head. "I won't be needing that anymore."

"I sure as hell hope not," Jordan growled.

When Gaines went back through the outer office, Muller pushed his chair back and jumped to his feet. Obviously, he had overheard the conversation in the colonel's office.

"Captain Gaines, sir!" he sang out.

Rat stopped and turned to face him. "Yes?"

"Glad to have you back, sir."

Gaines grinned. "Me, too."

By the time that Gaines pulled into his space in the parking lot in front of the Python operations shack, the word of his return had already leaked out. Everyone he saw had a big smile on his face.

It had not, however, reached Lance Warlokk. He had locked himself in Gaines's office so he could try to get the

274

last of the maintenance reports finished in time to make the deadline. He had threatened to kill anyone who interrupted him. No one had even dared disturb him with the news of Rat's return.

Gaines opened the door to face the muzzle of a .45-caliber pistol aimed right at him.

"Whoa," he said, his hands held out to show that he was not armed.

"What the fuck're you doing here?" Warlokk spat.

"Hey, nice talk, Lance," Gaines grinned. "I come down here to get the last of those reports finished up, and you say something like that to me?"

"You're coming back to work?" Warlokk's voice clearly betrayed his disbelief.

"Well, if you'd rather that . . ."

"No, no. You've got it."

"Okay, then get your dead ass out of my chair."

"Yes, sir." Warlokk grinned as he quickly stood. "It's all yours."

"I was afraid of that."

"Jesus, I'm glad you're back, Captain. This fucking bullshit paper work is about to drive me outta my fucking skull."

"Now you know what I have to put up with all the time."

"As far as I am concerned, Captain, you can have it. Every last piece of it."

"You mean that you don't want to be my new XO?"

"Not on your fucking life, Gaines."

Rat suddenly turned all business. "Okay, let's get to it. I want to have a meeting in fifteen minutes, Warlokk. Get the men together in the ready room."

"Yes, sir."

Gaines sat down behind his desk and looked at the mess that Warlokk had left for him. He reached for the top piece of paper on the pile. It was a request from MACV Headquarters in Saigon for a report on the utilization of mosquito nets at the company level. MACV wanted to know how many nets had been used per week for the last six months.

The information was to be broken down by the rank of the personnel using said nets and the length of time that they had been in-country. The number of cases of malaria, all three types, and dengue fever in the unit over the same period of time was also required. The report had been due the day before yesterday.

Gaines pondered the request for a few moments and then made a command decision. He wadded it up and threw it in his trash can. He had forgotten about the morons in Saigon who hadn't figured out that there was a war going on. He reached for the next piece of paper.

Brody and his people had the day off again. For the last week, they had been sitting in Camp Evans pulling routine bunker-guard duties while the Air Cav finished their preparations for the relief of Khe Sanh.

Most of the men had welcomed the break, but not Farmer. The young grunt had chafed at the long period of forced inactivity. He spent the first few days in his bunk when he wasn't pulling guard on the berm line, but he had soon gotten tired of sleeping all the time. He wanted nothing more than to get back out in the brush and kill somebody.

His ear collection was coming along very nicely. He had found an out-of-the-way place to dry them in the sun, where no one would find them. Being a kid from a farm, he had known enough to salt them heavily to help the drying process, and they were ready in only two days. When they were done, they looked like very dark, dried peach halfs, like the ones his mother used to make in the late summer. He grinned when he thought of what she would think if she saw his dried peaches.

He spent a lot of time counting and recounting the ears. He had eighteen, including the two he had taken from the cowboys down in the ville. He had almost thrown them out because they weren't from a field kill, worthy of inclusion in the collection. But in the end, he kept them, too. After all, dinks were dinks. Civilian or VC, they were all the enemy.

He was very careful, however, to keep his collection away from the other guys, particularly Strawberry. He really liked Strawberry, but he knew that the new man didn't understand what he was doing and that the ears bothered him. Farmer was confident, though, that after Strawberry had been in-country a little while longer, he'd understand. Then he could show the collection to him.

Even the other guys had been giving him real funny looks lately. Brody and Two-Step were keeping a close eye on him all the time, and Bunny would hardly even talk to him at all. This treatment by his buddies bothered Farmer. Regardless of his particular hobby, he was still a nineteen-year-old kid who just wanted everyone to like him. He had always been the squad's clown, and they had looked after him like a bumbling younger brother. Particularly Gardner. JJ had been the stronger, older brother that Farmer had never had, and now that he was gone, the young grunt was lonely.

Farmer had been making a real effort to get back in the good graces of the other men. He had resumed showering on a regular basis and was pulling his fair share of the work again. He was trying his best, but it wasn't working. The other guys wouldn't drink with him in the EM club and they didn't invite him to go to Sin City with them anymore. He was beginning to think that hunting down those two VC in the ville had not been a good idea.

He was sitting on his bunk considering one more time if he should throw out the ears he had taken from those two cowboys when Lindberry walked in.

"Hi," Farmer said hopefully. "You want to go to the club for a beer?"

To Farmer's surprise, Lindberry said yes.

"Great, let me get my boots on and we'll go."

All the way over to the club Farmer chattered away a mile a minute like he had always done in the good old days before Tet. Lindberry was surprised to see him so outgoing

277

and relaxed. Though Lindberry was fairly new to the squad, he remembered when Farmer had been cheerful all the time.

Lindberry also remembered Gardner. To him, the big man had not been the protecting big-brother figure that Farmer knew. Instead, he had seen Jungle Jim as a dark, brooding figure. He had never been quite comfortable around him. JJ had been friendly enough, but there had always been a cloud over his eyes.

Maybe there was something about Gardner that he had never seen, but one thing he was seeing was the effect of the war on men. Brody had a standoffish, almost superior attitude to everyone except the men who had been in-country as long as he had. Two-Step was a mystic figure, a modern incarnation of an Indian warrior living in a world that he did not freely share with many people. Corky was aggressive, touchy to all but his few friends. And it looked like Farmer was a little psychotic.

Only Bunny Rabdo seemed normal, the kind of guy you'd meet somewhere back home. Maybe that was because he was from New York and had learned to live comfortably with chaos before he came to Vietnam.

While Lindberry pondered the effects of the war on those around him, he did not consider what it was doing to him. It would be several more months before he would be able to see some of Brody, Two-Step, Corky, and Farmer in himself. And by the time that happened, he wouldn't care anymore.

The EM club was fairly crowded, and most of the crowd were grunts from the infantry companies. The Blues weren't the only unit waiting for Operation Pegasus to kick off. The two men found a table by themselves and ordered a beer when the waitress came by.

"I'll buy," Farmer said when she came back with two Millers.

"Thanks."

"No sweat, man, you're my friend."

Lindberry was a little taken aback by Farmer's announcement.

278

"Yeah," Farmer said, noting the look on his face. "I haven't had a real friend since JJ got killed. But since we work so well together in the woods, you're my best friend now—my bush brother."

Lindberry was secretly pleased. He had not really felt totally accepted in the squad. No one had been hostile to him, but he had always felt their reserve. They were veterans and he was the cherry. Now, though, Farmer had accepted him fully. Farmer hadn't been around as long as Corky or Brody, but compared to Lindberry, he was an old field hand.

"Thanks, bro," Lindberry answered with a big smile on his face.

"No sweat, Strawberry, my man," Farmer grinned. "Now you can buy the next round."

CHAPTER 38

LZ Stud

Though it bore the designation of a landing zone, LZ Stud was larger than many of the permanent installations in Vietnam. For the last twelve days, hundreds of combat engineers, both Marine and Army, had sweated alongside Navy Seabees to construct the base. They had built a fifteen-hundred-foot PSP runway, ammo-storage bunkers, vehicle- and aircraft-refueling facilities, a forward command post for Major General Tolson, the Air Cav's division commander, an air-traffic control tower, and even a passenger terminal.

The engineers had built a small city in just twelve days. Tonight their work was finished, and LZ Stud was in operation as the forward launch point for Operation Pegasus, the relief of Khe Sanh. General Tolson, the Air Cav's division staff, several long-range artillery batteries, and the 3d Brigade had already moved in and were ready to go to work.

The next day, April 1, 1968, would see the largest air-mobile operation in military history get under way. For the first time, an entire division would take to the air in a massive heliborne assault.

That night, last-minute checks were being made of the choppers that would carry the sky troopers into battle. Fuel was topped off, turbines were checked over, rocketpods and miniguns were loaded with death for the NVA. When everything had been given a final check, exhausted cavalrymen and aircrews sought their bunks.

In Khe Sanh that night, the six-thousand-man Marine garrison manned their perimeter and anxiously awaited the dawn. It had been seventy days since they had been cut off. Seventy long days and nights filled with exploding artillery and rocket shells and screaming NVA throwing themselves against the wire. Seventy days that the survivors would never forget.

The dawn would bring a new day in more ways than one. It would be the beginning of the end of one of the most incredible sieges in the history of modern warfare, siege noted for the most lavish expenditure of ordnance and airpower since the end of World War II.

The Marine and Army artillery batteries had fired 158,891 rounds during the siege, more than ten to one for every round they had received from the North Vietnamese. The combined aerial might of the Air Force, the Marines, and the Navy had flown 22,106 sorties in support of the Marines. The high-flying B-52's alone had dropped more than 90,000 tons of high explosive. These mission figures did not include the airlift resupply missions, the FACs, or the medevac flights, of which there had been thousands more.

Khe Sanh was a place that not one man who had been there would ever forget. That included the North Vietnamese survivors as well. The somewhat optimistic official estimate of the enemy dead was that more than 13,000 men had been killed or seriously wounded. Even were this figure to be cut in half, it was an ass-kicking of epic proportions.

Khe Sanh had been a nightmare, but the dream was quickly coming to an end. And while the skytroopers slept, the Marines watched and waited.

David Janson placed the typed pages of his news release inside a manila envelope and sealed it. When the Air Cav kicked off in the morning, he would have the first in-depth, eyewitness story on Operation Pegasus to reach print in the stateside newspapers. Once more he had been in the right place at the right time.

He quickly addressed the envelope and headed over to the battalion jump CP tent to give it to Lieutenant Muller to send out in the morning's mail to Saigon. In the brightly lit command post, he found Colonel Jordan standing in front of his tactical map board, going over the last-minute details of the mission with his staff.

"Hey, Janson!" the colonel called out. "You want to ride with me in the C-and-C in the morning?"

"I'd love to, Colonel," Janson replied. There was nothing like having a ringside seat to a massive air assault to give him enough material for more than a dozen stories. "When're you lifting out?"

"We're scheduled for ten hundred hours, but it's going to depend on the weather."

"Rain or shine, Colonel, I'll be there. You can count on that."

Jordan laughed. "I thought you'd feel that way."

"What's the plan?"

"Come on over and I'll show you."

Janson walked over to the large map covered with symbols. Arrows, boxes, LZs, axes of advance, refueling areas, and artillery batteries were all neatly plotted with unit symbols. The reporter had picked up enough map-reading skills in his years reporting on the war that he could read it.

"Jesus, this is some operation!"

"Isn't it just?" Jordan grinned. "We're going to kick ass and take names 'til there aren't any more asses left to kick."

"How long do you think it's going to take to break through?"

"The division three is planning for ten days, but my money's on less than a week." Jordan was in his element now. This was his kind of battle. Slash, cut, thrust, kick ass, and stack the bodies. He lit another smoke.

"The way I figure it, we just have to clear the mountain passes along the road. If we keep mobile and call for the

Buffs to hit the points of hard resistance we run into, I think we can punch right on through.''

"Airmobile all the way.''

Jordan grinned. "You got that shit right. As the troops say, choppers are what's happenin'.''

The next morning dawned dark and cloudy. A heavy ground fog lay in the valley around LZ Stud, effectively preventing the choppers from taking to the air. In the fog, ghostly figures stood around the hulking shapes of the choppers, talking quietly and watching for the sun.

"I wish that fucking sun'd come out," Corky said as he looked up at a solid ceiling of gray.

"What's your hurry?" Brody laughed. "Old Charlie ain't going anywhere. He'll still be there.''

"Fuck a bunch of Victor Charlie, man. I just hate this fog.''

"What's the time?" Two-Step asked.

"Ten-forty-five.''

"We're late.''

"No shit, Dick Tracy," Farmer said disgustedly. "If I'd have known this was going to happen, I could have gotten me a couple more hours in the sack.''

"Aren't you ready to go kill *cong?*" Brody asked.

"I'm always ready to waste dinks, but all I'm wasting here is my time.''

Sergeant Zack had overheard Farmer's bitching. "Keep a cool tool there, young troop. We'll get going as soon as we can.''

"Right, Sarge.''

Something in Farmer's tone of voice told Zack that nothing was going to calm the young grunt down today. He told Brody to keep an eye on him.

As noon approached, the fog slowly burned off and the outline of the sun could be seen in the clouds. An hour later, patches of blue were showing through. The men became restless. The only thing worse than going to war was waiting to go to war.

Finally, a red-star cluster burst in the air over the airstrip. Men scrambled for their gear, boarded the waiting machines, and took their places. Pilots and copilots in their armored seats, the door gunners in their pockets behind their pigs, and the grunts in the back of the slicks, sitting in the open doors.

Preflight checklists were gone over, radios were switched on, and commo checks were made.

"Gold Saber Lead, this is Gold Saber Three Niner. Radio check. Over."

No one answered Saber Three Niner.

"Any Gold Saber station, this is Three Niner. Commo check. Over."

Still no answer.

"Goddammit! Where is everybody!"

Saber Three Niner's copilot reached over and turned the radio master switch on.

After a few minutes, a green-star cluster burst to life over LZ Stud. The signal to crank up the turbines.

The sound started as a low whine when the first of hundreds of waiting helicopters fired up their turbines. It built into a screech. More and more machines cranked up. Soon there was a thundering roar as the rotor blades beat the air.

At exactly 1300 hours on the first of April, 1968, the first chopper pulled pitch and rose into the air. Hundreds more followed until the sky turned dark.

Operation Pegasus was under way, the Air Cav was moving out in the first division-level airmobile operation in history.

To the grunts of the Marine battalions trudging along Route 9, the sound began as a far-off drone, as if a huge flock of mosquitoes were on the wing. The droning grew louder and louder and took on the resonating throbbing sound of hundreds of chopper rotors churning the air.

"What the fuck is that?" one Marine asked, looking back over his shoulder. He did not believe the sight that greeted his eyes.

A cloud of helicopters was moving across the sky. The entire 3d Brigade of the Air Cav was in the air at the same time, headed for their initial objectives. Three battalions of infantry were being escorted by every gunship the Air Cav had on hand.

The Marine rubbed his eyes. "Shit, man, there ain't that many choppers in the whole world!"

The o.d.-colored metal cloud quickly passed over the sweating Marine battalions. Hundreds of Hueys flew in formation, with the Cobra gunships off to their flanks. Loaches scampered ahead, swooping down low to scout out enemy positions. The big twin-rotor shit-hooks brought up the rear with artillery guns and ammunition slings loaded under their bellies.

"It's the Cav," someone else shouted. "It's the entire fucking Air Cav."

A ragged shout went up as the grunts cheered the Cav on. One Marine, however, was not impressed.

"If they're so fucking great," he snorted, "what are we doing humping our asses off up and down these fucking hills, chasing after them? Why aren't they doing this shit all on their own?"

" 'Cause that's what the Marine Corps does best, man. We walk while others ride."

The first Marine spit on the side of the dusty road. "Eat the apple, fuck the Corps. The next time that re-up sergeant comes talking to me, I'm going to punch him right in the motherfucking mouth for getting me into this shit."

"You can always re-up for the Army and get in the Air Cav."

"You know, that ain't a bad idea. I'd hate to be a doggie, but riding around in a slick sure beats the hell outta humping these fucking hills."

CHAPTER 39

LZ Stud

Janson sat in Colonel Jordan's C-and-C ship, marveling at the display of overpowering aerial might stretching out on either side of him. It reminded him of the old newsreels showing the swarms of World War II B-17 bombers heading for their raids over Germany. Working with the Air Cav as much as he had, he was used to seeing the sky full of choppers in Nam. He had never seen anything as impressive as this.

The First of the 7th was to lead the assault by hitting LZ Mike, the top of a low hill only ten miles from Khe Sanh. Three of the battalion's rifle companies, Bravo, Charlie, and Delta would hit the LZ with Alpha Company, with the Blue Team of Echo Company holding back as a battalion reserve.

First, however, before the slicks dropped the grunts in, the landing zone would be extensively prepped by everything from long-range guns to Tac Air. Nothing would be left to chance today. If things went as planned, taking the LZ would be a walk in the sun.

Colonel Jordan's face wore a big grin. The chain-smoking battalion commander usually went through a pack of gum an hour when he was up in his C-and-C ship. Today, though, it was looking more like two packs an hour.

The artillery liaison officer and the S-3 Air kept the radio consuls in the chopper humming as they directed the prep fires. It was an intricate ballet of steel and high explosive being played out on the hilltop, a true dance of death.

As the lift ships carrying the three assault companies approached their objective, the long-range guns from LZ Stud were still hammering the landing zone, LZ Mike. Like raindrops, 155mm and 175mm shells fell on the large clearing on the top of the low hill. On the command of the artillery liaison officer, the artillery fire cut off. Tac Air fighter-bombers came in to make a high-explosive contribution to the preparation phase of the operation.

Two small O-2 push-pull FACs scampered over the smoking LZ as Marine F-4 Phantom fighter-bombers and Air Force A-1E Super Spads worked the place over. First the fast movers zoomed in, dropping their napalm and CBUs on likely targets. When no one shot back at the jets, the slow-moving prop planes motored over and dropped a few of their 500-pound H.E. bombs.

The Fox Fours had just finished doing their thing and were flying off for a rearm when the First of the 7th Cav appeared in their choppers. They went into a holding orbit off to one side, well out of the way of the diving Super Spads.

In the C-and-C, Jordan chomped his gum furiously and directed the battalion on the radio. Major Larson, the S-3, the artillery liaison officer, and the S-3 Air all shared the radio consul with him as the battalion went into its assault. It was a classic airmobile operation, the vertical envelopment in its purest form, and it was coming off as smoothly as a practice maneuver back at Fort Benning.

"Roger, Python," the S-3 Air called to Gaines's Python Flight gunships. "You are go to prep the LZ."

"This is Python Lead, Roger," Gaines radioed back. "We're rolling in now."

Jordan watched intently as the Cobras of the light-fire

teams peeled off and swooped down like hawks over the smoking landing zone. It didn't look like anyone could possibly be left alive down there after the massive working-over it had received from the artillery and Tac Air, but it didn't hurt to make double sure. Ammo was cheaper than lives.

Coming in behind the gunships in a long trail formation were the slicks carrying the three platoons of Bravo Company. They had been given the honor of hitting the LZ first. As the first lift carrying the lead platoon swooped lower, the doorguns opened up, hammering the tree line. When they flared out and touched down, screaming grunts leaped from the slicks and took cover in what was left of the tall grass.

The choppers immediately lifted off to make room for the next platoon. In minutes, the other three platoons were on the ground, fanning out to secure the LZ. So far, not a single shot had been fired at them. It was a walk in the sun.

With Bravo securing the LZ, Charlie and Delta Companies flew in and quickly off-loaded. As soon as they were on the ground, Bravo Company moved out deeper into the woods to extend the perimeter.

The minute that the last slick departed, Jordan ordered the pilot of his C-and-C ship to put him down in the clearing.

"Welcome to LZ Mike, sir," the Bravo Company commander said, rendering him a snappy salute.

Jordan stepped down to the ground and returned the salute.

"Okay, Fred," he said turning to his S-3. "Where do we go next?"

Major Larson flipped open his map case. "Here, sir," he pointed to the next objective.

"Okay," Jordan said, digging into his pocket for a much-needed smoke. 'Let's get 'em moving ASAP. I don't want them to get cold."

"Yes, sir, as soon as the arty shows up. We'll start the prep."

A flight of six big twin-engined CH-47 Chinooks soon approached the LZ. Each shit-hook carried a sling-loaded 105mm howitzer, with the gun crew and ammo supply riding inside. A seventh chopper carried the mobile fire direction center and the equipment needed to put it into operation.

In a cloud of stinging dust blown up by the huge twin rotors, the shit-hooks came to a hover one at a time and gently lowered the guns down in the center of the clearing. When each sling was released, the big choppers floated off to the side and landed to disgorge the gun crews.

When all six tubes of artillery were on the ground, yelling cannon cockers, stripped to the waist, wrestled their guns into a battery star formation and dug the trails in. While this was going on, other sweating Red Legs lugged the boxes of 105mm ammunition to each gun and quickly prepared the rounds for firing.

In minutes, the guns were in place, the ammunition had been broken down, and the FDC was ready to start computing the firing data. Jordan gave the word, and the howitzers sent their greeting card on to the next LZ.

Less than an hour after the first ships had touched down at LZ Mike, Jordan was back up in the air with Alpha and Charlie Companies, speeding for their next objective. Bravo Company had stayed behind to defend the artillery battery, and Delta Company had gone into reserve with the Blues.

The next LZ, however, wasn't quite as easy as Mike had been. For one thing, it had not suffered through the extensive pounding from the long-range guns. And the Air Force had only given it a lick and a promise. As a result, when the lead elements of Charlie Company choppered in, they found a warm reception waiting for them.

Jordan immediately sent Alpha Company around on the flank to roll up the enemy position. Over the LZ, choppers swarmed like mosquitoes. The Loach scout ships darted from one place to another, reporting enemy positions, while Gaines's Python gunships orbited higher, ready to drop down and blast anything that the scout ships found out of existence.

The grunts of Charlie Company slowly moved forward under the cover of heavy supporting fire and came up against a line of bunkers set up inside the tree line. These dinks had not been bombarded enough, and the will to fight had not been kicked out of them yet. They held their ground fiercely and fought back like cornered rats.

"Python Lead, Python Lead," came the call in Gaines's helmet headphones. "This is Dusty Joker Six. I have a fire mission for you. Over."

Gaines chuckled at the Charlie Company commander's use of the words "fire mission" to request a gunship attack. Those were the words used to get the artillery to shoot for you. Today his gunships were really living up to their official Army designation as an Aerial Rocket Artillery Platoon.

"Joker Six, this is Lead. Go."

"This is Joker Six, I'm up against a couple of RPDs in a bunker. They've got us pinned down and I can't seem to get around them. How 'bout giving me a hand with this? Over."

"This is Python Lead," Gaines radioed back. "Roger, Joker Six, always glad to help. Pop smoke on your frontline trace and mark the target for me. Over."

"This is Joker Six, Roger. Smoke out."

Gaines looked down and saw two columns of bright green smoke slowly rise directly in front of the tree line. In front of the green smoke, a dirt bunker sparkled with small-arms tracer fire.

"Joker Six, Python Lead, I've got your lime," Gaines said, identifying the color of the smoke. "And I've got the target. We're on the way. Over."

"This is Joker Six, Roger green. Out."

"Python guns, this is Lead," Rat transmitted over the choper-to-chopper frequency. "The Dusty Joker element has got their asses in a crack again. We're going to roll in and

290

see what we can do to take care of it for them. I've got the target spotted, so just follow me and let's do it 'rat' now."

A chorus of "Rogers" followed. Gaines nosed his Cobra over and lined up on the machine-gun position. In the front seat, Gaines's new gunner, Buck Davis, tightened his Nomex-gloved fingers around the firing controls to his weapons and peered through his gunsight.

"Make it good, Buck," Gaines called forward to him. "We don't want to have to do this twice."

From over a thousand meters out, Buck proved that even though he was an FNG, he could shoot. The first volley of 2.75-inch H.E. rockets that flashed out from the side-mount pods were right on the target. One of them flew into the front aperture of the position. The bunker belched flame from the firing ports when it exploded.

Gaines pulled up from his gun run and banked away before passing over the enemy position. There was too much heavy machine-gun fire on the ground. Most gunships took their hits from ground fire when they overflew their targets.

Lance Warlokk and Alphabet swept in right behind him, flying side by side in their Cobras, and completed the bunker's destruction.

"Dusty Joker Six," Gaines called down to the infantry commander. "This is Python Lead. How'd we do? Over."

"This is Dusty Joker Six. Nice work, Python. Thanks again, old buddy. It's always a pleasure to work with professionals. Over."

"No sweat, Joker Six. Just remember that the next time you see me in the club with an empty glass in my hand."

The Charlie Company commander laughed. "Roger, Python, I owe you one. Out."

Back up in the sky at three thousand feet, Gaines searched the ground below for more targets. He soon got a panicked call from one of the Alpha Company platoon leaders, who was meeting heavy resistance from a hidden trench line.

This time the gun birds swept up and down the trench line, blasting it with their nose turret–mounted miniguns and automatic thumpers. Two passes was all it took, and the infantry was able to move forward again.

This time when they regrouped in the sky, Gaines had his pilots check their fuel and weapons loads. His own machine was almost out of both, and he was sure the other two Cobras were in the same condition. After getting a status report from Warlokk and Alphabet, Gaines checked in with the S-3 Air and got permission to make a quick trip back to LZ Stud for a hot rearm and a top-off. The Hogs of the heavy gun team would remain on station and cover for the ground troops while they were gone.

It was a short flight and the three Cobras swooped down in tight formation, flaring out right next to the rearming point. Leaving the rotors spinning at flight idle, the three pilots jumped out of their birds and supervised. They didn't want to be away from the battle any longer than they had to.

In minutes, their gunships had been topped off with a full load of JP-4, and the empty weapons had been replenished. Gaines and the other two snake drivers clambered into their machines and lifted off.

While all this was going on, Alexander and his platoon were cooling their heels back at LZ Mike with the battalion forward CP, waiting to be sent into action as a ready reaction force. So far, though, the line companies were doing quite well by themselves, and they didn't need help.

Most of the men were satisfied to let it stay that way, particularly Corky. He had only a week to go now and had started to suffer from a bad case of short-timer's fever.

"Hey, Corky," one of the men in First Squad yelled. "How short are you?"

"I'm too short to be talking to a no-time, in-country FNG like you," he shouted back.

The grunt shot him the finger.

Farmer, on the other hand, was not at all happy to be sitting on his ass at a dusty firebase waiting for something to happen. He paced back and forth endlessly, his eyes scanning the sky for the slicks. Every time the radio in the

CP crackled with another message, he waited for Alexander to shout for them to saddle up.

"Hey, Farmer, you're going to have a nervous breakdown doing that," Brody said as the young grunt walked past him for the hundredth time. "Just take it easy."

Farmer didn't answer. His mind was locked on the image of the NVA in the woods. The enemy that he couldn't get to.

The rest of the afternoon, the gun birds of Python Flight continued taking out enemy hard points for the grunts on the ground. They had to go back to Stud two more times to rearm and refuel before the LZ was secure. As dark fell, Charlie and Alpha Companies formed an NDP, night defensive position, and settled in on their new real estate. In the morning, they would lift out and move in closer to Khe Sanh.

That night, at his new jump CP location back at LZ Mike, Colonel Jordan went over the operation plan for the morning. Since Charlie and Alpha Companies had had that unexpected little problem at their second LZ today, he decided to send the Blues in ahead of his line companies when they went out again in the morning. That's what the Blue Team was there for, to scout for him.

"Muller," he called over to the adjutant. "Get Lieutenant Alexander in here, will you?"

CHAPTER 40

LZ Mike

The next morning, the three squads of the Blues were standing tall by the makeshift chopper pad outside the wire at LZ Mike, waiting for the three slicks that would carry them into their recon AOs. Colonel Jordan wanted three different possible LZs checked out. Zack was leading one of the squads, Alexander was going with the second, and Brody was taking his people out by himself.

Farmer was in a real good mood, laughing, joking, and stuffing his face with C rations. It was almost like the old Farmer had returned.

"What're you so fucking happy about?" Corky growled.

Farmer grinned boyishly. "Hey! We're going on a mission, man. I get to kill me some more dinks."

Corky shook his head. "Man, you are one *dinky-dau* motherfucker, you know that?"

Farmer just grinned wider.

Lindberry watched the exchange between the two men. Farmer was talking crazy, but at least he wasn't depressed and moody today. Maybe talking it out had done him some good. He sure hoped so.

Just then, the three slicks appeared and flared out for a landing on the dusty pad.

"Okay, boys and girls," Zack shouted over the noise of the rotors. "Let's get it!"

The grunts scrambled into their assigned ships and took their places in the open doors. With a whirl of red dust, the slicks lifted out and turned toward the east and Khe Sanh.

"Treat, you'd better take a look at this," Two-Step said, handing him the binoculars.

Through the field glasses, Brody could see an entire company of NVA moving around back in the tree line. He carefully noted their position on his map before turning to his RTO. This was the second large enemy unit they had spotted in the last four hours. Obviously, this was not the best place in the world for them to be right now. They were pressing their luck to the breaking point.

"Bunny," he said softly. "Tell the ell tee that he'd better pull us the fuck outta here. This whole area is crawling with dinks."

Alexander, Zack, and the other two squads had finished their recons and were back at LZ Mike, waiting for new orders. The ell tee rogered the message but said that he'd have to get permission from the S-3 first. He told them to hold tight.

A tense fifteen minutes later, Brody received a radio call from Alexander. "Two, this is Six. You have permission to withdraw now. We're standing by, so keep me informed of your movement. Over."

"This is Two, wilco. Out."

Brody gave the handset back to Bunny and stood up. "Okay, let's go. Two-Step, you take point. I'll do slack. Corky, take drag."

They had only gone four or five hundred meters when Brody heard Corky's M-60 open up behind them.

"Bunny, call it in!" Brody shouted as he ran back to the drag.

Bunny keyed the mike. "Blue Six, Blue Six, this is Blue Two Tango. Over."

"This is Six, go."

"This is Two Tango, we are in contact with an unknown-sized enemy force at our rear. Over."

"Roger, Python is in the air, en route to your location. Do you need reinforcement? Over."

"I don't know. Over."

"Keep me informed. Six out."

Bunny crouched down at the side of the trail, his M-16 ready as he nervously scanned the jungle around him.

"I'm a goddamned FO, not a fucking grunt," he muttered to himself. "I'm not supposed to be out here all by myself."

As he huddled under a bush, Bunny fervently wished that there was some artillery close enough for him to call on. Even one tube of 105mm would get them out of this fucking mess. But they had been given the farthest recon area, the one outside the artillery fan. He vowed that he was never going outside the range of the guns ever again. A guy could get himself killed screwing around out in the woods without artillery support.

When Brody reached the contact, he saw that Corky had rolled behind a tree and was hosing down the trail. Two dead dinks were lying out in the open where the M-60 had cut them down. From the intensity of the enemy fire, however, he knew that there was still a squad or so of them out there. At least they didn't have a machine gun. All he heard was the distinctive clatter of AK-47 fire. That was bad enough.

He turned sharply and waved Two-Step around to their left flank. The firing wasn't as heavy there.

On the other side of the trail, Lindberry and Farmer were working together as a team. Every time Farmer rose up to fire his seventy-nine, Lindberry jumped up beside him and ripped off a magazine of 5.56mm on full auto to keep the dinks' heads down. So far, it was working really well. No one was giving them much trouble.

Lindberry poked his head up to take a look, and a burst of AK tracer cut through the air right in front of him. On second thought, maybe they weren't doing quite as well as he thought. Farmer whirled around and fired a thumper round at the source of the tracer. It stopped.

On the flank, Two-Step cautiously crawled up until the bark of the AKs sounded like they were right in front of him. He looked around the tree trunk and saw three NVA only a few meters in front of him. He ducked back behind the tree, pulled a hand frag from his side pocket and checked the load in his sawed-off.

He pulled the pin on the grenade, let the spoon fly off, counted off two seconds, and lobbed it fifteen feet to the NVA position. With the short count on the fuse, the grenade exploded in the air over their heads.

Before the frag had even stopped flying, the Indian stepped out from behind the tree, his deadly pump gun roaring flame. Working the slide as fast as he could, he emptied the magazine at them. The stainless-steel balls tore into the NVA. The two who had escaped the blast of the grenade were gunned down where they stood.

Two-Step ducked back behind his tree and quickly reloaded. Jamming the last shell up into the sawed-off's magazine, he ran out and dropped down among the bodies into their fighting hole. He scanned the jungle, looking for more dinks on his side of the trail.

When Brody heard the roar of Two-Step's shotgun, he yelled at Corky and charged. Cordova held the trigger down on his sixty, smoking the barrel as he sprayed fire into his side of the trail. Farmer quickly sent two grenades after Corky's tracer rounds. As soon as the echoes of their explosions died away, it was unnervingly quiet.

"Cease fire!" Brody yelled, rising from his cover. "Cease fire!"

The Indian stepped out of the brush and joined Brody. The two grunts quickly checked all the bodies they could find. "You see a radio?" Brody asked.

"No."

Brody turned and saw his RTO standing over one of the dead NVA. "Bunny, call the ell tee. Tell 'em that we're moving again and need a pickup ASAP."

Bunny passed the message on to Alexander. The ell tee rogered. The slick was just leaving.

Two-Step was loading shotgun shells in the magazine under the barrel of his sawed-off when he cocked his head to the side. "Quiet!" he hissed. "Listen."

The grunts froze. In the distance, they heard shouting voices, voices speaking Vietnamese.

"Hit it!" Brody shouted, and took off running. They all headed up the trail after him, running as fast as they could for the pickup zone. It was high time that they got the hell out.

Up at the point, Two-Step put his hand up to call a halt. The grunts stopped and took cover beside the trail. The panting grunts quickly spread out and dropped down into the brush. Right ahead of them was a small clearing, with a trail leading in the direction of their PZ. Two-Step went ahead to see if it was clear.

Farmer and Lindberry hurriedly rigged their last claymore with a trip wire fifty meters back the way they had come. They were fresh out of anything to leave behind to try to slow the dinks down, but if the trail leading away from the other side of the clearing was safe, they wouldn't have to stay and fight it out. With enemy units swarming all around them, Brody couldn't tell if the trail was still open until Two-Step reported back.

Once they were in position, the men checked their remaining ammunition and waited, hoping that they had gotten away from their pursuers. Brody kept looking over his shoulder for the signal that the way was clear. They were starting to run low on ammunition, and he didn't want to get into another heavy firefight in the thick jungle. Their only chance was to fade back into the brush and get going again as fast as they could.

Corky took a hundred-round belt of sixty ammo from around his chest and laid it out beside his sixty. He only had about three hundred rounds left for the gun. It was enough if they didn't get into a major pissing contest. If they did, they were going to be in a world of hurt. On full rock and roll, his M-60 would burn up over 550 rounds a minute.

The rest of the men were in little better shape than the machine gunner. They had ammunition for several short skirmishes, but no one had enough left to get into a mjaor firefight. After a tense ten minutes, Two-Step stuck his head out of the foliage on the right side of the grassy clearing. He gave them the arm-pumping signal for them to hurry up.

"Okay!" Brody hissed. "Let's go."

They could hear faint shouts of the pursuing NVA behind them. They had no time to waste.

The men got up from their hiding places and started across the tall grass into the clearing when a sudden storm of fire burst out of the tree line to their left front.

"Bunny!" Brody shouted as he scrambled for cover. "Get on the horn. We need the gunships! Now!"

While the grunts frantically tried to gain fire superiority, Bunny lay flat on the ground with the antenna of his radio stuck straight up into the air. "Crazy Bull, Crazy Bull, this is Blue Two Tango. Over."

"This is Crazy Bull. Send it. Over."

"This is Two Tango, we're cut off. We need gunships ASAP. Over."

"This is Bull. Send your location. Over."

Bunny almost wept. In all the confusion he had not kept track of where they were.

"Blue Two Tango, this is Crazy Bull. Did you roger my last transmission? Over."

"This is Two Tango," he sobbed. "I don't know where we are!"

"This is Crazy Bull Six," came Colonel Jordan's calm voice. "Don't panic, son. Help's on the way. Do you have a map? Over."

"Yes, sir."

"Then take your time and try to locate yourself on it. I've already got Python in the air. Over."

Jordan's calm tones helped steady Bunny. He brought out his map and quickly figured out where they were.

"Crazy Bull!" he shouted triumphantly. "I've found it! I think we're at seven three six, zero two eight. Over."

"Two Tango, this is Bull Six. Roger, good copy. I'll pass this on to Python. Just hang on. Out."

Farmer stuffed another 40mm grenade into the open breech of his thumper. As he rose to shoot it, a burst of fire sent him back down to the ground.

"Strawberry!" he yelled. "Cover me!"

Lindberry got up to one knee and ripped off half a magazine from his sixteen. The return burst slammed into him, knocking the rifle from his hands.

He looked down in shock. His arm was torn open. He was hit, but it didn't hurt!

Blood was pumping out everywhere. He could see the white of the bone and the salmon pink of his inner flesh, but all he felt was numbness and a light tingling sensation. He moved his arm and the pain hit him. A scream burst from his throat. "Medic!"

Farmer spun around at Lindberry's cry. "Strawberry!"

Dashing over, he dropped to the wounded man's side. Lindberry's eyes were glazed with pain.

"Farmer," he moaned. "It hurts. It hurts so bad."

Farmer snatched the field dressing from his First Aid pouch and ripped open the cover to take out the bandage. Gently taking Lindberry's hand away from the wound, he closed the jagged edges of the tear as best he could and placed the dressing over it.

"It'll be okay," Farmer tried to sound reassuring, but through his pain, Lindberry didn't hear him.

"Will I lose my arm?" he asked in a panic.

"No, no." Farmer tied the ends of the dressing tightly to stop the bleeding. "It'll be all right, I promise."

Being careful of Lindberry's arm, Farmer dragged him

deeper under cover, away from the crackling AK fire. He took off his rucksack.

"You just stay here now," he said, trying to make the wounded man comfortable. "I'll take care of you."

Farmer patted Lindberry on the head as if he were gentling a frightened animal. "Don't worry," he said. "I won't let them get you."

Lindberry closed his eyes.

A panicked Farmer reached down to check the wounded soldier's pulse. He was still alive, he had passed out from the pain. Snatching up his thumper, Farmer raced back out to the battle.

"Fucking dinks," he screamed as he triggered off a grenade. "You shot my friend!"

CHAPTER 41

LZ Mike

Lieutenant Alexander and the two other squads of the Blues were waiting at the makeshift chopper pad outside the battalion jump CP when Gabe and one of the other slicks landed in a flurry of dust.

"Go! Go! Go!" the lieutenant shouted as the grunts scrambled for their places in the two choppers. Alexander jumped into the lead bird with a map in his hand. He quickly pulled the spare flight helmet down over his head and plugged the radio cord into the intercom jack.

"Get moving, Gabe," he called up to the pilot.

"Pulling pitch now, sir," Gabe called back. He nudged forward on the cyclic and hauled up on the collective. The rotor blades bit into the air, and the slick's tail came up. In seconds, they were airborne and headed out to the contact as fast as the beating rotors could carry them.

Brody was cut off and he needed help fast.

"Where we going, sir?" Gabe called back.

Alexander checked the numbers he had scribbled on the combat acetate covering on his map. "Head out to the east. They're supposed to be at seven three six, zero two eight."

"Roger."

As fast as the slicks flew, the gunships charged well out ahead of them. Warlokk's and Alphabet's sleek Cobras led, with Gaines coming up fast behind them. The rest of the Python guns, the heavy team Hogs, would catch up with them when they could. Until then, the Cobras would do what they could on their own.

"Treat!" Corky said, looking up at the sky. "I hear choppers!"

Brody glanced up and saw the sleek shapes of the two Python Cobras in the distance. "Smoke!" he called out. "Somebody pop a smoke!"

Bunny snatched a smoke grenade from his assault harness, pulled the pin, and tossed it out as far in front of them as he could. Thick red smoke billowed up from the burning grenade.

The two lead Cobras saw the signal and went into a tight orbit high above the rising column. From a half a klick farther back, Gaines got on the radio to have Brody point out the targets.

"Blue Two, Blue Two, this is Python Lead on your push. Over."

Brody took the handset from Bunny and keyed the mike. "This is Blue Two. Go."

"This is Lead. What's your situation down there? Over."

"This is Two, we're in deep shit, sir. They've got us pinned down and we can't move. Over."

"This is Lead, Roger. Just keep your heads down. We're coming in, and the heavy guns will be here in just a few minutes. Over."

"This is Two. Roger. Out."

The arrival of the choppers was what the NVA had been waiting for. Initially, they had been hiding in the woods, hoping that the Americans would fail to notice them. Then they could pull back later that night and head for their sanctuary in Laos. But when Brody's squad had stumbled into them, that had ended their hope of exfiltrating to rejoin their comrades.

The NVA commander quickly decided to turn this situation to his advantage. Now that they had been spotted, there was no reason that they couldn't turn the tables on the Yankees. They were prepared to die, but they were going to take as many Yankees with them as they could. Particularly Yankee helicopters.

With that in mind, the NVA didn't try too hard to take out Brody's people. There were enough of them that it would have been a five-minute job. Instead, they kept them pinned down so the choppers would come in to rescue them. When they did, the NVA had a surprise waiting for them, a pair of 12.7mm Chi-Com surprises.

The first that Brody's people knew that anything was wrong was when they heard the *whoosh* of an RPG rocket launcher and saw the projectile leap into the air at the circling gunships.

"Break! Break!" he screamed over the radio.

Warlokk saw the puff of black smoke as the RPG rocket left the launcher, and reacted instantly. Kicking down on the rudder pedal, he dropped the nose of his ship and screamed down onto the target. The sleek Cobra dove, its guns and rocketpods blazing.

From deep inside the jungle, the trap was sprung. Twin fingers of deadly green tracer fire from the hidden Chi-Com 12.7mm heavy machine guns reached up at the diving gunship. Fire sparkled along the middle of Warlokk's Cobra fuselage as the armor-piercing rounds caught him in middive. Greasy black smoke, shot through with tendrils of angry orange-yellow flame, erupted from the exhaust of the howling turbine.

"Lead," he screamed in his throat mike as he battled the controls. "I'm hit."

The Cobra fell out of the sky in a skidding turn. Warlokk had been so close to the ground when he had been hit that he had almost no chance of bringing his machine to a controlled crash landing. Somehow he did the impossible. At the last moment, he corrected the skid and hauled up on the collective. The spinning blades bit deeper into the air and braked his descent just enough. When he hit, he had his nose up. The impact snapped the tail boom off, and the rotor blades shattered as the rest of the fuselage plunged down through the trees. The crew compartment made it all the way to the ground and turned over on its side.

From his orbit, Alphabet saw Warlokk's ship go down to the hidden chopper-killing guns. Without thinking, his right hand twisted the throttle to maximum RPM. He dropped the collective and stomped down on the rudder pedal to kick the tail around. The Cobra dropped down onto the target like a diving hawk.

In the front cockpit, Alphabet's gunner played his fire controls. Rockets lanced out from the side pods, trailing fire down into the thick jungle. The heavy ripping sound of the nose-mounted minigun filled the cockpit as he walked the finger of red tracer fire into the 12.7mm gun positions.

The North Vietnamese gunners on the fifty-ones didn't back away from Alphabet's gunship one millimeter. They had killed one Yankee machine so far and they would do their best to get this one, too.

The first burst of 12.7mm caught the Cobra in the left-hand stub wing. A round hit one of the rockets in the outside pod, detonating the warhead. The blast tore off the outer half of the wing. A second burst from the chopper-killing heavy machine gun smashed into his transmission and turbine. The armored skin stopped some of the rounds, but others got through and shattered the gearbox. The turbine wailed as it locked up. Fortunately, the rotor declutched and ran free. The overloaded gunship fell like a bird with broken wings.

Alphabet frantically tried to establish an autorotation as the machine headed into the jungle at the edge of the clearing. The rotor blades were windmilling above him, but he was too low. There was not enough time to build up the momentum he needed to cushion his descent. He threw his hands up in front of his face as they smashed into the tree line right in front of Brody's position.

The gunship's tail boom hit first, snapping it off clean behind the engine compartment. The crew cabin slammed into the ground with a rending, tearing crash, driving the landing skids up through the floor plates. Only the inertial reels of the men's shoulder harnesses saved them from going through the canopy face first.

For a moment, Alphabet was stunned, the wind knocked out of him by the impact. As he struggled to get out of his locked shoulder harness, a burst of AK fire raked his mangled chopper. He wrenched the buckle free and threw the canopy open. Bullets punched through the thin metal skin of the bird and whizzed through the cockpit area, smashing the instrument panel as he dived over the side.

Wrenching the gunner's canopy open, he struggled with the man's harness. The gunner seemed unhurt, but he was unconscious. Alphabet dragged him out of his seat, over the side of the cockpit, and laid him on the ground. They'd be safe there if the chopper didn't catch on fire.

From the air, Gaines saw Alphabet's gunship follow Warlokk's down into the jungle. Slamming his cyclic control forward, he threw his Cobra into a dive on the fifty-ones that had knocked the other two Cobras out of the sky.

Like an avenging angel, Gaines dove down on the gun positions. He switched to the pilot's override on the weapons system's firing controls and peered through the gunsight.

From several hundred meters out, he started firing his rockets two at a time, keeping the dinks under constant fire. He laid down on the minigun trigger, kicking the tail from side to side to spread the fire. He could see his rounds impacting, but the deadly strings of green fifty-one tracer still filled the sky in front of him. He jinked his machine out of their path, but took hits. He snapped back and kept on firing until he swept past the guns.

As he pulled up and circled around for another run, he glanced down at his instruments. Everything was still green.

On the ground, Brody and his men watched helplessly as Gaines started his suicide run. From where they were, none of their weapons could take out the fifty-ones, either.

"Bunny!" Brody shouted. "Get some artillery on those fucking dinks!"

"Red Leg, Red Leg," the FO called back to the artillery FDC at LZ Mike. "This is Red Leg Delta. Fire mission. Over."

"Delta, this is Red Leg. Wait one, we're tied up right now. Over."

"Brody," the FO shouted. "They can't shoot!"

"Fuck!"

On the approach to the LZ, Gabe had been monitoring the radio traffic between Brody and Gaines. He knew that the situation both on the ground and in the air was critical.

"Sir," he called back to Alexander on the intercom. "It's real hot down there. They've already taken out two of the Cobras."

"Just get us down there, Gabe," Alexander said grimly. "I'll worry about that later."

"Yes, sir."

The pilot switched his radio frequency. "Lead, this is the Gunslinger. Blue Six is going in. Can you cover for us? Over."

"This is Lead, Roger. I'll try. Wait 'til I make my move. Over."

"Roger."

Gaines took a deep breath and nosed his Cobra over again. He started firing rockets from fifteen hundred meters out.

The two slicks came in low and fast, keeping well out of the path of the gunship's firing runs, their doorguns hammering. They flared out at the last minute and touched down a few meters to the side of Brody's position. Screaming their war cries, Alexander and the grunts poured out of the choppers and ran for cover at the edge of the clearing.

Most of the dinks had been distracted by Gaines's diving, fire-spitting gunship, but there were still enough of them to bring accurate, deadly fire on Alexander's insertion.

A long burst of AK fire from the flank caught two of the men in the First Squad before they went three steps. One of them went down with a bullet in the head. The second one was hit in the shoulder. The others dove for cover in the grass.

Farmer lay with his face in the grass as the fifty-ones hammered at the diving chopper. First the dinks had hurt his new friend Strawberry, and now they were trying to kill Captain Gaines. The captain had been good to him, and he didn't want to see anything bad happen to him.

He crawled back to where he had left Lindberry. The wounded grunt was still unconscious. Farmer grabbed up his sixteen. Rummaging through his ruck, he got out all of his hand grenades and M-16 ammo bandoliers. He left his loaded M-79 near Lindberry's left hand in case he woke up and wanted a weapon.

With all the commotion going on, no one saw Farmer crawl off on the right flank and head for the wood line and enemy guns. He stopped inside the trees, loosened the knife in his boot sheath, and loaded a fresh magazine in the M-16 before moving on. He kept low as he headed for the heavy chunking sound of the 12.7mm antiaircraft gun.

A rustling in the brush stopped him cold. Slowly and carefully, he parted the brush in front of him and saw an NVA with an RPG on his shoulder, aiming it out at the men in the clearing. Drawing his K-Bar, Farmer launched himself at the NVA's back.

"Motherfucker!"

The startled North Vietnamese only had time to die as the big-bladed knife ripped across his throat. Steaming blood gushed out over Farmer's hands as the dink struggled under him. The man was dead before he had time to know it.

Farmer stabbed him twice in the back to make sure before he crawled off the body. He saw the RPG launcher lying where the dink had dropped it. The deadly antitank rocket round was loaded into it and the hammer was cocked back. It was all ready to fire.

He picked it up and took it with him.

CHAPTER 42

West of Khe Sanh

Out in the clearing, Brody looked around for Farmer. "Where the fuck's Farmer!"

"I saw him headed over that way," Bunny said, pointing to the wood line.

Then Brody heard Farmer's scream of hate ring out over the sounds of battle.

"Leo!" Brody shouted over to Zack's position. "Farmer's gone into the woods!"

Zack looked over in time to catch a glimpse of him as he ducked deeper into the jungle, the RPG launcher on his shoulder.

Farmer headed toward the sounds of the twelve-point-seven. None of the NVA manning the gun noticed him as he crept up close enough to get a clear shot with the RPG. When he found a good firing position, he tried to remember what Two-Step had told him about shooting the weapon. He checked to make sure that the firing hammer was back, and then looked for the safety catch. Flicking it off, he raised the launcher to his shoulder.

The iron sights had several graduations, and he puzzled over them for a second. He was only forty or fifty meters rom the gun, so he chose the lowest-range mark on the ight. Centering the sight on the gun, he held his breath and ulled the trigger.

The rocket ignited with a *whoosh* and sped to the target. The warhead impacted right under the breech of the ma- hine gun and exploded with a flash. The concussion sent he smashed gun and the bodies of its crew flying. Before he smoke even cleared, Farmer dropped the empty launcher nd charged, his M-16 blazing on full rock and roll. The NVA gunners never had a chance. The two who had not een killed by the RPG were quickly riddled with 5.56mm.

Farmer dropped down beside the wreckage of the gun nd slammed a fresh magazine in the bottom of the sixteen. One down, one to go.

Taking out the second gun was not so easy. When the RPG explosion rang out, followed by the rattle of an M-16 on full automatic, they knew that someone was in the woods with them. They moved quickly to protect their last heavy machine gun.

The two guns had been placed about 150 meters apart, and Farmer had to fight every foot of the way. It was an epic combat. One man was determined to do a job, and a dozen other men were equally determined to stop him.

While this was going on, the Hogs of the heavy gun team had finally arrived. When Alexander saw them coming, he quickly got on the radio and warned Gaines that Farmer was in the jungle on a one-man mission. Gaines cursed, but told the gunships to hold off until Alexander could get Farmer back under control.

The first two NVA Farmer ran into had their backs to him. He simply cut them down and moved on. The third one saw him first.

He was bringing his sixteen up when a round cut into his upper right arm. The shock knocked the rifle from his hand. He rolled to the side and snatched at it with his left hand. Rolling over again, he brought the weapon up and triggered off a one-handed burst. The 5.56 caught his at- tacker in the chest.

He looked at his arm. It was not badly hit. He transferre
the sixteen back to his right hand and pulled a grenade from
his pocket with his left. He heard shouts in Vietnamese an
dove for cover in a clump of bushes. Three NVA ran pas
him in the direction of the first gun. He calmly shot them
down, putting an entire magazine into them. One of th
dinks was only wounded, however, and sprayed AK fir
back at him. Farmer ducked down and lobbed the grenad
with an overhand motion. The crump of the grenade ende
the shooting.

Farmer had won again, but the brief fight had been ove
heard by even more NVA. They converged on his position
AK fire smashed into the brush around him. He spun aroun
and crawled deeper under cover.

Back in the clearing, the men could hear the rattle o
Farmer's M-16 over the clatter of the AK fire. They ha
made several attempts to go to his rescue, but each tim
they had tried to move, they came under blistering fire fro
the wood line. As long as he was in there alone, the
couldn't use the gunships, and without them, they wer
pinned down.

The storm of fire in the jungle ended with the crump o
a grenade explosion and a last long burst of M-16. Agai
Farmer won, though he did not remember how he had don
it. Nor did he remember how he had taken the small fra
wound he saw in his chest. He tore his shirt open. It wa
minor. At least it didn't hurt much.

Farmer had been running on pure adrenaline for almos
half an hour now, but his overworked body was starting t
betray him. He was suddenly tired. He wanted nothing mor
than to stop and rest, but he knew he could not. The jo
was not done. JJ had never quit when there was still wor
to do.

He put another full magazine into the rifle and found tha
he had only one left. Where had they all gone? It didn'
matter. He still had the grenades.

Unknown to Farmer, the remaining NVA had retreate
to surround the gun emplacement. They didn't know exactl

what they were facing, but they would keep whoever it was away from the last twelve-point-seven as long as they could. The antiaircraft gun was all that was keeping them alive. When it was gone, the choppers would come in again.

The jungle was quiet as Farmer slowly made his way forward again, deadly quiet. A single shot rang out. The AK round took his leg out from under him and he went down. Hugging the dirt, he reached into his pants pocket for another grenade. There was only one left. Painfully, he crawled closer to the machine gun.

A burst of AK fire sent him flat on his face again. He was very tired, and his strength began to bleed out of the hole in his leg. He rested with his face in the damp earth of the jungle floor. A picture of Gardner flashed through his mind, a smiling JJ reaching down to help him to his feet the day he had jumped out of the chopper, tripped, and landed on his face.

Again JJ reached down to him and helped him get up. On his knees, he pulled the pin on the last grenade and threw it as hard as he could for the gun emplacement.

"JJ!" Farmer screamed right as the grenade went off.

Farmer's grenade landed right in a supply of Chi-Com stick grenades stored inside the enemy position. Their detonation reached a store of RPG rockets and their launch charges. Everything went off, and a boiling black-and-orange fireball rose above the treetops.

For a few moments, no one in the clearing said a word. A column of smoke rose from the last NVA gun position. Obviously Farmer had taken them both out, but they weren't safe until his grunts were holding the ground. Alexander slowly rose to his knees and saw the figures of the NVA fleeing deeper into the jungle.

"Let's go, Blues," he yelled, waving them forward. "Follow me!"

With a ragged cry, the grunts jumped to their feet and charged across the clearing, firing from the hip. No one shot

313

back at them. The dinks had seen the destruction of the heavy guns as a bad omen. Without them, the chopper would cut them to pieces. They were getting the hell out of the area as fast as their feet could carry them.

Brody and Zack ran ahead of the others. "Farmer!" Brody cried out. "Farmer!"

At the site of the first heavy machine gun, none of the NVA were alive, but there was no Farmer. The two men tore through the thick brush for the other gun site. Brody saw a small body lying by the smoking rubble of the second fifty-one position.

"Farmer!"

Brody dropped to his side and checked his pulse. It was weak, but he was still alive. His fatigue jacket was torn open and his chest sprinkled with a dozen or more small oozing frag wounds. His upper right arm had a shallow furrow cut into it where a round had grazed him. His left leg had taken a rifle round below the knee and was bleeding badly. Brody quickly tied a field dressing around the leg wound, but there was nothing he could do for the multiple frag wounds in his chest. Suddenly an AK fired from close by. The short burst hit in the dirt beside Brody.

"Sniper!" he shouted, spinning around to loose a quick burst back into the jungle.

Zack reached down and scooped the slightly built Farmer into his arms. Clutching him to his chest like a father holding a sick child, Zack raced back for the clearing.

Brody laid down a base of fire to cover him. As soon as Zack was clear, he jumped to his feet and raced after him.

"Bunny!" he yelled as he ran out into the clearing. "Call a Dustoff! Priority!"

"It's on the way!" Bunny shouted back. "I already called it for Strawberry and the other guys."

Zack gently laid Farmer on the ground and checked his wounds.

"Is he going to make it?" Bunny asked.

"I don't know, he's hit bad." Zack shook his shaved

ead. "Poor crazy little bastard. What in the hell made him
lo something like that?"

"I don't know," Brody said. "But he sure as hell saved
ur asses."

"Yeah, he did that," Zack nodded. "Those heavy guns
would have chewed us up as soon as they got through work-
ng on the choppers."

The sniper had been the last of the enemy resistance.
Alexander and the grunts of the Blues now owned this as
et unnamed LZ. Someone in 3 Squad had even planted a
mall American flag in the clearing next to where the cas-
ialties waited for the Dustoff. American blood had been
hed to take this place, and it was fitting that the Stars and
Stripes should fly over those who had shed it.

"Brody!" Bunny shouted. "The Dustoff's coming in."

Brody waited until he saw the medevac chopper in the
listance, and popped a smoke. When the Huey flared out
or a landing, the wounded and dead were quickly carried
n board. Farmer was still alive when it lifted out again for
he flight back to the hospital at Camp Evans. With luck
ind a lot of blood expander, he'd make it.

Bunny was on the radio, calling for the slicks to come
back down when Alphabet and his gunner limped up. They
aad dug themselves out of the wreckage of their crashed
bird. Except for sprains and bruises, they were unhurt.

"You okay, Schmuchatelli?" Alexander asked.

"Yeah, we're both fine," the pilot answered. "How
about Warlokk?"

"I've got Williams bringing them in now. Both of them
made it, too."

"Out-fucking-standing," Alphabet grinned.

As soon as the first slick touched down in the clearing,
Zack told Brody to get the rest of his people rounded up
and loaded on board. Brody, Two-Step, Corky, and Bunny
climbed on with Alphabet and his gunner. He tapped the
pilot on the shoulder, and the slick lifted off.

When the chopper broke free of ground effect, Brody
made his way back to the door gunner's compartment. A

315

substitute gunner was already back on the door sixty. Brod
found a place among the canvas seats and sat down heavily

Jesus, he was tired. This mission should have been
breeze, but two of his men had been hit, and both badly
At least Corky had come through it okay. Now, he shoul
be able to sit out his last few days without having to go ou
again.

He looked over at Two-Step. The Indian's face was im
mobile, his eyes locked on some kind of inner vision. Cork
was going home, but there was always Two-Step. Brody wa
going to need him more than ever now.

On April 6, a grunt from the Cav reached out across th
wire at Khe Sanh and took the hand of a Marine. The sieg
of Khe Sanh was broken.

"Hey!" the Marine said. "What took you guys so fuck
ing long?"

"Well, you know how it is," the grunt quipped. "W
had to stop off for a beer and a short time."

"You bring me some?"

"I ate all the pussy, but more beer's coming on the re
supply bird. It'll be here any time now."

Across the blasted hill, the thrilling notes of the Cavalr
charge sounded. They were played on a captured NVA bu
gle.

"The war's over, guys," one of the Marines in th
trenches yelled. "The fucking Cav's here."

CHAPTER 43

Khe Sanh

The hills around Khe Sanh were quiet. For the first time in over seventy days, there was no artillery fire incoming or outgoing, there were no air strikes, and no antiaircraft fire aimed at the swarms of choppers that were landing and taking off from the battered airstrip. Men strolled around both inside and outside the perimeter as though they were on a holiday. A few of the Marines still scurried around, half bent over, their ears cocked for the all-too-familiar sound of whistling incoming. Old habits die hard.

Sweating men stripped to the waist hurriedly off-loaded bales of sandbags and bunker timbers from sling loads under hovering twin-rotor CH-47 Chinooks. Out on the perimeter, Army Engineer bulldozers were throwing up a new berm line and digging bunkers. The Marines watched all this feverish activity in amazement.

In the center of the base, a huge Army mess hall had been erected, and grinning cooks were dishing up hot meals to Marines who had lived on nothing but C rats for over two months. Steaks, fresh corn, salad, and ice cream; nothing was too good for the Marine grunts of Khe Sanh. The Army usually ate that way whenever they could, but the

Marines didn't know that. They thought they'd died an gone straight to heaven.

Outside the perimeter, another bulldozer was digging a hug sanitary fill, a garbage dump. That was another thing abou Army operations, they loved garbage dumps. In just a day o two, most of the debris of the two-month siege would be po liced up and thrown away, as if the siege had never happened At one end of the runway, sergeants were already supervisin the lines of Army grunts detailed for police call.

Janson stood with his adopted Marine squad and watche the feverish activity going on all around them. It wasn't new t him. He had seen the Army in full-bore operation many time before. But it was strange to see it happening at Khe Sanh.

To the Marines, however, it was as if Disneyland ha been magically transported into their private backyard. The had never seen so many men and so much equipment be fore, and more of it flew in with every shit-hook sling load

Bear slowly shook his head. "Shit, where were thes fucking doggies and all this candy-ass shit when we reall needed it?"

Janson clearly understood the Marine's undisguised bit terness. The Marines operated as light assault infantry, un burdened by much of the support equipment that the Arm took for granted. Also, the Marines had an offensive men tality that did not do well in a defensive situation such a they'd had to endure for seventy-seven days at Khe Sanh The Army always saw to their defenses first, then tried t make their troops as comfortable as possible. With the Ma rines, all too often troop comfort was whatever the me could scrounge up or steal.

"They're even digging latrines!" Bear said disgustedly "I went to take a piss behind the bunker, and some Arm E-6 jumped dead in my shit for not using the piss tube!"

Janson smiled to himself. That was probably the sam sergeant who had caught him doing the same thing. La trines, showers, hot food, dry bunkers with overhead cover Life was never going to be the same at Khe Sanh now tha the Army had moved in. He had even seen a bunch of Ai

318

Cav troopers putting up a sign reading, Khe Sanh. Under New Management. Delta Company 27th Cav, as if they had liberated a captive town.

Maybe the Cav was right. Maybe they had liberated Khe Sanh from legend. Now the siege would pass from reality into the annals of Marine Corps history, to be remembered long with their other desperate fights whenever Marine veterans gathered.

The reporter glanced at his watch. "Look, guys, I just wanted to stop by and say good-bye. I've got to catch my hopper back to Camp Evans."

Bear took the reporter's hand in his meaty paw. "It was real nice to see you again, Mr. Janson. You take care now, you hear?"

Janson grinned. "You, too.

"Oh, one thing I almost forgot." He reached into his shirt pocket and came out with a letter that he handed to Bear. "Here's the recommendation for that medal for Wee Willie."

"Thanks," Bear said. "I'll see that it gets sent through. By the way, Willie's okay. He's going home."

"I'm glad to hear that."

The First of the 7th Cav had set up their jump CP inside the perimeter, and Janson went there looking for Colonel Jordan.

"You seen the colonel?" he asked the adjutant as he walked in.

Muller looked up from his field desk. For once he didn't jump to his feet. "I think he's down on the berm line inspecting the bunkers, sir."

"What sector?"

"The northern."

"Thanks."

On the way out of the GP large tent, Janson saw Rat Gaines coming his way. "Hey! Rat!" he called out.

Gaines walked over to him. "It looks like you're headed out."

"Yeah, you know how it is, I've got to go where it's

happening. Khe Sanh is old news now, so I've got to move on. You still planning on leaving the Cav?''

"Well, not really," Gaines grinned. "I just took a six month extension. It looks like Python Flight just can't get along without me."

"Well, I'm real glad to hear that it worked out for you."

"Me, too."

"Look," Janson said, sticking his hand out. "If you ever get away to someplace civilized, like Nha Trang, look me up at the press camp. I'll show you the sights, buy you a drink or something."

Gaines took his hand. "I just might take you up on that. I've been planning on going down there to visit a friend of mine."

Janson glanced down at his watch. "Well, I've got to run, there's a chopper waiting for me."

"Keep your head down."

"You, too."

The reporter found Jordan talking to some of the men of the Blues. The colonel was shaking Corky's hand and wishing him well. When he was done, he turned and saw the reporter standing there.

"You leaving, too?" Jordan asked.

"Like I told Rat, Khe Sanh isn't news anymore, it's history."

"Where you going?"

"First back to Nha Trang for a hot shower, a decent meal, and clean sheets. Then I'll look around and see what's happening."

"Well, you're always welcome to stay with us if you get back up this way."

"Thanks, I'll keep that in mind."

As soon as the colonel walked off, Brody called out "Hey, Janson, you're not taking any pictures."

The reporter looked over at what was left of the 2d Squad of the Blues. Lindberry was still in the hospital, recovering from his wound, and Farmer had been med-evaced back to Japan already. There was only Brody, Two-Step, Corky, and Bunny left, and Corky was flying out with him.

"There's nothing to take pictures of," Janson said with a grin. "You boys have gotten everything so calmed down around here that I've got to take my business somewhere else where I can find a little action."

"Keep your head down," Brody said.

"You boys be good now," Janson said. Clutching his AWOL bag, he climbed up into the waiting courier slick. Once he was on board, the pilot leaned out of his window and yelled at Corky, who was still saying good-bye to his buddies.

"Hey, troop! If you're going with me, son, you'd better get your ass on board."

Corky waved to the pilot and turned back to his friends. "Well, it looks like this is it, guys. I'd better get going."

Brody put his hand on Corky's arm. "You take care now, you fucking bean bandit."

"Yeah, you, too, asshole."

Two-Step took Corky's hand. "Write us, let us know how you're doing."

"I will."

Behind them, the pilot lit the Huey's turbine, and it fired up with a whine. The rotors started turning slowly. It was time to go.

"Catch you guys later," the machine gunner shouted over the chopper's noise. He shouldered his duffel bag and climbed up inside without looking back. He took a seat next to the reporter.

Corky felt strange to be sitting in the canvas jump seats of the slick instead of in the open door, with his legs hanging over the side. It felt even stranger not to have the comforting weight of the M-60 machine gun lying across his lap.

The pilot pulled pitch and the tail came up. He waved one last time to the friends he was leaving behind. Brody shot him the finger. He turned his head away so they wouldn't see that he was a little red-eyed.

As the slick lifted off and climbed for altitude over the base, Corky realized that this might very well be the last chopper flight that he would ever take. Suddenly he felt very much alone and wanted the pilot to turn around and take him back to the Cav.

"What're you going to do when you get home?" Janson asked him, trying to make conversation.

Corky paused for a moment. "I don't know." He shrugged his shoulders. "Just hang out at home for a while I guess, 'til I find something to do."

"You've got the GI Bill, why don't you go to school. You've sure as hell earned it."

"I don't know, man." The ex-machine gunner shook his head. "I don't know what the hell I'd study. I don't really know how to do anything but hump the brush as a fucking grunt."

Janson realized that Corky was right. After two years in the woods with the Air Cav, what else did he know? That was the worst thing about this war. What were these men going to do when they got home?

The two men flew on in silence over the lush, green jungle-covered hills.

Brody and Two-Step leaned back against the bunker, having a smoke and watching the sun go down over the blackened bomb-blasted hills to the west of Khe Sanh.

"It's going to be strange not to have Corky around here anymore," Two-Step said.

"Yeah, it's just you and me now, bro." Brody flicked the cigarette butt away. "We're all that's left."

"There's Leo."

"He don't count, he's a fucking lifer."

"You'd better lighten up on lifers, man. You're one, too now." Two-Step grinned. "Or did you forget?"

"That's different, man," Brody protested. "I'm a Nam lifer. I'd get out if I had to go back to the States and put up with that peacetime Army horseshit."

"What're you going to do, stay here forever?"

Brody's eyes swept out past the bomb-pocked, napalm blackened hills to the jungle-covered mountains in the distance. "You know, I might just do that."

322

Two-Step looked at his friend, trying to read his thoughts. "That's a dead end, man. This fucking war's got to end someday."

Brody laughed. "If that ever happens, then maybe I'll run me a fancy bar in Saigon with a whorehouse upstairs and a poker game in the back room."

"Yeah." Two-Step grinned. "I can just see you doing something like that."

Brody turned. "How long're you gonna stick it out?"

Two-Step got a serious look on his face. "I don't know, man. I've been giving it a lot of thought lately. I've got a DEROS coming up in a couple of months and I may take one last burst of six so I can help you break in all the cherries you're going to get. But I'm starting to get real tired of this shit."

He lit a another cigarette. "This ain't the same Air Cav that you and I came over with. These fucking kids we're getting for replacements now just aren't like you and me were when we came here. They're fucking *dinky-dau* before they even get out in the woods. You know all that shit we read about that's going on back home—race riots, peace creeps, fuckin' flower power—it's messing up their minds. It's just not like it used to be."

Brody nodded his head as he thought about Farmer. That poor bastard was going to be living in a rubber room at a VA hospital for a long time. "Yeah, it sure as hell isn't like the good old days."

"Shit, man, nothing's like the good old days. Even the good old days weren't."

Brody laughed. "You got that right, my man."

The two grunts stood in silence and watched the sun slip behind the purple mountains in the distance. Even at a place like Khe Sanh, the sunsets in Vietnam were spectacular.

Two-Step ground his cigarette butt out under his boot. "We'd better check in with Leo about the guard roster tonight."

Brody's eyes automatically swept the perimeter. "Yeah, this shit isn't over yet."

EPILOGUE

29 April, 1975, Billings, Montana

Montana State Trooper Chance Broken Arrow slowly sipped his midmorning coffee in the roadside truck stop on U.S. Highway 10, a few miles outside of Billings, Montana. It had been a long time since anyone had called the Vietnam veteran by his old nickname Two-Step. That was far behind him now. But watching the reporter on the television set behind the counter brought it all back.

He knew that reporter on the tube and he also knew what he was talking about. The screen was filled with the images of Huey choppers lifting off the roof of the American embassy in downtown Saigon. The old familiar whop-whopping sound of the rotors could be clearly heard over the reporter's voice.

Almost five long years had passed since the one-time grunt had left the jungles of Vietnam and the Army for civilian life. It all came flooding back to him as he listened to David Janson's calm, measured tones reporting on the hurried evacuation of the last Americans to leave Southeast Asia.

"One last footnote to the conclusion of this long and tragic chapter in our nation's history. I have just received word that one of the evacuation helicopters has been shot down. It crashed in the Cholon district in the outskirts of the city, killing

324

all those on board. One of the casualties was a man that I have known for a long time, Army First Lieutenant Treat Brody, late of the First Air Cavalry Division.''

Broken Arrow's coffee cup clattered to the counter top. Oh, fuck! Not Treat!

He leaned across the counter and turned up the sound on the television set. A truck driver seated at the other end of the counter looked up. Broken Arrow glowered at him. The man wisely kept his mouth shut.

"Lieutenant Brody arrived in Vietnam with the first deployment of the Air Cav in 1965. He rose in the ranks as a member of one of the famed Aero Rifle Platoons and was given a battlefield commission as a second lieutenant for his bravery. Though Brody had seen far more than his share of combat and could have returned home with honor, he remained in Vietnam, trying to save this small country from falling to the communists. He was a brave man, committed to the goal of freedom.

"It is ironic, but somehow fitting, that Treat Brody should die on the last day of the American presence in Southeast Asia. It may even be that he will be the last American to die in Vietnam, but it is too soon to tell. The day is not over yet.''

The TV camera panned down from the embassy roof to swarms of panicked Vietnamese trying to fight their way onto the grounds, in hopes of being evacuated. The scattered Marine guards beat them back with rifle butts as they stormed the front gate.

"I have just been told that I must leave now,'' Janson continued. "But before I go, I wish to join Lieutenant Brody's friends and family in bidding good-bye to a brave man. We will all miss him.''

Through the tears in his own eyes, Broken Arrow thought that he could see tears running down the reporter's face as well. The camera showed one last scene of the crowded embassy grounds before the station switched to a deodorant commercial.

Chance picked up his Smokey the Bear hat from the

counter and slowly walked over to the cash register at the end of the counter.

"Have a nice day, Officer Broken Arrow," the cute young thing behind the cash register said as he laid a quarter down for his coffee.

The ex-grunt stared at the girl for an instant. "My name's Two-Step," he shot back gruffly. As soon as he said it, he felt ashamed for snapping at the girl. What the fuck did she know about anything, anyway? She had been in grade school when he had been killing dinks in the jungles.

The Indian turned abruptly and pushed his way out the door into the bright spring morning. Overhead, a civilian Huey from an oil company flew past in the distance. The faint, familiar sound of the beating rotors brought a surging rush of adrenaline shooting through his body. Some things were never forgotten.

For a split second, the barren, red Montana hills faded and he saw once more the faces of his old buddies from the Air Cav days in the Nam. Brody, Corky, Snakeman, Em Ho, Zack, Gabe, Warlokk, Gardner, and Farmer against a backdrop of jungle green. Some of them were long dead, but he had managed to keep track of most of the survivors of the old Echo Company.

Leo Zack had finally retired in Columbus, Georgia and was working as a civilian at the infantry school. Corky was somewhere back in L.A., running a real estate office. Farmer, that poor bastard, was still in a VA hospital somewhere in the Northwest. Captain Gaines was a pilot for Delta Airlines, and Gabe was running a flying school in Arizona with Lance Warlokk.

The only one he had lost track of had been Brody, and now he finally knew what happened to him. Of all the goddamned things, he had become a real lifer, an officer. Two-Step blinked back the sudden tears and opened the door to his patrol car, murmuring the final words before stepping inside.

"Good-bye, Brody."

GLOSSARY

ALPHA The military phonetic for *A*

AA Antiaircraft weapons

AC Aircraft commander, the pilot

Acting jack Acting NCO

Affirm Short for affirmative, yes

AFVN Armed Forces Vietnam Network

Agency, the The CIA

AIT Advanced individual training

AJ Acting jack

AK-47 The Russian 7.62mm Kalashnikov assault rifle

AO Area of operation

Ao dai Traditional Vietnamese female dress

APH-5 Helicopter crewman's flight helmet

APO Army post office

ARA Aerial rocket artillery, armed helicopters

Arc light B-52 bomb strike

ARCOM Army Commendation Medal

ARP Aero Rifle Platoon, the Blue Team

Article 15 Disciplinary action

ARVN Army of the Republic of Vietnam, also a South Vietnamese soldier

ASAP As soon as possible
Ash and trash Clerks, jerks, and other REMFs
A-Team The basic Special Forces unit, ten men
AWOL Absent without leave

BRAVO The military phonetic for *B*
B-40 Chinese version of the RPG antitank weapon
Bac si Vietnamese for "doctor"
Bad Paper Dishonorable discharge
Ba-muoi-ba Beer "33," the local brew
Banana clip A thirty-round magazine for the M-1 carbine
Bao Chi Vietnamese for "press" or "news media"
Basic Boot camp
BCT Basic Combat Training, boot camp
BDA Bomb damage assessment
Be Nice Universal expression of the war
Biet (Bic) Vietnamese for "Do you understand?"
Bird An aircraft, usually a helicopter
Bloods Black soldiers
Blooper The M-79 40mm grenade launcher
Blues, the An aero rifle platoon
Body count Number of enemy killed
Bookoo Vietnamese slang for "many," from French *beaucoup*
Bought the farm Killed
Brown bar A second lieutenant
Brass Monkey Interagency radio call for help
Brew Usually beer, sometimes coffee
Bring smoke To cause trouble for someone, to shoot
Broken down Disassembled or nonfunctional
Bubble top The bell OH-13 observation helicopter
Buddha Zone Heaven
Bush The jungle
'Bush Short for ambush
Butter bar A second lieutenant

CHARLIE The military phonetic for *C*

C-4 Plastic explosive

C-rats C rations

CA A combat assault by helicopter

Cam ong Vietnamese for "thank you"

C&C Command and control helicopter

Chao (Chow) Vietnamese greeting

Charlie Short for Victor Charlie, the enemy

Charlie tango Control tower

Cherry A new man in your unit

Cherry boy A virgin

Chickenplate Helicopter crewman's armored vest

Chi-Com Chinese Communist

Chieu hoi A program where VC/NVA could surrender and become scouts for the Army

Choi oi Vietnamese exclamation

CIB The Combat Infantryman's Badge

CID Criminal Investigation Unit

Clip Ammo magazine

CMOH Congressional Medal of Honor

CO Commanding officer

Cobra The AH-1 attack helicopter

Cockbang Bangkok, Thailand

Conex A metal shipping container

Coz Short for Cosmoline, a preservative

CP Command post

CSM Command sergeant major

Cunt Cap The narrow green cap worn with the class A uniform

DELTA The military phonetic for *D*

Dash 13 The helicopter maintenance report

Dau Vietnamese for "pain"

Deadlined Down for repairs

Dep Vietnamese for "beautiful"

DEROS Date of estimated return from overseas service

Deuce and a half Military two-and-a-half-ton truck

DFC Distinguished Flying Cross

DI Drill instructor

Di di Vietnamese for "Go!"

Di di mau Vietnamese for "Go fast!"

Dink Short for *dinky-dau*, derogatory slang term for Vietnamese

Dinky-dau Vietnamese for "crazy!"

Disneyland East The Pentagon

Disneyland Far East The MACV or USARV headquarters

DMZ Demilitarized zone separating North and South Vietnam

Dog tags Stainless steel tags listing a man's name, serial number, blood type and religious preference

Donut Dolly A Red Cross girl

Doom-pussy Danang officers' open mess

Door gunner A soldier who mans a door gun

Drag The last man in a patrol

Dung lai Vietnamese for "Halt!"

Dustoff A medevac helicopter

ECHO The military phonetic for *E*. Also, radio code for east

Eagle flight A heliborne assault

Early out An unscheduled ETS

Eighty-one The M-29 81mm mortar

Eleven bravo An infantryman's MOS

EM Enlisted man

ER Emergency room (hospital)

ETA Estimated time of arrival

ETS Estimated time of separation from service

Extract To pull out by helicopter

FOXTROT The military phonetic for *F*

FAC Forward air controller

Fart sack sleeping bag

Field phone Hand-generated portable phone used in bunkers

Fifty The U.S. .50 caliber M-2 heavy machine gun

Fifty-one The Chi-Com 12.7mm heavy machine gun

Fini Vietnamese for "ended" or "stopped"

First Louie First lieutenant

First Shirt An Army first sergeant

First Team Motto of the First Air Cavalry Division

Flak jacket Infantry body armor

FNG Fucking new guy

FOB Fly over border mission

Forty-five The U.S. .45 caliber M-1911 automatic pistol

Fox 4 The F-4 Phantom II jet fighter

Foxtrot mike delta Fuck me dead

Foxtrot tosser A flamethrower

Frag A fragmentation grenade

FTA Fuck the army

GOLF The military phonetic for *G*

Gaggle A loose formation of choppers

Get some To fight, kill someone

GI Government issue, an American soldier

Gook A Vietnamese

Grease gun The U.S. .45 caliber M-3 Submachine Gun

Green Berets The U.S. Army's Special Forces

Green Machine The Army

Grunt An infantryman

Gunship Army attack helicopter armed with machine guns and rockets

HOTEL The military phonetic for *H*

Ham and motherfuckers The C ration meal of ham and lima beans

Hard core NVA or VC regulars

Heavy gun team Three gunships working together

Hercky Bird The Air Force C-130 Hercules Transport plane

Ho Chi Minh Trail The NVA supply line

Hog The M-60 machine gun

Horn A radio or telephone

Hot LZ A landing zone under hostile fire

House Cat An REMF

Huey The Bell UH-1 helicopter, the troop-carrying workhorse of the war.

INDIA The military phonetic for *I*

IC Installation commander

IG Inspector general

IHTFP I hate this fucking place

In-country Within Vietnam

Insert Movement into an area by helicopter

Intel Military Intelligence

IP Initial point. The place that a gunship starts its gun run

IR Infrared

JULIET The military phonetic for *J*

Jackoff flare A hand-held flare

JAG Judge advocate general

Jeep In Nam, the Ford M-151 quarter-ton truck

Jelly Donut A fat Red Cross girl

Jesus Nut The nut that holds the rotor assembly of a chopper together

Jet Ranger The Bell OH-58 helicopter

Jody A girlfriend back in the States

Jolly Green Giant The HH-3E Chinook heavy-lift heli copter

Jungle fatigues Lightweight tropical uniform

KILO The military phonetic for *K*

K-fifty The NVA 7.62mm type 50 submachine gun

Khakis The tropical class A uniform

KIA Killed in action

Kimchi Korean pickled vegetables

Klick A kilometer
KP Kitchen Police, mess-hall duty

LIMA The military phonetic for *L*
Lager A camp or to make camp
Lai dai Vietnamese for "come here"
LAW Light antitank weapon. The M-72 66mm rocket launcher
Lay dead To fuck off
Lay dog Lie low in jungle during recon patrol
LBJ The military jail at Long Binh Junction
Leg A nonairborne infantryman
Lifeline The strap securing a doorgunner on a chopper
Lifer A career soldier
Links The metal clips holding machine gun ammo belts together
LLDB *Luc Luong Dac Biet*, the ARVN Special Forces
Loach The small Hughes OH-6 observation helicopter
Long Nose Vietnamese slang for "American"
Long Tom The M-107 175mm long-range artillery gun
LP Listening post
LRRP Long-range recon patrol
LSA Lubrication, small-arms gun oil
Lurp Freeze-dried rations carried on LRRPs
LZ Landing zone

MIKE The military phonetic for *M*
M-14 The U.S. 7.62mm rifle
M-16 The U.S. 5.56mm Colt-Armalite rifle
M-26 Fragmentation grenade
M-60 The U.S. 7.62mm infantry machine gun
M-79 The U.S. 40mm grenade launcher
MACV Military Assistance Command Vietnam
Ma Deuce The M-2 .50 caliber heavy machine gun
Magazine Metal container that feeds bullets into weapons; holds twenty or thirty rounds per unit
Mag pouch A magazine carrier worn on the field belt

Mama San An older Vietnamese woman
MAST Mobile Army Surgical Team
Mech Mechanized infantry
Medevac Medical Evacuation chopper
Mess hall GI dining facility
MF Motherfucker
MG Machine gun
MI Military intelligence units
MIA Missing in action
Mike Radio code for minute
Mike Force Green Beret mobile strike force
Mike-mike Millimeters
Mike papa Military police
Minigun A 7.62mm Gatling gun
Mister Zippo A flamethrower operator
Monkey House Vietnamese slang for ''jail''
Monster Twelve to twenty-one claymore antipersonnel
  mines jury-rigged to detonate simultaneously
Montagnard Hill tribesmen of the Central Highlands
Mop Vietnamese for ''fat''
Motengator Motherfucker
MPC Military payment certificate, issued to GIs in RVN
  in lieu of greenbacks
Muster A quick assemblage of soldiers with little or no
  warning
My Vietnamese for ''American''

NOVEMBER The military phonetic for *N*. Also, radio
  code for north
NCO Noncommissioned officer
Negative Radio talk for ''no''
Net A radio network
Newbie A new GI in-country
Next A GI so short that he is the next to go home
Niner The military pronunciation of the number 9
Ninety The M-67 90mm recoilless rifle
Number One Very good, the best

Number ten Bad
Number ten thousand Very bad, the worst
Nuoc nam A Vietnamese fish sauce
NVA The North Vietnamese Army, also a North Vietnamese soldier

OSCAR The military phonetic for *O*
OCS Officer candidate school
OCS Manual A comic book
OD Olive drab
Old Man, the A commander
One five one The M-151 jeep
One oh five The 105mm howitzer
One twenty-two The Russian 122mm ground-launched rocket
OR Hospital operating room
Out-country Out of Vietnam

PAPA The military phonetic for *P*
P Piaster, Vietnamese currency
P-38 C ration can opener
PA Public address system
Papa San An older Vietnamese man
Papa sierra Platoon sergeant
PAVN Peoples Army of Vietnam, the NVA
PCS Permanent change of station, a transfer
Peter pilot Copilot
PF Popular Forces, Vietnamese militia
PFC Private first class
Piece Any weapon
Pig The M-60 machine gun
Pink Team Observation helicopters teamed up with gunships
Phantom The McDonnell F-4 jet fighter
Phu Vietnamese noodle soup
Point The most dangerous position on patrol. The point

man walks ahead and to the side of the others, acting as a lookout

POL Petroleum, oil, lubricants

Police To clean up

POL point A GI gas station

Pony soldiers The First Air Cav troopers

Pop smoke To set off a smoke grenade

Prang To crash a chopper, or land roughly

Prep Artillery preparation of an LZ

PRG Provisional Revolutionary Government (the Communists)

Prick-25 The AN/PRC-25 tactical radio

Profile A medical exemption from duty

Project Phoenix CIA assassination operations

PSP Perforated steel planking used to make runways

Psy-Ops Psychological Operations

PT Physical training

Puff the Magic Dragon The heavily armed AC-47 fire support aircraft

Purple Heart, the A medal awarded for wounds received in combat

Puzzle Palace Any headquarters

PX Post exchange

PZ Pickup zone

QUEBEC The military phonetic for *Q*

QC *Quan Cahn*, Vietnamese Military Police

Quad fifty Four .50 caliber MG's mounted together

ROMEO The military phonetic for *R*

RA Regular army, a lifer

Railroad Tracks The twin-silver-bar captain's rank insignia

R&R Rest and relaxation

Ranger Specially trained infantry troops

Rat fuck A completely confused situation

Recondo Recon commando

Red Leg An artilleryman
Red Team Armed helicopters
Regular A well-equipped enemy soldier
REMF Rear echelon motherfucker
Re-up Reenlistment
RIF Recon in force
Rikky-tik Quickly or fast
Ring knocker A West Point officer
Road runner Green Beret recon teams
Rock and roll Automatic weapons fire
Roger Radio talk for "yes" or "I understand"
ROK The Republic of Korea or a Korean soldier
Rotor The propellor blades of a helicopter
Round An item of ammunition
Round Eye Vietnamese slang for "Caucasian"
RPD The Russian 7.62mm light machine gun
RPG The Russian 77mm rocket-propelled grenade anti-tank weapon
RTO Radio telephone operator
Ruck Racksack
RVN The Republic of Vietnam, South Vietnam

SIERRA The military phonetic for *S*. Also, radio code for south
Saddle up To move out
Saigon commando A REMF
SAM Surface-to-air missile
Same-same Vietnamese slang for "the same as"
Sapper An NVA demolition/explosives expert
SAR Downed chopper rescue mission
Sau Vietnamese slang for "a lie"
Say again Radio code to repeat the last message
Scramble An alert reaction to call for help, CA, or rescue operation
Scrip *See* MPC
SEALS Navy commandos
7.62 The 7.62 ammunition for the M-14 and the M-60

SF Special Forces

Shithook The CH-47 Chinook helicopter

Short Being almost finished with your tour in Nam

Short timer Someone who is short

Shotgun An armed escort

Sierra Echo Southeast (northwest is November Whiskey, etc)

Sin City Bars and whorehouses

Single-digit midget A short timer with less then ten days left to go in The Nam

Sitrep Situation report

Six Radio code for a commander

Sixteen The M-16 rifle

Skate To fuck off

SKS The Russian 7.62mm carbine

Slack The man behind the point

Slick A Huey

Slicksleeves A private E-1

Slope A Vietnamese

Slug A bullet

Smoke Colored smoke signal grenades

SNAFU Situation normal, all fucked up

Snake The AH-1 Cobra attack chopper

SOL Shit Outta Luck

SOP Standard operating procedure

Sorry 'bout that Universal saying used in Nam

Special Forces The Army's elite counterguerrilla unit

Spiderhole A one-man foxhole

Spooky The AC-67 fire-support aircraft

Stand down A vacation

Starlite A sniper scope

Steel pot The GI steel helmet

Striker A member of a SF strike force

Sub-gunny Substitute doorgunner

Sweat hog A fat REMF

TANGO The military phonetic for *T*

TA-50 A GI's issue field gear

TAC Air Tactical Air Support

TDY Temporary duty assignment

Terr Terrorist

Tet The Vietnamese New Year

"33" Local Vietnamese beer

Thumper The M-79 40mm grenade launcher

Tiger suit A camouflage uniform

Ti ti Vietnamese slang for "little"

TOC Tactical Operations Center

TOP An Army first sergeant

Tour 365 The year-long tour of duty a GI spends in RVN

Tower rat Tower guard

Tracer Ammunition containing a chemical that burns in flight to mark its path

Track Any tracked vehicle

Triage The process in which medics determine which wounded they can best help, and which will die

Trip flare A ground illumination flare

Trooper Soldier

Tube steak Hot dogs

Tunnel rat A soldier who goes into NVA tunnels

Turtle Your replacement

201 File One's personnel records

Two-point-five Gunship rockets

Type 56 Chi-Com version of the AK-47

Type 68 Chi-Com version of the SKS

UNIFORM The military phonetic for *U*

UCMJ The Uniform Code of Military Justice

Unass To get up and move

Uncle Short for Uncle Sam

USARV United States Army Vietnam

Utilities Marine fatigues

VICTOR The military phonetic for *V*

VC The Viet Cong

Victor Charlie Viet Cong

Viet Cong South Vietnamese Communists

Ville Short for village

VNAF The South Vietnamese Air Force

VNP Vietnamese National Police

Void Vicious Final approach to a hot LZ, or the jungle when hostile

Vulcan A 20mm Gatling-gun cannon

WHISKEY The military phonetic for *W*. Also, radio code for west.

Wake-up The last day one expects to be in-country

Warrant officer Pilots

Waste To kill

Wax To kill

Web belt Utility belt GIs use to carry gear, sidearms, etc.

Web gear A GI's field equipment

Whiskey papa White phosphorus weapons

White mice Vietnamese National Police

White team Observation helicopters

WIA Wounded in action

Wilco Radio code for ''will comply''

Willie Peter White phosphorus

Wire, the Defensive barbed wire

World, the The United States

X-RAY The military phonetic for Z

Xin loi Vietnamese for ''sorry 'bout that''

XM-21 Gunship weapon package

XO Executive officer

YANKEE The military phonetic for *Y*

Yarde Short for Montagnard

ZULU The military phonetic for Z

Zap To kill

Zilch Less than nothing

Zip   A derogatory term for a Vietnamese national
Zippo   A flamethrower
Zoomie   An Air Force pilot

ABOUT THE AUTHOR

The author served two tours of duty in Vietnam as an infantry company commander. His combat awards and decorations include the Combat Infantryman's Badge, three Bronze Star Medals, the Air Medal, the Army Commendation Medal, and the Vietnamese Cross of Gallantry. He has written six novels and many magazine articles about the war. He and his wife make their home in Portland, Oregon.